Prai...

Tyburn

"Unapologetic highwaymen, harlots, dual personalities, honor among thieves, murder, desire and lesbian prostitutes combine to create a novel of substance and the only fluff seen for miles is perhaps the puff in the ladies gowns. The seedy streets of London come absolutely alive and feels like a character in and of itself."
Smexy Books

"The twists and suspense as *Tyburn* unfolded were just right and kept me cheering for good to triumph--although I must give emphasis to the darkness written so poetically and truthfully in Tyburn, giving a great contrast."
Luv My Books

"Jessica Cale's characters are multi-faceted. They are complex, morally ambiguous and fully human. The author has a gift with words, creating vivid images of a London infested by "rodents" of various kinds —two and four legged. She displays a keen observation of detail and unfiltered representation of London society after the Great Fire. I can count on one hand, the number of times I was this heavily invested in the characters of a book."
Carmen Stefanescu

"Jessica Cale has written a romance that will remain one of my all-time favorites. With characters who could belong in a Dickensian classic, a sweet romance to make the spirit soar, and heroes who have to surmount incredible odds, *Tyburn* has it all."
Rosanna Leo

Tyburn

Other books by Jessica Cale

The Southwark Saga
Tyburn
Virtue's Lady
The Long Way Home
Broken Things

2017 Corbeau Media LLC Edition

www.authorjessicacale.com

ISBN: 1503292215

ISBN-13: 978-1503292215

Second paperback printing: March 2017

To my grandmother, for the typewriter.

Acknowledgements

This book would not have been possible without the support of a lot of amazing people. I would like to thank my family, my beta readers, Matt and Dana, for their humor and enthusiasm, Neil Austin for helping me with the nuts and bolts, and David Oprava for asking, "Whatever happened to Sally?"

A very special thank you to Jen and Keiran, two of the best friends a person could ever hope for, and to my husband, John, for proving that romantic heroes exist in real life, too.

Tyburn

THE SOUTHWARK SAGA, BOOK 1

Jessica Cale

Chapter 1

Sally was there the day they hanged Claude Duval.

It was madness in the January snow, the stands filled to capacity and creaking beneath the weight of too many bodies. Spectators filled the pit surrounding the gallows shoulder to shoulder. The grounds were packed and still they let them in.

The usual families with picnic baskets were disappointed at the lack of open ground on which to lunch. The vendors had sold out of hot potatoes and cakes and stood uselessly between the stalls, their hands in their pockets to protect their profits from the Tyburn Blossoms, young pickpockets who could hear two pennies rub together at one hundred paces. Prostitutes of every age and disposition sauntered through the crowd, anticipating a very profitable day. At least a dozen apothecaries, sorcerers, and quacks waited at the base of the gallows, jars at the ready to collect pieces of the corpse.

There was magic in a dead man's blood.

Claude's execution was remarkable, not only for the falling snow that so seldom blanketed London, cold as it could be, but for the staggering number of ladies in attendance.

The pit swarmed with them. From fashionable residences in Leicester Fields and St. James they came, traveling all the way to Tyburn in private coaches and hired hacks, sacrificing their silk shoes to stand in the muddy snow. They must have ruined ten thousand pairs among them.

They chattered happily, trading daring stories of times Claude had robbed them of their jewels or better, some of them true, all of them embellished. They speculated as to how he was caught at long last, and bemoaned the loss of such a handsome face. Their fans churned their sighs and scent in a gale that assaulted Sally's senses with the smell of lilies and idleness.

Why anyone would require a fan in January was beyond her. She pulled her ragged cloak closer around her shoulders to fend off the wet chill of the morning. The ladies, their dresses no doubt ordered for just this occasion, pouted and postured in plush fur capes, their little hands encased in gloves and muffs of sable and mink, impervious to the punishing cold.

Rounded cheeks flushed and eyes alight, they were quite breathless at the prospect of seeing Claude in person, deriving no little thrill from the knowledge that they were about to see him die. They gasped over copies of his "Last Dying Confession" so recently printed that the ink rubbed off on their gloves.

Sally hated every one of them.

They took up places that should have belonged to the people who knew him and loved him as she did, ragged wretches obliged to crowd outside of the gate, too poor to purchase a seat, or too late to find room to stand.

Sally had arrived hours early, standing in the cold in threadbare finery with an empty belly. She waited alone, not a blood-thirsty spectator or a sighing ninny, but a friend.

She had met Claude in Normandy when they were children, long before Charles had regained the throne, neither of them ever dreaming they would end up in England. They had been respectable in those days, but in the dank, stinking streets of London, Claude had become a robber and Sally a whore.

The crowd fell silent, parting as he rolled up in a lacquered cart behind an enormous black horse. Claude stood proudly in his long coat and wide-brimmed hat, hands tied behind his back.

The ladies collectively gasped.

The cart stopped abruptly. He gave a measured bow.

The crowd erupted in cheers. The woman beside her clapped wildly and reached out to him, her gentleman escort reddening.

Claude stepped off the cart and began his slow walk to the gallows.

He nodded and smiled pleasantly as he passed, greeting people and winking at the ladies. He was the very picture of a swaggering hero, handsome at twenty-seven, proud to meet his end among so many devotees.

Then he saw her.

His eyes were empty and his expression rigid. His pale, ghostly face belonged not to her first love, but to a man who had already died. He paused before her.

2

"Celestine." He called her by her childhood pet name and ventured a sad smile. "Send me off right?"

Tears clouding her eyes, she took his cold face in her hands. He closed the distance between them with a chaste kiss.

Claude Duval, beloved of ladies everywhere, gave Sally his very last kiss.

It was the last kiss of a condemned man.

The woman beside Sally swooned into her escort's arms. Several others whined in protest, ready to fling themselves at his boots if not for the watchful eyes of their husbands and guardians.

Claude felt their disappointment. Perhaps was afforded some satisfaction from it. As he continued forward, smiling at those he passed, Sally contemplated her fate. His kiss was cold as death and tasted of ashes on her lips.

A chill ran up her spine.

The horse beneath the gallows stomped impatiently, the falling snow melting into his glossy coat. Steam rose from his nostrils in great clouds, a promise of brimstone. As far away as she was, Sally could have sworn that horse was breathing down her neck.

It felt like a curse.

"Hats off!" someone bellowed, and the cry was repeated throughout the crowd until every hat had been removed. It was not a gesture of respect for Claude. They did it so everyone would have a good view.

At last at the gallows, Claude climbed onto the second cart. They removed his hat and lowered the noose around his strong neck. His face was blank. He gave one last devilish smile as the signal was given. The horse sprung into a trot and pulled the cart from beneath his feet. Sally looked away before he began to swing.

Claude.

She choked back a sob and forced her way back through the cheering crowd. He had marked her with that kiss, and she knew she would be next.

♠

1671

One Tuesday afternoon, Sally awoke to the sharp jab of a walking stick to her ribs.

"Wake up, Sally."

She opened her eyes to see Wrath and his manservant, Charlie, standing over her, the harsh light of the sun casting halos of hellfire around their hardened faces. Wrath was smiling again. "We're going for a little ride."

Sally closed her eyes against a splitting headache. "Where are we going?"

"Never you mind, darling," he said, very slowly. "Make yourself pretty now. There's a good girl."

She climbed out of bed, slipped her dress over her head, and nonchalantly tugged at the laces. It wasn't fear of another beating inspiring some as yet unseen obedience. She went without resistance, as she had many times before, because she knew that wherever she was going was likely to be better than where she was.

After she gave her hair a lazy comb with her fingers, she snatched a green velvet ribbon off of her dresser and wound it around her head in a lopsided bow.

Wrath looked her over, nodded, and Charlie tossed her shoes at her.

She stepped into them, the white tips of her toes visible through the worn patches. Wrath marched down the stairs without a backward glance. He had no doubt Sally would follow.

Charlie slammed the door behind them as they left. He didn't bother to lock it. He was little more than a ruffian from the docks dressed in the frilled livery of a footman, and did not trouble himself with niceties. Sally's heart raced at the thought of someone finding her hiding places, but she tried to keep an indifferent expression as they passed through the lower parlor.

She need not have worried. Bessie, the housekeeper, was busying herself with ordering the few servants around. The only other person present was Camille, Wrath's newest girl, fast asleep at the foot of the stage.

To Sally's considerable surprise, a richly appointed carriage waited in the street. The wood was black and polished to a high shine with a crest of a lion rampant affixed to the door.

She wondered whom Wrath stole it from.

Wrath opened the door for her and gave her arse a hard slap as she climbed in. She sat down on the bench, clenching her teeth in silent fury, hating his touch. With Charlie's considerable girth taking up the rest of the bench beside her, Wrath took the seat opposite and yanked the curtain closed.

Sally had nothing else to look at but him. "Not showing me off today?"

"We're going to see a very good friend of mine."

She'd had quite enough of Wrath's very good friends. The better the friend, the stranger the perversion. "Who is he?"

"That is none of your concern. You must do as he tells you, and speak as little as possible."

They sat in silence as the coach bucked through the street, the horses' hooves clattering over cobbles, then dirt. Fresh air wafted through the curtain with the sound of birdsong, and Sally knew they were passing through St. James Park.

It would be good for her to know where they were; Wrath liked to leave her to find her own way back from assignations. She was always watched at a distance, and knew she wouldn't get far if she ran.

Sally didn't like to remember the last time she had tried.

At last the carriage stopped. Wrath threw open the door and jumped out. Sally climbed out carefully, gazing in wonder at the white mansion. It was the brightest building she had seen in all of London. Even the best-kept houses bore traces of the fire in soot-darkened windows and the murky shadows that the constant rain never seemed to wash away.

The estate was some ways north of Hyde Park and surrounded by several acres of ornamental gardens and a lush forest. Though much of the nobility had suffered great losses during the war, Wrath's friend had clearly not been among them.

Wrath strode purposefully across the yard toward the servants' entrance. Charlie gave Sally's shoulder a shove and walked her through the kitchen garden, past a little tabby cat hunting in the bushes, and into the back door.

They walked through a corridor past the kitchens and

climbed up a creaking stairway that snaked along the backside of the building to a long hallway that stretched across the second floor. Most of the doors were shut and it was quiet except for the sound of a low, mellow voice.

The voice was coming from behind a half-open door at the end of the hall. It was even, soft, and pleasant, and as they drew closer, Sally realized it was a man reading aloud. She glanced into the room as they passed and saw two small boys sitting in matching chairs, paying close attention to their lessons. She smiled to herself, wondering what that was like.

Wrath's very good friend that afternoon was a flagellant of some fifty-odd years introduced to her as Lord H. Wrath never used real names around his girls to protect the reputations of his high-born clients should they start "telling tales." The fact that Sally could easily discover his name by knowing which estate was his didn't seem to concern him, so long as he maintained the appearance of discretion.

Regardless of the secrecy they had taken pains to maintain, it was obvious Lord H was a prominent member of the nobility. Sally looked up to see a coat of arms proudly displayed over the fireplace, a raven splayed rather eerily across a plain white field. She thought of Claude's dark figure in the snow and shivered.

Lord H looked her over with a frown. He addressed Wrath over her shoulder. "Was this the best you could do?"

"Sally is full of surprises. Aren't you, Sally?"

She was not in the mood for compliance. She fixed her coldest glare on Lord H and prayed he would dismiss her.

His face lit up. "My, my. What ferocity!"

"She has a cruel heart and a quiet tongue."

Lord H's face quirked with a tight-lipped smile. "Very well, then. We shall see."

Wrath left the room without a word. Sally heard his steps retreat down the hallway toward the stairs, Charlie stomping along behind him. There would be no one there to guard her should things get out of hand, but equally, no one would see what she got up to. She was on her own.

As Lord H crossed the room to retrieve something from the armoire, Sally sized him up. He was only slightly taller than her, but a good deal heavier. As hungry as she was, she could put up a good fight. Her eyes settled on his neck and she thought of the thick velvet ribbon in her hair. If she managed to run, this far out into the country, how long would it take them to find her?

Carefully closing the cherry doors of the armoire, Lord H paced the room with a well-oiled birch cane in his hands. He rubbed his palms lovingly along its length, and at last stopped between Sally and the hearth. He licked his lips. "Do you know how to use one of these?"

Sally chose to heed Wrath's warning about keeping speaking to a minimum, and at once seized the cane and gave him a sound rap across the back of his right hand.

His eyes lit up and he held perfectly still. Sally swung the cane idly as she surveyed the room. A large canopied bed hung with deep blue velvet stood against the wall to her right, and a suite of sumptuously upholstered chairs was arranged artfully to her left. The windows were wide open, and the room was bathed in sunlight. She stepped toward the window and took a deep breath of the sweet spring air.

She heard Lord H start to shift and she turned toward him. He watched her with impatient expectation, and she was at once flooded with such hatred that she could not contain it. She kicked a plush footstool to his feet and struck his backside with such force that he fell over it onto the floor.

He let out all his breath at once in a huff as his ribs hit the stool. Bracing himself with his hands against the floor, he struggled to take another breath and she struck him again. He wheezed pitifully, and began to fumble with his trousers. Sally watched with growing disgust as he managed to unlace them and pull them down, exposing his arse to the cane.

She clenched her teeth and hit him harder.

He wasn't the first flagellant sent her way, but he was by far the easiest to beat.

He had talked over her like she wasn't there.

Smack.

He was the lord of this beautiful estate in the country, while she would be returning to a dirty room in a run-down theatre on a street that reeked of horseshit and rotten fruit.

7

Smack.

He had at least two healthy children being taught by someone else only yards away while he chose to spend his afternoon being beaten by a common whore.

Sally hit him so hard that the cane snapped.

Her skin burned and her blood pounded behind her eyes as she pulled the ribbon from her hair. She sat down heavily on his back, wrapped the ribbon around his throat, and pulled it tight. She felt tears rolling down her cheeks as his neck started changing color, his choking giving way to terrible silence.

The image of Claude standing beneath the gallows flashed before her eyes and Sally let the ribbon go with a sob.

Lord H jerked violently and fell to the floor, coughing as he tried to regain his breath. Sally crushed the tears against her face with the heel of her hand and realized she was still clutching the splintered end of the birch cane.

He rolled over onto his back and she saw that he had spent against the footstool while she had been choking him.

Curling a lip in disgust, she dropped the remains of the cane to the floor and re-tied the ribbon in her hair.

Chapter 2

Looking down into the bored, young faces of the Ramsey twins, Nick Virtue wondered for the second time that day if he should look for a position elsewhere.

The nine-year-old twins paged idly through their copies of Mallory's *Le Morte D'Arthur*, looking at the crisp new paper more than the words.

"What do you think of this passage?"

Leaning their faces on their palms, unconsciously mirroring each other, James sighed as William looked absently out the window.

"Did you think it was exciting when Lancelot saved Guinevere?"

William shook his head and James said, "I thought it was foolish."

Nick looked slowly from one to the other. "You thought it was foolish?"

They nodded.

"Why?"

"He defied the King," said William.

"She had to die. It was the law."

Nick took a deep breath and tried to ignore the pain of his empty stomach. "Why do you think he did it?"

They looked at him with identical, blank stares.

"Lancelot saved Guinevere because he knew that although she was accused of adultery, sorcery, and treason, she was a good woman, and he loved her," he suggested.

James wrinkled his nose. "Perhaps she bewitched him to think she was good, but really she was tempting him into sin."

William nodded vigorously. "Ladies do that."

Nick sat back in his chair, regarding them carefully. "Do you think it was possible that she wasn't tempting him, and they did really love each other?"

"No," they replied in unison.

"Why not?"

"She was married to Arthur."

"Everyone is a victim of circumstance, to some extent. Do you think she wanted to marry the king?"

They looked at him blankly.

"What if she didn't want to? What if she would have chosen Lancelot instead?" Nick asked.

"That doesn't matter." James shook his head. "She belonged to the king, and he had the right to kill her."

"Why?"

"She betrayed him with Lancelot."

"So you don't think Lancelot should have risked his life to save her?"

"She's just a girl." James sniffed.

"You don't think girls need saving sometimes?"

William shook his head. "Father says girls are evil."

"Jane's evil," James declared.

"All sisters are evil," William agreed.

Nick ran a hand over his face. "What else does your father say?"

The dinner bell rang and the boys sprang out their chairs and ran down the hallway, sparing him more of Lord Hereford's second-hand wisdom. Hereford wasn't alone in his mistrust of women, but Nick had to admit that hearing it parroted by nine-year-old boys left him feeling rattled. If there was no reasoning with them now, what hope did they have for the future?

The smell of roasting meat and garlic rose warmly up the back staircase and found its way into the parlor used for studies. It hit Nick like a punch to the gut. He kicked the wall with his boot and sank heavily into the window seat.

He hadn't eaten all day. Hereford had no great love of education, and as tutor, Nick often found himself on the receiving end of his disdain. He was not permitted to eat with the family except for Sunday lunch, and his elevated status ensured the servants kept him at a safe distance. There was not much use in asking them for anything. More often than not, he went hungry.

Nick looked out the mullioned window to see that dusk was settling over the grounds. It would be better to leave quickly if he had to make the long walk back into town, though he knew he could find his way in the dark.

He rose wearily and took the servants' staircase down toward the kitchens. The intoxicating smells grew stronger as he reached the ground floor and raised a hand to open the door.

Mrs. Turner, the head cook, blocked his entrance with her stout frame. "Mister Virtue. How can we be of service?"

He cleared his throat and nodded politely. "Good evening, Mrs. Turner. I was wondering if I might take something for supper."

She sucked air noisily through the gaps in her teeth. "We haven't anything to spare, I'm afraid."

Behind her two serving boys struggled to balance a roast boar on an enormous silver platter between them. His eyes widened at the sight of it.

"I don't require overmuch, perhaps any bread or cheese left over from dinner?"

Mrs. Turner put a hand on her ample hip. "Not possible. You know how Lord Hereford feels about that. Learned men don't need so much sustenance. Keeps them closer to God."

Nick swallowed, his dry throat chafing painfully. "I understand, Mrs. Turner, but I haven't had a thing to eat since yesterday."

Mrs. Turner rolled her eyes impatiently and motioned as if she was needed back in the kitchen. Her wide white apron was spotted with patches of flour, grease, and, if he wasn't mistaken, pie crust. She was twice as wide as he was and half as tall; clearly Hereford had no reservations about feeding his kitchen staff. "Go into the village and get something at the inn."

"I haven't been paid in months, Mrs. Turner."

"That's between you and his lordship, isn't it? I'm sorry, Mister Virtue, we haven't got anything for you here. Master's orders."

She shut the door in his face.

Nick stared at the whitewashed wood, overcome with frustration.

He tried to be upstanding, to be the very model of piety and virtue that tutors were held up to be, but respectability wouldn't keep him from starving to death.

Mind made up, Nick marched back up the stairs to his small, windowless room in the attic. He was not required to stay there, but when he did leave, he took great pains to conceal his path as Hereford would not approve of his destination. Southwark was a great many things, but pious was not one of them.

He took his long coat off the peg beside the door, and removed his pistol from its hiding place beneath the dusty copy of *Paradise Lost* in his only drawer. He slipped it into his coat pocket and put his hat on his head as he closed the door behind him.

There were a number of doors for the servants along the back of the property. He favored the one that led him straight into the long shadows of the hedge maze. He slipped his coat on at the third bend and was safely hidden in the forest in minutes. Years of practice had taught him to move through brush without a sound, and again he had used this skill to his advantage since he had run out of money weeks before.

Nick had been spending his evenings in the company of his brother, Mark, a carpenter who lived and worked in Southwark. Since the fire five years before, carpenters had found themselves out of work by the dozens, and many were forced to leave or find other positions. Having inherited the business on the death of his old master, Mark had been determined to stand his ground, whatever the cost may be. Now he was not strictly a carpenter, although he introduced himself as such, and indeed, had taken on apprentices. Ever intrepid, Mark Virtue had found a way to thrive in the crime-ridden slum that was Southwark.

When the death of Nick's patron had forced him to abandon his medical studies at Cambridge, Mark had taken him in and taught Nick to survive as he had. He owed Mark his life.

It was a long walk, but he knew he would be welcome. Mark was generous with his provisions, the quality of which varied wildly depending on the previous week's take, and he asked almost nothing in return. On good nights Nick was welcomed with a portion of beef and beer, but lately his suppers had been limited to days-old pottage of God-only-knows and peas.

That his position was taking a toll on him was evident; his large frame, healthy and well-muscled before he had begun working for Hereford only a year before, was thinning out considerably. His near-constant hunger made him tired and weak, but there was nothing he could do to remedy that while remaining on the right side of the law.

For months he had refused to consider falling back on his old occupation, to his brother's dismay, but the hungrier he got, the better it looked.

Of course the penalty for stealing anything worth more than a shilling was death, so he would have to take care not to get caught. He supposed he could claim benefit of the clergy if he was tried, though he was not a religious man. Mark had told him that if he could prove his education by reading a verse from the Bible, they would stay his execution and have him transported abroad instead. Every man, woman, and child in Southwark had committed the same one to memory.

"*The sacrifice of God is a troubled spirit, a broken and contrite heart,*" he recited, reaching for his pistol.

If reading was what they wanted, he could read to them all day.

Transportation could hardly be worse than working for Lord Hereford.

He strode through the forest confidently, keeping to the side of the road without so much as casting a shadow in the ditch. Hearing the rattle of a carriage in the distance, Nick raised the pistol.

It wasn't robbery if he was only taking what was owed to him.

Chapter 3

Dusk had fallen over the gardens when Sally made her way down the servants' stairway toward the kitchens. The smell of roasting meat and fresh bread rose through the stairwell and she realized she was famished. She hadn't eaten since the day before, and it had been weeks since she'd had anything hot. Sally clutched her stomach, feeling dizzy.

The kitchens were full of activity; several people were engaged in cleaning, boiling, plucking, and serving, and not one of them noticed as she slipped into the shadow of the open larder.

Gossiping voices grew louder as they approached her hiding place. She crouched under a table as two ladies bustled in.

A slight blonde girl asked the matron, "Was that him?"

The burly matron groaned. "He was after something to eat again. I sent him on his way."

"He's handsome enough. It's no wonder Lady Jane has her eye on him." The girl hefted a haunch of venison under her arm.

"If she has any sense at all she'll stop making eyes at him like a fool and turn her attentions toward someone suitable." The matron pulled a sack of onions from a deep wooden bin and swung it over her shoulder. "He's the base-born son of nobody from nowhere and he's a *tutor*, for pity's sake!"

The tutor?

The little blonde one sighed. "It may not matter, in any case. He's sure to leave us if Hereford don't pay him one of these days."

So Lord H was Hereford. Sally tried to breathe silently, convinced they could hear the rapid beating of her heart from under the table. Seeing that the edge of her skirt was just visible in the shaft of light that spilled through the doorway, she yanked it back into the shadows.

They didn't seem to notice the movement, and continued chatting without pause. "Don't be foolish. Every brat in London that wants a tutor's got one. He's got nowhere else to go."

"Seems a shame not to feed someone who's hungry." The

girl rested her toe on the hem of Sally's dress. She held her breath.

The matron made an unladylike noise. "We're stretched tight enough as it is without feeding the whole of London as well. Mister High-and-Mighty can see to himself. Thinks he's better than us with his fancy books. He doesn't know nothing about life, you mark my words!"

They left together, swinging the door shut behind them. Sally held her breath as she listened for a lock, praying she would not be trapped inside.

There was no lock. She sighed in relief.

She silently crawled out from under the table and pushed the door open a crack. The sliver of light revealed several large wheels of cheese piled high on the table. She snatched a wedge, thrust it into one of the deep pockets she had sewn into her petticoat, and watched as the servants began to leave the kitchen with trays.

When many had gone to serve and the others had begun furiously working on the second course, she slipped back out into the hallway, hoping no one saw her. Sally was just about to escape into the garden when she felt a gentle tug on her hand.

Her heart nearly stopped. She turned to see the girl who had been in the larder. The girl raised a finger to her lips and passed Sally a linen bundle of food. Sally felt tears sting her eyes for the second time that day. The girl smiled at her and quietly returned to the kitchen.

Clutching the bundle, Sally rushed into the night, wanting to put as much space as possible between herself and the Hereford estate before she feasted. A thick, rolling fog had settled over the parkland making it impossible to see more than a few yards at a time. She kept to the side of the road and followed the sound of the river.

A mile or so up the road, she found a log to sit on and unwrapped the parcel. Inside was round loaf of fresh bread and half a chicken, still hot, roasted in butter and fragrant herbs. Sally could have walked all the way back to kiss that girl's feet in gratitude. She had just torn open the loaf of bread, inhaling the steam that rose from its warm insides, when she heard hooves beating down the road toward her.

She froze. In a city with thousands of horses, it was

unreasonable to fear them, but they had held a certain terror for her since Claude's execution. She clutched the bread and thought she might hold very still until the danger had passed.

"Stand and deliver!"

The horses reared as a large man in a long black coat and mask leapt out of the bushes from the other side of the road, brandishing a pistol. Sally watched, wide-eyed, her bread nearly forgotten as the driver struggled to reign in the horses. The highwayman approached the side of the carriage and Sally was taken aback by the sight of Hereford appearing at the window in his evening clothes.

For one thing, she was amazed he could sit down.

"What is the meaning of this?"

The highwayman leveled the pistol at Hereford's forehead and repeated, deliberately, "Stand and deliver."

"Julian! See this fellow off at once!"

The driver held the reins and kept his seat. "Best stay calm, my lord."

The highwayman thrust a bag at Hereford and waved his pistol.

With a great deal of grumbling, Hereford dropped his purse into the bag along with a polished silver pocket watch.

The highwayman took the bag and tipped his tricorn to Hereford. "My thanks. Good evening to you." He smacked the rump of the nearest horse and the carriage sped off into the night, Hereford's curses echoing through the forest as they disappeared from sight.

There was something about the whole spectacle that struck Sally as absurd. It didn't matter to her that he was robbed. He was a pervert and a cheapskate and he probably deserved it. She thought of him bouncing along on his bruised arse in the speeding carriage, headed for the theatre, and she couldn't help it.

She laughed.

The highwayman heard her. He stuffed the pistol into his coat and made his way toward her slowly, as if he was afraid she was going to bolt.

Most people would have been scared out of their wits, but Sally wasn't. She had known her fair share of conmen and cutpurses and she knew that she had less to fear from him than she did from the likes of Hereford and Wrath.

"Sorry," Sally said. "Struck me as funny."

His eyes were dark above his mask, and she could have sworn he was smiling beneath it.

Sally remembered the food in her lap and offered him half the loaf of bread.

She heard a chuckle and the log moved as he sat down beside her. His face was lost between the darkness of the night and the shadow of his hat, and she could not get a good look at him even as he removed his mask to take a bite of the bread. Sally ripped off the leg of the chicken and handed it to him. He accepted it gratefully, and they ate in silence.

He was a big man, tall and broad, and from the way he moved easily through the forest, Sally could tell he was fairly young and agile. She wondered if he would ravish her. Most men, coming upon a young woman alone in the night would, wouldn't they?

Besides, Sally was clearly a harlot and he would hardly be stealing her virtue.

She wondered if it would be so very bad if he tried.

When all the food had been eaten, he stood up, brushed the crumbs off his coat, and reached one big hand into his pocket.

Instead of the pistol she had anticipated, he pulled out a heavy coin and pressed it into her palm. She held his fingers and smiled at him in the dark, not knowing if he could even see it. He touched her cheek affectionately, the rough callus of his thumb brushing her cold skin as he tilted her face up into the moonlight.

Sally froze. She was not accustomed to men touching her in kindness. Her breath caught in her throat and she willed herself to be still, to revel in it. It was not likely to happen again.

He regarded her face, his no more than a shadow beneath the brim of his hat. Sally couldn't see a thing, so she closed her eyes and relaxed against the soft heat of his hand.

She felt his breath against her skin, a warm caress within the night's chill, and she wondered if he would kiss her.

Sally's face cooled too quickly as he pulled away. Closing her fingers gently over the coin, he gave a silent, gallant bow and headed into the forest, leaving her to her bread.

17

She rubbed the coin in her hand, not quite believing her luck.

Chapter 4

Nick knocked twice before letting himself in. Receiving no answer, he crossed the workshop, sidestepping piles of wood and tools left lying around the floor. He emptied his pockets onto the dining table, a weathered church door mounted on makeshift legs. Smooth silver coins dripped through his fingers like rain, tinkling into shining puddles over a panel of carved rosettes.

The sound succeeded in summoning Mark where the knock had failed. He threw open the backdoor with a grin, tracking dirty straw from the alley into the rushes on the floor. "Just when I'd given up on you." He ran a hand through his dirty blond hair. "Where did that come from?"

"Hyde Park," said Nick, taking off his hat.

Mark pulled up a chair and began to sift through the pile. "Not bad, not bad. Got anything else?"

Nick withdrew the remaining loot from his pocket and passed it to Mark for inspection.

"The pin's nice, but this pocket watch won't sell in town. It's got his crest on it! One for the coffin." Mark tossed the watch into the pine coffin that sat open on the floor.

Nick glanced at the contents. The bottom was littered with jewelry, snuff boxes, and even odd gilt details pried off coaches or harnesses. Before long, it would be full enough for Mark to wrap it in a shroud of wool and rosemary and ship it out of the city for sale.

The coins they divided up between themselves.

"Where is everybody?" Nick asked.

"They went off to the theatre. Some bawdy nonsense on Maiden Lane. No more food in the house, so off they went."

Mark had converted the old warehouse in Southwark into a home of sorts. The ground floor was an open workroom with a hearth that barely heated the cavernous space. The back end was used as a kitchen, with a second hearth and a disused oven that served as storage for Mark's few dishes. The upper floor consisted of a gallery overlooking the workroom that had been divided up into small rooms with pallets on the floors for the apprentices. Mark had the attic to himself.

Nick slipped his portion of the take into the inner pocket of his coat. There had only been one gold piece that night, and he had given that away. "Fancy a drink?"

"Go on, then." Mark threw an unfinished lid on the coffin and grabbed his cloak from a peg beside the back door.

They walked companionably down the side alley to the main road, away from the burnt shell of London Bridge toward The Rose and Crown, a newer tavern run by the vast Henshawe family. When they entered, they were greeted by one of the five Henshawe girls, who appeared to be falling out of her dress in her eagerness to be of service.

Nick looked around the room and spotted their friends sitting down for a drink at a table beside the bar. He left Mark to the attentions of the barmaid and took a seat across from Will, Mark's partner in the business, and Jack, their young apprentice.

"I thought you lot were going to a play." Nick raised his eyebrows.

"It was awful." Jack laughed.

"Nothin' but a lot of poxy-doxies strutting around in Cleopatra wigs." Will took a gulp of dark beer. "Mark was right to stay home."

Nick turned to see Mark, still occupied by the barmaid in the doorway. He looked to be trying to get away. Nick smiled. "It looks like he could use some help."

"Some help, he says." Will rolled his eyes. "I'd like to be in that kind of trouble."

"Where's Harry been? I haven't seen him in a while."

Will shrugged. "Started seeing some bird in Cheapside, over there whenever her father's away. Probably there now."

Another barmaid set a tankard of beer in front of Nick and he sipped it slowly, trying to remember the last time he'd been to the inn. His belly was full for once as well, and his thoughts returned to the girl in the forest. He smiled to himself.

They heard the sound of a hard slap over the din of the bar, and turned to see the barmaid skulking off, Mark rubbing his cheek.

Jack tried to get a look. "What's he done now?"

Nick shook his head and sipped his beer.

"She got me good, she did." Mark rubbed his reddened cheek as he approached the table.

"What did you say to her?" Will asked.

"I didn't say nothing," Mark protested, feigning shock. "Why would you think that?"

"Because we know you." Will smirked.

They looked at Mark expectantly.

Mark sat down with a dramatic groan, setting his beer on the table. "I merely complimented her on her dress, and I asked if it used to belong to her sister."

"Her sister?" Jack repeated.

Mark sipped his beer. "Yeah, her sister, Meg. Lovely girl. The last time I saw that dress, I says to her, Meg was halfway out of it."

The others laughed and Nick gave a weary sigh.

Hearing her name, Meg sauntered up to the table with a jug of beer. "Mark Virtue, have you been torturing my sister?" She pouted, leaning over the table lower than necessary to top up their drinks.

Meg was a curvaceous woman with masses of dark blonde hair piled loosely on top of her head in a messy knot. The jug emptied, she put a hand on her hip in a saucy pose.

"Torturing? I never!"

"She fancies you, you know." She sat on his lap and draped her arm around his shoulder.

Mark was unfazed. "Does she now?"

"You'll have to let her down gently."

"Come now, there's enough of me to go around." He grinned.

Jack rolled his eyes, world-weary at sixteen.

"When are you going to take me out again?"

Mark raised his eyebrows. "I'll take you out right now. We can go down to the fights at Bear Gardens and see the boxer I hear you've been keeping company with."

Meg gasped. "I didn't take you for the jealous type!"

"And I didn't take you for a virtuous woman." He laughed.

21

"Honestly, love, you can do as you like."

Meg jumped to her feet and slapped him. "Virtuous indeed!" She marched to the bar, shouting over her shoulder, "Stay away from my sister!"

Will shook his head, laughing. "How do you do it?"

Mark sipped his beer. "Do what?"

"Every time we go out, you're fighting them off. Even now, you've been slapped twice in ten minutes, and I can see four more giving you the eye. Yes, I'm talking about you." He nodded to a girl with ginger hair across the bar. She saw that he was addressing her and turned bright red.

Mark turned toward the girl Will indicated and smiled.

She smiled back.

Mark turned back to the lads and shrugged. "What can I say? Perils of being a Virtue. We're irresistible. Nick knows what I'm talking about."

Nick shook his head. "I bloody don't, and I'm not a real Virtue."

Mark waved his hand. "Close enough."

"Obviously not," teased Will. "I don't think I've ever seen you with a girl."

Nick sipped his beer.

Jack frowned. "But aren't you? A Virtue, that is? I thought that was your name."

Nick shrugged. "Mark's my half-brother. Different fathers."

"What's your name, then?"

Mark answered for him when Nick hesitated. "It's Virtue now, innit? You're my brother, at any rate." He raised his beer with a knowing look.

Nick gave him a look of gratitude and raised his own.

The door flew open and in swept a young woman in a heavy cloak, her hair disheveled and her cheeks flushed from exertion. She looked around the bar frantically, spotted Mark, and rushed to their table.

"Mary," Mark greeted, and Nick braced himself to witness another slap.

It didn't come. She leaned down toward them, eyes wild, and said as quietly as she could manage said, "Harry's been nicked."

"What? When?"

"Three days ago. I've been searching for you ever since, I didn't know where to turn. They've taken him to Newgate. You have to do something."

Mark's face went pale and he set down his beer. "Jack, Will, finish your beer and make sure Mary gets home safe. Nick, come with me."

Chapter 5

London.

Years had passed and it still took Sally's breath away.

Coming from the darkness of the park at night, the lanterns hung outside the houses began to appear, one by one, like stars in the night. The streets were peaceful outside the city, and she fancied the houses looked sleepy, all tucked into bed with their curtains drawn. She wondered at the people who lived in them, what peaceful lives they led.

All she had wanted growing up was a quiet life, a home of her own, and a kitchen, of course. Then her "father" ruined everything.

She was sixteen when she discovered that the man who had sold her into work as an infant and every week beat her and drank her wages, was not her real father. Needless to say, she didn't take this discovery with the grace of a well-bred woman.

One thing led to another. She may have killed him. She didn't wait around to be sure. Three years had passed, and she could not find it within herself to regret it.

That night she had been forced to flee the Chateau, and Monsieur Claude Duval, a relative of the kitchen matron, happened to be taking his leave. He hid Sally under a blanket until they reached Calais.

They boarded a ship there and took it all the way to Greenwich, where they reached the sprawling poverty that was London in 1668. They rode through the cinders of buildings that had been burned two years before, past slums built so hastily that they collapsed before their eyes. Her back still charred from Bertrand's burning switch, Sally felt an odd affection for the city due to their shared condition.

She was deeply upset that she had been unable to bid farewell to Madame Toulouse, but consoled herself with a hopeful vision of her future in this new city. She would work hard and someday, she thought, she would manage the kitchen of a grand estate, and she would look after orphans as Madame had looked after her.

They rode down the narrow passage between the remaining shops that lined London Bridge, passing dozens of stalls and bakeries selling everything from feathers and gleaming silver ornaments to coarse bread and exotic fruit. A man sang ballads from an overturned box, and Sally felt like he was singing just for her.

Her delight at the sights and sounds of the city departed abruptly as she caught a glimpse of three heads mounted on pikes at the north gate of the bridge. Every trace of flesh was gone, and they were no more than skulls bleached by the sun.

Claude caught her looking as they passed. "Regicides."

"What is that?"

"They signed Charles I's death warrant. When the king was restored, he made short work of them."

"They've been up there for ten years?"

"Take care not to upset the King."

Sally had heard little of this King, confined as she had been to the kitchens. Seeing those heads up there, she imagined him to be stern and merciless. "This King, is he very cruel?"

"Cruel?" Claude snorted. "No worse than most. Those men killed his father. What would you have done?"

They rode in silence until they reached Charing Cross, where Claude left her with the address of an acquaintance and a purse of coins. "Your face is all healed up now. You'll have no trouble finding work here."

Sally's exhaustion gave way to curiosity as she was left on her own in the city. She began to walk.

Gazing in naïve wonder at the long rows of enormous houses, she listened to passing people speaking English, picking out the few words she knew, and hoping there would be some who spoke French as well.

Coming from a village of no more than a hundred people, London was perhaps a thousand times bigger than anywhere Sally had ever been. There were no numbers on the buildings, and the street signs were odd, when there were any at all. She would walk down one long road and, without turning off it, find it called three different names in three different places.

Sally walked for hours without reaching countryside, until night began to fall. Her feet ached. She was tired from the journey and she still had not found anywhere to sleep. She was lost and alone, and that was when the woman found her.

At first glance, Bedford Street had appeared to be a street of inns right in the middle of the fashionable new area of Covent Garden. The houses were beautiful. People bustled in and out of the bars, well-dressed and appearing to enjoy themselves. Taking comfort in their smiles, Sally had imagined herself to be very safe until a little old woman with unnaturally orange hair bumped into her in her haste to get into one of these inns.

"*Excuse-moi, Madame,*" Sally called to her. "*Est-ce un hotel?*"

She turned suddenly and looked Sally over, a slow, sly smile curling across her face. "You're French," she observed. "*Parlez-vous Anglais?*"

"Yes, a little," Sally replied.

"Are you looking for work?"

Music began to play from a nearby inn. Candles appeared in the windows overlooking the street, their flickering light like so many curious eyes. Sally had started to feel nervous, but she didn't know why. "Yes. I can cook."

The woman grinned at Sally, her chalk-white face sinister in the night. "What's your name, poppet?"

"Celeste."

The woman stepped up to her and took her arm companionably. "Come along, Sally, my girl. I reckon I have just the job for you."

That was how she learned that it is not wise to speak to strangers.

The wonder she had felt at seeing London for the first time never left her, although time passed and showed her quite another side of the city.

The people smiling in the inns were smiling because they were dead drunk, paid to smile, or both. The houses were inordinately expensive and filled with pests, and the conversation, once she understood it, was nothing she wanted to hear. When she learned to read a little bit of English, the street signs took on a different light altogether.

Dead Man's Walk. Melancholy Lane. Dog and Bitch Yard. Labour in Vain Hill.

Gropecunt Lane, it so happened, was exactly what it sounded like, and there were no maidens to be found on Maiden Lane.

Not one.

As Sally passed the murky marshes in Upper St. James Park, she heard the all-too familiar sound of dramatic moaning coming from behind the icehouse. It was easy to imagine that every woman in London was a whore. Just about every one Sally had met certainly had been. Even Bessie, the evil old bat who had taken her in that first night had been, at one point or another. Now she had a hand in creating them. The circle of life on the street.

The further Sally got into the city that night, the more ladies were out. They stood in doorways and hung off balconies in St. James, they promenaded in Leicester Fields. There were young ones, olds ones, half-dead ones, poor ones with pockmarks, successful ones in their patron's coaches, all the way up to the aristocratic ones who could be found warming the King's bed on any given night. Barbara Palmer, the Countess of Castlemaine and the King's long-favorite mistress, was widely hailed as the queen of the whores. When the city's harlots had grievances, such as when so many were attacked by mad apprentices in the Shrove Tuesday riots of '68, it was she whom they petitioned for justice.

Many of them, of course, were common shop girls off work looking to supplement their income with a penny or two. Food was expensive in London, and a woman could be cheaper than a loaf of bread, depending on which street one walked down.

Arriving in London as a runaway baker, hunger had been a cruel surprise. Sally thought of the highwayman and opened her fist to see the coin he had given her, gasping at what she saw there.

It was a whole mark.

Sally had never had so much money in her life. It could buy dozens of loaves of bread, would easily keep her fed for months if she was careful, or she could rent a clean room in a boarding house for *weeks*.

She laughed out loud and clutched it to her heart. She could have danced. It would serve her well, if she was ever able to escape.

That man had given it to her as if it were nothing, for nothing.

Perhaps there were good men in London after all.

Reaching Covent Garden after her long walk in the chill of the night, she passed Bedford's and was treated to the rich smell of good coffee. It was early yet and the evening had not truly begun, surely she had time for a dish?

Sally squeezed the mark in her hand and walked in.

Chapter 6

Lord Henry Marshall, the young Viscount Beaumont, had just arrived at the Bedford Coffee House in Covent Garden for what he thought of as his morning coffee, taken, as it was, at the true start of his day. He removed his perfectly cut silk jacket with the ease of someone who had practiced in front of a mirror, and handed it as well as his hat, to John Cooper, the proprietor, who had attached himself to Beaumont immediately upon his entering the establishment.

"Coffee, my lord?"

Beaumont answered him with a gracious gesture of his gloved right hand, and Cooper rushed off toward the bar.

Arranging himself carefully into the red cushioned chair in his usual corner, Beaumont breathed a sigh of relief at having escaped his house. The housekeeper his mother had hired for him suggested he would accomplish more of God's work if he were to begin his day earlier. He had responded by pointing out he left the house immediately after waking, taking his chocolate in bed, and dressing, and no man could hope to do better than that. Beaumont got little enough sleep as it was, and his friends were no better. No respectable young man he knew would show his face in public before the sun had gone down. Beaumont was quite ashamed that he had been the first to arrive at Bedford's this evening, but assured himself it would not happen again.

Cooper brought over his coffee, and Beaumont relaxed as he artfully swirled cream into it with a dainty silver spoon. "That will be all, Cooper."

Cooper remained still, distracted by something. He motioned to his daughter behind the bar.

"Cooper, what is it?"

"I'm terribly sorry, my lord, it's this girl. She causes a stir every time she comes in. I've told her to keep out, but here she is again."

Beaumont looked toward the door, where Miss Cooper was

engaging in an animated conversation with a woman in a vibrant green dress with a ribbon in her hair. In spite of the distance, he could see she had an excellent figure and a lovely face. "Bring her to me, Cooper."

"But sir, she's a black cat! Misfortune follows her wherever she goes! Why only last week--"

"I'll keep an eye on her, Cooper."

"You'll regret it, my lord."

Beaumont smiled as he raised his coffee to his lips. He watched Cooper approach the woman and speak to her, then motion toward him in his corner. The woman looked up at him with an expression of consternation before she relaxed and gave him a nod. She swept past the Coopers with a roll of her generous skirts and walked, hips swaying, to his table. "My lord, I am indebted to you."

"Please, sit down, miss. It troubles me deeply to see a lady denied the pleasure of a morning coffee." He motioned to Cooper for another.

She sat back into the large red chair, eyeing him carefully. "You're very kind."

"You're far too lovely to be unescorted. What are you doing here alone?"

She lowered her kohl-darkened lashes over her wide, dark eyes. "The same thing you are, I'm sure."

"And what is that, my dear?"

"Drinking coffee." At that moment, Cooper brought two more cups, the china clattering as he unceremoniously set hers before her.

Beaumont looked at her carefully. She had the bearing and flawless skin of a lady. Her black hair, curled and arranged carefully, shone in the light. She sipped her coffee and raised a perfectly arched eyebrow as she met his eyes. "Thank you."

She crossed her small hands over her lap, covering a threadbare patch that belied the age of the magnificent dress. For all her manners and her posture, this woman was clearly not a lady in the proper sense. Her dress was cut quite low and she wore nothing to protect herself from the elements and wandering eyes but a shawl so thin it was nearly transparent. She did not have the cultivated meekness of a well-bred woman; she held his gaze shamelessly from across the narrow table. Her eyes had a slight yellow tinge about them, and the kohl had fallen from her eyelashes to form soft, dark rings around them. If she had been a lady once, she wasn't one now.

"Forgive me. I have neglected to introduce myself. I am Beaumont."

"Sally."

♠

In the alley behind Bedford's, Beaumont could still taste that coffee.

He smelled her sweat and the starch of her dress as he came, his face buried in her hair. The frayed edge of the ribbon taunted his skin.

He heard a pack of boys pass by the dark passageway, paying no attention to them. He was sure they would be doing the same thing later that evening. Other alleys. Other women. Perhaps the same woman.

Here, against the wall with Sally in his arms, he felt odd. He dismissed the idea it could be love by any definition. Instead he felt a sort of vigorous freedom running through his veins as if he had reached a depth of vice never previously experienced.

But how?

She was certainly not his first bought woman, but there was something about her that separated her from the others. He could not place it.

Relaxing his hold, he looked at her. She was breathless, her eyes closed in pleasure, her skin glowing in the light from the open kitchen door.

He had never seen such an expression on a woman. She appeared to have enjoyed it.

When she saw the look on his face, Sally must have known what he was thinking. She laughed.

"I must see you again," he gasped, his voice suddenly gone.

She smiled enigmatically. "Perhaps."

Chapter 7

Returning to the Opera House with the mark hidden in her corset and the crown that Beaumont had given her in her hand, Sally almost felt sorry for him.

She had been thinking of the highwayman throughout the very brief ordeal, and Beaumont had assumed otherwise. Now he was in love.

It wasn't the first time it had happened, to be sure. This was one of the ways Sally dealt with her unfortunate circumstances. The other came in a bottle.

Well and good, we learn to survive.

Her habit of daydreaming had inadvertently contributed to her popularity. High and low, Wrath sold her to anyone who could pay. He kept it for himself, of course, occasionally throwing her a penny or two for food. Not often. The gin he kept in ready supply and it was the gin to which Sally returned.

Gin was a Dutch drink that she had taken to without undue persuasion. It had not quite gained a foothold in London yet, but it would in time. It was cheap, it was dirty, and it brought on a blessed forgetfulness that was all too welcome. If she'd had more money and fewer morals, she'd have opened a gin palace in St. Giles and lived off the misery of the masses.

Unfortunately for Sally, she was burdened with said morals, she had no money to speak of, and she was plagued with constant shame at the life she was forced to live. Part of her believed some part of the violence that had led to her confinement had been her fault. She never should have walked down that street. She should not have called to that woman. She should have run faster.

Hindsight can be unforgiving.

Sally crossed the threshold of the Opera House and saw Wrath standing at the bottom of the curving staircase, surrounded by courtiers.

"Sally, my dear," he greeted with a dangerous look in his eyes as he approached her, tucking his arm around her waist. "Where have you been?"

She opened her fist and dropped Derby's coin into his hand.

"Good girl." He patted her arse. Sally cringed. "I have some gentlemen I would like you to meet."

"I'd like a moment, if I may."

"Don't be long." He returned to the courtiers who openly ogled her as she ascended the stairs.

Sally sauntered along the high gallery to her room at the front end of the derelict building as if she was in no particular hurry, and shut the door behind her.

Satisfied she was alone, she scrambled beneath her sagging bed to her secret cache of tributes and hid the mark beneath the false bottom of the small box. She put it back into its hiding place, pulled the coverlet down to conceal the space below the mattress once again, and sat at her dressing table.

None of Wrath's other girls had been afforded a room with both a dressing a table and a window, but she was by far his biggest earner. She would have traded any one of them. They were free to come and go as they pleased.

Sally uncorked the new bottle Wrath had left beside her mirror and looked at her foggy reflection.

She would never be a beauty. Her features were large and irregular, too obviously Gallic. She had never been aware of her nose until the first courtier Wrath had introduced her to had advised him that it was a problem.

Sally had never thought a nose could be a problem, but she had to admit, it was *enormous*.

Nevertheless, the courtiers kept coming. They all seemed dreadfully fascinated by it. They called it "stately" and wrapped themselves up in her crazy black hair. She shrugged it off and waited for the day they tired of the indelicate-looking Frenchwoman and moved on to other girls.

It hadn't happened yet.

Sally took a deep drink of the green-tinged liquor and was rewarded by a familiar rush of warmth as it filled her body and dulled her mind. It was a peculiar kind of drunkenness, unlike beer or wine, as everything slowed down but became remarkably clear at the same time.

She took another drink. Bettie said he had never experienced it like that. She suspected that was because she drank too much.

With another deep drink, Sally had put away half the bottle. She applied more kohl to her eyes and tidied her hair. By the time she was done, the drink had taken over and she saw little black devils dancing around her reflection.

Sally paid them no mind. They were not the most frightening thing she had seen.

Leaving her room, she was aware of every tingling nerve in her body, and the men waiting for her did not seem as repulsive as they had. Bettie's door was closed as Sally passed, and she thought for a moment that she heard him weeping.

Nonsense, she thought. *Bettie doesn't make a sound when he cries.*

Sally descended the staircase slowly, seeing a flurry of flickering silver lights filling the atrium like falling snow, the ground covered in great white drifts, and the crowd hungry for blood. She reached the open arms of the men at the bottom of the stairs as she saw an enormous black horse walk through the wall, steam rising from his nostrils.

Sally laughed, mad as anything, to the delight of the courtiers. Claude's execution played around them in excruciating detail. She felt terror somewhere in the back of her mind, dull, like a thought she couldn't quite remember.

The horse walked up to her, crushing patrons in its path, and sniffed her face. She reached out to touch it and missed.

"She's perfectly charming," one of the men congratulated Wrath. "She's having a lovely old time!"

Wrath grinned, baring his yellow teeth and raised his black eyebrows. "Yes, she is."

"Yes, I am!" Sally repeated, her voice floating like ashes to the ceiling. "Prick."

"Did she just call you a prick?"

She sank backward into someone's perfumed arms as one of the buggers touched her nose. "Damn me! It's remarkable!"

The touch was followed by four more like it. "It's real!"

"Mad bastards," she muttered. When no one commented, she realized she had lapsed back into colloquial French.

One of them took her face in his hand and looked into her

eyes. "Who is your father? Where were you born?"

As Sally looked at him, she saw a noose lower over his wig and settle around his fat neck.

She laughed.

Chapter 8

Nick smelled Newgate before he saw it.

Feces, human and otherwise, bile, refuse, rotting flesh. He had tried to prepare himself as they walked the short distance across the rubble and reconstruction of London Bridge into the City and up Newgate Street to the looming prison at the end of the road.

Nothing could have prepared him for the reality. The voices grew louder as they neared. Moans of pain, cries for help, the ravings and laughter of the criminally insane. A long cell opened out onto the street and dozens of arms reached through its bars, palms up, begging for food or money. Nick reached for his purse but Mark laid a hand on his arm. "Harry's gonna need that."

Mark trudged on, his mouth set in a line of grim determination. They reached the public entrance where a group of well-heeled girls in various shades of pastel dresses waited as their chaperone paid for their entrance to gawk at the unfortunate.

"Nothing changes," Mark muttered to himself. "At least I'm on the right side this time, eh?"

"You didn't have to come," Nick said in a low voice. "I could have come for you."

Mark shook his head. "Harry's one of mine and I'm gonna see to it he's got everything he needs. Can't let a man rot."

Admission purchased, the girls ahead of them entered the gaol, handkerchiefs aflutter as they skipped in their excitement. Mark spat in the dirt. "Useless bits of fluff. Deliver me from a woman who's never been dirty."

They approached an open window in the gatehouse where a turnkey collected admittance. "Two." Mark slapped six shillings on the ledge.

"Mark Virtue," the turnkey greeted. "Been keeping out of trouble, have you?"

"Morning, Steve. How's the missus?"

"Not bad, not bad. Who's this fella?"

"He's my brother."

"Ain't he a physician? They're extra."

"No, mate. Never finished. He's a carpenter, like."

The officer looked him up and down and Nick resented his examination. "What's in the bag?"

Nick cleared his throat. "Bread." He lifted the flap of the satchel to reveal the golden crust of the loaf concealing his medical supplies.

"No feeding the prisoners." The turnkey dismissed them, seizing the bread from Nick's hands.

Mark gave an exaggerated sigh. "Come along, Nick."

Nick shot a look of contempt at the man as they passed through the iron gate. Unfazed, the man returned to his newspaper, tearing into the confiscated bread.

"Arse," Mark muttered. "Stupid as he is greedy, what'd I tell ya?"

Mark led the way inside the dank prison, stopping at a set of turnkeys at the second gate. "Evening, lads. We're looking for a cousin of mine, Harry. Young guy, blond, handsome like me." He winked.

The guard on the right scratched his head. "We got a new blond boy, but I can't say he's looking too handsome these days. He's in the begging grate."

Mark nodded his thanks and passed them, Nick following close behind.

Down a flight of stairs into a cold cellar, Nick found himself looking into the other side of the cell that opened out into the street. Mark paced the length of the long, narrow galley that held dozens of unwashed bodies of both sexes and every age, children, men, and women, some pregnant, others nursing infants. They vied for space within the overfull cells, standing tightly packed along the inner side while others, begging at the street, shivered as they stood in the foot of water that flooded the far end.

Even from where he stood, Nick could see blood and feces polluting the water. In the far corner, there was a corpse of an old man sitting, his chalk white head slack against the grate. From the state of the body, he had been dead for days.

A fat rat scurried out of the water that surrounded the corpse and ran across Nick's boot. A woman scrambled for it, missing it by inches.

"Damnation!" she shouted, eyes wild. "You should have caught it!"

Were they really obliged to eat rats? Nick withdrew a penny from his pocket and placed it in her moist, dirty hand. She held it close to her chest.

Another woman saw the penny and tried to snatch it from her. They began to fight, pulling hair and striking each other feebly as the prisoners surrounding cheered them on and watched for opportunities to steal it.

"Nick!" Mark shouted over the melee.

Nick rushed to the far end of the passageway, deeply dismayed at having caused so much chaos. Mark gave a crown to a turnkey at the far end, who opened the gate to expel Harry's limp body.

Harry landed at Mark's feet. He looked up, bewildered, as Mark stooped to help him up. "Mark?"

Mark slipped his arm around him to support his weight. Harry's feet were bare, his boots apparently stolen, and a wound festered on his foot.

"We need a clean, private room with a bed," Mark snapped at the turnkey.

The turnkey crossed his arms over his chest and drew his breath through his teeth. "It's gonna cost ya."

Nick reached into his purse and pulled out a crown.

The turnkey snatched it and tucked it into his vest. "You're having a laugh. That'll get him a blanket, if that."

Nick reached into his purse and Mark shot him a look. He paused, his hand hovering over his few coins.

"Get Matilda," he demanded.

The turnkey raised his eyebrows and disappeared down the corridor.

"I haven't got much more," Nick whispered.

Mark shifted Harry's weight onto Nick. "You take Harry, and keep quiet."

A coarse female voice boomed over the wails of the inmates. "Who presumes to disturb the warden? I ought to give you a slap!"

The woman did not look like any Matilda Nick had ever met. A medieval name, Matilda was likewise a fearsome battle axe of a woman, at least as wide as she was tall, her heavy fists resting like great hams where he supposed her hips must be. Her cheeks melted into rosy jowls, flapping around her open, scowling mouth. She looked at Nick holding Harry up with disgust.

"Hello, Tilly." Mark winked.

Matilda noticed Mark at last, and her face transformed from something that wouldn't look out of place on a gargoyle to that of a blushing schoolgirl.

Nick wasn't sure which was more terrifying.

"Why, Mister Virtue," she purred. "What can I do for you?"

"Didn't I tell you to call me Mark?" He gently chucked her on the cheek with his knuckle.

The warden *giggled*.

"Listen, Tilly my girl, my cousin Harry here needs some medical attention. We were hoping to get him a room of his own, like. Would you be able to help us out with that?"

She sucked in air through her teeth as the turnkey had before her. "I don't know Mark, rooms is expensive. You're looking at a guinea at least, plus more besides if you want a bed. A moidore'd get you the whole...package."

"Prices have gone up," he observed. "How about a guinea for a room of his own, with a bed, sheets, *clean* sheets, and a blanket besides?"

"I knew you was a robber, but I never imagined you'd take such advantage of a lady..."

Mark leaned against the wall and treated her to one of his best half-smiles.

She visibly trembled.

Nick watched the whole spectacle because he could not bring himself to look away.

"Now, Tilly, I know you to be a fair and kind-hearted lady. My cousin is in a terrible state and I've no more than a guinea to my name. Do you think we could work something out?"

"Yeah, we can work something out. Let's discuss the particulars in my office." She looked Nick up and down appraisingly and turned back to Mark. "What about him?"

Mark's eyes widened. "What, Ni – Father Nick? He's a man of the Church. Married to God, yeah?"

"He's a papist?"

"Protestant as you or me, but he takes his calling very seriously." He leaned in and explained in a whisper loud enough for Nick to hear, "He ain't got much to work with, to be honest. Dreadful accident when he was a boy."

"Oh!" She gasped, regarding Nick with pity. "Shame. He looks like a nice big lad."

"He was...once." Mark looked over his shoulder at Nick and grinned.

For all Nick felt like choking him, he knew Mark was doing him in a favor and he kept quiet.

Matilda rounded the corner with great effort and had a quiet word with the turnkey who had been so unhelpful when they arrived. Mark followed her down the corridor and the turnkey led Nick and Harry up two flights of stairs to a private floor, letting them into an empty cell with a bare, narrow bed.

Nick helped Harry onto the bed as the turnkey locked the door behind them.

The sound of the bolt sent a shiver down Nick's spine.

"Nick, I'm so glad you've come, I can't even tell you..."

"I'm sorry we couldn't come sooner. We only just found out you were here. Let me see your foot."

Harry raised his leg onto Nick's lap with some difficulty. The gash crossed the top of his foot from his toe to his ankle and didn't appear to be deep, but was badly infected as he had been forced to stand in that filthy water for days. Nick examined it carefully, satisfied it had not yet begun to putrefy, although it was swollen and must have caused him great pain.

Nick set to work, pulling his surgical tools out of his bag, along with fresh bandages and a bottle of brandy.

"Is it bad?" Harry asked.

"It's a miracle it's not worse. Try not to look."

Nick cleaned Harry's foot and placed it on a fresh length of linen, deftly lancing the wound and draining the infection into the cloth.

Harry groaned in pain and collapsed on his side into the flea-bitten mattress. "Mother of God! What are you doing?"

"Saving your foot, with any luck. Take heart, the worst is over."

Once he was satisfied the wound had finished draining, Nick cleaned it again and dressed it with the fresh bandages. When he was finished, he packed his tools back into his bag and gently swung Harry's legs onto the bed so he could lie down.

Harry blinked, his breath uneven. "That's feels better, actually. You're a good sort, Nick."

"Thanks, Harry." Nick sat on the floor and leaned back against the bed.

"I haven't gotten to lie down in three days."

"When's the trial?"

"Don't know."

They sat in exhausted silence until they heard the bolt turn in the door.

Mark stumbled in, straightening his shirt. The turnkey thrust a pile of provisions into his arms and bolted the door behind him.

He set the bundle on the edge of the bed, sorting through clean sheets, a thick blanket, a thin little cushion for Harry's head, and a newspaper from the previous week. "This isn't everything." Mark banged his fist on the door. "Oy! Where's the rest?"

They heard a shuffle outside and the turnkey returned with a tray loaded with food, a pipe with tobacco, and a small bottle of prison gin.

"That's more like it," Mark said as the door was bolted once more.

Harry accepted the tray with tears in his eyes. "Mark, how did you..."

He ran a hand through his hair. "Don't ask. Listen, we ain't got much time, so we got to talk fast. Can you talk and eat?"

His mouth full of stew, Harry nodded.

"Good. What did they catch you with?"

Harry shook his head. "It was the take of a lifetime. You wouldn't have believed it. Enough to buy Whitehall outright, make no mistake."

"Did they find it?"

"No." He took a bite of coarse bread. "I was at Mary's place in Cheapside. Stashed it under the floorboards of the house. She don't even know it's there. Only, I took too long hiding it, and they got me at the back gate. I didn't have anything on me at all, only a few pennies, and they took those. Says I stole them."

"How much?"

"Maybe four pence."

Mark breathed a sigh of relief. "You might keep your neck after all. When's the trial?"

"No date."

"They got to let you out if you can pay the discharge fee and whatever they says you owe when the time comes. We'll be there and we'll pay it, but you might be in here for a while." Mark withdrew a small purse of coins from his jacket and gave them to Harry. "You can get anything you need for a bit of rhino, so keep this where you can feel it at all times, yeah?"

"What about the loot?"

"We'll go back for it when we can."

The bolt popped and the door swung open. The turnkey hollered, bored. "Time's up, unless you fancy another go at the warden."

"God bless you both," Harry said.

"Don't worry about it. We'll be back before long."

Nick left several clean bandages at the edge of the bed. "Change these every day while it's weeping, and as often as you can when it closes. Keep it as clean as you can, and you'll be fine."

Before Harry could say another word, Nick and Mark were ushered out, the door slamming behind them. As the dank staircase opened out into the courtyard, Nick had to shield his eyes. Even the cloud-shrouded sun was blinding after traversing the bowels of Newgate. They walked in silence until they reached the bridge.

"Was it like that when you were inside?" Nick asked.

Mark rubbed the back of his hand under his nose, his face white as chalk. "It was worse."

"How long were you there?"

"Two months, before they let me out. No friends on the outside and no ready money. You have to cozy up to the guards to get anything to eat. Lucky for me the warden liked me."

"Christ's tears! I wish I would have known. I would have come for you."

"I wouldn't have wanted you to leave university. Then Mum went..." He sighed. "Look here, it wasn't all bad, so don't go feeling sorry for me. I learned the way of the world, that's for certain, and there's not a crook in these parts who don't owe me a beer, and that's a fact."

Nick laughed in spite of himself.

After they crossed the bridge, The Rose and Crown came into view and Mark smiled his easy smile. "I could use one after that."

"I've still got a couple shillings." Nick smiled at his brother. "Let me buy you a beer. You've earned it."

Chapter 9

Lady Jane Ramsey was bored.

Standing on a short stool in her dressing room, she held still as a doll as she was measured for yet another white dress. Taking shallow breaths as the tailor pinned carefully around her narrow rib cage, she fought the urge to sigh.

This would be her fifth white dress in as many months. Her closet was filled with them. Every shade of pale lavender, the softest blue, and baby pink was crammed into the narrow space among the white, long shapeless confections trimmed with lace and pearls. Children's clothes.

On the few visits she had been permitted off the estate to the fine homes of her father's peers, she had been awed by the daring necklines and vibrant colors the ladies had worn, deep crimson, gold, violet, and azure, their fine long necks weighed down by elaborate jeweled collars gleaming in gold and rubies. She longed to touch the sumptuous velvets and fine silks she had otherwise only seen covering odd pieces of furniture and hanging from the walls that looked so lovely draped over the curvaceous figures of London's most fashionable women.

Jane's room did not have velvet on the walls. Everything was as white as the kitchens, which she had seen but once, when she had gotten lost as a child. The external wall was covered in a tapestry embroidered with the tale of *Tristan and Isolde*, and as little regard as she had for the story, she could not imagine her father would approve if he had known what it was about.

Pinning completed, the tailor carefully took a length of fine French lace from his apprentice. "A little lace for the bodice, Lady Jane?"

Jane absently grasped it in her hand. It was at least four inches deep, and spotted with pink pearls throughout. She rolled her eyes and handed it back to him. "Do you have anything red?"

The tailor looked taken aback. "Red, my lady? On a white dress?"

"You're right," she sighed. "I want a red dress. With black ribbons."

The tailor cleared his throat and his apprentice hid a smile. "I do not believe your father would approve, my lady. He has been very specific in his color selection."

Jane sighed. "Yes, he is very specific, isn't he?"

"Indeed, my lady. Do consider the lace. It would look very fine against your lovely pink complexion." He motioned for his apprentice to bring the looking glass as he held the lace across the top of the gown.

The lace, as she had surmised, covered every inch the dress did not up to the base of her throat. The pearls did bring out the flawless pale rose of her skin, and the burnished copper of her hair contrasted violently against the white. It would have to do.

Greta, her maid, stood from her stool and admired the lace. "It is quite beautiful, my lady. You are without compare."

Jane was aware she was considered a great beauty by the few people who had seen her, but as she had no basis of comparison, she did not know if it was indeed her face or her father's wealth that inspired their admiration.

Jane conceded with a shrug. "Do as you will."

The tailor bowed and he and his assistant began to carefully remove the dress in progress. Jane waited until they had packed up their supplies and left the room before letting out a deep breath and stepping off of the stool.

"How tiresome." She sighed.

Greta withdrew a pale lilac dress from the closet. "I should think it would be wonderful to have so many lovely dresses, my lady."

Jane raised her arms as Greta carefully slipped the dress over her head and began to lace it up the back.

"They're all so boring," Jane protested. "I long for something vibrant and daring. When is he going to realize I'm not a child anymore?"

Greta raised her eyebrows and took the horn handled brush from the dressing table. Jane sat down with a huff and Greta began to gently brush the long waves of her hair. "When you are married, my lady, I expect you can wear what you like."

JESSICA CALE

"When I am married," she repeated. "What if I don't want to get married?"

"Don't be silly, my lady. Everyone wants to get married."

"I don't." She narrowed her wide gray eyes. "I want to be kidnapped."

Greta sighed. "You don't want that, my lady. You will be ravished and no one will want you."

"No one will want me, you say?"

Greta cleared her throat, "Not to say you aren't a very desirable young lady, but I daresay your father might have a time of it finding someone willing to take a lady who's been ruined, as wealthy and beautiful as she may be."

Jane watched the brush swish quietly through her hair and did not reply.

"You mustn't think of it, my lady. Your father has taken every precaution to ensure your safety and would never let you come to any harm."

Jane smiled at Greta and feigned a yawn. "I would like a rest now, Greta."

Greta smiled gently and set the brush on the table. "As you wish, my lady. I will wake you for supper."

"Thank you," Jane said as Greta closed the door behind her.

As Jane heard her footsteps retreat down the hallway, she leapt from the bench, pulled the strings of the lilac dress and tore it over her head, discarding it in a pile of at the foot of the bed. She ran her fingers through her hair, willing it to be wild. Sighing in disappointment as it fell in soft, uniform waves down her back, she flopped dramatically across her feather bed.

At eighteen years old, Jane was well past the age most ladies were introduced at court. Her father's reasoning was, as he had explained many times, that he was wealthy enough to receive more offers than he could entertain, and a little mystery never hurt anyone.

Instead of meeting men at court like a civilized person, Jane was obliged to bide her time, confined to her rooms, taken out on occasion to meet one lord or another or, in all likelihood, his parents. If she passed inspection, and she always did, she would be introduced to the men. They were all either scandalously old or

46

young curious creatures without chins, who lisped terribly and spoke of nothing but hunting various animals with other various animals, be it dogs or hawks, or on one occasion, a bloodthirsty monkey. She could not possibly entertain the notion of spending the length of an afternoon with one of them, let alone her entire life.

Jane shuddered at the thought. She knew exactly what men and women did together, thanks to finding some romances among her late mother's possessions, and she could not –would *not*–think of doing *that* with any of them.

Rolling out of bed, Jane opened her closet and went to her mother's trunk. Jane had been allowed to keep a few mementos after her death and, while the trunk appeared to the untrained eye to contain only religious texts and sewing supplies, it hid a wonderful secret. Shoving the fabric aside, Jane removed the false bottom and smiled. Inside were her mother's romances, her diaries, and a blue velvet dress.

Jane removed the dress and hugged it close to her chest. Her mother had been wearing this dress the day they had been robbed by Claude Duval.

Finding the carriage containing only Jane, then perhaps nine years old, and her mother, the highwayman had proclaimed Lady Hereford so beautiful he could not possibly relieve her of her jewels, and prepared to send them on their way. Lady Hereford handed over her pearls, a brooch, and her wedding ring, with a kiss.

Jane had relived the day many times, reading the diaries until every detail of his face and lovely manners was burned into her heart. It was all over for her at nine. How could she hope to be happy with any kind of match her father would approve?

She couldn't.

Thinking of her brothers' young tutor, she smiled wickedly to herself. He was a little dull, perhaps, but he was deliciously handsome. Perhaps she could seduce him and get out of marrying someone vile. Or perhaps she would go walking along the road one day, and get scooped up by a band of dashing criminals, never to return again.

Thus inspired, Jane put on the blue dress and her walking

47

shoes.

Chapter 10

There was a dream that haunted Sally many of the nights she slept in the Opera House.

A dingy room, the meager bars of sunlight stretching across the dirty walls, the smell of blood. Always the smell of blood. She lies flat on a filthy grey bed, half conscious with pain and hysteria. Wrath is there, lurking in the corner. He wears his ever-present grin, slowly smoking with Charlie in the corner. He watches her face. He's enjoying this. Sally is certain she is about to die.

She digs her nails into the flea-ridden mattress and screams as the old woman pushes down on her belly once more. She feels another current of blood between her legs. It soaks her skirt. It overflows the porcelain pot and floods the floor. Sally can hear a voice praying in the distance, not realizing the voice is her own. The pain is blinding; she takes comfort in the knowledge that it will stop when she dies. She prays for forgiveness. She prays for peace. She prays for a life after death.

"It is done, Sir," Sally hears the old woman say. "I doubt she'll live through the night."

"She'll live," he replies. Sally feels him approach on her right side. He slaps her face. "Wake up, you silly bitch. This is important."

Sally opens her eyes. Through the tears she sees his face; yellowing skin, black hair, glowing eyes. That strange smile.

"You're mine now. You're ruined. What man will have you now that you're barren? What God will save you now that you're a whore?" He growls, his face blocking the light from the window. "I'm all you've got now, and you will do as I say."

Sally grimaces in pain and lets her head drop against the filthy, sweat-soaked sheet. She doesn't know how long she has been locked in the room, but she half-remembers kindness between the screams. "Where's Bettie?"

The old woman shakes her head.

"Get him," Wrath says to her. Sally closes her eyes with a grimace and she does not open them again until she is certain he is gone. She hears light steps enter the room and the door closes with a soft click. Silk skirts swish as

*he sits beside the bed and rests a cool, sweet-smelling cloth across her forehead.
Sally opens her eyes to see the gently smiling face of her only friend. "I lost the
baby," she says.*

"I know." He rests his large hand on her shoulder.

"I'm dying."

"You're going to be just fine," he lies.

Sally woke with a start and reached for one of the bottles
beneath her bed, drinking deeply. Three years had passed and she
still had not escaped that day. With shaking hands she straightened
her chemise. She felt frantically for the necklace she had hidden
within her bodice, sighing in relief once she found it. Although she
had her own room, the other girls were not above rifling through
her possessions, so Sally had taken to hiding them. She slid the
bottles under her bed to the side, not thinking twice about the
noise they made as they clanged together. There were a lot of loud
noises there; self-preservation taught her to ignore them.

Sally had managed to work the third floorboard behind the
gin loose with a pair of scissors one night after a sizeable ruby had
been taken from her bureau. Underneath she hid her jewelry case
full of precious things. Wrath had taken what little she had of value
when she was taken into his brothel, but let her keep her little box,
as it was only plain and wooden. Her hair combs he had taken,
along with a brooch and her mother's rosary.

Now, as she opened it to hide her latest sapphire, it looked
very different. Aside from her few letters, it was packed full of
beautiful colors--gold, silver, reds, blues, rose, violet, jonquil, and
at least ten shades of green, all winking at her from the darkness.
She smiled as she added the sapphire to her collection, and took
out a small opal that had been given to her by a fat barber. She
replaced the board, lined up the bottles over it once more, and
took the opal to her bureau. Sally placed it carefully under the false
bottom of the top drawer as a diversion from the real treasure
beneath the floor.

From the street she could hear the merry voices of the
whoring young gentry, already drunk at four. The sun seemed to
be setting earlier those days, although it was never too early to start
drinking in that part of town. She lit a few candles to stave off the

darkness a while longer. She needed the light to arrange her hair for the evening.

Sally jumped involuntarily as Bettie snuck in, bottles in hand. "They're already mad out there. It's going to be a busy night. Drink up." He set a bottle of gin between her and the mirror.

She pulled out the cork and took a deep swig.

Bettie's reflection appeared behind hers in the mirror and he began to fuss with her hair.

"I haven't started yet."

"Give me your comb."

Sally passed the comb over her shoulder and he began to pin her hair into its usual high coif. She took another sip of gin. "Why are you so good at this?"

"I used to be a ladies' maid, can't you tell?"

Sally giggled. He told her a different story every time. She didn't know which, if any, of them were true.

Hair forgotten, Bettie leaned over her shoulder to take her pot of carmine from the dressing table. Rubbing a little on his finger, he began to dab it onto his lips. "Will you do my eyes tonight? I want to look like you."

"Why would you want to look like me?" She laughed, reaching for the kohl.

"I'm going to the theatre tonight." He smiled. He closed his eyes as she began to tap the oily black powder over them with a small brush. "Rochester's meant to be there. I need to look perfect."

"That's very daring." As common as male prostitutes were, homosexuality was still a capital offense. Unlike Sally, Bettie worked for Wrath of his own free will, but seldom ventured outside the confines of the playhouse for his own safety.

"'Tis," he agreed. "We're going to try to catch him backstage."

"You would do well in Versailles. The whole court is mad for pretty boys. Close your eyes." She coated the brush in more kohl. "How have you been feeling?"

"Fine." He shrugged and his eyelid twitched almost imperceptibly beneath the brush. "I haven't been bad again in weeks."

51

"Have you been taking your mercury?"

"Can't you tell? I've been salivating like a wild dog."

Eyes finished, Sally set the pot on the table. "You be careful, dearest. We don't want anyone suspecting."

He straightened the neckline of his dress and pulled up his corset. "You, too. Don't forget to check for the signs."

"I never do."

He smiled tightly and took a drink. "How do I look?"

Bettie was a lean man of medium height, broad of shoulder with a strong jaw. He wore a dress of dark pink embroidered all over with maroon flowers. Its low, square neckline was filled with lace and a small bustle over his hips set off his waist, a masculine shape in spite of the corset. His face was powdered as white as hers, his lips and cheeks set off with carmine, and his laughing blue eyes emphasized with the kohl. She wondered how long his looks would last before the syphilis reached his face.

Sally reached up and adjusted his new wig, an expensive but well-made mop of carefully formed golden curls. "You're beautiful."

Chapter 11

Wrath stood as a knock sounded on the door to his office. Charlie crossed the room to admit Lord Hereford a full five minutes before he was expected. Hiding a smile, Wrath greeted, "Well met, my lord."

Hereford offered a half-bow, out of courtesy more than necessity.

"Please, have a seat." He motioned to the small chair on the other side of the table. "Charles, the wine."

Charlie brought a bottle of darkest claret with two crystal glasses and poured as Hereford settled uncomfortably into the narrow seat.

Hereford raised his glass to Wrath and sipped the wine, unsure of where to start. "Sally," he sputtered, at last.

Wrath leaned back in his chair with a cocky smile. "I trust she met your approval?"

Hereford shifted in his chair with an uncharacteristically candid expression on his face. "Oh, yes. Wherever did you find such a creature?"

"It was not easy," he began with feigned humility, "but I would go to great lengths to please those whom I consider to be my friends, in faith that they would do the same for me."

"I would do anything you ask, as I hope I have demonstrated in the past," Hereford answered, showing his interest too quickly. He would never make a businessman.

Wrath would use this to his advantage. He sipped his wine.

Hereford filled the silence. "What do you want for her?"

There it was.

Wrath set down his wine and attempted to look surprised. "Want? What ever could you mean, my lord?"

"Don't play coy with me, Wrath. You have something and I want it. Name your price."

"What are your terms?"

"Full rights. Exclusivity. She will be mine alone to keep where

I will and to do with as I see fit."

Wrath had been waiting for this day for years. Since the moment she had walked through his door, he knew Sally was the key to securing his future. She had been the card up his sleeve he'd been holding for the hand with the highest stakes. He had to play this just right.

He let out a long breath, "My dear fellow, that is impossible. Quite impossible, I'm afraid."

"You understand I am a very wealthy man?"

Wrath knew precisely how wealthy Hereford was. "Indeed, sir, but Sally is no common whore. She is sought by the very highest in the kingdom. Even this week I have entertained offers from certain dukes of our mutual acquaintance," he lied.

"Buckingham?"

"I couldn't possibly say." Wrath waved a hand. "Anonymity, you understand."

"Of course."

Wrath leaned forward slightly, the shadow of his hat falling across Hereford's glass. "I trust you are aware of her parentage?"

"I am aware of what you had told me before our meeting, but is that terribly likely?"

Wrath chuckled. "Come now, it is as plain as the nose on her face, is it not?"

Hereford reddened.

"Your late wife was a Stewart, I believe?"

"You know very well that she was."

"I regret that I was unable to meet her. Did she bear any resemblance to Miss Green?"

Hereford looked down into his wine. "None at all, but very beautiful. Brilliant auburn hair, quite a temper." He laughed. "Jane looks just like her. The very picture."

All or nothing. "Of course, your lovely daughter. She must be getting close to marriageable age. How old is she now?"

"She's only eighteen. I've received some handsome offers, naturally, but I'm in no hurry to decide."

"Very wise, very wise." Wrath sipped his wine. "Would you consider the suit of an earl?"

Hereford visibly shuddered, "You can't be suggesting..."

"Why ever not?" Wrath motioned for Charlie to refill Hereford's glass. "I'm well-situated, as you know. There is the house in St. James, the estate in the West Country, and a good yearly income besides. Not to mention my little business." He smiled.

Hereford sputtered. "I'm afraid I had assumed otherwise. If your income is adequate, why bother with business?"

Wrath smiled, his eyes glittering dangerously, "I like to make my friends happy."

Hereford sipped his wine and began to negotiate in earnest. "You are out of favor, I believe."

"Not so much out of favor as out of fashion, but I imagine making your lovely daughter a countess would remedy that."

Wrath watched Hereford consider his offer. He could almost hear the wheels turning in his head. For all his wealth and connections, Hereford was only an earl, and a fairly new one at that. He was no better than Wrath when it came down to it.

Hereford took a deep breath, "You understand that Jane's dowry is substantial, in addition to the estate in Inverness. Her portion would bring you another several thousand annually."

"Indeed, my lord."

"You would want all that, and what else, besides?"

Wrath threw up his hands. "You wound me, my lord. I propose nothing but an honest trade. A Stewart for a Stuart."

"It's not quite the same thing, is it?"

"No, but Sally is trained to satisfy the most discerning of patrons with the most particular of..." *perversions* "...preferences. Do you deny her value?"

Hereford did not meet his eyes. "I will need time to consider your offer."

"Of course," Wrath conceded, sensing he was losing him. "In the meantime, shall we see what Sally is up to?" He stood, motioning to a door to the side of the office.

Hereford looked up in surprise. He drained his wine and moved to follow him through the dark corridor and up a narrow set of winding stairs.

Wrath led the way past the door to the street and up to the top floor, past peepholes drilled to better view the rooms from every conceivable angle until they reached the room at the end that faced the street. He could hear Hereford breathing behind him, short of breath from exertion or anticipation. Charlie closed the door behind them and followed them up the stairs with heavy footsteps. Wrath smiled to himself and removed the planks that covered the peepholes.

Hereford gasped as he saw Sally on the other side. "She's in there with a molly!"

"Quietly, my lord. These walls are thin."

"Of course, of course," he whispered.

They watched together as Sally dipped a brush into a pot. She took Bettie's masculine jaw in her delicate white hand and leaned forward to apply the kohl to his closed eyes with an enigmatic little smile, her dress tantalizingly low. Her lips were inches away from Bettie's face. They were the very picture of sensual beauty together, her curves and his angles, dressed head to toe in gleaming silk. Sally set down the brush and took a blonde wig from her dressing table, placing it over Bettie's short hair and carefully adjusting it to frame his face. Smiling at her handiwork, Sally whispered something Wrath could not hear and gave Bettie a sisterly kiss on his lips.

There were many who would pay a great deal to watch this very thing, and Hereford was getting it for free. "Shall I have them put on a show for you?"

Wrath could see Hereford's expression of horror even in the dark. "Good God, man! He's wearing a dress!"

"He can take it off." He rolled his eyes.

Hereford shook his head. "I do not like the idea of other men touching her, regardless of what they are or are not wearing."

Wrath led the way back down the stairs and Hereford reluctantly followed. "You understand that until you have purchased her, Sally will continue to entertain other patrons?"

He could almost hear Hereford shudder behind him. "Of course."

Back in his office, Wrath returned to his high-backed chair. "I hope you will consider my offer, my lord."

Hereford did not sit down. He stood, shifting from foot to foot. He was practically salivating. "I will consider it. Am I correct in assuming you would not object to the conditions in which she will be kept? I am to have absolute authority over her person?"

Wrath nodded. "As well as her disposal, should you tire of her."

Hereford nodded sharply. "I hope you will remember the favors I have done for you in the past."

How could he forget? "How is Mister Virtue?"

Hereford shrugged. "He is a passable tutor. His views are a bit fanciful for my taste, but the children seem to have taken to him. Jane especially," he added.

Wrath cringed. "I trust she is still a maiden?"

"Of course!" Hereford sputtered, "To think I would allow such a thing!"

"I have every confidence you have the utmost control over your daughter," Wrath offered. "Our Mister Virtue, he's not too comfortable, is he?"

Hereford chuckled. "I should think not."

"Is he still confined to the estate?"

Hereford's eyes shifted to the left. "Naturally."

"My thanks, my lord." It was plain that he didn't have the slightest idea what his tutor got up to when he couldn't see him. Wrath shrugged it off. He didn't truly care as long as Mister Virtue was not causing him any problems.

Hereford wrinkled his nose. "Remind me again, why is it that you asked me to keep him under lock and key?"

"I couldn't possibly say. I am the very soul of discretion, you understand."

Chapter 12

"The master wishes to have a word with you."

The voice of the old woman creaks like a rusted hinge from the doorway, sending a cascade of goose bumps down Sally's neck.

Reluctantly leaving the knife she has been using on the table, she wipes the butter from her hands on a cloth and follows her into the hallway.

She leads Sally without a word through a short corridor that empties into the atrium of the Opera House, the once serviceable stage covered in half-conscious harlots, already in their cups at noon. They pay her little heed as she passes.

Opening a door at the far end of the atrium behind the enormous sweeping staircase, the woman ushers Sally into an office and closes the door behind her. Sally's heart begins to pound in earnest.

Dark as it is, she can make out stains marring the green silk wall coverings. Heavy curtains are drawn across the windows and the room is lit by a single burning lamp. Clutching her skirt in fear, she turns to see that she is being observed by two very well-dressed men.

Clearly in the presence of nobility, Sally curtsies, regretting that she has not been permitted to wash before leaving the kitchens, and hoping she will not be reprimanded for smelling of kippers.

The men approach her, slowly. Both are older gentlemen. One is tall, thin, and dark wearing a black coat with a brilliant red waistcoat. The other is stately and graceful, resplendent in a suit of embroidered silks. He would be handsome if not for his look of self-satisfaction. Sally holds still as they draw closer, her every nerve standing on end.

The dark man asks, "What do you think?"

The other man takes her face in his hand and her eyes widen at the firm, steady pressure of his fingers on her jaw. He takes his time examining her face with curiously objective blue eyes, seeing her eyes but not looking into them. As he turns her face to the side to look at her profile, she hears a sharp intake of breath.

Taking a curl of her hair between his thumb and forefinger, he asks the other, "Does he know?"

The dark man's face splits into a grin. "No, I thought to call upon you first."

Dropping Sally's hair, he asks, "Why?"

The smile falters. "I thought she might be of some use to you. I know you two have your little intrigues..."

"You can't be suggesting..." the man beside her is taken aback. "Come now, that's unnatural."

"Y-you misunderstand, my lord. I merely thought she might serve some purpose, whatever it is is no concern of mine. Perhaps Rochester, or Arlington "

Holding up a hand, he responds, "Say you're right, which you cannot prove, what good would it do to bring this to his attention now? Say you find a use for her, as you put it, and he finds out, what do you suppose he would do to you? Our friend is forgiving but he has his limits. Take my advice, forget you ever saw her, and send her on her way."

Without a second glance at Sally, he leaves the room, the door slamming shut behind him.

The dark man stands quietly for a moment, shaking with barely contained rage.

Sally takes a tentative step toward the door and he seizes her painfully by the shoulders, hissing into her ear, "If Buckingham doesn't want you, I will take you for myself."

Sally woke up screaming for the second time that week.

Long, lean arms tensed around her, holding her firmly. "Shhhh! Sally! Sally! Wake up, it's only a dream. It's a dream. Sally!"

Her eyes adjusted to the sunlight glaring through her dirty window and she relaxed against Bettie's chest with a relieved sigh, willing her heart to slow its rapid pace.

Bettie rested his face against her shoulder, the short waves of his sand colored hair soft against her skin. "Was it the rape again?"

She rubbed a hand over her eyes. "Which one?"

Sally felt his sadness in the slope of his broad shoulders and his slight weight leaning limply against her back. Nothing she could have said would have made it better. She regretted saying anything at all.

"You woke me up before it happened," she said, a consolation. "Was I screaming again?"

"You were tossing a bit. Someone's taken my room so I

thought I'd sleep here. Didn't think you'd mind."

"I don't." She snuggled against him. "You're the best kind of company."

He kissed her cheek affectionately and sat up, stretching his arms. His reflection in her mirror was blurry, the red silk of his corset glowing in the sunlight like the petals of an enormous blooming rose, an image that would not have been out of place in one of her pleasanter gin-soaked dreams. He caught her watching his reflection and turned to stretch across the bed on his stomach with the grace of a dancer, smiling sleepily.

"You are wasted on those awful men," Sally lamented. "How can they know how beautiful you are?"

"I could say the same for you, my dear." He took her hand and gallantly kissed the back of it. "We shall have to go on appreciating each other to make up for their oversight."

"I love you to distraction," she said. "Let's a run away and get married and live out our lives in peace."

"Yes, let's. The pox-ridden molly and the barren French runaway. We'll disappear in Devon and appreciate each other until death do us part."

"You can have all the men you like and I will...garden?"

"You're bad at this game." He hit her with a pillow. "You need to think of something more sensational. I will be a glamorous gentlewoman with more handsome lovers than there are days in the week, and you will take to the roads dressed as a dashing highwayman, relieving the gentry of their jewels for the mad thrill of it."

She laughed. "Some highwayman I would make. I'm afraid of horses!"

He rolled his blue eyes dramatically. "Why, I shall simply throw a saddle on one of my lovers and compel him to take you wherever you wish to go."

"How gracious!"

"Quite."

They stayed quiet for a moment, contemplating the ceiling through the holes in her canopy.

"I would marry you, if I thought it would get you out of here," he consoled.

"I know."

He sat up suddenly. "Do you want to go to the shops with me? Get out of here for a bit?"

"What, now?"

"It's early yet. Everyone's still sleeping, unless you woke them."

She raised herself up on her elbows. "They don't like me to go out on my own."

"You won't be on your own. You'll be with me." He smiled.

She raised an eyebrow. "Do you mean to go out like that?" His wig was gone and he wore no shift. As fetching as his bare chest looked cinched into the red silk, he could not safely leave the house dressed as he was.

"No worries, dearest. I won't be a moment." He rose, bunching his skirt in his hands, and tiptoed out of the room, closing the door softly behind him.

Climbing out of bed, Sally shivered as her bare feet touched the cold floor. A handful of new cundums was scattered across the floor, pink ribbons asunder, soaked in the contents of a shattered bottle of gin. She must have struck her nightstand in her sleep. She would have to purchase more of both.

She threw her only dress on over her shift and took her thin shawl from her dressing table, wanting it for modesty more than warmth. Slipping her shoes on, she edged the shattered glass under the bed with her toe to further deter anyone who might go looking for her jewel box beneath the floor.

The door swung open with a soft creak and a well-dressed man walked in. Sally jumped backward with a gasp before she recognized him. "Bettie?"

He splayed his arms in feigned offence. "You didn't know me?"

"Good Lord, Bettie! You're handsome!"

"And you're surprised?" Bettie had scrubbed the makeup off of his face and wore the suit of a gentleman.

"I'm impressed."

"I try not to disappoint." He straightened his posture theatrically and offered her his arm. "My lady."

Sally giggled in spite of herself. "Good sir. Oh, but what shall

I call you? I can hardly call you Mister Bettie!"

"You certainly could," he assured her, "but if you like, you may call me Benedict."

"Is that your real name?"

"It's one of them." He shrugged. "I prefer Bettie. I chose it myself."

He could have invented any number of names, and likely had, but she had caught a glimpse of unguarded pain in his eyes, and knew this one was real. Her heart swelled at having been taken into his confidence. As close as they were, so much of him remained a mystery to her.

They walked arm in arm down the hallway through a cacophony of snores, creaking beds, overzealous fucking, and even the beginnings of a catfight in the room at the end of the hall. Bettie smiled brightly. "You see? We were hardly the loudest up and about this morning. No one will even hear us leave."

The inhabitants of the atrium were still sleeping, for the most part, drunk to various stages of blindness, and they managed to walk out the front door without any comment. They were mere yards down the street when Sally heard the door open again and glanced over her shoulder to see Charlie following them at a distance.

She shouldn't have been surprised.

"What is it, my love?"

"Charlie is following us."

Bettie raised his chin an inch or two and puffed up his chest. "Pay him no heed. We shall simply have to have a pleasant outing in spite of the stench."

He could have referred to the gutters, overflowing in the summer heat in defiance of the gentility of the neighborhood, but they both knew what he meant. Passing a flower cart, he gave the vendor a penny for two small nosegays of violets, handing one to Sally with a grin and burying his nose into the other, inhaling deeply. "Much better."

They passed carts piled high with turnips and leafy vegetables, caked in dirt and pests. There were great wheels of cheese, loaves of heavy bread, and crates of live chickens. They walked past Bedford's, already open for the day and packed with patrons, and reached the sun-dappled walls of the church at the edge of the piazza. "I hope you're not taking me to confession," Sally joked.

"Goodness, no! I don't have all day! Besides, I hear it's bad form to burn a priest's ears off before breakfast. Where would you like to go?"

She looked around at the shops and lovely new houses around them, their white walls cheerful by the light of day, and almost forgot Charlie was following not far behind. "Not far, I imagine," she said with no little regret. "I should buy more cundums. Mine got soaked in gin."

"Bedford's, then?"

"They only sell them at night, and every time I go in there, John Cooper gives me the evil eye. I don't know what kind of clientele he thinks he has if he chases me away when he's the one selling cundums."

"I abhor hypocrites. Unfortunately for us, my dear, London is overrun with them. To the apothecary, then?"

"Are you suggesting we poison them?"

He almost laughed. "Don't tempt me."

They ducked into the apothecary's at the end of the street and Sally was relieved to see Charlie keep to the shadows of the inn across the way. Better he did not know what they were there for.

She kept close to Bettie as he purchased the mercury he took to fight the symptoms of the pox, examining the blue and green bottles behind the counter, the names of the potions scrawled on white tags in a narrow hand that she could not read, even had she known what they were meant to be called. At the edge of the shelf nearest her, she recognized Borage and Dandelion, and wondered what medicinal purpose the herbs could serve.

The apothecary handed Bettie an unlabeled bottle without being asked. Clearly he recognized him from his previous visits. Bettie passed it to Sally across the counter, their proximity to each other disguising the exchange, and she slipped it into her pocket for him along with a stack of new cundums.

Although many considered their use to be risqué, cundums were as common as snuff, and one shop in four sold them beneath the counter to people from all walks of life to protect them from disease. Sally no longer blushed when she purchased them. The alternative was worse.

Supplies purchased and stashed away, they left the shop for the market, stopping for sticky buns to break their fast.

Though the quality was poor, Sally ate hers quickly and was sucking the honey off her fingers when she heard Bettie gasp.

"What is it?" she asked, her thumb in her mouth.

His eyes wide, he lightly rapped her shoulder with the back of his hand and nodded enthusiastically toward the nearest inn, where a group of young nobles staggered onto the street.

Sally looked them over with indifference. With their wigs and their ridiculous clothes, they all looked much the same to her. There were about a dozen of them, and from the state of them, they had been drinking for days. They were led by a handsome man in burgundy velvet, dark-featured with a devilish smile. Sally fancied she could smell the drink coming off him in waves, though he wore it better than the rest, managing to hold himself up a little higher, walking a little straighter, with the commanding air of someone who knew he was very important indeed.

"Who is that?" she whispered.

"Who is that?" Bettie repeated, aghast. If he had been holding a fan, he would have struck her with it. "That, my darling, is Rochester."

"He's pretty." She shrugged.

"He certainly is." Bettie sighed.

"Does he like boys?" she asked, perhaps too loudly.

"He will when I get through with him," he growled into her ear, setting her giggling again.

Sally elbowed him gently in the ribs. "Go talk to him."

"Are you mad? One doesn't simply talk to the Earl of Rochester."

"What *does* one do with the Earl of Rochester?"

Bettie inclined his head to one side and she could tell he was thinking about it. Her laughter interrupted his reverie.

He blushed rather prettily for a handsome young man. "Cheeky baggage," he muttered under his breath.

Sally had turned to buy another bun when she recognized one

of the final two members of Rochester's party to stagger into the street. "Bugger!" she cursed, ducking behind Bettie.

"What is it?"

"It's Beaumont! I don't want to work until I have to. Hide me!"

"Sally?" Beaumont called.

"Hellfire and damnation!" She cursed even as she smiled in greeting.

Bettie chuckled at her discomfort and threw an arm around her shoulders. "Never fear, darling."

Beaumont made his way to them, an impossibly wide smile plastered across his face. "Sally! It's you. Where have you been?"

"Good day, my lord." She bobbed a reluctant curtsy.

His eyes were bloodshot and his right eyelid drooped slightly. He needed a bed. "Who is this gentle...ham?"

"Did he just say...?" Bettie murmured.

Sally stifled a laugh. "This is my friend, Mister--"

"Benedict," Bettie supplied. "Lord Benedict, that is."

She raised an eyebrow. Bettie was enjoying this.

"I am Beaumont."

He remembered his own name, at least.

"It is a pleasure." Bettie gallantly bowed.

"Charred, I'm sure."

Sally did laugh at that one.

Bettie winked at her. "If you will pardon us, my lord, Sally and I have an appointment."

Beaumont looked stricken, and she did feel for him, though she wondered what he imagined she was doing out on her own with a man who was not actively trying to sell her. "Of course," he said with some regret. He took her hand and attempted to kiss it, but missed. "Until we meet again."

"Lord Beaumont." She nodded as Bettie tipped his hat.

Bettie wrapped his arm possessively around her waist and led her quickly down the street. While Beaumont still watched, Bettie let his hand slide down and gave her arse a good squeeze.

"Bet--Benedict!" She gasped, smacking his shoulder.

He gave a dirty laugh. "Had to see what all the fuss was about."

"Are you satisfied?"

"Not by half. I wish I looked like you in a dress."

"You're much prettier than me." Sally sighed.

"Nonsense. You are a goddess, my dear, and everyone knows it. Why, that poor fellow back there was ready to burst into tears when I mentioned our appointment."

"You shouldn't kid so. You're lucky he's too drunk to ask what you're the lord of."

A wicked smile spread across his face. "I am the petticoated lord of Bedford Street. I am the very king of the catamites!"

Sally giggled nervously. "Keep it down, your majesty. You don't want to attract the wrong kind of attention."

"I believe I attracted enough of the right kind of attention for one day." He smiled smugly.

"What do you mean?"

He leaned down to meet her face and raised his eyebrows. "Your Beaumont, of course! A little jealousy is good for a man. Stirs the blood. Mark my words, he'll make an offer for you before the week is up. We may get you out of here yet."

Chapter 13

Beaumont couldn't sleep.

Rolling out of bed after a long day of tortured insomnia, silk sheets and feather mattress notwithstanding, he rang for his chocolate and sat in his long shirt at his dressing table.

He wearily peered at his reflection in the polished mirror. His hair was frightfully unkempt and he had deep circles under his eyes. Gently touching his puffy skin, he observed that his face had not been shaved in days. His mouth was dry and tasted like he had licked a beach.

He looked a mess.

Two weeks of continuous debauchery with his libertine compatriots had taken its toll, leaving him looking far older than his twenty-two years. He remembered little of what had taken place, only that John Wilmot, Earl of Rochester, was back in town. The return of their beloved friend and the leader-in-all-but-name of their band of miscreants had inspired a celebration to rival the return of the King some ten years before.

There had been days of rich food and endless drink, and his stomach ached as though he had been sick several times. His hair still smelled of tobacco and he detected a note of saltwater, dimly recalling being slapped with a smoked fish.

Had that been a dream?

There had been women, a gaudy procession of brightly dressed women, and catamites as well. He had lost count somewhere after the third day, their painted faces and heaving bosoms melding into one nameless, horrifying beast with dozens of legs and hundreds of thieving fingers.

The one thing he was certain of was that Sally had not been there.

Two weeks of untold pleasures, heavy drink, and otherworldly terrors and he had not been able to get the girl from Bedford's out of his head.

Their encounter had been brief, yet memorable. Her hair

between his fingers, the taste of coffee on her breath...her wicked laugh echoed through his memory. *Perhaps...*

Morton, his valet, appeared silently and set his chocolate before him, opening the heavy curtains before he left the room. Beaumont cringed at the deadly invasion of natural light and blinked in pain as his eyes began to adjust. He might still be drunk, but there appeared to be two dishes of chocolate on the tray.

He heard a moan and turned toward the sound. An unfamiliar shoe hung off an unfamiliar foot protruding from the floor behind his bed. Beaumont grabbed his velvet dressing gown from the floor and belted it around his waist before investigating the disturbance.

Peering around one curtained pillar, Beaumont beheld Geoffrey Conley, his university friend and fellow libertine, sprawled across his Oriental rug wearing nothing but a pair of heeled court shoes.

"Christ's blood, man! Cover yourself!"

Conley sat up gingerly, slowly looking about himself in confusion. "Beaumont?"

Beaumont crossed the room and searched his closet for something suitable. Finding the previous season's dressing gown toward the back, he pulled it down, gave it a shake, and threw it at Conley, hitting him in the face.

Conley stroked the velvet dumbly. "What time is it?"

"Too bloody early," said Beaumont, returning to his chocolate and finding there were, indeed, two dishes there. He took the tray to the table beside the window and sat in one of the upholstered chairs there.

Conley joined him, taking the seat opposite. "That was a long revel," he said, sipping his chocolate.

"Indeed."

"It's not late, is it? We agreed to meet Rochester at Bedford's."

Beaumont shook his head, blinking. "I can't do another night. You go on without me."

"But we were going to try to get Sally tonight. I thought you'd want to go."

"Sally?" Beaumont blinked dumbly, "Rochester has an

interest in Sally?"

Conley shrugged. "We all do. You wouldn't shut up about her after you saw her with that lord. You piqued our interest."

"What lord?"

"You don't remember seeing her outside the Tangier? You wept into your beer at the injustice and that's what started it. Rochester wrote a verse about her on the spot from what you said." He laughed. "You must remember that."

"Rochester can't have her–she's mine!"

"Try telling him that."

"But–but–he's got the pox!" Beaumont sputtered.

Conley laughed. "You're worried about getting a whore sick? That's a good one."

Beaumont set down his chocolate, sloshing some on the table, and rang for Morton.

"What are you doing?"

"I'm going out," he said.

Two hours later, Beaumont had washed, shaved, and dressed. Conley had departed after a long, fruitless search for his clothes, having been obliged to take his leave wearing some borrowed items of Beaumont's. Fortunately, Beaumont had gotten up in the early hours of the afternoon, allowing ample time to tidy himself up before running off to Covent Garden to try to beat the libertines to Sally.

He was not yet certain of his feelings for her, but he would be damned if he would knowingly take a pox-ridden mistress.

Beaumont arrived at Wrath's place just after sundown. A rambling old theatre that had survived the war and had somehow avoided being replaced when Covent Garden had been rebuilt years before, it was often referred to as the "playhouse" or, more generously, the "Opera House," as it still had a disused stage in the atrium and all of the walls were draped with brilliant red curtains. It was lit throughout by the soft light of towering wax candles, the open flames, and boiling blood of the closely packed punters raising the temperature inside.

Several dozen rowdy men of all ages and stations were congregating at the bottom of the wide, sweeping staircase that connected the atrium to a long row of rooms in the gallery above.

A few girls in low-cut dresses shuffled amongst the crowd like orange girls at a play, the excited conversation around him building to a fever pitch.

He turned to the man beside him, a sailor, by the looks of him, and asked, "What are we waiting for?"

"Like you don't know." He laughed. "The Green Devil's coming down. We're waiting to see who gets picked."

"Picked by whom? For what?"

The sailor glanced at him impatiently. "Man comes out from behind the stair and picks who gets her. Could be anyone."

As promised, a tall, thin man in a black coat emerged from behind the stairwell to cheers from the crowd. He was tailed by a hulking giant with a menacing look. Paying little attention to the crowd surrounding him, he stepped to the base of the staircase and waited.

"What now?" Beaumont asked.

The sailor shushed him and watched the top of the staircase.

Moments later, a tall, willowy redhead in a gown with a shortened skirt showing off miles of legs in striped stockings sauntered down the staircase with a cheeky grin. She was greeted with wolf whistles and applause.

"That's Rosey," the sailor said.

Rosey was followed by a petite blonde in a red dress that looked at least ten years too old for her. "She's a child!" Beaumont protested.

"That's Camille. She's older than she looks."

Beaumont very much doubted that.

Camille was followed by another half dozen reasonably attractive women in cheap dresses of vibrant jewel tones, and even, to his surprise, a boy in a rose colored ball gown and a blonde wig. There was a belief among his circles, at least, that men could not transmit the pox in the way that women could, so some of his compatriots had taken to entertaining themselves with their own sex to avoid infection. Beaumont thought the idea was nonsense, but as the boy elicited at least as many cheers as did the ladies, he suspected he was alone in that regard.

He was beginning to grow impatient when, at last, she appeared at the top of the stairs.

The crowd fell utterly silent for an instant as she paused at the top, resplendent in that emerald green dress, her eyes glittering dangerously beneath heavy lids painted black with kohl. As she began to descend, one hip-swaying step at a time, the crowd began to cheer wildly. The fearsome looking man in black at the bottom of the stairs even cracked a smile.

"Sally." Beaumont sighed.

The sailor threw himself toward the man with a purse of coins in his hand. "How much for the Green Devil?"

The man didn't even glance at him. "Too much for you, mate," he dismissed.

Undeterred, the sailor waited, watching Sally's descent into the greedy crowd.

"Why do they call her the Green Devil?" Beaumont asked him.

"Cause she wears green," he said.

Beaumont rolled his eyes. "That's it?"

The man shrugged. "Tempts men into sin, don't she?"

"Is that the best you can do?"

Another man to his other side cut in. "They say she's one of the King's bastards! She's almost a princess!"

"Which king?" Beaumont demanded.

"How many kings we got, mate? Are you daft? Look at her!"

He did.

Sally was beautiful, to be sure, in an unconventional way. Her eyes were black as night, her lips a shade more sensual than the smaller, rosebud pouts so beloved of the poets. Her nose was prominent and burdened with a bump at the bridge. She was tall for a woman, though not unreasonably so, with flawless skin the luminous white of fine porcelain stretched over curves that made his mouth water. Her black, black hair was piled on top of her head in a fetching coif, much darker than the brighter tones aspired to by the ladies at court, who took to lightening their own with secret concoctions to emulate the court favorites like Lady Castlemaine.

No, by the standard of the day, Sally was far too striking to be considered truly beautiful, but she had a fierce magnetism that was impossible to ignore.

But the King's daughter?

"Preposterous," Beaumont dismissed.

"You ever seen him?"

"Of course," Beaumont huffed. "But if there were any truth to it, do you suppose His Majesty would allow her to set foot in a place like this?"

The man looked confused for a moment. Shaking his head as if ridding himself of Beaumont's troublesome logic, he turned his attention back to Sally.

Patience well and truly spent, Beaumont approached the man in black at the bottom of the stairs. Sally was better than this place, and he would get her out of it. "How much do you want for her?" Beaumont asked.

The man barely glanced in his direction. "For the hour or the night?"

Beaumont had a vague recollection of seeing him before, but he could not place where. The man stood half a head taller than he did. Beaumont stood up a little straighter, pulling himself to his full, not insignificant height. "For good."

He laughed. The scoundrel *laughed*. "No price on this earth could persuade me to part with her."

Beaumont tossed him a small purse with enough gold in it to buy a good horse.

The man weighed it in his hand, unfazed.

"Will that cover the month?"

The man laughed. "Try the night."

Beaumont made no attempt to disguise his contempt. "Very well," he agreed reluctantly. "But I'm taking her with me."

"Sally!" The man called up the stairs. "You've been sold!"

A disappointed hush fell over the crowd and many of them left. Others paired off with the remaining girls, and a few milled around, waiting and smoking while an old bawd brought them beer and wine. Sally stepped over to him, smiling in recognition. "My lord."

Beaumont offered his arm and she took it, following him out into the night.

72

Chapter 14

As Sally left the opera house with Beaumont, the crowd thinned considerably. The remaining girls offered little temptation to the Friday night crowd, and she was certain they would vent their frustration on her over the following week, as they often did through pranks and cruel words.

It may have bothered her, had she taken any pride in her work or position in society, but as she did not, she was impervious to their attacks. In any case, no one took the words of common whores to heart, least of all other whores.

A wave of misery overtook her, as it did whenever she had the misfortune to remember herself, and she had a fierce craving for more gin. She glanced over her shoulder as they turned the corner toward the piazza to see the Opera House disappear behind the baker's and she wished, as she did every day, that she had never wandered onto Bedford Street. Sally pulled her thin shawl tighter around her shoulders with a shiver, and crashed into the broad chest of man, breaking her connection with Beaumont.

"I beg your pardon, Sir," she apologized, and looked up into the kindest eyes she had seen in Covent Garden.

"Not to worry, miss. Are you all right?" He smiled at her gently, and for the second time in her life, she found herself quite unable to speak.

"Come along, Sally," Beaumont called.

Sally nodded at the man, and made an attempt to return his smile, wondering where her voice had gone.

"Sally!" Beaumont took her arm and began to lead her down the street, away from the handsome man.

Sally's gaze followed him as Beaumont dragged her away. He gave her a half-bow before disappearing completely as she was pulled into the crowd.

"Did you know that man?" Beaumont asked as he helped her into his carriage.

The bench was upholstered with deep indigo brocade, and

she sat down carefully, running a hand over the fine embroidery. "I do not, my lord, although I confess he reminded me of someone," she said, thinking of Claude.

Beaumont sat beside her, resting his hand on her knee and kissing her shoulder. "And who is that, my dear?"

"My brother," she lied, looking out the window into the night. She couldn't say what had made her think of Claude. The strange man was tall and handsome, certainly, but had lighter skin whereas Claude had been swarthy, and soft green eyes when Claude's had been sharp and black.

Sally thought of Claude's eyes, the light gone out of them as he kissed her, and shivered.

"You've gone quite pale, my dear. Does your brother live nearby?" Beaumont asked, withdrawing a snuff box from his coat.

"No," she replied. "He's dead."

Chapter 15

Nick shifted in the narrow pew, trying in vain to reach some relative level of comfort. As tutor in Lord Hereford's household, it was his duty to oversee the religious education of his young charges, a duty Hereford seemed all too happy to relinquish as he pardoned himself early from the service.

The subject of the sermon was, appropriately enough, Virtue. The vicar muddled through several examples of the failings of humanity to retain Virtue, and of the hopelessness of regaining Virtue once it has been lost. Nick observed that the boys were still awake and had not yet begun beating each other and considered this to be progress.

Jane sat directly in front of him between the boys and her stepmother. She squirmed in her seat, tilting her head this way and that, sweeping her hair over her shoulder and stroking the blue velvet ribbon that tied it together in a long, copper lock. Lady Hereford elbowed her gently, and Jane held perfectly still for a measure of a couple of moments before resuming her grooming.

Nick struggled to pay attention to the sermon. It wasn't the distractions, of which there were many--minute gestures between the twins that might lead to violence later on, a pigeon cooing from a crumbling arrow loop, Jane shaking her head to and fro, sighing--it was the monotonous tone of the vicar's voice and the stagnant warmth of the little chapel. He felt a twinge in his right eyelid and tried to shake himself awake. Nick often struggled with early mornings without breakfast, but he consoled himself that he would be eating with the Ramseys and the vicar after the service, the Sunday luncheon being the only meal he could count on during the week.

Jane reached into her hair to fondle a curl and quickly dropped a folded note out of her glove onto the floor between Nick's feet. He glanced from side to side to see if anyone had noticed, and, satisfied that they were as drowsy as he, pushed the note back under her seat with the toe of his boot. It was not the first of such notes, and Nick suspected bothering to read them would only serve to encourage her inconvenient infatuation.

He didn't know what, if anything, would discourage it. Jane was very young and of quite another station, as he had pointed out to her on other occasions. There was also the fact that she bored him senseless with her conversation and deeply embarrassed him by her constant advances. He couldn't imagine what she thought could come of it, even had he been willing, and suspected she hadn't thought beyond that fact that he was a relatively young man, and certainly one of the only men she'd ever had the chance to meet on the estate who was not related to her. Nevertheless, she was sure to be introduced at Court within the year, and then she would leave him alone.

At the bleak thought of remaining in his current position for another year, Nick stifled a shudder. As much as he despised Lord Hereford, it was that or highway robbery. Tutoring was less likely to get one hanged, at least.

The congregation rose suddenly and began to shuffle toward the aisle. Nick stood with a start and reminded himself of his surroundings. The Ramseys were already halfway out the door. He took his place behind them, the vicar, and the highest ranking members of their household in their procession toward the Hall.

Nick followed the gentlemen into library for a glass of wine as lunch was being laid out. He dutifully waited until the gentlemen had been served before taking the last glass for himself and sitting on the window bench, his presence necessary to raise Lord Hereford's status, but unobtrusive so that he was not a nuisance.

Hereford met them in the library, wearing the wide, fish-mouthed smile he saved for Sundays. His neighbors were in attendance, as was Sir George Conley and his wife down from Berkshire. While his wife had retreated to the parlor with the ladies, Conley took a healthy drink of claret and cornered Hereford. "Jane is a lovely girl. So delicate and well-mannered! When will you bring her to Court?"

Hereford issued an ungentlemanly snort. "Court? Bah! I'm not letting her near the place until she is safely married. Jane is pious and good, and there's far too much wickedness and debauchery there for such a gentle soul."

Conley's eyebrows shot up into his hairline. "Our son, Geoffrey, has gone only this last year, and he is making brilliant connections. I did not think you would object, as you have been such a presence yourself as of late."

"I know too well the kind of alliances one makes at Court. I am resolved they shall not get their hands on her, to warp her weaker mind and corrupt her very soul. No, no! My Jane is staying here until a suitable match can be arranged, and then the matter will be decided by her husband."

Nick cringed silently in the corner. No hope she would be taken off of his hands, then.

Conley tsked kindly. "Pray, think of the matches she could make! If only they knew how lovely she is--why, she looks like a young Lady Castlemaine!"

"That is precisely what I'm afraid of," Hereford seethed. "Only think of what could happen to a young girl fallen into the wrong hands."

Chapter 16

Sally woke up in a clean, sweet-smelling bed, bathed in the sunlight that poured through the open windows. A tea service had been left on a table at the foot of the bed, polished to perfection and shining brilliantly in the morning light. She rose without a sound and carefully made her way towards it, afraid any sudden movement would cause her to wake to find it a dream. It would not have been the first time she had dreamt herself elsewhere, but the earthy smell of the tea, steaming from the spout of the pot, was reassuringly real.

Reaching the tray, she took a delicate porcelain cup and began to fill it when she saw, to her intense delight, a plate of apple tarts resting behind the sugar. She ate one greedily while she poured milk into her tea, taking a second one with her to a chair beside the window, where she sat, tea in hand, to watch the people passing by on the street below.

Resting in the marigold velvet chair, she thought that she had reached the very height of comfort. She could have happily sat there all day in only her corset and shift, nibbling apple tarts.

A moan from the bed startled her. She looked in the direction of the interruption to see Beaumont sitting up. In her bliss she had forgotten he was even there.

"Good morning." He yawned, a slow smile spreading across his face. "You're up early."

"I have to go back." She sighed with a mournful glance at her crumpled dress lying in the corner, still damp from the previous night's rain.

"You must stay at least a little longer," he said with a look that attempted seduction.

She looked down at the last bite of tart in her hand with no little regret. "I'd like to, but I really must go. If I leave it much longer, he'll come to collect me."

Beaumont stretched across the bed and rested his chin on his wrists. "He doesn't even know where you are."

"He always knows where I am," she said, popping the last delicious bite into her mouth. She rose and resignedly began to dress.

"Did you know that you have an unusual scar on your lovely little bottom?"

"It's a brand," she said, lacing the front of the dress.

Beaumont chuckled, "I may have been too drunk to get a good look, but it was hardly a brand! You're having a laugh."

The brand was something few people had seen, and she never joked about it. She crossed the room, hiked up her skirt, and pulled down the edge of her smallclothes. He stopped laughing.

"My God." He carefully touched it. "It looks like a lion."

"I've never seen it," she said, dropping her skirt to the floor with a swish.

"What a dreadful shame it is not a rose." He smiled, taking her in his arms, "Everyone would know that you are mine."

Sally sighed, breaking away, and slipped into her worn shoes. "I belong to no one. The price is too high."

Beaumont reached into his purse and withdrew an enormous garnet suspended on a gold chain. "Let this be a small payment toward the balance," he whispered with a kiss, willfully misunderstanding.

Sally fastened the jewel around her neck, knowing she would need to conceal it in her dress before arriving back at the Opera House. "My thanks, my lord, but I'm afraid I really must go."

Beaumont sank back into the mattress with a sigh. "You must take my carriage. I will call on you again." He kissed her hand.

As tiresome as he could be, Beaumont was kind, and Sally knew that she could do much worse. She was under no illusions that his fascination with her would last any length of time, but she was determined to accept every cup of tea he offered while it pleased him to do so. His carriage turned onto Bedford Street, and she jerked the garnet from her neck. It glowed deepest red in the sunlight, and brought to mind an enormous drop of blood. She shook off the image and dropped the jewel down the front of her corset.

No sooner had she left Beaumont's carriage than Wrath loaded her into another one. It was the same carriage that had taken her to Lord Hereford the first time, and she found her gaze lingering on the lion crest emblazoned on the door. Lions appeared in a great many places, and while hers signified ownership rather than nobility, she wondered how the brand had come into Wrath's possession.

They rode to Hereford's estate without a word. Wrath seldom spoke to her unless he was trying to intimidate her in some way. He led her up the stairs when they got there, and bade her wait in the hallway while he conversed with Hereford. They greeted each other warmly.

"I have arranged for her to appear in a play for you," Wrath said. This came as some surprise to Sally.

She could not hear Hereford's response, but he nodded vigorously and gave Wrath an overfilled purse and a decanter bearing his family's crest, filled with some kind of amber liquor. Sally had received a good many tributes since arriving in London, but never had she known gifts to be given to Wrath.

Wrath led her into the bedroom, the same place as before, and left discreetly.

Sally began looking for a cane. Seeing one, she reached for it, only to be stopped by Hereford taking firm hold of her waist. "Not so fast," he said, his breath reeking of wine.

As she pulled away from him, Beaumont's garnet fell from its hiding place onto his plush blue rug.

"What is this? Something you have stolen from my wife, no doubt."

"It was a gift."

He slapped her. "Dirty girl. And what did you do to get it?"

"I did nothing. It was a gift."

He slapped her again. "You're a liar and a whore. How did you get into my wife's room?"

"I didn't--" He hit her with his closed fist, knocking a tooth loose. She flung up her arms to defend herself, and he delivered two more blows, knocking her to the floor. She landed hard on her hip, and nearly cried out in pain.

Hereford dropped the garnet into his pocket. "You thought you could get away with this? By God, I will teach you to behave." He knelt over her and took her shoulders in his fat hands. He shook her vigorously and demanded, "What were you doing with that molly?"

Sally's blood went cold. *How had he seen her with Bettie?*

When she didn't answer, he lifted her off the floor, pulling her face close enough to his that she could smell his fetid breath. "With both of you in skirts, who goes on top, I wonder?"

Sally recoiled from the fury she saw in his ice blue eyes.

He slapped her. "Answer me!"

"I did," she said through her teeth.

Hereford slapped her again. "Unnatural slut. You admit it! You fucked him!" He dropped her to the floor, the back of her head hitting the hard wood with blinding force. He stood, his shapeless shadow falling across her prone body. "You are not to see him again. You will soon be mine, and I will not have you sullying yourself with another man, or whatever it is that he calls himself."

Sally spat a mouthful of blood at his shoe and grasped the cane, swinging it with all the strength in her body for his knees. He fell to the floor with a pitiful scream.

Tearing the garnet from his pocket, she kicked him in the ribs for good measure. "I've had quite enough of men telling me whom I belong to."

Dropping the cane, Sally sat firmly on his chest, driving the air from his body with the weight of her hips. She struck his horrified face once, twice, three times with all of the force she could muster. His arms tangled themselves in her skirt and when he tried to shout, Sally found herself once again cutting off his airways, this time with her hands.

She lowered her face to his, letting him see the depths of the hatred in her eyes, and growled, "Yes, I've fucked him. It was at the behest of some cretin like you. It was like fucking my brother. Are you happy?" She shook him. "That molly is worth a thousand of your sort, and I will fuck whomever I please when it pleases me to do so. Am I making myself clear?"

She tightened her grasp around his throat, not caring if they killed her if she got to take this bastard with her to hell, when all of the sudden, his chest began to convulse and his purple face broke into a delirious smile.

He was *laughing*.

Sally dropped him abruptly and saw, to her disgust, that he had soiled himself in much the same way as before.

He was playing a game with her. A game that may have cost her a tooth, and a perverse game besides.

She glared at him with disdain and left the room to the sound of choking laughter.

Limping down the hallway, Sally heard the sound of the tutor reading from a room at the far end. Her heart leapt into her throat and her eyes began to tingle with the promise of tears.

She could see just the end of his boot, caked in mud. He was reading a poem to the children. She wanted to stay, to sink into the floor and listen to him read, and to forget. Willing herself not to cry, she steeled her shoulders and slipped into the back staircase without a sound.

Chapter 17

Dusk settled over the grounds as Nick made his way through the woodland toward Southwark. In spite of their visit to Newgate, he still had some coins in his pocket from his apprehension of Lord Hereford and was looking forward to meeting Mark and Will at The Rose and Crown for dinner.

Nick glanced over his shoulder toward the estate, making sure he was alone. Jane had not obviously followed him all day, but she had managed to appear in front of him several times in various poses that were meant to be enticing. As firmly as he had resisted her advances, he knew he was lucky to be leaving with his trousers on.

"Nicodemus," she had called to him, her use of his first name too informal for comfort. She leaned against the library door, twisting her long hair absently with her fingers. "Do you know anything about erotic literature?"

He had looked up from Geoffrey of Monmouth's *The History of the Kings of Britain*, and blinked.

"Father doesn't like to keep it in here, but I know he has some." She had approached him with a slow slink and smiled coyly. "I do so love a good romance. Tell me, where does he keep them?"

"If you like romance," he said, clearing his throat, "you might consider Braithwaite, or Chrétien de Troyes. *The Knight of the Cart* is particularly moving."

She rolled her eyes and gave a laugh. "No, no. I want something positively sinful. Do you have anything?"

"I don't believe I understand your meaning," he said, giving her an opportunity to back off. "Please excuse me, it's getting late and I have lessons to prepare."

Jane closed the distance between him and captured his arms in her grasp. "I heard you reading that poem to the boys this afternoon and I know you love me as I love you!"

Nick tried to shrug out of her grasp without hurting her.

"You misunderstand; my lesson today covered Roman poets, and although Catullus can be perceived as romantic, the reality behind the circumstances of his writing the poems is that he had a very unsatisfying courtship with a dreadful woman called Clodia."

Her eyes began to glaze over and he saw his out.

"Given the nature of this ill-fated romance, it really is remarkable that his poems convey so much beauty, although many are laden with clever jokes and double meanings. You should really read them in depth sometime, I'm sure you would enjoy them." He put his copy into her hands and excused himself before she thought to follow him.

Escaping through the trees as fast as his long strides would take him, he wondered what he could do. Her advances were becoming more brazen by the day. If he submitted to her impulse and began courting her, he would certainly lose his job, and much as he wouldn't mind seeing the back of Hereford, there was the small issue that she repulsed him. The best case scenario would be that Hereford would lose his wits completely and allow them to marry, in which case Nick would be stuck with a pampered, empty-headed harridan, and that was a hell he could not abide.

Nick pulled on his coat and hat as he reached the river. No, he sighed, he would just have to keep trying to bore her until she lost interest.

Remembering her stunned, grey eyes looking at him blankly, he shuddered. That beer would be most welcome.

He heard a branch snap in the distance and looked up to see what looked like a skirt disappearing behind a tree. "Who's there?" he called.

The girl stopped and peeked out at him from behind the trunk. After getting a good look at him, she stepped out into the moonlight. It was the girl who had shared her dinner with him the night he had robbed Hereford. She hadn't been afraid of him in his mask. What was she doing alone in the forest?

"It's me," she said. "I don't have any more chicken."

He smiled before realizing she probably couldn't see him. "Pity. Where are you off?"

"I'm headed back to town."

"Let me walk you there, you shouldn't be alone at night."

"Thank you." She smiled. "Heaven knows what kind of brigands I could happen upon in the dark."

"These woods are crawling with highwaymen," he replied, deadpan.

"Indeed," she agreed, with a hint of a laugh in her voice.

He could just make out the shape of her face illuminated in blue, and her dark hair shining like the river at night. She looked small and soft to him, and she walked with an uneven step. "Did you hurt yourself?"

She raised her hand to touch her cheek. "I had a bad day. You don't need to slow down for me."

"I don't mind. It's very warm out tonight and I was just going for a beer with my brother. Would you like to come with?"

She looked at him strangely for a moment, considering. Dropping her gaze to her feet, she said, "I can't. I would love to, but I must get back."

"Your parents will be worried about you," he suggested.

She laughed. "Something like that."

They saw lights in the distance as they approached the edge of town. There was a noisy farm with a yard full of clucking chickens across the dirt road from an inn, all lit up for the night. "What luck," he smiled. "How about here?"

The girl glanced at the inn longingly and looked at him with large, luminous eyes. "I really shouldn't be seen."

In the poor light he could see her tattered dress and the bruise forming on her jaw. "You've been hurt." He frowned, stepping closer to examine her face. She hesitated, but did not resist as he gently took her small face in his hand. "It's beginning to swell. What happened?"

"It's nothing." She didn't meet his eyes. "I'll live."

"Are your teeth all right?"

She nodded. Her long lashes cast dark half-moons on her pale white cheeks. Lips softly parted, her breath caressed the inside of his wrist.

He swallowed.

When he didn't immediately take his hand away, she looked up, her gaze at once soft and weary. She looked so sad and beautiful, half-submerged in shadow. He had never wanted to comfort somebody so badly in his life.

"I'm sorry," he murmured. "I can't seem to let you go."

Her eyebrows raised slightly at his confession, and she tilted her head up toward his face. He glanced down at the sweet curve of her lips, wanting very badly to kiss her, and caught sight of the bruise once more.

He remembered himself at the sight of the injury and took a half-step back. "You must be hungry, allow me to repay your kindness. Will you wait here for a moment?"

She nodded.

Nick half-ran to the inn, not at all certain the girl would be there when he returned. With a few words and some coins to the serving girl, he had his arms full in minutes, and took his bounty back to the edge of the forest.

He found her sitting beneath a tree in the dark. Sitting beside her, he passed her a skin of ale and broke the savory pie into two large pieces. She drank deeply and passed the skin back to him when he handed her half of the pie. "Thank you." She looked up at him with those beautiful eyes. "You're very kind. You don't even know me."

"You shared your dinner with me when I was hungry. That was enough." He took a bite of the buttery pie crust. "Why aren't you afraid of me?"

"Are you joking? Anyone who waves a gun in that cretin's face is a friend of mine."

It took him a moment to realize she was referring to Hereford, and he nearly choked on his pie. "Not a friend, then?"

"They sent me here for him," she confessed after a moment's hesitation. "He likes me to beat him."

Nick paused with his dinner halfway to his mouth. He had thought he had heard some commotion that afternoon but had assumed Hereford was beating another one of his servants. "You beat him?"

She nodded. "That's it. He likes to get hit. I nearly killed him this afternoon."

His eyes returned once again to the swelling at her jaw. "Did he hurt you?"

She shrugged. "He knocked a tooth loose. I've had worse."

The idea of a rodent like Hereford putting his hands on the girl made Nick clench his fists in rage. "I hope you hit him hard."

"I may have broken his leg," she replied.

Nick nodded grimly. "Good. He touches you again, you tell me. I'd love an excuse."

She looked down at her hands. "How would I find you?"

"Shout," he offered, thinking of his daily proximity to Hereford's parlor. "I'll come get you."

The girl gave him an odd smile that went a ways to erasing the pain on her face.

"What is it?"

In one fluid movement, she leaned across his lap, took his face in her hands, and kissed him sweetly on the mouth. Dropping the remains of his pie, he closed his eyes and lost himself in the warmth of her kiss. Too soon, she let him go.

Nick sat there, blinking dumbly.

"I have to go," she stood. "Thank you for the pie."

"Where can I find you?"

"Come to Covent Garden." She smiled sadly. "I'm difficult to miss."

Chapter 18

Sally thought her room felt brighter with people in it, and Bettie was the brightest.

She returned home that night to find him sitting in her bed with a half-empty bottle of gin. "Welcome home, poppet." His eyes sparkled with drink.

He and most of Wrath's girls had embraced their fates and set about enjoying the short, gaudy lives of whores, taking every indulgence, every drink, and every moment of tenuous pleasure they could grasp while they were still young and beautiful enough for the work to keep coming in.

Many were fraying around the edges. It wasn't something apparent to the casual observer, but Sally had seen their bruises, scars, missing teeth, and pock marks. More than one struggled to hide their lesions and the mercury they took to delay the onset of disease.

The rest were dead.

When they succumbed, they were cast out, or so she had assumed at the time. Whether by disease, poverty, or violence, Death would come early and surely as the sunrise.

Bettie made it bearable somehow. He shook the bottle invitingly, reclining on his elbow with a cheeky grin.

Kicking off her shoes, Sally sank onto the bed with a sigh. "Give me some of that." She reached for the gin and took a sharp swig.

"My, my. Long day?"

"No longer than most." She passed the bottle back to him and felt her loose tooth with her thumb. It was too early to know if she would lose it.

Bettie grasped her jaw in his hand and she winced. He gasped and sat up on his knees too quickly, knocking over the bottle and spilling the gin. "Damnation!" He cursed, grabbing the bottle with his left hand while he held her face too tightly with his right.

"Careful!" Sally chided through squished cheeks.

"Look at your face! He's got to stop hitting you. No good's gonna come of wrecking that face. Let me get you a cloth."

"I'm fine." She held up a hand. "Really, I'm fine. It wasn't Wrath this time."

"Who was it?"

"That pervert he's been making me see past Hyde Park. I got a few good ones in, though."

"Good girl." He looked at her curiously. "You look awful. Why are you smiling?"

Sally grinned. "I ran into that highwayman again."

"You didn't! He's still there?"

"He's not always there."

He took a drink of gin and handed it to her. "What happened?"

Sally shrugged. "Not a lot. He bought a pie and we ate it in the woods."

"You ate a pie? Please tell me that's not the only thing you did in the woods."

She blushed to the roots of her hair. "No...I might have kissed him."

"You kissed him?"

She nodded.

"You are the most celebrated courtesan since Nell bloody Gwyn and you *kissed* him?"

"It was nice." Sally shrugged. "Really nice."

Bettie shook his head in disapproval and leapt from the bed. He threw her shoes at her and said, "Come on."

Sally didn't move. "Where are we going?"

"We're not going anywhere. *You* are going back there and you are going to find that highwayman and show him the night of his life."

She laughed. "Right, Wrath would love that."

Bettie sprawled out across the bed with a dramatic sigh, throwing his slender arm over his eyes in a swoon. "Right. That rat bastard. How very tiresome. How's a girl to have any fun around here?"

Sally stretched out beside him, lying on her stomach with the bottle in her hands. She drank.

"Is he very handsome?" he asked.

"Wrath?"

"Dear God, no! Have you been listening? Do you hear anything that I say?"

Sally laughed. "I beg your pardon. Yes, he is very handsome. I think. I still haven't gotten a good look at him." She passed the bottle back to him. "How did you get on with Rochester the other night?"

"I didn't. By the time we got there he'd already left. Apparently he came back here and spent the night with Rosey. Bloody men."

"Good thing there aren't any of them around here," she teased.

"Too right!" he said, drinking.

"Not worth the trouble."

"Oh, yes they are." He pointed a finger at her. "You might not know it because you've only met abject scum, but there are some great ones, you mark my words."

"How would you know?"

"Ah, little girl." He patted her head condescendingly. "I've been around a lot longer than you have, and I've seen a great many things..."

"What things? Tell me of this fantastical creature." She laughed.

"Well..." He suddenly grew serious. "There exists, in this world, men who are courageous and good, men who will treat you kindly whether you are a lady, or a whore, or a skinny boy in a dress. They are few and far between, and when you find one, you must not let him get away."

"Did yours get away?"

He drank. "That's not a story for bedtime."

"It's early yet. Tell me, pet."

He shook his head. "You don't want to hear my stories."

"I want to hear all of your stories."

His face became animated as he told her another one. "Well, I used to be a very beautiful little girl. My mother would not stop bragging about me, wherever she went. One day a band of gypsies came through town and cursed me to punish her for her pride,

90

turning me into a gawky young man. She was so horrified that she cast me out, and I was forced to roam the countryside with the gypsies until they grew weary of my face and left me here."

"I have asked you fifty times how you came to be here, and every time you have told me a different story."

"All of them are true." He drank.

Sally took the bottle. "I used to think my mother was a gypsy."

"Was she?"

"That's what my father told me. She was unfaithful to him. He beat me every Sunday to punish her for it. He wasn't my real father. When I found out, I hit him back with a bottle. I might have killed him. I escaped with Claude Duval, who brought me to England and left me to find his friends, only I got lost, looking for my real father, and wound up here."

"That's a good one. How much of it is true?"

Sally smiled at him and drank.

"You did know Claude Duval, didn't you?"

"Yes, I did."

"What was he like?"

"He was one of your good men," she said. "One of the very best. Did you know that he could sing?"

Bettie laughed. "Singing highwaymen!"

"It's true. Beautiful voice. He taught me some English, before I met you and you taught me the naughty words."

"Naughty, indeed. Did you love him?"

"I thought I did." Her eyes misted. "He was more of a brother, I think."

"You do like your highwaymen." He sobered. "Did you ever find your father?"

She shook my head. "Never. Madame Toulouse told me he was an Englishman, young, and very handsome. A party of them traveled through the Chateau on their way to the Hague."

He sat up suddenly. "Sally, how old are you?"

She shrugged. "Twenty, maybe. Twenty-one. Why?"

He looked at her carefully, then waved a hand.

"What?"

"I was wondering if there was some truth to it, is all."

"To what?"

"Come now, you must know what they say about you?"

"What who says? What is it?"

Bettie leaned in conspiratorially. "There is talk that you bear a certain resemblance to certain people, if you catch my meaning. You were born during the war, and at that time, certain people were doing quite a bit of travelling between France and The Hague, yes?"

Sally shrugged. "I assumed he was a nobleman. What of it?"

"You don't look like anyone I have ever met," he began. "But--"

The door burst open and they were interrupted by Camille, breathless and spilling out of her dress. "They've arrived. Lots of them. We need everybody, come on."

Bettie sat up with a start. "Who's here? Are they handsome?"

Camille shrugged, her small breasts bouncing over the low neck of her crimson dress. "I don't know, they've got masks on."

"Masks?" Sally asked.

"Libertines!" Bettie swooned.

"Look at my face," Sally protested, gesturing to her bruise. "No one wants to see this. Let me stay here in peace."

"One of them is asking for you," Camille argued, turning to look down the stairs.

"Which one?" Bettie asked.

"Does it matter?" Sally shrugged.

Camille leaned back into the room. "He's young and dark. I think it's Rochester!"

"Good heavens!" Bettie gasped. "Send him up!"

"What?"

Bettie elbowed Sally in the side to keep her quiet. "Send him up and we'll put out some of the candles so he won't see her bruises."

Camille nodded and ran down the stairs.

"Bettie, what--"

He slammed the bedroom door behind Camille and blew out half of the candles, leaving the room a shade darker than it had been. He opened the small wardrobe, empty but for a spare shift and a pair of shoes, and deftly shoved her into it. "Never say I didn't do anything for you." He winked at her and locked her in.

Chapter 19

Wrath held still as the little bald tailor measured the length of his arms and around his neck. The man scribbled some numbers on a pad and cleared his throat. "The same as before, my lord?"

Adjusting his collar, Wrath replied, "Not this time. I need something remarkable. I will shortly be announcing my engagement and I mean to outshine Buckingham when I present my new wife at Court."

"Ah, my felicitations." The tailor pushed his spectacles up on the bridge of his nose. "And who might the lady be?"

"I am not at liberty to discuss it until the final arrangements have been made," he purred.

"Of course, of course." He moved behind the desk and pulled a ledger from the drawer. "I will add this to your account, shall I?"

"Quite." Wrath began to look through the bolts of fabric on display, running the edge of his thumb along some particularly fine black brocade.

The tailor cleared his throat again. "There is the small matter of the balance, my lord."

Wrath looked disdainfully at the little man. "Send it to my clerk."

"As you wish, my lord."

Wrath sat in an upholstered chair for the remainder of his appointment as the tailor suggested fabrics, buttons, and flounces. The resulting suit would be exquisitely embellished and scandalously expensive. He would return in triumph, his wealth restored, and the Court would embrace him once again.

His fantasy was interrupted by the tailor's incessant throat clearing. He hesitated before speaking, and kept adjusting his spectacles in an irritating habit that surely signified disapproval, or some other such nonsense he had no business feeling toward his betters. Wrath felt his scowl deepening until the appointment concluded and he left the shop for the solitude of his carriage.

Though Wrath was in no mood to deal with people that day, he was obliged to make his way through the bustling crowd as he made his way out of Westminster Hall. The dressmaker he used for his girls was a half-blind old man with a shop off Fleet Street who knew the value of keeping quiet. Though he preferred that anonymity, a man of his station had a duty to keep up with the latest fashions and to patronize only the best for his sartorial needs. His tailor was expensive, to be sure, but he outfitted many of the most prominent members of the nobility, and Wrath would settle for nothing less.

A lovely young woman in a pale blue dress crossed his path and he looked at her appraisingly. Her skin was unblemished and becomingly flushed, her tawny hair arranged in neat curls. His lips twisted into a slow smile and he considered approaching her. Not one of his girls wore blue. The way he saw it, there was an opening at the Opera House.

As he moved toward her, a young man appeared and took her arm. Clearly a husband or suitor, she smiled prettily at his arrival. Disappointed, Wrath slowed his step. She wouldn't work at all; someone would miss her if she was gone. He shrugged it off. He preferred virgins anyway.

The girl looked above him and gasped. He glanced up to see that he was passing beneath the rotten heads of Cromwell and his generals. As the shops shared their space with the law courts, heads were known to appear above the shoppers from time to time. Wrath rolled his eyes. She must have been new to Westminster Hall, as those heads, in particular, had been in a place of prominence for years.

It served them right. The war had ruined his family and had taken him from his rightful place at Court. He only regretted that there were not more heads on display.

"Repent! Repent!"

Wrath was taken aback as a man leapt before him, naked as the day he was born, with a chafing dish of smoking brimstone on his head. His face was red with heat and pain, his features contorted into an expression of ecstatic madness. "Repent!" He cried as he rushed through the crowd.

Most of the shoppers paid him little heed as he ran between

them. They averted their eyes at his nudity, stepping out of the way of any cinders falling out of the chafing dish in his wake. He ran to the end of the hall and back again, shouting, "Repent! Repent!"

Wrath increased his pace. He was nearly out of the hall and Charlie waited with his carriage in the street outside. He'd had quite enough madness for one day.

The man crossed Wrath's path once again, and he stopped so abruptly that the chafing dish flew from his head and extinguished itself on the floor. He stood in Wrath's long shadow, his red face glistening with sweat. His mouth hung open slightly, and he stared at Wrath as if he could see into his soul. It was unsettling, to say the least.

Wrath cleared his throat. "I suppose you're going to tell me to repent?"

The man's face twitched. He sat on the floor beside the chafing dish, covered his eyes, and began to weep.

Wrath felt a chill go down his spine but dismissed it. He pushed the man out of his way with the end of his polished black cane and walked through the exit.

"Bloody lunatics," he muttered to himself as he spotted his carriage. Charlie opened the door for him and Wrath climbed into the safety of the interior, breathing a sigh of relief as the door was closed behind him.

They had just begun to roll away from Westminster Hall when the carriage was jostled to a halt.

"Damnation," Wrath muttered as he adjusted his hat. Pounding on the front wall with his cane, he fidgeted in his seat and waited for movement to resume. When it did not, he drew the curtain to see what manner of nonsense had caused the unhappy disruption.

Leaning out the window expecting to see an injured horse or perhaps a beggar who had the effrontery to die before his carriage, he found, instead, Beaumont, reclining in an open-topped coach.

"Sir, may I have a word?"

Wrath could not imagine a greater irritation than meeting Beaumont in his current state. He knew that Beaumont was not aware of his identity outside of Covent Garden, as most of the visitors to his Opera House were not. He went to great lengths to keep his secret, but dressed as he was and riding in his best coach with his crest emblazoned on the doors, they might as well have been introduced at Court.

"Beaumont," he acknowledged, curtly.

"How serendipitous. I thought I saw you leaving the tailor, but I couldn't imagine what business you might have at Westminster Hall. Yet, here you are."

Wrath caressed the ivory inlay of the pistol in the pocket of his coat and briefly considered shooting the smug smile off Beaumont's face. "What do you want?"

Beaumont was looking at the crest on his door with great interest. "I had hoped you had time to reconsider my proposition regarding Miss Sally Green."

Miss Sally Green. Wrath answered Beaumont's laughing gaze with his most intimidating stare. "Sally is not for sale. She belongs to me, so you can stop trying to sneak her letters."

The mirth on Beaumont's face faded but he smiled nonetheless. "I daresay someone's been working on their elocution. Good heavens, is that a lion? I feel I should recognize such a distinct sigil but I've lost the name. Pray tell, what is it?"

Wrath clenched his fist around the gun. He leaned forward, looked straight into Beaumont's eyes, and said, "Piss off."

"How very charming. Good day to you, *my lord.*" Beaumont tipped his hat to him and laughed as his coach pulled away.

Chapter 20

Intermission at the theatre, Sally was backstage re-applying a thin coat of ceruse to her face with a damp cloth, focusing on her dim reflection in the mirror and struggling to remember her lines for the second act surrounded by the chaos of actresses fighting, drinking, and turning tricks behind worn red velvet curtains.

Sally was one of two leads in some vulgar production written by a local hack designed to advertise Covent Garden's evening wares. Admission was next to nothing, but with enough backless benches for a few hundred bodies, boxes for the better classes, and commission from the pimps and madams besides, the theatre owners would walk away with a handsome profit.

Naturally Sally would be receiving no compensation, and she was expected to be grateful for the demand her starring role would generate.

"Sally! Pass us some carmine, darling."

She turned on the bench and handed the little tin pot to Thalia, a whore of vaguely Italian origin belonging to Madame Beatrice, whose house, across the piazza, had a better reputation but higher prices. She deftly seized the pot, leaving traces of red powder on Sally's palm, and returned her attention to Camille, who would be making her first appearance on the stage and was made up in layers of paint in an attempt to make her look less like the child she still was.

Sally's role had won her a dressing table of her own slightly removed from the benches of the others. From her seat beside the curtain, she could hear the shrill giggles of orange sellers above the ferocious roar of the crowd, already in their cups and worked up from the bawdy first act with its poorly disguised references to the sexual habits of the nobility. Her enviable complexion and distinctive features had earned her the part of the unnamed Lady, whose virtues would be compared and contrasted to Thalia's Jezebel.

Sally had thusly been spared the sparse, breast-bearing

costume of the harlots' chorus. A small mercy, though her tight, low-cut taffeta gown left little to the imagination.

She had been dressed in black to emphasize both the affected sobriety of the more respectable ladies and the extraordinary paleness of her complexion. Others had taken to drawing pencil-thin veins across their breasts in an effort to imitate the skin tone of fair ladies who had never had to stand in the sun without a parasol.

This was not a fashion Sally admired. The heavy coats of ceruse, cracking over the course of an evening beneath patches and veins that smudged when they were touched created a frightfully garish appearance that made the wearer look hideous in the wrong light.

Well and so; they had their tricks and she had hers. She took her little jar of kohl from her pocket and began to retouch her eyes with a short broken paintbrush. It was not a common practice, but the smoky black smudges around her eyes brought out their darkness and gave her a distinctive, slightly feral appearance that suited her mood as well as her face.

"She's doing it again!"

Sally heard a flurry of whispers and giggles behind her as she became the object of speculation and ridicule once again. Sighing to herself, she finished her eyes, applied a small, spade-shaped patch high on her right cheek, and dropped the kohl back into her pocket.

Suddenly Martha, stage mistress and local bawd, grasped Sally's arm and dragged her from her seat. "You've got a visitor," she hissed, her eyes bright at the potential for a siphoned commission and something else that Sally didn't recognize. She led her through the maze of curtains to a partitioned area near the side door to the street, where Sally saw what had made her so excited.

Beaumont was waiting in an exquisitely cut coat of indigo brocade, embroidered all over with his family's emblem of six-pointed roses. He stood apart from the shadows, illuminated strikingly by the lantern beside the door.

When he saw Sally, he smiled and took her hands in his. Martha hastily withdrew into the shadows, but Sally had no illusions that they were alone.

"Sally." He sighed. "Death has never looked more beautiful."

Sally blinked, terror suddenly seizing her chest. "My lord?"

"You're Lady Death, surely? Or perhaps Fate?"

She glanced down at her black dress and sighed. "I don't think I have a name."

His clear blue eyes softened as his hands moved to her waist, gently pulling her into his arms in the shadow of the partition. "Why won't you see me?" His cheek caressed the crown of her head as he bent to kiss her neck. His hair was clean and shining, and he smelled of wine and smoke.

"I have never denied you, my lord. I have not seen you this fortnight past."

He held her shoulders and studied her face. "He said that you would not see me. I made him a handsome offer and he said you did not care to take it."

"What offer?"

He laughed to himself and took Sally's face in his hands. "Exclusivity, Sally. I want you to be my mistress."

It did not surprise her that it hadn't been mentioned. Although Beaumont would no doubt bring a great deal of money to his house as well as a measure of prestige, she was Wrath's most jealously guarded possession, and a favorite of more than one of his friends.

Beaumont watched her expectantly. He was elegant, young, and well-situated, and being kept by such a man for any length of time was the best someone of her station could ever hope for. The idea of living in her own private quarters, seeing only one agreeable man and being otherwise left to her own devices was so divine that she couldn't bear to entertain the notion for more than a moment.

Of course, being kept by someone would mean there would be no more stolen kisses from highwaymen in the forest. Her cheeks warmed at the memory.

Sally looked at Beaumont's soft, expectant face, and sighed. "You know I would like nothing more, but he'll never let me go."

Far away as she was from the stage, Sally could hear the melee as the signal was given that the second act would shortly begin. She began to pull away to take her place and Beaumont held her fast and kissed her soundly.

100

As his cool, dry lips touched hers, Sally realized that she felt nothing. His kiss was inoffensive, to be sure, but it wasn't particularly memorable.

It was *nothing* like that kiss in the forest.

"I'm so pleased, Sally. I swear I'll look after you and you will want for nothing. I'll make the arrangements tomorrow."

Sally felt her heart sink at his mirth. "You don't understand. You don't know what he's done to me; he's obsessed with me. I can never leave."

"Fear not, my dear. Now that I know we are in agreement, I will make him a better offer and you will be mine. If he refuses, I'm certain I can persuade him."

She laughed in disbelief. "How on earth do you plan to do that?"

"Sally! You're on!" She heard Martha call from the direction of the dressing room, unseen.

"I have to go," she said.

"Sally, listen. He's leading a double life. He's not who you think he is."

"Sally!"

Running his hands up her back, he buried his face in her hair and murmured, "I can protect you. Come with me."

More than a little puzzled, and perhaps even hopeful, Sally resolved to ask him more about it later. She kissed him quickly and pulled away. "Come see me soon," she said.

"I will." He kissed her hand. "Farewell, my love."

She kissed him on the cheek one last time before running to the stage, skirts swishing, and taking her place as the curtains opened to the roar of applause.

Chapter 21

Sidestepping a pool of vomit as he followed Mark into the theatre, Nick asked, "Why go to a play if you miss the first half?"

Mark headed swiftly for the pit, dodging the imprecise swing of a bottle lobbed from the drunken brawl taking place in the lobby. Shoving the velvet curtain aside to reveal the open pit, teeming with unwashed dock workers and bawdy girls selling oranges, Mark paused to allow Nick to catch up. "Cheaper, innit? How long since you've been?"

Nick couldn't remember. He sighed and followed Mark into the pit. The crowd was so tightly packed that Nick had difficulty following Mark's lean frame as he wove between scores of rowdy men quite relieved of their senses. At last he found an open space on a bench toward the front of the crowd and Nick joined him, his height allowing him a clear view of the stage and whatever mischief Mark had planned.

The makeshift orchestra began to play over the roar of the crowd. Worn red velvet curtains were drawn, and out danced a line of girls completely naked from the waist up. Mark cheered wildly, elbowing Nick and pointing at the stage. Nick ran a hand over his eyes and laughed.

The girls danced about and sang a rude little song, shaking their short skirts and kicking this way and that in mismatched stockings. It went on for some time before they retreated to the back of the stage and the music changed ominously.

Strutting out from stage left was a woman draped in nothing more than a series of vibrantly colored transparent scarves. Her hair was a pile of curls on top of her head, and her face was caked in so much makeup that she appeared to be wearing a flawless white mask with spots of rouge on her lips and cheeks.

Nick thought she looked ridiculous, but from the way Mark was hooting beside him, he supposed most of the men in the audience weren't looking at her face. Rolling his eyes, he stifled a yawn and looked for the exits.

A second woman appeared on the stage, and to his shock, he recognized the girl from the forest. In contrast to the other actress, she was fully covered, wearing a rigidly constructed gown of black taffeta that hugged her little waist and showed her perfect bosom to advantage. Her hair was a river of black curls running down her back accented by a close fan of black feathers pinned at the side. She was not wearing so much makeup as the rest, but she had covered her eyes in some kind of black powder, making them look unnaturally large and giving her an otherworldly appearance.

He heard Mark laugh at him and realized he had been gawking like a school boy. Taking a deep breath, Nick attempted to slow the blood rushing through his veins. He felt a sudden horror as he realized she might be forced to do something humiliating in front of the crowd, and he was overcome by a possessive desire to protect her from their greedy eyes.

The girl wrapped in bits of silk appeared to taunt her with a suggestive dance and an unladylike gesture. The girl from the forest responded by withdrawing an enormous paddle from beneath her skirt and, to the crowd's delight, began to chase the other woman across the stage. The building shook as the crowd stomped their feet and shouted rude suggestions. As the chase continued, the scarves somehow unwound themselves and lo-and-behold, the Jezebel character was naked. The girl hefted the paddle and was just beginning to give the other a jolly good beating when Nick felt his throat close and made for the exit.

The fresh sting of cold night air hit his face as he escaped into the street.

"Nick!"

Nick paused before the alley as Mark caught up to him.

"Are you all right? You look like you're going to be sick."

Shaking his head, Nick looked nervously toward the entrance of the theatre. "I feel like I'm going to be sick."

"Go on, get some air and then we'll go see us some more girls, eh?"

Nick shook his head, "No! I don't want to go back in there. It was humiliating."

Lowering his voice, Mark said, "No worries. No one saw you."

103

"It wasn't me, it was her. They were all...looking at her."

Mark rocked back on his heels and nodded slowly. "I should think so, she was bare-arse naked."

Nick sighed and headed down the alley toward Southwark. "Not her, the other one." He grumbled over his shoulder.

Mark followed him reluctantly. "Gor, she was a nice bit of crumpet. Let's go see her some more then."

"No!" Nick shouted, stopping. He raked a hand through his hair, and muttered through his teeth, "I know her."

Mark's face lit up. "Have you got a lady-friend?"

Nick groaned and kept walking.

Laughter echoing down the alley, Mark scoffed. "Don't fall in love with an actress, Nick. I'll ruin the surprise for you—they don't love you back."

"She's not like that. We met a couple of times, is all. She's a good person."

"So go get her, then," Mark half-sang as he danced down the alley like a pan.

Nick cursed under his breath in frustration. "And what do I have to offer her?"

"God's teeth, Nick. You don't have to marry her."

Nick stared at him.

Mark sobered at the expression on Nick's face. "Come on, then." He threw an arm around his shoulders and steered him into the nearest alehouse.

Nick had reached the bottom of his second beer before he felt like talking.

Mark sat at the other side on the table, watching him carefully. "The way I see it, the girl has to go for you. You're a good-looking guy, you've got all your teeth and no pock marks besides. You can come back and work for me, fill your pockets, and get a little apartment."

Nick leaned back into his chair, glancing at the half-empty bar. "Be serious. I'm doing well if I have a sovereign to my name."

Raising his eyebrows, Mark leaned in conspiratorially. "But you do have the name."

"It isn't my name, is it?"

"It bloody is. I never believed for a second the old man didn't leave you a penny. Something don't add up there. Say I make a few inquiries--"

"Don't bother. Why would he leave me a thing?"

Mark looked at Nick as though he were a dim-witted. "Didn't you ever wonder why he paid such an interest in you when you were growing up?"

"He thought I was clever, is all."

"You don't give children your surname just because you think they're clever."

Nick shrugged. "It was a respect thing, is all. Mother was grateful to him and wanted to pay tribute."

"On the day you were born?" Mark shook his head and laughed. "I remember. I was there. That man was your--"

"It doesn't matter." Nick cut him off. "At any rate, it's all Arthur's now. I don't want anything to do with him, and he certainly doesn't want to see me."

Nick thought back to the last time he had heard from Arthur, the swine. The day Lord Somerton had died, his villain of a son had written to Nick, forbidding his return. Arthur immediately had his income cut off, abruptly ending his studies. After years of kind patronage from the elder Somerton, Nick had not even been permitted to pay his last respects. Nick clenched his fist.

"That's up to you, then." Mark drained the rest of his beer. "Look, if you like this bird, go talk to her."

"Just like that?"

"Yeah, just like that." Mark stood and headed to the bar for another round.

Nick stared into the bottom of his glass and thought about it.

Chapter 22

The week after Christmas, 1669, Sally had been staring into an empty glass when she felt a hand on her shoulder.

"Celestine? *C'est-toi?*"

It was late evening at the Hole in the Wall and she had the night off. The holidays had taken Wrath away from town temporarily, and Bessie had allowed the girls a few hours to themselves, here and there, so long as they did not go far. The tavern in question, a dingy but warm establishment, was around the corner on Chandos Street, not one hundred yards from her prison. She had taken the better part of a bottle of sherry to an empty seat as near to the fire as she could get and attempted to drink the cold from her bones.

It could not have been more than a couple of hours before she found herself sitting across from the now infamous Claude Duval. He was looking at her with concern, and more than a touch of pity.

"Claude." Sally smiled, her breath clouding like smoke in the chill of the room.

He leaned in closer and lowered his voice. "What happened to you?"

Her eyes welled up and again she was the naïve country girl he had rescued years before. "I got lost. I was trying to reach your friend's house, and I came upon a terrible place, and they will not let me leave! Claude!"

He took her in his arms and held her as she sobbed. "Shhhh...*ma petite*, you must not call me that here."

"I'm so sorry." She hiccupped. "Of course."

Stroking her hair gently, he asked, "What do you mean, they will not let you leave?"

Sally looked up at him, finding comfort in his presence, though no longer attracted to him as she once had been. He was a good man, and a true friend. Her heart swelled, and she started to believe that maybe he would be able to save her.

Two large hands gripped her arms and began to pull her away. "Come on, Sally, time to go back."

Sally turned to see Charlie pulling her, Wrath standing in the doorway with his arms folded across his chest.

Claude held her fast with one arm as he reached for his sword with the other. "The lady does not wish to leave."

Charlie laughed. "That ain't no lady, and she's coming with us."

Claude slapped him hard in the face. "I will not see the lady dishonored. I demand satisfaction. Name your second."

Charlie looked at him, hopelessly confused.

Wrath appeared to be studying his nails. "How very tiresome. Gentlemen." He addressed the bar. "That man is Claude Duval. I believe there is quite the bounty on his head. You may take him away."

Chairs crashed to the floor as the men in the bar collectively surged to seize Claude.

"No!" Sally screamed as they tore her from his arms. "You are mistaken!"

"Celeste!" He called, but it was too late. Charlie held both of her arms behind her back and pushed her out the door as Claude was dragged to the nearest cart and thrown in.

He was imprisoned for a month before his execution. After they cut him down, they displayed the body of Sally's first friend at the Tangier Tavern for those who had been unable to see him off at Tyburn.

He had been caught because of her. Years of avoiding capture, careful never to cause anyone any real harm, and he was brought down because she had refused to go along quietly.

Another night, another bottle of gin.

Sally looked at herself in the mirror and rubbed the last bit of stage makeup from her skin.

With Claude died the only person in England who remembered her from before she was captured. What proof did she have that there was life before Bedford Street? Who would remind her if she ever forgot?

The gin made things feel foggy much faster than any beer or wine. Sally threw her curtains open wide and looked to the corners of her room in terror.

Although it looked empty, Sally knew he was there. Was it truly Death, or some demon sent to torment her?

She could feel him watching her as she rubbed her arms for warmth. She could almost hear him breathing through the walls as she crawled into her empty bed and prayed for sleep.

Chapter 23

"Does she always cry like that?" Hereford whispered.

"Don't trouble yourself," Wrath replied.

The passageway between the rooms was black as pitch. Hereford had followed Wrath through the tight, winding corridor to watch Sally in her room after the play, and now he was growing impatient.

She had barred her door before lighting a couple of candles on her dressing table. Wrath could almost hear Hereford salivating beside him as she undressed down to her worn linen shift and dropped her famous green dress carelessly to the floor. *Ungrateful bitch.*

Hereford leaned closer and watched as Sally removed her makeup and drank a glass of gin. Wrath smiled. The gin he had replaced with some of his own potion and left for her to find beside her mirror. She hadn't noticed the cork had been removed.

Sally looked at her face in the mirror, gazed out the window, and poured herself a second glass. They watched for some time as Sally sat perfectly still, looking around the room. She threw open her curtains a little wider and held her arms against the chill. Leaving the candles burning, she climbed into bed and started to cry.

"I must confess, this is quite a contrast to how she behaves at our...meetings."

Wrath rolled his eyes. Who would Sally beat when she was all alone? The chair? He took a deep breath. "Perhaps she senses your presence and is doing it to tease you."

"To tease me! Saucy wench."

"Would you prefer it if I sent up a man to give you something to watch?"

"Good Lord, no. I can't abide the idea of anyone else handling my purchase. By the by, I have heard that she has been seen in the company of young Beaumont."

Would he ever be rid of Beaumont? "I believe he has visited

the house, yes."

"I will not stand for it. If she is to be mine, she will belong to me only. Am I understood?"

"Of course. I will make it so."

"Well and good. I am paying a great deal for the privilege, as I'm sure you are aware."

How could he forget? "Certainly."

Hereford wiped the corners of his mouth with a handkerchief. "Jane is my only daughter, you understand. I expect you to take care of her."

"Without a doubt, my lord. You believe she will be compliant?"

Hereford waved the handkerchief in the air in a gesture of dismissal. "Jane would love to be a countess, of course she will consent. She is a good girl and she obeys her father."

He lowered his eyes to the peephole once more, and Wrath began to grow impatient. "When shall I send her to you?"

"Not for some time, I shall be visiting some tiresome relations in Sussex." He made a blustering noise of distaste. "I will send word when I have returned."

"As you wish, my lord."

With that, Hereford retreated down the passage. Wrath waited in silence until he heard the click of the door at the bottom of the stairs.

In her room, Sally had fallen asleep, as she always did when he put wormwood in her gin. He listened for the shallow breathing on the other side of the wall. When several minutes passed and she did not stir, he crept into her room through the secret door.

The candles flickered in the soft breeze coming through her window and he snuffed them out. He walked across the floorboards with light, careful steps, until he stood over her sleeping form.

Removing his boots, he climbed into the bed beside her. He lay on his side, smelling her warm skin and the black torrent of her hair across the pillow. He didn't have to drug her to have her, he knew, but he did wish she wouldn't fight so very much.

As he slinked his hand up the curve of her waist, her body shook and she began to cry again in her sleep. He wouldn't take her tonight. He didn't often care to, but he looked at her and he understood precisely what it was about her that compelled men to part with so much of their money. A smudge of black above thick lashes, bitten lips that formed her words so beautifully with the merest hint of a fashionable French accent, and of course, the nose.

That nose, long and distinctive with the slight bump at the bridge, was a smaller, feminine version of the Stuart nose known so well to Court and the underworld alike. As beautiful as she undoubtedly was, that nose had brought in untold amounts of gold and had inspired many to visit his house to see his secret for themselves.

With her familiar features and waving black hair, she was a miniature china doll version of King Charles. How fitting that his daughter should be a whore. Though what drove so many men to seek her out to possess, for a fleeting moment, a piece of the King, Wrath would never understand.

Wrath rolled onto his back and looked at the ceiling with a smile. Whatever it was, it was making him richer, and in time, through Hereford's stupidity and lust, would double his already sizeable fortune.

He had, in his possession, the most sought after harlot Covent Garden, and he was about to trade her for one of the richest heiresses in England.

Chapter 24

Late the night after the play, Sally was alone in her room again. The candlelight cast long shadows over the wood-paneled walls, the heavy brocade curtains overhanging the bedposts keeping the mattress in a perpetual state of darkness. She was sitting at her dressing table in her corset and shift, leaning her face against her palm and listening to the sounds of the street through the half-open window. It was midsummer, and the stale breeze that blew through the streets of Covent Garden that night carried with it the occasional howl of a cat, the slam of a door, and the high-pitched whittering of girls too-long out of work.

The murky smell of the Thames in summer had bled through the streets and alleys until, just after sundown, it filled her room with an oppressive scent of sea and sewer. Sally absently dipped a hand into the now-tepid water of her basin and stirred the lavender buds through her fingers. Although the heat wave had initially brought in restless men with heated blood and burning pockets, its persistence had quite undone the city and its men, having lightened their purses on women and drink, had been absent for days.

Although she would have been grateful for the reprieve most nights, that night she was unusually lonely and woefully low on gin. Sally gazed out over the bright windows of the narrow houses. She spotted the full moon through a break in the clouds, and thought of Beaumont's offer. She hadn't heard from him since the previous night, but she was sure to see him soon.

It was the fondest dream of every girl she knew to be kept by a gentleman, but she knew Wrath would never let her go. Whether it was because she was so popular or because he derived a certain pleasure out of torturing her, she did not know. But the fact of the matter remained, the only way Sally could ever leave would be in a coffin, like the others.

The room seemed to darken as she thought of Claude.

Sally could almost feel his cold fingers on her cheek.

She shuddered.

The shadows themselves seemed to be watching as she crossed the room and took her shawl from the chair beside the bed. Suddenly chilled, she reluctantly put her dress back on and wrapped the shawl around her shoulders before returning to her seat by the window. The moon appeared again, a pool of light on the rooftop across the street illuminating a single crow. He was looking at her curiously.

The door swung open and Bettie stumbled in, gripping his stomach, his brows knit together in pain.

Sally leapt to her feet and rushed across the room, slamming the door behind him before drawing him into her arms. "What is it, dearest?"

"It's back," he said. Beads of sweat were forming across his forehead. She helped him into the bed and grabbed a cloth from the dressing table, dipping it in the lavender water and quickly wringing it out. He grimaced and turned to his side as she sat beside him on the lumpy mattress.

She applied the cool cloth to his forehead. "Has Wrath seen you like this?"

"No." He took a deep breath. "Just got back...I held it together until he left."

"Shall I fetch your mercury?"

"Blast the mercury!"

"You need a physician."

He closed his eyes, pained by the candlelight. "We mustn't draw attention. Do you know what he did to Rosey when he found out? Do you *know*?"

Sally blew out the candle beside the bed. "You must leave. I have some things we can sell to pay for your care."

"I can't leave," he insisted through clenched teeth.

"You must. He doesn't keep you as he keeps me. You can escape. You must seize your chance."

"Who will look after you?"

"I can look after myself." Sally rested on the pillow beside him, hoping to give him some small comfort with her presence. He had dropped his wig on the floor and she stroked his short sandy hair. "You're going to be fine."

Tears rolled down his cheeks. Sally wrapped her arms around him and held him.

She had just begun to relax when she heard the sound of heavy footsteps coming up the back staircase.

It wasn't an unusual sound, but something about it seemed ominous. Sally hovered near sleep, hearing Bettie's breathing evening out as the pain began to subside, and it seemed a distant danger. She began to dream, hearing nothing at all until a sudden choking cough roused her with a start.

Her eyes shot open to see Bettie's horrified face, his eyes wide and blood bubbling from his mouth. Feeling a sharp edge against her breast, Sally glanced down to see the angry red point of a stiletto blade emerging from his heart. He collapsed against her and died in her arms.

Sally screamed.

She hadn't heard anyone come in. Wrath stood beside the bed, cleaning the blade with the edge of her coverlet. Charlie dragged Bettie's lifeless body away from her and she sat shock still and covered in blood.

"You're a very bad girl, Sally." Wrath smiled at her. "You've been hiding something from me."

Sally stared at him, mouth agape.

He hit her across the face, hard. "Did you think I didn't know about you two? He's been lying for months and you've been helping him."

She didn't deny it.

He shouted, his eyes wild. "Have you got it, too? Did he give you the pox, you stupid whore?" He hit her again. "Clean yourself up. Lord H's valet is waiting for you downstairs. See if you can get rid of the sheets."

Sally watched them leave down the back stairs, dragging Bettie's body with them. She looked down at her blood-soaked dress and it only took a moment to decide.

She grabbed her shawl and ran.

Anyone could have seen her go. She was in such a state that she didn't attempt stealth, praying the fog would hide her as she ran for her life toward St. James.

Shoes forgotten, her bare feet splashed through puddles as

114

she kept to the muddy back alleys, the paving stones of the streets too slippery for haste. By the time she reached Beaumont's townhouse, her throat was burning and her feet ached. She crashed against the door, frantically pounding her fists against it.

She glanced at the street behind her to see if she had been followed. The street was eerily quiet. She saw nothing but shadows.

Beaumont himself opened the door in his nightclothes. "Sally!" He looked at her dress. "What happened?"

Sally gasped for breath, struggling to get the words out. "Please--"

Pain ripped through her body and she fell to the ground, blood soaking through the green velvet of her dress from a wound in her chest. She held the wound, blinking against the searing pain. As she lay bleeding on the doorstep, Charlie leapt over the threshold and attacked Beaumont, stabbing him repeatedly.

She screamed.

A booted foot hooked itself around her shoulder and pushed her onto her back in the gutter. She saw Wrath staring down at her, his head surrounded by heavy clouds, rain rolling off of the brim of his hat. "Silly bitch." He sighed. "You can't escape me."

The pain was blinding. Sally closed her eyes against the rain pelting her face, the cobblestones cool beneath her back. A tepid river of rainwater and blood rushed beneath her and soaked her skirt through, warming her bruised heels. Her fingertips and her toes were already growing cold. She heard the click of Wrath's heels retreating down the street, Charlie loping behind him, and she died.

Chapter 25

"Thou rob'st my days of business and delights, of sleep, thou rob'st my nights."

After days of half-remembered fevered dreams in which she was sure she was dead and enduring the uncertain torment of Limbo, Sally woke to the sound of the even, honeyed voice of a man.

"Ah, lovely thief, what wilt thou do? What? Rob me of Heaven, too?"

A cool breeze caressed her cheek and she settled deeper into a soft straw pallet. Clean wool bedclothes enveloped her in a delicious warmth she was certain she had never before experienced. Every inch of her skin tingled in sensuous delight.

She took a deep breath as she stretched her legs beneath the thick, homespun blanket and inhaled the fresh smell of sawdust and lavender.

Heaven smelled *nothing* like Covent Garden.

"Thou even my prayers dost steal from me. And I, with wild idolatry, begin, to God, and end them all, to thee."

The voice was quiet and had a roughness to it that contrasted with its educated accent. He was reading from something she did not recognize, and yet he sounded familiar.

Sally relaxed further and let every vowel, every consonant, and every delectable sentence roll over her like waves falling into the sea.

Certain she had somehow reached Heaven, she had begun to drift off once more when recognition firmly woke her.

The tutor.

She sat up in bed with a start, fearing herself locked away somewhere in Hereford's enormous house. *How else would these miracles be possible?* Expecting to see him lurking in the doorway with some newly devised torture, Wrath perhaps in tow, Sally saw only an empty room.

The room was an enclosed loft, sparsely furnished, with one small window and a serviceable hearth. The walls and floor were newly paneled in unfinished wood, and lavender and rushes carpeted the floor. She looked down to find herself wearing a clean, white linen shift, and covered in layers of fresh bedclothes and blankets. She twisted around to see the rest and was overcome by an intense burning pain in her back.

"Careful! You'll tear the stitches."

Sally sunk back into her mountain of pillows and finally got a good look at the man with the beautiful voice.

Although he was sitting on the floor beside the bed, she could tell he was unusually tall. He was a little thin, but it was evident from his broad shoulders and large frame that this was not his natural state.

His thick hair was deepest brown, and was cropped unfashionably short. His skin was perfect save for a small scar on one of his high cheekbones, and a few days' growth of dark beard covered his magnificently square jaw. His lips were full and beautifully formed, and Sally was struck with a sudden desire to bite them.

He was quite the handsomest man she had ever seen.

There was something about his eyes that she could not place. Wide-set eyes the green side of hazel looked down at her with real concern.

The kindest eyes in Covent Garden.

Sally had walked into him that night near the piazza with Beaumont.

Memories of the attack flooded back into her head, and she saw Beaumont, lying in a growing pool of blood, trying to reach for a weapon, even as he died.

Silly bitch.

She could still feel Bettie's lifeless body in her arms and the sharp sting of the knife between her ribs.

You can't escape me.

Sally struggled to slow her breathing. The handsome man rested a large, warm palm on her forehead. "Your temperature is better. How are you feeling?"

"Where am I?"

He smiled at her gently. "You're safe. No one will hurt you here."

Her eyes darted around the room. "Who are you? Are we in London?"

He rested his hand reassuringly on her arm. "We're in a carpenter's in Southwark. My name is Nicodemus Virtue, and you're in my room."

Nicodemus Virtue. Sally didn't need to have all of her wits about her to realize that wasn't his real name. Too fitting for a tutor, it had to be a fabrication. "How did I come to be here?" She asked him. "Was it a dream?"

His face paled. Taking a deep breath, he explained, "You were attacked, and I found you lying in the street. You were losing blood quickly, so I brought you back here, and myself and my brother patched you up. You had a long fever. I was—we were afraid we were going to lose you."

She tried to sit up, acutely feeling the pain of her wound. Nicodemus' face showed concern, and something else that she did not recognize. She asked, "Does anyone know I'm alive?"

"Only me, my brother, Mark, and the lads downstairs." He reached for a pamphlet behind a pile of books and she noticed for the first time that there was a jug of wilting flowers beside the bed. "Can you read?"

"A little," she replied, accepting the paper from him.

On the front page in sensational detail was a rather unflattering woodcut of Sally wielding a knife. "Infamous harlot murders Lord Beaumont, commits suicide." Sally looked up at him, mortified. "I didn't do it."

"I know." He nodded. "I sewed you up."

Taking one of his hands in hers, she looked into his eyes and said, "Thank you."

He smiled and looked down at the floor, his hand gently contracting around her fingers. "Anyone would do the same."

"No, they wouldn't." Sally watched his downturned face, wanting to see those eyes again. He looked a little flushed, but he did not strike her as a man given to blushes. *Why did he look away?*

Remembering the pamphlet on the bed, her heart sank.

He knew who she was, or who she had been not so very long before.

It was apparent that he was a good man, and respectable.

Tutors were known to be serious, godly people, and were held up as examples of righteousness and dignity.

He had found her, a scarred, half-starved prostitute, bleeding into a gutter without any shoes.

I must have disgusted him. Why did he save me?

Sally thought that he looked like an angel sitting there in the sunlight. His tunic hung loosely off his wide shoulders, the linen pale against his golden skin. The dark waves of his hair were deliciously disheveled, casting a shadow over his downturned eyes.

His beauty made her dumb, and hungry for something she could not name.

Sally looked at his big hand in hers. Her first impulse was to kiss it. She wanted to press it to her cheek, to hold it to her breast, to feel those fingers against her skin.

She was not a virtuous woman.

Forcing herself to look away, she squeezed his hand lightly instead.

He looked up with a smile playing on his face, eyes bright without a hint of shame or lust.

He was better than her.

Sally sank back into the pallet with a disappointed sigh. "What were you reading?"

He cleared his throat. "Abraham Cowley. It's a new poem I purchased. I can find something more...exciting, if you like?"

Exciting? With his voice, he could have read her the household ledgers and she would have listened with rapt attention. "I liked it very much," she assured him. "What is it called?"

He ran a hand through his hair and lowered his voice. "*The Mistress*, actually."

"How very fitting," she murmured. "Please continue."

Nicodemus took the book from the floor beside him and began to look for his page.

"I wasn't, you know," Sally added.

"What's that?" He looked up.

"The man in the pamphlet, Beaumont. I wasn't his mistress. He was my friend."

"I confess I'm pleased to hear it, though I am sorry for the loss of your friend."

"Thank you."

As Nicodemus began to read once more, Sally tried to relax beneath the coverlet, focusing on the rolling sound of his voice, each syllable floating like music from his lips.

Bettie would have told her to bugger the stitches and climb into his lap, ask for a demonstration of what those lips could do.

She would have laughed, had Bettie been there.

Sally stared blankly at the ceiling with a heavy heart, willing herself not to cry.

Chapter 26

Once she had fallen asleep again, Nick quietly crept down the stairs to see if there was any broth left in the kitchen. Sally, as the papers had called her, had been at turns unconscious and delirious since he had found her near death in the street.

Having finally made up his mind to go talk to her, he had set out toward Covent Garden on a quiet midweek night with a posy of wildflowers, hoping he might be allowed to buy her a drink and perhaps talk to her somewhere they could see each other properly.

She had said she would be difficult to miss, and she was absolutely right. After seeing her in the play the previous night, he set out for Covent Garden, expecting to find her onstage again. He had reached the edge of Upper St. James Park when he heard a scream tear through the night.

Running toward the sound, he darted down the street, and seeing no commotion, he almost missed her. Lying at the side of the road in front of a townhouse, the girl was unconscious, a gaping wound in her back bleeding angrily into the street.

Swearing under his breath, he dropped the flowers and rushed to her side. Checking her pulse and finding it slow, he took off his coat and wrapped her in it, finding the wound went all the way through to her back. He lifted her limp body into his arms, struggling to apply pressure to both sides of the wound without dropping her or causing her further injury.

Nick looked around for the attacker. The streets were empty and quiet, the rain-slick cobblestones of St. James Square shining by the light of a lone streetlamp outside the house. Inside, the hall was in disarray, and Nick found the body of a young man in a dressing gown sprawled across the threshold. He had numerous stab wounds in his chest, and his face was frozen in an expression of horror. There would be no saving him now.

Hearing a commotion as the servants began to stir, Nick took to the street with the girl in his arms, careful not to disturb her wound. It would not do for the servants to find the man dead with no one around except for Nick. No one would save the girl if he was hanged for murder.

Nick had carried her down several streets before finding a carriage for hire. Piling into the back, he gave the driver the contents of his purse for a swift ride to Southwark.

As they reached Mark's warehouse, Sally had begun to grow cold. The flow of blood was slowing, but so was her heart.

"Mark!" He called as he kicked open the door, carrying Sally toward the kitchen table. "Mark!"

Pulling on a shirt as he jogged down the stairs, Mark yawned. "I heard you the first time." Seeing Nick carefully lying the girl face down on his blood-soaked coat, Mark joked, "Jesus, Nick, you didn't have to knock her out."

Ignoring him, Nick grabbed a knife and split her dress from her waist to her neck. "I need hot water, a needle and thread, and some brandy."

Mark lit the lamps in the kitchen, built a fire in the hearth, and headed out to the back garden to get some well water to boil.

Nick had sliced through the laces of her corset and deftly tore her shift until her back was exposed. The wound was not large, but more of a seeping puncture that passed through the muscle tissue beneath her shoulder blade and exited through a small wound in her chest. Thankfully, her breath was even and clean. Whoever had stabbed her had missed her heart and her lungs.

Within minutes, Mark had a pot of water boiling and they had set to work.

Days later, Sally was awake.

Her fever had burned ferociously, giving her nightmares and causing her to cry out at all hours. Reading aloud seemed to calm her, so he sat by her side and read to her for days, checking and cleaning the wound, and praying.

The wound was healing well with no signs of festering, and given the state in which he had found her, Nick counted this as a miracle.

In the kitchen, Mark was sanding the rough edges of a coffin lid when Nick walked in. Will was at the hearth stirring a pot.

"Good morning." Mark smiled brightly

"Hey." Nick nodded. "What's that smell?"

"Making coffee," answered Will. "You want some? You look like you could use it."

Nick ran a hand over his face and sat down at the table. "Thanks."

"How's she doing?" Mark asked, setting his file on the table.

"She's awake." Nick smiled wearily. "The wound is looking better. I think she's going to survive."

"That's great! Want to grab a drink?"

"I can't." Nick shook his head. "She's still in and out, and I want to keep an eye on her. Do we have any of that broth left? It would be good to get her something to eat."

"Finished it last night." Will shrugged. "We'll have to go out if you want anything."

Nick nodded and took a sip of the coffee. It was vile. "I'll go quickly. Will one of you check on her if she wakes before I get back?"

"Perhaps you'd better let me go out," Mark offered. "We wouldn't want to give her a scare with our ugly mugs. You stay here, and I'll be back."

"Thanks." Nick nodded, braving another sip of coffee.

"What's Hereford got to say about you being gone so long?"

"The whole family's away," explained Nick. "I told the housekeeper a relative was ill and I'd be gone for a while. I doubt they'll notice."

Chapter 27

Lady Jane hated the country.

For the long weeks she had been confined to her aunt's estate while her father and brothers embarked on one tiresome hunting excursion after another, she sat in the library, of all places, and waited.

The Ramseys were not known for scholarly pursuits. A fashionable and expensive formality, the library was filled with books, yes, but served mainly as an informal armory showcasing weapons used by the Ramseys in every war or skirmish the family had been directly or indirectly involved in since the Norman Conquest. The few bookcases were flanked on every side by battleaxes, maces, spears, and swords.

Above the hearth hung an enormous oil painting of her grandfather and great-grandfather prevailing at the battle of something-or-other against a backdrop of slain foes and horses beneath a blood red sky.

It was all dreadfully dreary.

The books themselves seemed to shrink beneath the weight of all those centuries of violence painstakingly preserved against the red, floral papered walls.

The library was the only place in the house she was certain she would not be disturbed in the day before the men returned from the hunt, cheeks aflame and calling for wine. They would drag their muddied boots across the rugs, bearing foxes and hares swinging over their shoulders from snares, and would relive every moment of the day's hunt and of hunts of days past until they inevitably fell asleep in their chairs.

Yet every morning, the floors were gleaming, and the stains had miraculously disappeared from the rugs.

It was this time in the morning, when the maids had left, that Lady Jane would tip-toe into the library, take her place at the window seat with a romance, and sigh.

Every day she would lean her cheek delicately on her palm,

look absently across the fields, and dream of Nicodemus.

In all of her eighteen years, she had never met such a man. It was true that she had not met many men at all outside of her family and their servants, but she very much doubted they could be as clever, or conscientious as he. He was a shining light of beauty and virtue in the household, a badly needed antidote to her father's bile and the triviality of her stupid little brothers.

Yes, it was his virtue that she admired, and her affection had nothing whatsoever to do with his magnificent shoulders, his towering stature, or his dark, sensual features far too tempting to belong to any common servant. No, his devastating beauty was quite secondary to his calm and pleasant soul, although it served to further her belief that he was meant for far more than a life of demeaning servitude.

Nicodemus Virtue, she had decided, was destined to marry her.

Her father would not initially approve, she was certain, but she had every confidence she would win him over. She was, after all, quite irresistible when she put her mind to it. The fact Nicodemus had been able to resist her thus far only proved that he cared too deeply about her to show any outward signs of affection before they could marry, no matter how difficult it must be for him.

Jane sighed dreamily and counted the days until their return to London. If she had her way, she would be married by Christmas.

Thus inspired, Jane left her perch at the window and crossed the room to the writing desk. Withdrawing a piece of parchment from the drawer, she carefully grasped a long, white quill, and dipped it into the ink pot, gently shaking off the excess before beginning:

"My Dear Mister Virtue--"

Jane chewed at the nib, considering. Remembering the wet ink, she spat it out, hoping it had not stained her lips. Wrinkling her smooth brow in concentration, she decided, at last, to keep it brief.

There would yet be time for sentiment.

"My Dear Mister Virtue," she read aloud.

"I fare well in Sussex, though the country is darker for the lack of your shining spirit. I look forward to the day we are reunited and wish you all the very best in all things."

Jane read the short note over half a dozen times or more, wondering if, perhaps, she should be bolder.

What else could she say?

Leaning her face on her hand, careful to avoid the ink-dampened quill, she stared at the missive. Suddenly, she shook her head. "It is better to leave some things unsaid."

She signed her name with a flourish, shook a handful of sand over it to dry the ink, and folded it carefully. Lighting a blue taper, Jane wished once more for a more exciting color. She watched the wax drip onto the loose edge of the thick paper in fat droplets, firmly pressed down the lion seal of Hereford, and blew out the flame.

Chapter 28

Sally couldn't breathe. Every pitiful attempt at movement caused a shock of pain to burn through her chest and into her shoulders. Struggling in vain, her arms were pinned to the sides of her body by a tightly wrapped shroud of clean wool, scratching the surface of her paper-thin skin. The smell of dried flowers and herbs hung in the air, heady and sweet.

He had finally killed her.

The vague sound of deep voices engaged in conversation drifted from beyond the darkness, followed by heavy booted footsteps descending wooden stairs.

She couldn't see a thing, and yet she felt certain that she was back in her room, laid out for further molestation, disposal, or whatever else he chose to do with her body. A shadow seemed to fall over the room and Sally felt a presence, a formless evil menacing from the corners of the small room. She could hear it dripping thickly down her bedposts and feel it pooling under her back; could see it slithering across the dirty floor boards, an amorphous torment come to claim her once and for all. Sally thrashed back and forth, half-mad with pain, until the shroud fell away and she sat bolt upright, clutching her chest.

She found herself not in her old room, but alone in a strange bed without posts in a vaguely familiar, clean smelling place lit only by the borrowed light of burning lanterns below stairs. The door was ajar, and in the cascade of light that poured through the opening, Sally could see dry straw and lavender rushes across the floor and a vase of wilting flowers beside the bed. A bead of sweat dripped into the corner of her eye and she wiped her face with the back of her hand to find it hot to the touch and damp with perspiration.

Not dead then.

The pain in her chest persisted and she looked down at her shift to find a spot of blood darkening the pale muslin.

Not yet.

She wadded the muslin together in her hand and held it tightly over the wound, looking for anything to help still the flow of blood.

Why was she bleeding?

Sally stood uneasily and walked softly to the hall, unconsciously avoiding the floorboards that creaked in her own room, although she seemed to be in a different place. Peering over the railing, she saw tables bearing tools and piles of wood and scrap materials scattered over the floor.

Again, the sound of conversation from below; words punctuated by deft hammer blows and the fluid rush of chains slithering against each other. Sally held perfectly still and listened. There were at least two of them gathered below. A door snapped shut and another man walked in, footsteps muted by the sawdust that appeared to cover everything below the stairs in a thick drift.

A carpenter's in Southwark. The handsome man had told her that they were in a carpenter's in Southwark. The conversation hovered, half-remembered, at the edge of her mind. He had the voice of Hereford's tutor, but that couldn't be right, unless this was some new plot of Wrath's to convince her she was mad.

Why was she bleeding?

The men below stairs sounded carefree, but Sally knew enough of men not to trust them in groups.

She sat heavily on the floor outside the room and listened for any signs that they might be slowing their work or even leaving. Weary as she was, she would need something to staunch the blood before long, and she was very hungry.

Sliding to the top of the stairs, Sally silently lowered her legs over the first two steps, and began to climb quietly down, stopping every few steps to listen for changes. She reached the bottom of the stairs undetected, and waited. Beyond the open work space was a kitchen area where three men milled around a narrow table which appeared to hold, to her horror, an open coffin.

Sally clutched the banister and tried to make herself small behind it. One man set down a hammer and began to sand the edges of the coffin, while another loaded what looked like treasure into it, and a third stirred a pot of foul smelling coffee over a small fire in the hearth.

128

As bad as it smelled, her stomach ached for anything. The sweat was quickly cooling on her skin, the fire looked very inviting indeed.

At that moment, the man carrying the treasure looked up from the coffin to see her at the foot of the stairs. He looked startled at first, then smiled warmly and waved her over. "Good Lord, you're up and about. Do you want some coffee?"

The other men looked at her curiously. The one sanding the coffin was short, no more than a boy, really, with wild dark hair, and the one stirring the coffee was tall, blond, and lanky. They didn't look particularly aggressive or dangerous. The man who had spoken to her dropped the remaining treasure unceremoniously into the coffin and approached Sally with slow, effortless swagger. "I'm Mark, Nick's brother."

His accent was very thick and he sounded like a tradesman. It sounded as though he said Nick was his *bruvva*. Fortunately it was an accent that Sally had had a great deal of experience with, or she may have had more difficulty understanding it in her fevered state. Still, it was heavier than Nick's cleaner, educated accent, and yet they were brothers.

English is a strange language.

"Nick," she repeated, remembering. "Nicodemus Virtue." She smiled.

"That's right." Mark laughed. "Come sit with us," he said, leading the way to the kitchen. "This is Jack." He motioned to the boy, likely an apprentice. The boy stopped sanding and nodded politely. "And this is Will."

The lanky man stood up from the hearth. He was older, and Sally placed both him and Mark in their late twenties. "Morning," he greeted.

Sally curtsied out of courtesy, though it was not strictly necessary. She cleared her throat nervously. "My name is Celeste, but most people call me Sally."

She wondered how much they knew of her and where she came from. She noticed them looking at the loose fabric of her shift gathered in her hand. Sally looked down to see that the spot of blood that had driven her out of bed was still there. *Not a dream, then.* "I beg your pardon," she started. "But there is blood..."

Mark came forward and rested a hand carefully on her arm, taking the muslin in his hand. Without a word, he turned her around and examined her back. "Mother of God!" he exclaimed.

"What is it?" Sally asked.

"Your stitches must have torn in your sleep. Come sit and we'll take a look at you."

Stitches? Sally followed him to a bench beside the coffin. Glancing inside, she saw that the coffin was half filled with precious metals, jewels, brass buttons, and carriage embellishments glinting in the warm light of the burning lamp. She could not know how deep it went, but the collection made her little jewel box look very paltry indeed.

Sally wished she'd had the presence of mind to take it with her. Now she was lost again in London without a penny to her name. She felt the bridge of her nose tingle with the promise of tears and she blinked them back, feeling alone once again.

She sat down carefully and began to untie the cord that held the shift high on her shoulders. The boy called Jack blushed and turned away to protect her modesty, while Will filled four heavy cups with coffee, carefully avoiding looking at her exposed skin.

Not since leaving the Chateau had Sally been afforded such consideration. She was no lady. *Was there a chance they didn't know?*

She held the shift to cover herself while allowing it to hang down her back. Mark gave a low whistle. "Will," he said. "Get the linen Nick left, and his liquor, too."

"We were going to drink that." Will shook his head even as he obeyed. "You can always trust Nick to get the good--"

His sentence trailed off as he circled behind Sally and saw her back.

Mark removed a signet ring from his left forefinger and set it on the table. He took the liquor and applied some of what smelled like adequate scotch to a square of fresh linen Will brought. He gently dabbed the blood from the wound in silence, while Will held the extra linen. Jack took a mug of coffee off of the table and brought it over to Sally, his head lowered. "Thank you," she said with genuine affection.

He colored faintly and returned to his seat on the other side of the table.

130

"It's not as bad as it looks," said Mark, finally. "Your stitches tore a little, you were bleeding quite a bit, but it seems to have stopped now. We'll have Nick take another look when he gets back."

"What happened?" She asked.

"He just went off on an errand. He'll be back soon."

"I mean, to me. Why am I bleeding?"

Mark handed her the linen and she dabbed at the drying blood on her chest. As he said, it appeared that the flow had stopped. "You don't remember?"

She shook her head and began to re-tie her shift. Will took the rest of the liquor and linen and packed it into a trunk beside the hearth.

Mark leaned over and felt Sally's head with the back of his hand. "You still have a bit of a fever. You woke up a couple days ago, but you've been in and out ever since." He sat back and took a sip of his coffee, making a face at the taste.

Sally looked down into the black depths of hers suspiciously.

"Nick found you in St. James Square a couple of weeks back and brought you here to mend. Somebody stabbed you right in the back and nearly did for you. Do you know who it was?"

Sally remembered running in the rain. She could see a man's face, contorted in pain, Beaumont, and then she was lying in the street, looking at a pair of black leather boots.

"Yes, I remember now," she said, her voice cold. She took a sip of coffee. Terrible, yes, but it was something to drink. "Did Nick see him?"

"No." Mark shook his head. "Scoundrel got away before Nick could go after him. In any case, he wanted to get you patched up first."

Sally tried to picture Nick in her head, and wondered if he really had been very beautiful, or if that had been a dream. "Is Nick a tutor?"

Mark watched her carefully. "Sometimes. Why?"

Sally took another sip of coffee, shifting under his scrutiny. "He was reading to me."

Mark offered a small smile but Sally did not kid herself. He didn't trust her. She couldn't find it in herself to blame him. "How did you two meet?" he asked.

Sally remembered bumping into him as she left with Beaumont that night. The warmth of his chest, his smile. She blushed. "We haven't, really."

Mark tilted his head almost imperceptibly to the side. "Are you certain?"

Sally didn't know what he was implying, but she wasn't sure she wanted to know. "I may have run into him once or twice, but we have never actually *spoken*, I don't think."

Mark's golden eyebrows shot up in surprise.

Sally realized how that had sounded and her cheeks flushed with embarrassment. "He wasn't a client, if that's what you're asking."

Jack's eyes widened and Will busied himself with the coffee. Mark didn't blink. "It wasn't."

"Why did he save me?"

The façade of affability was beginning to slip and Sally could tell Mark's guard was well and truly up. "He's the sort to look after the needy, taking in injured dogs, and helping the infirm and the like. He doesn't know what's good for him."

The message was clear. Mark thought Nick was a fool and he had taken it upon himself to protect him from her. Sally didn't know who he thought she was going to seduce in her state. She bristled a bit at the insult. "Someone tried to kill me and very nearly succeeded. It's very fortunate for me that your brother has such affection for *injured dogs*."

They regarded each other carefully for a moment. His steely blue eyes flickered and he changed his approach. He reluctantly offered a slow, crooked smile by way of apology. "Pretty girls as well, hey?"

He really was disarmingly handsome. He knew it, too.

If he had hoped that a pretty face was enough to set her bumbling like a lunatic, he would be sorely disappointed. At any rate, Sally was certain that it would take nothing short of an act of God for her to willingly let another man into her bed now that she was free.

She thought of Nicodemus reading to her in the sunlight, his lips reverently forming the words of the love poem like a blasphemous prayer and nearly shuddered in pleasure.

Well, *almost* certain.

Looking at the coffin behind Mark's head, Sally changed the subject. "What manner of place is this?"

"It's a carpenter's, and I, Mark Virtue, am the Master Carpenter," he said, proudly.

Sally looked from the piles of loot on the floor to the long coat hanging beside the door, pistol jutting out of the pocket. "You are highwaymen," she observed.

Jack looked surprised and Will laughed out loud.

Mark didn't flinch. "Yes, we are."

"Good." She smiled.

"You've a lot of experience with highwaymen, do you?"

"Enough to know I like you better than most."

"Any one in particular?"

Sally blinked, taken aback. He couldn't know about the highwayman from the forest, could he?

Good God, it wasn't him, was it?

Mark was of medium height, taller than Sally but probably only just. He was lean without being too thin, with the well-developed arms and shoulders of a man in his trade. He regarded her with a strange combination of distrust and interest, and try as she might, Sally could not imagine him coming across a willing girl in the forest and stopping at a kiss. Mark was a fine looking man, to be sure, but he was not her highwayman.

She looked at the others. Jack couldn't be older than about fifteen and although Sally was tall for a woman, he was inches shorter than her, so he was out. Will was tall enough, certainly, but had a slightness of frame that could only have come from a lifetime of hunger.

All three of them, in fact, looked in need of a decent meal, and her heart ached for them. Sally wished for a working kitchen. She could set them all to rights.

If she was there for any length of time, that is. She didn't expect to be.

"Not anymore," Sally answered, finally. Her highwayman was not there. "It was a highwayman who first brought me to England."

He raised an eyebrow, "Anyone we would know?"

"Claude Duval. Did you know him?"

Mark's eyes lit up with real interest and the others stopped pretending they weren't listening. "Can't say I had the honor. Were you his, um..." he tried to think of a kind way to ask.

Sally shook her head. "We grew up together. He was sort of a cousin."

Jack gasped. "You're the girl he kissed!"

Mark glanced at him quickly, as if he'd forgotten he was there.

"At the hanging," Jack said. "Remember?"

Mark looked at Sally again, trying to place her in that snowy field more than a year before, face white as death, wearing a dingy shawl of no particular color. The ice of that morning had found its way into her bones and had never quite left.

"Yes, I am," she confirmed. "You were there?"

"Everyone was there," said Mark. "I'm sorry for your loss."

"Thank you. So am I."

The door screamed on its hinges as Nicodemus walked in, his wide shoulders spanning the doorway and blocking the dawn's first light. His smile faded as he saw Sally. "Sally, you're up. Are you well?"

He didn't so much as pause to take off his long coat before he rushed to her side. Her heart fluttered in spite of her best intentions. She opened her mouth to speak, and to her horror, emitted a sort of weak squeak.

So much for not behaving like a madwoman.

Mark watched the exchange with a widening smile. "She's all right, just had some trouble in the night, didn't you, poppet?"

"My stitches tore a little, is all. It's nothing."

Nick's face paled. "Does it pain you?"

"Not anymore." Sally hugged her arms to her chest, conscious she was sitting in her undergarments.

"Do you mind if I see it?"

Sally shook her head. "Please."

"Would you prefer to go upstairs?"

He wanted to protect her modesty. Sally had already spent much of the morning with his brother in a state of undress. Suffice to say, she didn't mind if he looked in front of the others, but she would have appreciated a break from Mark's shrewd judgment. She nodded her consent. "Thank you."

Nick smiled gently, going some way toward melting that ice in her bones. "You go on ahead. I'll gather some things and be up in a moment."

Sally stood and repeated her half-curtsy, stumbling a little.

Chapter 29

Once Sally had returned to her room, Nick took his coat off and hung it on the peg, taking his surgical instruments from the inner pocket and setting them above the hearth for later cleaning.

"How's Harry?" Mark asked.

Nick took the coffee off the pot hook and poured the remains into a heavy cup. Jack took the pot without him asking and rushed out the back door to refill it with fresh water. Although he was young, Jack had had enough adventures to know that the instruments would have to be boiled.

"He's still in that room by himself, but he could use a bath. The conditions are appalling. It's a wonder his foot is doing as well as it is. He seems to have been spared jail fever, at least. No more word on when he might be released. They haven't even set bail yet."

"What can we do?"

Mark rested his chin in his hand, thoughtful. "Whatever we got to."

Will sat down at the table. "He's good with a file. If we could get him one, maybe--"

"Is he strong enough?" Mark asked.

Nick shrugged. "Should be, before long, but he's not running anywhere with his foot the way it is. It'll be some time before he's fit enough to stand."

"Might be able to buy him out by then," suggested Will.

"We'll have to see what happens, but we should get him that file." Mark sighed. "How's the rhino holding up?"

Nick shook his head. "Gone. I gave him everything we had."

Mark nodded gravely. "Good."

Jack returned with the water and set it to boil over the fire. Nick thanked him and began to gather linen and liquor from the chest.

Mark sat up with a jolt. "Nick."

Nick turned, arms full of bandages.

Mark pointed at the ceiling. "She said you hadn't met before. You sure you saved the right girl?"

"Of course, we met in Hyde Park." Weeks had passed and he hadn't been able to get that kiss out of his mind.

"She said you'd never spoken, and she wasn't lying. Looks like your girl don't know about your evening activities."

Will snickered.

Nick paused, surprised, before closing the chest. He had seen her, clearly enough. Would have recognized her anywhere. Then again, she was an unusually pretty girl, and would not be difficult to pick out of a crowd. Could it be possible that she didn't know him?

Would she think less of him if she knew?

Nick cleared his throat. "No matter. As long as she recovers." He turned to head up the stairs and almost walked into Jack, who stood holding a plate of toasted bread.

"This might help," Jack offered.

Nick smiled at him and accepted the plate. "Thank you, Jack."

♠

Sally waited at the foot of the pallet in his room, her eyes wide.

She was nervous. Nick smiled at her and nodded toward the stool in front of the window. "I apologize, I didn't mean to upset you. Please, sit here in the light."

Sally crossed the room and sat carefully on the stool. The morning sun caressed her hair, giving the black waves a blue sheen as she casually pulled them over her shoulder. Her breath was shallow and her shoulders trembled almost imperceptibly beneath the thin white shift.

Nick felt a wave of unwelcome desire, startling in its intensity, and willed himself to play the measured physician. He rested his hand gently on her shoulder and felt her jump beneath his touch.

Poor thing. She's scared out of her mind.

"You don't need to fear me," he said, in a voice he hoped was soothing.

"I don't," she replied, her voice hoarse. She cleared her throat. "Thank you for saving me."

As Nick sat on the edge of his trunk behind her, he settled his thighs around her hips, pulling her close enough to allow him to see the even silk stitches he had placed a fortnight before. Her head swayed with the movement and he caught the sweet smell of her skin as she drew near. He closed his eyes and took a deep breath before answering, "You don't need to thank me. I'm glad I was able to."

He eased the shift off her shoulders, his hands skimming her smooth sides. Her arms crossed her chest to clutch the loose linen over her breasts. Every inch of exposed flesh revealed a new piece of a pattern of crisscrossing scars that ran all the way up her back, culminating with the fresh knife wound beneath her right shoulder blade, angry and red.

He had seen the scars as he had sewn her up, and again the many times he had checked on the wound's progress, but he had not been prepared for the sight of them in the unforgiving light of day. Nick let his breath out slowly, trying to hide his shock.

"You haven't seen them in daylight."

"I beg your pardon?"

Sally's shoulders relaxed slightly. "I felt your breath on my back."

Nick swallowed. "There are so many of them."

"Years."

Years. What kind of monster could do such a thing? He traced the edge of his thumb along a thick scar that crossed her spine from beneath her left shoulder to just above her right hip.

She shuddered.

"Forgive me." He dropped his hand.

When she answered, there was a tremor in her voice. "It doesn't hurt."

Nick rested his hand beside the wound and checked the stitches, finding them still in place and the wound closing well. He dampened a square of clean linen with the brandy and gently patted the surface of the wound. There was no evident infection, and he intended to keep it that way. "It looks fine," he said. "It reopened briefly, but it appears to be healing properly."

"Good." She sighed.

"How does it feel?"

She hesitated before answering. "Better now."

He set the brandy on the windowsill with the used linen, and lifted the voluminous shift onto her shoulders, tying the ribbon together in a bow at the base of her long neck. She sighed and seemed to settle into the chair, and he became aware of the slight movements of her hips against the sore muscles of his thighs.

Nick swallowed. He raised his eyes to the ceiling and took a deep breath, beseeching God or anyone who happened to be listening for the strength to calm himself before she noticed his arousal. *She was ill, for Heaven's sake!* The last thing she needed was another man pawing at her.

Another man.

Nick's heart sank at the reminder that there had been others, and God only knew how many. She was no less beautiful for it; her skin was smooth and fair, her hair the color of a moonlit night. He breathed a sigh that was almost a laugh, chiding himself for his romantic heart.

"Is something wrong?" She glanced over her shoulder.

"Not at all." He ran a hand over his eyes. "Something amusing just came to mind."

"What was that?" A hint of a smile played on her soft lips.

He was very much aware that she hadn't moved. She was nearly in his lap and she seemed perfectly comfortable there with her back to him. It would be so easy to pull her into his arms and kiss the length of her lovely white neck.

Nick coughed. "Poetry."

"Poetry?" She turned in her chair to face him, her soft dark eyes fixed with interest.

His face began to warm under her gaze. Nick pulled the remaining bandages into his lap. "Only a fanciful thought. I'm sure I've been reading too much."

"I'm not sure that's possible." As her smile widened, her lips parted to reveal a narrow gap between her front teeth.

If they had been in the forest, he would have kissed her by now. Here, in a half-finished room in his brother's house, he was a physician, and she had a fever--

He raised his hand to her forehead and cursed himself. "I am ten times a fool! Here I am going on about poetry and you still have a fever. Let's get you back into bed."

Nick stood abruptly and offered his arm to help her to stand. She took it, though she seemed strong enough, her long fingers resting on his bicep. He helped her into the bed, and as he tucked the coverlets around her, she looked up at him with something that looked like interest.

Gratitude, he told himself.

He gave her the plate of toasted bread and sat on the floor beside the bed.

She ate the stale bread quickly and without complaint. It was the last food they had in the house. He wished he had more to give her.

Sally settled onto the pillow and yawned. "Would you read to me? That is, if you don't mind?"

"Gladly." Nick smiled.

He took up *The Mistress* and began to read from where they had left off before Sally had woken up. She was asleep in minutes, but he read on for some time. He skimmed over the parts about the fickle nature of the woman, and read the sweeter parts instead, taking care over every word.

After a while, he paused, listening to her deep, even breath. He daringly reached out and smoothed an errant curl away from her face.

Nick sighed. It wasn't like him to act like a besotted schoolboy. He was nearly thirty, and she was not the first woman he'd seen.

He barely knew her, really. She had been kind to him, of course, when few others had. She was beautiful and generous, but given her night terrors, quite possibly mad.

Then there was the kiss.

He leaned his head against the wood paneling and closed his eyes.

There was no changing her past, but he didn't hold it against her. There were many reasons people did the things they did. He had no desire to punish her for it, only wanted to keep her to himself, to show her that he could be the man to make her happy.

But could he?

At best, he was an unpaid tutor. An unqualified physician. A highwayman who, by the grace of God, had not yet been caught. He couldn't support himself on his tutor's pittance, let alone a wife. As for highwaymen--ha!--women were willing enough to offer themselves to them when their husbands and fathers were away, but no one in their right mind would actually *marry* one.

He could pretend to be respectable all he wanted, but he was little more than a common footpad. *A criminal.*

She said she hadn't seen him those nights. She didn't know what he was.

Maybe he had a chance after all.

Chapter 30

After countless days of fever, Sally woke up shivering.

The fire had gone out, and there was no sign of the handsome physician masquerading as a tutor who had, until that point, been sleeping beside the bed on a blanket on the floor.

A cold grey sky was visible through the window. Her throat burned with thirst and her limbs ached. She rose from the bed carefully and padded across the unfinished wood floor to see the world outside.

The room was two or three floors up, and overlooked dozens of shabby rooftops in uneven rows leading to the river. White gulls glided over the boats, the only color in a dreary morning. Across the river lay the ruins of the city, and beyond to the west, new developments built to house the ever growing gentile classes. Covent Garden had been one, and twenty years on, was already ridden with thieves and whores eking out a living between the plush apartments and townhouses.

Bettie used to walk to the river on nice days. Something about the water soothing his spirit. Why, she could not say. Cluttered with boats and unfathomable rubbish, it was a far cry from the beaches of Dover.

Her heart ached at his loss and she blinked back tears. There would be no funeral for her only friend. She wondered what had happened to his body.

She feared she knew.

Sally found her old dress ripped beyond repair in a basket of rags to be discarded. She grasped the velvet hesitantly, running her thumb over the dried blood that had crusted the ruined bodice. Her blood, almost certainly, mixed with Bettie's and the filth of the gutter.

Beaumont's blood would be in his hall.

Sally rubbed her eyes with the heel of her hand. Two more gone because of her.

At least Beaumont would have a funeral. He would be buried

with all of the appropriate ceremony in sacred ground, or perhaps a family crypt.

There was no one left to mourn Bettie but her.

Sally reached her hand into the secret pocket in the ravaged skirt and took out the few pennies she had left. She tip-toed down the stairs, clutching her shift in her hands, and was relieved to find the house empty. There was a long coat on the peg by the door and she put it on, buttoning it over the shift and hoping it would be enough to disguise the fact that she had no dress.

She had no shoes, either. Determined to go without them, if need be, Sally was nevertheless pleased to find a pair of battered men's boots beside the hearth. She slipped them on, her feet lost in the loose, soft leather, and easily pulled them up to her knees. They belonged to someone tall, then. She thought of Nicodemus, and wondered if they were his.

Sally left through the back door, clutching the pennies within the pocket of the coat and keeping her eyes on the ground ahead of her. She didn't know Southwark, and she hoped she would be able to find her way back.

The Thames is never far from anywhere in London. Sally had seen where it was from the window, so she pointed herself that way and followed the smell, keeping to the alleys until she reached the riverbank.

She had never seen the river from the south side. It was early morning, and the bank was already teeming with sailors and laborers starting their days. There were dozens of them, many of them glancing at her with curiosity, others leering openly. Very few women ventured near the docks unless they had something to sell. She shuddered and kept her eyes to herself, hurrying past the boats as fast as the too-large boots would allow her to go.

Her stomach rumbled as she reached a cluster of carts selling food overlooking the river. She paid a man a penny for two buns. They were vastly overpriced but she was in no mood to argue. She took the buns and as she stopped in front of a cart selling flowers, she had the familiar feeling she was being followed.

A chill ran up her spine and she stood very still.

Had they found her?

Sally looked around herself and saw no one. Dozens of

sailors and laborers walked past and vendors paced the shore calling out to them, promising good food at fair prices, bread, oysters and beer. Their booming voices muddled with the whisper and snap of the ships' sails billowing in pockets between the ropes that held them fast, and the shrill cry of the gulls echoing over the water. There were no familiar faces. No tall black hats, no ominous silk-clad figures waiting in the shadows to drag her off. No thug of a footman, following her from a distance as she wandered town. Charlie had never been a subtle man, and she had always been aware of him lurking on the few occasions she'd gone out. If he was anywhere near, she would have no trouble spotting him.

If not Charlie, who followed her?

Sally chided herself for being foolish. Neither Wrath nor Charlie would ever set foot south of the river. There was no money to be had in a slum.

Willing her hand to stop shaking, Sally told herself she was imagining things again. Her mind hadn't been quite right in years. She paid another penny for a posy of violets and walked to the shore.

Sally found an empty bit of grass a few feet above the bank and sat down.

Clutching the buns in her hands to protect them from the gulls overhead, she took a deep breath of the sour river air, detecting a note of salt from the sea beyond. Wishful thinking, perhaps. She watched the water lick the shore in murky ripples, swirls of black, green, and darkest brown, thinking of Bettie and looking for the beauty he had seen in it.

Finally, ribbons of silver revealed themselves in the waves, and she saw it.

The sky.

Sally tossed a bun into the river along with the violets.

She didn't realize she was crying until a handkerchief appeared in front of her face.

"The bread can't have been that bad."

Sally looked up to see Mark, and hesitantly took the handkerchief.

He sat beside her at a respectful distance, regarding her carefully.

"You've been following me," she said.

"You're wearing my brother's coat. I thought he'd shrunk a foot and went wandering the docks. You can understand my concern."

"You don't trust me," she observed.

"Had to be sure, didn't I?"

"Are you satisfied?"

He nodded toward the river. "Who are the flowers for?"

Sally wiped her nose on the handkerchief as delicately as she could. "Before they caught me, they murdered my friend."

"Beaumont," he remembered, confirming her fear that he was aware of the pamphlet.

"Him, too." She sniffed. "Bettie was my only friend, and he died because of me."

He nodded, accepting. "Gentleman friend?"

"He was a whore, and he was the only good person I knew. Do you think less of me?"

He shook his head, blond waves catching the breeze beneath the brim of his hat. "Not at all. Not many would befriend a molly. It's all well and good when a woman plays the game, but a man?" He whistled. "You've gone up in my estimation."

A small victory. Sally smiled a little and shrugged. "It wasn't difficult to be his friend."

"So you're here to say goodbye," he observed. "Why the river?"

"Everything ends up in the river."

"I'll give you that."

Remembering the bun in her hand, she tore it in half and offered a piece to Mark.

He took it and nodded his thanks.

Sally took a bite of hers, tasting the grit of the poorly sifted flour and immediately spat it out. She looked down to see some suspect looking black specks in the grain.

Mark laughed. "So it *is* that bad!"

"Worse." She cringed. "Was that an oven I saw in your kitchen?"

"It was, though we just use it for storage."

"Does it work?"

"Can't say I've used it."

Sally counted the pennies in her pocket with her fingertips and asked, "May I use it?"

"Be my guest, though it'll take some doing to get it cleaned out."

She nodded. "I can handle it."

"I believe you can." He smiled. "So you're coming back?"

"If I may." Sally tucked a strand of hair behind her ear. It hadn't occurred to her that they might not want her back. It should have, of course. *Who wants to look after an ailing prostitute?*

"Of course." He chuckled. "We've got to get Nick's boots back to him at the very least."

Mark stood and took her hand, helping her up. The wind took the edge of her skirt as she rose, scattering the rest of the crumbs to the wind.

They walked companionably back into Southwark down the main thoroughfare and stopped for butter and flour along the way. Mark attempted to pay for the lot, but Sally thrust her last pennies at the seller, desperate to pay her own way. He didn't press the issue, and for that she was grateful. He did, however, insist on carrying the heavy sack of flour over his shoulder.

"Thank you for allowing me to stay," Sally said at last.

He smiled his crooked smile, "It's nice to have a lady in the house. Keeps the girls down at The Rose on their toes."

She smiled. "I hadn't thought of that. Are you courting someone?"

"Not exactly courting," he looked sheepish, "and not exactly one."

"I'm sure you're very popular."

"I can't complain." He grinned.

They rounded the corner and Sally recognized the alley that led to the back of the warehouse. She swallowed. "What about your brother?"

"He's not to my taste."

Sally laughed. "I daresay. I mean, is he courting anyone?"

Mark attempted to suppress a smile. "You like him," he observed.

"Who wouldn't?" Sally shrugged. Mark opened the back gate

and she hurried after him, carrying the butter. "Why did he save me?"

"You'll have to ask him that," he said, dropping the sack of flour onto the table beside the coffin.

Sally had forgotten it was there. She felt an involuntary jolt of fear at the sight.

Jack and Will set down their tools and rose to greet them.

"New plan this morning, lads," Mark announced. "We're going to set the kitchen to rights and then Sally's going to make us breakfast."

Chapter 31

After walking for nearly four hours, Nick was famished.

He had woken at dawn and set out for the Hereford estate in search of his late pay. Knowing full well that Hereford was not in residence, he hoped to prevail upon his clerk to settle their account in his absence. Finding the clerk absent and his wages nowhere in sight, Nick turned back toward home.

It was late morning by the time he made it back to Southwark. His pockets were filled with a few fresh eggs one of the kitchen maids had passed him on his way out, so he walked as quickly and carefully as he could without crushing them or signaling to pickpockets that he had anything to steal--not an easy task. His long black coat with the deeper pockets would have been infinitely more suitable, but harder to explain.

Along with the eggs, the maid had slipped him a carefully folded missive bearing the Hereford crest. Hoping it held word of the wages owed to him, he tore it open, reading it on his way through the maze.

"My Dear Mister Virtue,

"I fare well in Sussex, though the country is darker for the lack of your shining spirit. I look forward to the day we are reunited and wish you all the very best in all things.

"Until we meet again, Jane"

Nick had crumpled the letter with a curse and raised his hand to throw it into the woods, but thought better of it. It would do no good for someone to happen upon it and give it to Hereford. Better to burn it. The girl was bound to cost him his job as it was, and he didn't need Hereford calling him out over some imagined affair.

He sighed as he neared Mark's shop. He would boil the eggs and give some to Sally and share the rest around. It wouldn't be much, but it would be most welcome.

Nick had woken beside Sally's bed before dawn to find her sleeping soundly. Her fever persisted, though not in full force. He had watched the wound for days, and was satisfied that she was recovering, but she still had nightmares that caused her to wake in the night.

It was plain that her trauma still haunted her. The sound of hooves outside could make her rigid with fear. It would be better if he could stay by her side until the terrors stopped. Fortunately, the Ramseys were still away from the estate.

The longer he stayed with Sally, the more he was convinced that he was observing the effects of some poison leaving her system. While the fever resulted from her wound and could explain some of the early delirium, it did not explain the short bursts of shaking, or the terror of common things. Either she had been drugged for a very long time or she was completely mad, and as she had periods of remarkable lucidity, he was inclined to believe the former.

As he reached the back garden, he heard the light sound of a woman's laughter. Unusual thing to hear in these parts, unless it was at someone's expense. Sally would surely still be in bed, and he would surprise her with eggs and coffee for breakfast. He smiled at the thought.

Increasing his pace, he walked briskly into the heavenly smell of baking bread. Nick's stomach growled angrily. The bakery was two streets down and he didn't have any money to speak of, so bread would have to wait. He would get the eggs to Sally first, and if he could find a penny or two, he would buy a stale loaf later in the day when it was discounted to a price he could afford.

Nick pushed open the garden gate and again heard the sound of laughter. It was unusually early in the day for Mark to have a girl over, and most who lived in these parts would have been away at dawn, working or attending their families. Nick opened the back door cautiously.

Inside was a scene he had not been expecting. The sawdust had been swept off the floor, fresh rushes strewn across the kitchen, and every surface had been cleaned. The bread smell was coming from Mark's oven, along with a pot of coffee bubbling fragrantly over the fire. The coffin was on the floor, and Mark,

Jack, and Will sat on benches around the table eating warm rolls slathered with fresh butter.

Nick stood in the doorway, dumbstruck, until Sally came strolling around the corner wearing an old shirt and a pair of loose trousers that he was certain belonged to Mark.

She stepped around the table to the hearth, stirring the pot of coffee with a smile. "It's ready. Who needs more?"

The lads all made noises of consent, their mouths filled with bread. Sally collected their cups and quickly refilled them, passing them around the table.

"Where have you been all my life?" Mark grinned as he tore open a fresh roll and inhaled the steam.

"Are you talking to me or the bread?" Sally joked.

"Both, by God!" He declared, making them laugh.

Sally looked lovely, healthier than he had ever seen her, and happy. Perhaps she had finally recovered.

Perhaps it was Mark.

His heart sank.

She looked up suddenly, as if sensing his presence, and smiled.

Seeing Sally look up, Mark noticed him standing in the doorway at last. "Nick!" he greeted, his mouth full. "Welcome home! We made you breakfast."

Will leaned back with his hands behind his head, smiling, as Jack grabbed another roll from a basket sitting on the image of Saint Francis carved into the center of the table.

When did they get a basket?

Since when did they use the table for food?

And where in the world did they get butter?

"Good morning, Nick." Sally reached for another cup from the shelf, both of which were miraculously clean. "Would you like some coffee?"

"Certainly, thank you." He sat on an empty stool between Mark and Jack, before remembering the eggs. "Damnation!" He cursed, and pulled them out of his pocket, one by one, setting them on the table.

"Eggs!" She gasped. "I haven't had a fresh egg in ages. I shall cook them at once. Thank you."

Nick stood to take the coffeepot from her, pouring himself a cup as she took the eggs. "Are you quite sure you're feeling up to it? I can cook them."

"You saved my life." She smiled. "The least I can do is cook you breakfast."

Nick blushed in spite of himself and sat down with his coffee. He reached for a roll and Will and Jack watched him, smiling smugly. "What?"

"Nothing." Will nodded toward the basket. "Have some bread."

Nick looked suspiciously at the roll in his hand. It was a knot shape, soft and brown with a dusting of flour on the top. He tore it open, spread a little of the butter on it, and took a bite.

He could have wept. It was the best bread he had eaten in years.

The boys laughed at the look on his face. "These are delicious," he said as he reached for a second. "The bakery's aren't this good. Where did they come from?"

"I made them," Sally said from the hearth, dropping the eggs into a pot of hot water.

"You did?"

"I was sold to a great Chateau as a baker's apprentice when I was a child. Baking is a way I can be useful."

Nick looked around the tidy kitchen. "Tell me they didn't make you clean."

"You wound me," said Mark with a smile, his hand over his heart.

Sally made an unladylike noise. "Why would I do that when I have such helpful men so hungry for bread?"

Will chuckled and Jack looked like he was in love. Mark watched Nick carefully.

"That's good," said Nick. "You don't want to overexert yourself." He watched her bend over the pot, carefully pulling boiled eggs out with a spoon. The shirt was far too big on her and it skimmed the curves of her back and her hips beautifully. He had never seen a woman wearing men's clothes, but he expected Sally would be stunning in anything. "What happened to your shift?"

She set the plate of boiled eggs down on the table and sat

beside him, reaching for a roll. "I had to wash it. Mark was kind enough to lend me these old things of his." She quickly peeled a hard-boiled egg and ate it in two bites.

Mark wiggled his eyebrows at Nick. "Can I keep her?"

Nick felt another flash of jealousy and glared at Mark, hoping he was joking.

Mark laughed at his expression and grabbed a hot egg.

"I'm sorry you have to wear men's things. I will try to find you a dress later, if you would like," Nick offered.

Sally smiled at him warmly. "You've been so kind to me, I couldn't possibly ask you for anything else."

Her smile made Nick feel warm from the roots of his hair to the ends of his toes. He felt quite certain he could pull a dress out of thin air, if she asked him to.

"Go on, bruv, you've got some money coming to you from the last haul," Mark said. "Get her something nice."

Nick tossed Mark a dirty look. Mark was well aware that Nick adored Sally and would not get in the way of that, but he wouldn't stand for him dragging his heels in courting her, either. With Mark's fair hair and easy smile, he had always been popular with ladies. Nick didn't fancy his chances competing against him.

"It would be my pleasure. What do you need?"

Sally smiled as she sipped her coffee. "Not much, I can make it myself. Just some thread, a needle, and a length of linen, or linsey-woolsey. Any color but green."

Chapter 32

After breakfast, Nick collected his wages from Mark and took Sally to the shops.

At the first sight of people outside, she felt a flash of embarrassment and pulled Nick's tricorn lower over her forehead.

Nick sensed her hesitation and came back to where she stood in the doorway.

He gave her a warm half-smile and said, "It's not far. You won't be in any danger."

Sally found herself smiling back, although she must have looked a fright, wearing Nick's coat over Mark's clothes. In the bustle of the market, no one seemed to notice. She hurried to keep up with Nick's long strides. He was so sure of himself, picking his way through the bustling street. As busy as Covent Garden could be, Sally wasn't often up and about at such an hour, and she certainly wasn't allowed out. Such fast-paced crowds were new to her, but fear of being trampled kept her moving.

Nick was a natural. Weaving between people, over mud puddles and around carts of rotting vegetables and crates of laying hens, he never once let go of her hand, and was careful to lead her around the obstructions. She held his big hand and did not take her eyes from his shoulders until they escaped the midday crush.

Now that her wits had returned to her, Sally was quite certain he was most decidedly handsome.

Surreptitiously studying him over breakfast as he held the bread she had baked like a holy thing, Sally prayed her silent thanks to God and Madame Toulouse that she remembered her baking so well. The look on his face as he bit into it was a thing of beauty; she recognized the pleasure of eating something delicious on an empty stomach and her heart ached for him and his hardships. There were few enough ingredients available in the kitchen, but she was resolved that she would put them to good use feeding this man and his friends. She needed to prove, to herself as much as anyone, that she could be useful.

He had been so kind to her. Seeing to her wound, he hadn't turned away from her scars. The feel of his hands on her back had been a shock, she could not remember a time someone had touched that part of her in kindness.

She *liked* it.

Nick's warm, firm hands on her skin, his callused thumb dragging along her scar...God help her.

She would never make a lady.

They crossed the street and Nick led her into a shop on the corner of Love Lane. The small space was packed to the rafters with bolts of muslin, linen, wool, and some silks and velvets in vibrant jewel tones that would have to been too rich for even the highest earners off the Piazza. Southwark was not an area of means, and Sally wondered who purchased them.

Nick glanced around at the bolts of fabric and looked lost. He turned to her and raised his eyebrows. "Do you see anything you like?"

Feeling shy, Sally drifted toward a length of brown homespun much like the cloth she had worn working in the gardens of Chateau. It was sturdy, it wouldn't show dirt, and she knew it was cheap. If Nick insisted on buying her cloth, she would at least try to be sure it wouldn't cost him much.

Most women she knew would have taken that opportunity to spend every penny he had on silk, ribbons, and every other frippery they could fit onto a single gown, but Sally would be damned if she repaid his generosity by bankrupting him. In any case, she was anxious to separate herself from her old life insofar as she could, and if that meant forsaking silk, well, that was a sacrifice she could live with.

The shopkeeper, a plump blonde woman of middling years, chose that moment to approach them. "Nick, my lad!" She gave him a noisy kiss on the cheek. "How have you been keeping? How's Mark?"

"He's much the same, as you can imagine. Maggie, this is my friend, Sally. Sally, this is Maggie Townsend, my mother's cousin."

As Nick called her his "friend," Maggie Townsend took notice of her hiding in Nick's shadow, wearing his hat. She looked Sally up and down appraisingly. "Good Lord, there's a girl in there!

What have you done to her dress, you naughty boy?"

Nick blushed to his ears. "Sally was set upon by brigands and it got ruined, and now she's wearing Mark's trousers, God help her. Do you have anything she can wear?"

"Brigands! Not here, I hope!"

"Not here. Near Upper St. James Park. We brought her back to Mark's to patch her up."

"St. James Park," she sneered. "Bloody parading ponces, they've got no respect for young girls. You're a saint, Nicholas. A saint! Your mother would be so proud, God rest her soul." Maggie turned her full attention to her, and Sally nearly jumped back at the force of the warmth in her face. "You poor dear! Imagine having to wear Mark's trousers! He's a lovely lad, but I wouldn't wish that fate on anyone. God only knows who's been in them!" She laughed at her own joke. "Come with me, and we'll get you sorted!"

Sally glanced helplessly over her shoulder at Nick, who waited in the doorway. How strange that a cousin would call him by the wrong name. Thinking she had merely gotten caught up in her own histrionics and it was a slip of the tongue, Sally shrugged it off. Maggie seemed eager enough to help, although the last time an older woman had said she was going to help Sally, she had wound up imprisoned at Wrath's, so she was understandably nervous as Maggie led her around the corner to a small side room out of Nick's sight.

Maggie took the borrowed coat from her shoulders and set Nick's hat on a table strewn with fabric scraps and scissors. "My, but you're a pretty thing," She clucked. "Have you no corset? Undergarments?"

Sally's voice cracked as she answered, "I have a plain shift, but I had to take it off. My back bled in the night."

"Good Lord!" Maggie shrieked, "Set upon by brigands indeed! Did you let Nick look at it? He is a physician, you know. Well, almost a physician. He went to Cambridge, until Lord Somerton died, but he was doing very well, indeed. You could certainly do worse, my dove."

Sally hadn't blushed in a long while, but that almost did it. "He sewed me up. He saved my life."

"Lucky girl. Not a girl in five miles wouldn't stab herself in the back to get our Nick to take a look at it." Maggie gathered up a soft white cotton shift in her arms and held it in front of Sally. "This should do nicely. Put this on."

With a moment's hesitation, Sally discarded Mark's clothes and threw the shift over her head, but not before Maggie saw the stitches in her chest. Maggie gave a low whistle. "That go all the way through?"

Sally turned around, showing her back.

After a moment, Maggie let out a long breath. "I daresay you didn't do that to yourself, did you?"

Sally shook her head.

"You're quiet," she observed. "Are you shy?"

"I'm unaccustomed to kindness."

"Lift your arms," she instructed, and Sally did. Maggie fastened a corset around her waist and began to lace it firmly but not painfully up her back. "I would believe that. Were those whip scars?"

"Some of them," Sally admitted.

Maggie turned Sally around and she was shaking her head. "You poor dear." She pulled a pair of long cotton drawers out of a trunk and handed them to her. Sally slipped them on under the shift as Maggie disappeared into a closet at the end of the room. "You're in good hands now," she called over her shoulder. "Nick will take care of you."

Sally sank gently against the work table. It had been a long time since anyone had wanted to take care of her.

Maggie emerged moments later with a length of red fabric draped across her arms. "This will do nicely," she assured.

To Sally's surprise, it was a completed dress. Maggie lifted it over Sally's head and tied it up the front, pulling the lace-edged shift above the bust and through the elbow-length sleeves. It was a long, lightweight dress of fine linen dyed the rich red of fresh strawberries and trimmed at the bust and sleeves with silk ribbon embroidered with flowers. The laces were a darker shade of the same red, and came together in a bow at the top. It was girlish but modest, embellished yet serviceable. It was the kind of dress Sally imagined would belong to a common, respectable woman not too

156

troubled by strenuous work.

It was the nicest thing she had ever worn.

"There you are." Maggie smiled. "Much better. Let's get you some nice hair ribbons and give Nick his hat back, eh?"

Sally looked down at the yards of red and pristine white and held the skirt in her hands, delighting in the feel of the soft linen beneath her fingertips. "This is so beautiful. I cannot possibly keep this, it is too expensive."

Maggie made an unladylike snort. "Don't be soft. Any friend of Nick's is a friend of mine. At any rate, the lady who ordered this paid for it and never came back, so it's yours now, I reckon."

Maggie marched into the main room, expecting Sally to follow. She grabbed Nick's hat and the borrowed clothes and coat and walked after her, relishing the feel of the soft, clean fabric swishing around her legs.

She led Sally behind the counter of ribbons and thread and started fussing with her hair. Nick had been watching the street from the only window, and he turned to them as they re-entered the room.

Sally carefully studied the ribbon display, avoiding his eyes, afraid of seeing judgment there. A harlot dressed as anything else would surely look ridiculous.

Maggie tied her hair back with an embroidered ribbon matching the trim on the dress and handed her the comb she had been using. "You keep hold of this. Men never appreciate the need for such things."

Sally smiled at her in thanks, and tried to work up the courage to look at Nick. It wasn't like her to be shy around men. *What made him different?*

Finally, slowly, Sally met his eyes.

Nick stepped toward the counter, looking at Sally as though she might disappear.

"What do you think? Our girl looks nice, don't she?"

"She's lovely," he said. "Do you like it, Sally?"

That did it. Sally blushed. As popular as she had been, few had ever called her lovely. "I like it very much."

"Good." He smiled. "We'll take it."

"Of course you will." Maggie bustled around the shop

gathering up odd pieces as she went. "It's yours. The underthings and comb as well, and some bits and bobs besides. Won't be a moment."

Sally crossed the small space and handed the coat and hat back to Nick. He tucked the coat under his arm and put the hat on his head. He looked up at her under the brim and it knocked the breath out of her body.

He looked very much like the highwayman from the forest.

"Here we are." Maggie dumped a bundle of supplies into Sally's arms, another set of underwear, a hat, a pair of slippers, and more ribbons, from what she could see. "This should sort you out for now. You come back if you need anything."

Nick took some coins from his pocket and pressed them into her palm. "Thank you, Maggie."

"You're a good lad, Nicholas. You take care of this girl and keep Mark out of trouble, you hear?"

He laughed. "I can't swear to the last part, but I'll do my best."

"Thank you." Sally clutched the bundle of extra undergarments tightly to her chest. It had been so long since she had any new ones, she was prepared to protect them with her life.

The walk back from the shop was somewhat less frightening. The effect of the dress on her mood was remarkable; it was clean, it was soft, and most importantly, it wasn't green.

Sally smiled all the way back to the warehouse, stealing glances at Nick in that hat, trying to imagine his face draped in shadow. She thought of that kiss in the woods. *Was it possible?*

She could hardly come out and ask him, and certainly not in public where someone might hear. She settled for an easier question. "Mark says you're a tutor. What's that like?"

He gave her a half-smile, but it was half-wince as well. "It's not so exciting. I tutor a couple of young boys who would rather be somewhere else most of the time."

"Have you ever thought of going into business with Mark?" Anyone listening would have thought she was referring to carpentry.

He let out a breath. "I did, for a while, but there's no future in it. I wanted to do something that wouldn't be so dangerous."

"As carpentry?"

His shrug gave nothing away. "I've no talent for it. I would be a very poor carpenter. Better to build a life from my love of books."

"I should think being a tutor would be wonderful."

"It's a respectable position, as my mother would say."

"You want to be respectable?" Sally asked.

"I did." He sighed. "Imagine my surprise when I discovered just how much respect tutors often get."

It wasn't difficult to believe that Hereford would mistreat his staff. Sally looked down at his scuffed boots, remembering seeing the toe at the edge of the door. If only she could have thrown open that door and run to him then...

He would have seen a ragged harlot in a cheap dress and he would have been horrified.

He had seen that awful pamphlet, but how much did he really know about her? Would it make a difference?

Why did he save me?

"I came to London to be a baker," Sally said, at last.

"Your bread was great. You could do that."

"The bread?" She shrugged. "They were only plain rolls. I want to make you something lovely, to thank you for the dress."

His smile made her skin feel warm. "You don't need to worry about that. You need to rest until you're well again."

"I feel fine." She looked at the carts for supplies as they passed. "I can cook many things. Do you like pies?" She watched for any reaction that might indicate a memory of that night in the forest, clinging to the impossible idea that he might be her highwayman.

"There's not a lot of food I don't like," he said honestly. His eyes didn't flicker, and Sally tried to hide her disappointment.

He could not possibly be her highwayman. He was careful and kind, and she would have bet that he had never so much as fired a pistol. Though they had similar builds, to be sure, Nick was hardly the only man in London in possession of a tricorn, as new as the style was, and he was clearly too virtuous to lead a life of crime.

Either way, it had been a long time since Sally had eaten

159

properly and she was itching to put Mark's kitchen to good use. If she could thank Nick and his friends with the recipes she had committed to memory, so much the better.

"Do you know where we could get some almonds?"

Chapter 33

Sally was closing the oven as Nick walked into the kitchen through the back door, Mark following close behind.

"Hellfire and damnation!" Mark cursed, striking the top of the table with his fist.

Jack leapt from his chair beside the hearth. "Any word?"

Mark ran a hand through his hair. "They're talking transportation."

"Transportation?" Jack repeated. "For four pence?"

Nick set his medical bag on the table with a heavy sigh. Sally watched the exchange with rapt attention, her hands white with a dusting of flour.

"Anyone else and they would have set bail by now. Mary's father sussed what they were about and has it in for him. Right connections, as it were."

Jack stared blankly into the fire.

Mark sat in front of Jack and looked him in the eyes. "We'll get this sorted."

"He can't be transported. He'd never survive seven years in the colonies. He's barely older than I am."

"I'll think of something, I promise you. In the meantime, practice your Bible verses in case you need to claim benefit of the clergy one day."

"Does he have a court date?"

Mark shook his head. "Not yet."

"Then we have time. Can we get him a file? Take it to him in Nick's bag?" Jack suggested.

Nick opened the bag and began to withdraw the instruments for cleaning. "They've caught on to us. Searched my bag. Couldn't imagine what a minister would need with all of these."

"A minister?" Sally asked.

Nick shrugged. "Mark has them all convinced I'm a man of the Church now. Physicians are extra."

Mark sat heavily on the bench beside the table and pointed a finger at Nick. "I saved your hide with that little piece of genius, make no mistake."

Nick crossed himself. Jack laughed in spite of everything, drying his eyes with his sleeve.

Sally gathered the bread dough she was working and began to knead it between her hands, leaning her back against the edge of the hearth. "I think I've missed the joke."

Mark chuckled. "The gaol has a lady warden, you see, a great, hulking monster of a woman, and she wanted a piece of Nick in payment for Harry's room and board."

"Over my dead body!" Sally gasped.

All three of them looked up at her outburst, and Nick realized he was holding his breath. *Why would she care?*

Sally coughed. "That is to say, no one should have to do such a thing. How awful! What did you tell her?" She smacked the dough against the table.

Mark smiled at her, eyes sparkling with suppressed laughter. He didn't miss a thing. He leaned back and folded his arms behind his head, explaining, "I explained that our Nick here is a man of God and is above such things."

Sally wrinkled her nose in distaste and looked at Nick. "You're not, are you?"

Not with the kind of thoughts he'd been having. Nick blushed to his ears and Mark and Jack laughed out loud.

Sally put a hand on her hip and turned to Mark. "And was she satisfied with that answer?"

"Alas, she was not, so I had to satisfy her with something else."

Jack laughed so hard he nearly fell on the floor. Mark's smile didn't extend to his eyes, and Sally noticed. She left the dough on the table and wrapped her arms around his shoulders, hugging him from behind the chair. "You're a good brother."

Mark smiled at the sudden affection and Nick looked on sadly. They seemed to get along so well, and Nick was still having trouble just talking to her. If she preferred Mark, he supposed he would have to accept it. He could never begrudge his brother a chance at happiness. Still, Mark had so many girls, and Nick had only ever wanted one.

The smell of caramelizing sugar and almonds reached them at the table and Sally rushed to the oven, taking two cloths in her hands. She pulled a tray of tarts from the oven, releasing a current of warm air into the kitchen through the open door.

Mark moaned loudly. "What are those?"

She set one in front of him. "Try one and see."

Sally handed hot tarts to Nick and Jack with a smile, and watched in satisfaction as they made short work of them. Steam rose from the sticky filling as Nick bit into his, crumbs falling onto the table.

He closed his eyes in pleasure, the taste of the burnt sugar mingling with the hot crunch of the nuts and the buttery base. Nick thought it was the most opulent thing he had ever tasted. When it was gone, he opened his eyes and Sally was watching him. She held his gaze, gently biting her lower lip.

He swallowed.

Sally took a deep breath and began to slap the bread dough between her hands. "You need to get him a file and you can't take it in your medical bag, right?"

Nick nodded. "Right."

"Have you got a file?"

"Several," offered Jack. He rose to grab one off of the workbench in the next room and handed it to her.

She dusted it off on her skirt and folded it into the bread dough, rolling a quick demi-baguette.

"They're not good with food," Mark said. "We'll have to sneak it in."

"What if it's charity?" she asked. "We've got a man of the Church."

"For one prisoner? Bound to get suspicious."

"For all of them. How many prisoners are there in Newgate?"

Mark snorted. "Too bloody many. In any case, they know us. They'd never buy it."

"They don't know me," she said.

Newgate was hell on earth. By entering it as a woman, Sally would be exposing herself to physical danger, disease, and horrors the likes of which should never be seen. To say it was not a place for ladies was putting it mildly. "You would do that?" Nick asked.

"Of course," she said, unfazed. "You would have to go with me."

Nick nodded. "I will."

"Wait," Mark held up a hand, "you reckon we can make enough bread to feed everybody in Newgate?"

"That depends." She shrugged. "How much flour can you get me?"

♠

Hours later, the sun had gone down and the table was covered in round loaves of crusty bread.

Jack had run out to have a word with the nearest miller, another cousin of the vast Townsend family, and within an hour, they had more flour than they could reasonably use in a week. Sally didn't blink as the sacks were brought in, only thanked the miller's boys with almond tarts, tied up her hair, and set to work.

When Will returned from the job he'd had that morning, Sally put them all to work mixing and kneading dough, and setting it to prove in batches over the hearth before it was put into the oven. Dozens of loaves later, the lads were exhausted, but Sally pressed on, baking until the supplies ran out.

She stood at the table, kneading the last of the dough, when Mark stopped at Nick's elbow on his way out the door. "We're knackered," he said quietly. "Going down to The Rose and Crown for a bite to eat. Bring the missus when she's done."

Nick nodded, unsure of whether Mark was assigning Sally to Nick or himself. He shrugged it off and approached Sally as he heard the door close.

A few strands of hair had come loose and they framed her face in black waves. Her cheeks were flushed and her arms were covered in flour up to her elbows. Her shoulders rose slightly with every knead. They had baked most of the day, and she had already made bread and tarts before the work had begun. She must have been exhausted, but she pressed on, determined to finish.

Sally formed the last of the dough into a ball and put it above the hearth to prove with a sigh. She wiped her forehead with the back of her hand, leaving a streak of flour across her face.

Nick grabbed the bucket of water they had been using to wash their hands and set it before her.

"Thank you." She plunged her hands into the icy water and scrubbed her arms, scraping the dough from her fingernails.

Nick took one of the oven cloths from the side and dipped it into the water.

Sally looked up at him and smiled.

"You've got, um..." He laughed awkwardly and took her upturned face gently in his hand. Her smile faded, her eyes widening. Nick thought he could hear his heart beating in his chest. He wondered if she could hear it, too. "There's a bit of flour..."

"Oh." She gave a little laugh.

He squeezed the water out of the cloth into the bucket and Sally closed her eyes as he gently wiped the flour off of her face.

"You're a wonder," he said.

She opened her eyes. He still held her face in his hand. It would be so easy to kiss her. Would she want him to?

Of course not. He wouldn't press his attentions on a poor, tired woman, trapped as she was alone with him. What kind of animal was he?

He dropped his hand and felt her sigh as he pulled away. *Was it disappointment?*

Or relief?

Nick draped the towel over the edge of the bucket and dried his hands. He smiled weakly and moved to stand behind her, laying his hands on her shoulders and massaging them firmly. She collapsed against him, the length of her body pressed against his, her head resting back against his shoulder.

"You must be knackered," he said into her sweet-smelling hair. "The lads have gone out to The Rose for supper. Would you like to go meet them?"

Sally turned in his arms abruptly and put her hands on his shoulders, distressed. "I forgot to cook! I'm so sorry."

He held her there, his hands resting above her hips. They fit together perfectly. He smiled. "You were busy. We can fend for ourselves. Would you let me buy you supper? To show my thanks?"

165

Her face relaxed into a beaming smile and Nick felt himself weaken at the knees. "I would like that very much. Thank you."

"Good." He reluctantly let her go and took his hat and coat from the peg beside the door. He put his hat on and passed her the coat. "You can borrow this, if you like. It's a little cold tonight."

Sally took it with a smile and held it close to her chest.

Chapter 34

The Rose and Crown was a bustling inn a good ten minutes' walk into town. Though Sally was near boiling from the long hours working in the kitchen, she had accepted Nick's long coat and wore it over her dress, fancying the loose fabric was only a few steps removed from having his arms around her. They hurried through the streets, and she realized that the hour was indeed late if it was so dark in midsummer.

"Will they still be serving food?" Sally asked.

"Oh yes," he assured her. "They're open all hours."

"And they admit ladies?" she asked shyly. Strictly speaking, she was no lady, and had many years of going places ladies were not allowed. Still, she had begun her new life, and dearly wanted to avoid any situations that made her feel that cheap again.

"I should think so. The Henshawes have five daughters, and all of them work there in some capacity. We've seen other ladies there most nights. You will be made welcome."

Sally smiled at his back as he turned away, a step ahead of her. She grasped the lapel of the borrowed coat and held it over her nose, inhaling his smell of sawdust and soap.

"Are you well?"

Sally opened her eyes to see him looking back at her. She dropped the coat. "Yes, quite well, thank you," she stammered, embarrassed.

"We're almost there." He smiled, confident as anything, and reached back for her hand.

Surprised, she took it and held it all the way to the inn, warming inside.

The lads were sitting around a table towards the back when they arrived, and Sally let Nick lead her through the throng. As he had said, there were many ladies present, more than a dozen amongst the men, and to her surprise, a few small children running underfoot. She had never seen children in an inn before, and took care not to walk into them as they approached the table.

"There's the lady of the hour," greeted Mark, taking her hand and kissing it affectionately.

Sally struggled to hide her disappointment. Perhaps they were accustomed to holding ladies' hands and Nick's gesture had not been the romantic overture she had hoped for.

She smiled at Mark just the same.

Nick hesitated before taking a chair, as if he was trying to decide whether he should sit beside Mark or let Sally sit there. After an uncomfortable pause, he chose the seat on the bench across from Mark, leaving her to choose her own place beside either one of them. She felt very much that she was being tested, as Will and Jack looked on. Sally shrugged off the feeling, telling herself she was reading too much into it. All she wanted at that moment, and every moment, if she was honest, was to feel Nick close to her, so she stepped toward his bench.

Her foot hooked over a boot and she lost her balance, falling sideways into Nick with an involuntary shriek.

He caught her in his arms before her head hit the table, crushing her to his chest. "Are you hurt?"

Sally brushed the hair out of her reddening face as she looked up to see his lips inches from hers.

"I'm well," she assured him. "Only unbelievably embarrassed. Thank you for saving me. Again," she added.

He smiled as he easily set her on her feet again, helping her to sit on the bench beside him.

Sally rearranged her skirts under the table, feeling a bruise forming on her knee, and saw the boot she had tripped over.

It was Mark's upturned foot.

She gasped and looked up at him accusingly.

He grinned from ear to ear and passed her a mug of beer.

Sally kicked him under the table and felt some satisfaction as she saw him suppress a yelp.

A barmaid approached the table bearing a tray laden with more tall mugs of beer. She passed them around to the lads and skipped Sally as she saw hers was full. Staking her claim, she saucily perched her generous bottom on Mark's knee and looked her over appraisingly.

Sally was more than used to being given the once-over, and

she'd received it from more frightening women than her. She met the woman's icy stare and she did not flinch.

The woman turned up her nose and addressed Mark. "Who's this, then?"

"Meg, I am pleased to introduce Miss Sally...er, Remi, Nick's lady friend. Sally, this is Meg Henshawe, the eldest of the Henshawe girls and the best barmaid in Southwark."

"Pleased to meet you." Sally smiled politely.

Meg ignored her, looking at her and Nick sitting beside each other and wrinkling her nose in distaste. "So it's like that, is it?"

"Yeah, it's like that." Mark smiled, but he was clearly becoming irritated with her offishness.

"What about my sister?" Meg asked Nick.

"I beg your pardon?"

"She likes you." Meg jutted her chin defiantly. "Or isn't a barmaid good enough for you?"

Sally looked at Nick, silently praying he didn't have a sweetheart. There was nothing but confusion on his face.

Mark answered for him, "Meg, I think you're confusing my dear brother with yours truly."

Meg put her hand on her hip and looked down at him angrily. "I am not."

"You are so," he corrected. "I've already taken three of you to bed. Who's left? Alice?"

Meg stood and slapped him, the sound echoing through the bar. "How bloody dare you! You're still cross with me!"

Mark rubbed his red cheek and smiled. "I'm not cross about your damned fighter and I never was. Calm yourself. In the meantime, we'll have five pots of stew. Run along now and see if you can't find one of your sisters to bring it out to us. The rest of them were sweeter, if I remember right."

Meg slapped him again, and that one he had coming.

"I think I've caused some trouble," Sally said after she stormed off. "I hope they don't spit in the food."

Mark waved a hand. "She loves me, really, but she's a bit mad, you see."

Nick smiled at Sally and her cheeks warmed. With all the excitement, she hadn't fully processed Mark introducing her as

Nick's lady friend, and she felt a little flustered at the thought. She had known more than her fair share of men, but not one of them had wanted to be hers. She reminded herself with some difficulty that saying a thing didn't make it real, and she fought the urge to take his hand under the table.

Mark watched her knowingly with a sly smile on his face. She avoided his eyes.

Within a few minutes, a girl brought up a tray to the table and passed around bowls of stew with a loaf of crusty brown bread. She was young, certainly no older than thirteen, and delicately pretty with mousy hair and fair skin. The food passed out, she bobbed a polite curtsy and moved to excuse herself.

"Good evening, Alice," Mark greeted warmly, and Sally surmised she was the fourth Henshawe sister.

Alice cleared her throat and gave a quick smile. "Good evening, Mister Virtue. Mister Virtue. Madam. Mister...Will." She tucked her hair behind her ear and looked up with large, oddly grave grey eyes. "Jack."

They greeted Alice in turn and Sally smiled at what she saw in those grey eyes, relieved that at least one of the Henshawes was not in love with Mark.

"Alice," Mark started, "is there any chance that your darling sister did not spit in my stew?"

Alice shook her head. "I wouldn't let her. I poked her with a fork," she confessed.

The lads laughed and she smiled at Jack's response.

Alice cleared her throat and touched Sally's arm lightly. "Madam," she lowered her voice, "I heard what you're doing for Harry. Thank you."

Sally took her hand and gave her best smile. "It has been my great pleasure. Please, call me Sally."

Alice curtsied quickly and disappeared behind the bar.

Sally inclined her head toward the middle of the table, inhaling the strong, savory smell of the stew, and asked, "Does everybody know?"

Will raised his eyebrows but did not stop eating. On the other side of Mark, Jack smiled. "Alice has a way of knowing things."

"Slips here and there unnoticed. We take it for granted now,"

Mark added.

Sally wondered if Alice knew everything, or just what Jack was doing.

She would have to remind herself to ask her one day.

Chapter 35

Sally woke the next morning feeling anxious.

Newgate.

Nick was just waking as she sat up in bed, his hair mussed, with an expression of sleepy contentment despite his place on the floor. He sat up in his long shirt and stretched, the wide, untied neckline shifting to reveal a glimpse of a particularly well-developed shoulder. Successfully distracted, Sally sat there and stared.

He smiled slowly and asked, "Coffee?"

Her mouth had gone quite dry. She nodded.

Nick stood and crossed the room, pulling on his loose trousers and tucking the shirt into them. Sadly, Sally was not afforded a glimpse of much more than a fine pair of strong calves. He glanced at her curiously and she tried her best to look innocent. "You go ahead and get dressed," he said. "I'll meet you downstairs."

"Thank you," she croaked, and watched him walk out the door.

The effect that man had on her was like nothing she had ever experienced. She had dreamt of his hands on her, inside her, and woke up feeling so aroused it was uncomfortable. She slid a hand between her legs with a sigh, finding herself wetter than she had ever been, and withdrew her fingers to see they were covered in blood.

"Lord have mercy," Sally breathed, wiping the blood with her washing linen.

Wrath had ruined her. Surgically, permanently ruined her. She could not conceive, and had not bled in three years.

She stood, feeling her belly for any unusual changes. Finding it the same as it had been the previous night, she dressed quickly, folding the linen into her smallclothes to staunch the flow of blood.

Sally paced the room nervously, imagining every terrible

thing that could have caused it, dismissing the hopeful notion that it might indicate a return to health. She cleared the soiled bed linen off of the pallet to wash and sat beside the window, looking at the river.

Perhaps she had not escaped Death after all.

She did live with a physician, but she could not imagine asking him about such things.

Sally took a deep breath and began to comb her hair for the day ahead. She would go through with the plan as discussed, and as she otherwise felt fit and well, she would go on hoping very much that she did not die. If it got worse or did not go away, she would simply have to work up the courage to ask Nick about it, and hope she did not die of embarrassment in the meantime.

Satisfied with this compromise, Sally followed the smell of coffee downstairs.

Nick stirred the pot, fully dressed in a somber black coat that must have been part of his tutor's garb. He did not look like any minister Sally had ever seen, but then few of them she had known were young and handsome. She smiled in thanks as he handed her a mug of coffee, attempting to put her worries aside.

The lads had already loaded the bread into big sacks, and would help them to carry it as far as Newgate Street. Harry's file was baked into the long demi-baguette that Sally had intentionally burned and slipped into the bottom of the sack she carried. The rest were round in shape and baked to an even golden brown. They were counting on them to take the bread at face value, and to not look too closely at the loaves themselves.

The five of them crossed the bridge in the early hours of the morning, walking in silence until they reached Newgate Street. Mark handed Sally the bag he carried and kissed her cheek in gratitude. Nick took the others. "We'll see you at the Cheshire Cheese after."

Mark nodded and Will and Jack followed him down Newgate Street into the City.

"It's unlike them to be so quiet," Sally observed. "They must be nervous, too."

"Are you nervous? You can go with them, if you like, and I can try to do it myself."

"I'm not that nervous." She smiled. "Let's go."

The formidable gaol loomed in the distance, the sounds of wails and the stench of excrement reaching them several hundred yards away. Sally steeled herself and they trudged on, their arms loaded with bread.

As they approached the gate, Nick stopped short and handed Sally a small Bible.

"I can't read English very well," she said.

"Neither can most of them." He shrugged. "Use any of it that you know. Keep it close."

Sally nodded and followed him through the gate.

A turnkey greeted them at a low window, charging for the privilege of entering the gaol. Sally struggled to hide her disgust as Nick handed over six shillings.

"What's all this, then?" the turnkey asked.

Nick brought himself up to his full height and set his jaw. "Charity."

"Not on my watch," the turnkey pointed at Sally. "Who are you?"

Nick answered for her. "This is Celeste Virtue, one of our cousins from the country. She's very pious."

"That true? You pious?"

Sally withdrew a loaf of bread and thrust it through the window with the Bible. "I've come to feed the hungry," she said. "You look like you're hungry. Would you like some bread?"

The man looked at her suspiciously, holding the bread in his hands. He tore it open and inhaled its soft insides. He took a bite.

"How much have you got there?"

Sally gave him her best impression of a wide-eyed innocent and shrugged. "Enough for everybody, I hope."

"Where'd it come from?"

She blinked. "The goodness of my heart, of course."

Nick cleared his throat. "She's very wealthy."

The turnkey nodded. "Give us another then." She handed him another loaf and he thrust the Bible back at her. "Saves us feeding them today, at least." He motioned to a guard to meet them as the gate.

Struggling to hide her relief, she met Nick's eyes and he

nodded very slightly in response.

The guard led them first through the begging grate. The stench was overpowering, the sight of so many unwashed, starving bodies a trial. Of everything that Sally had lived through up until that point, nothing had prepared her for Newgate.

She took a loaf of bread from her bag and dozens of arms thrust into the passage to grasp at it. Sally handed it to the first she saw, followed by another, and another. "Please calm yourselves," Nick shouted over the din of laughter and howling. "There's enough for everyone."

Sally handed it out down one side and Nick took the other, emptying one bag, then two. They were led into another long hallway of damp, dingy cells and they emptied the second bag. By the time they got to the final hallway on the ground floor, they were down to two bags and they had not even reached the upper floors. Sally glanced into the bottom of hers to be sure the baguette was still at the bottom.

It was.

"I see you, Sally Green."

The voice sent a familiar chill ran down her spine and she raised her head to see Rosey on the other side of the bars.

Rosey, the red haired beauty with perfect legs who, to Bettie's dismay, had so recently entertained the Earl of Rochester himself, was huddled in a filthy blanket in a cell with half a dozen other women, all prostitutes.

"I'm sure I don't know what you mean."

She slinked toward Sally, her bones jutting through her thin clothes. The light hit her face and Sally could see that her nose had half rotted from the pox. Much thinner, filthy, and no little insane, Wrath's once prized earner was all but unrecognizable. She looked at Sally sideways from behind a curtain of lank, pest-ridden hair. "How did you do it?"

"Do what?"

"How did you die?"

Sally handed her a loaf of bread through the bars. "I didn't." She hiccuped, rigid with fear.

Rosey snatched the bread and tore into it with the teeth she had left.

"You take care of yourself, Rosey," Sally said, passing out loaves to the other women in the cell, gaunt as corpses, the flesh rotting from their faces though they continued to draw breath. It was the final stage of syphilis, and they would be dead within weeks.

So easily, they could have been her.

If he had survived, they might have been Bettie.

Tears rolled down her cheeks, angry and hot, and she pressed on through the other cells, finding more prostitutes, but none she recognized. More importantly, none recognized her. They took the bread and Sally gave it to them gladly, seeing in each face a fate that could have been hers. She passed it through the bars, weeping openly.

Within a matter of cells, the prisoners had stilled their raving to watch her weep, accepting the bread with something like wonder. Whispers echoed down the hallways behind them, and as Sally reached the cells on the upper floor, they were expecting her.

She passed out the last of the bread until they ended at Harry's cell, and she caught a glimpse of a handsome young man through the bars with a face not unlike Mark's. He saw Nick first, and then met Sally's eyes with an uncertain green gaze.

Sally thrust the baguette through the bars, and he took it.

"That's all I have left." She sniffed, for the benefit of the guard. "Mind your teeth. They burned it."

Nick passed Harry a purse of coins when the guard turned his back and they were led down another flight of stairs to the front gate.

Sally shielded her eyes against the sunlight, too bright after the darkness of the gaol, and wiped her eyes on her sleeve. The guard looked at her curiously as he led them back through the gate to the street outside.

She stood there for several moments, listening to the gulls cry overhead, carts rolling down the street, chickens clucking in crates from the market down the street. Her hair blew across her face and she heard her skirt crack against the wind, but Newgate was silent.

Nick offered her his arm and they walked in tense silence to Fleet Street.

176

Once they were at a safe distance from the gaol, Nick asked, "How are you feeling?"

Sally rubbed at her eyes one last time and gave him a small smile. "That was...difficult."

He nodded his understanding. "You were brilliant."

She held his arm with both of her hands until they reached the Cheshire Cheese, growing a little more nervous with every step they took down Fleet Street. Sally was aware that it had a reputation as a dangerous place, but so did Southwark, and she had never felt threatened there. She looked up at the tall houses as they passed, thinking she had seen them before and trying to place them.

At last they saw the sign in an alley and Nick led her through the door into the tavern.

From the outside it appeared to be little more than a hole in the wall, but like so many places in London, it was much larger on the inside. The first bar was paneled in dark wood and lit with a few lanterns, eerily dark at midday. There were already several people drinking at scattered tables, each one of them watching them from over the rims of their glasses as they walked by.

Sally shivered and grasped Nick's hand as they went through a rambling series of small bars and up the stairs to yet another bar with a window that faced the street. Mark and the lads were there, as promised, drinking at a table with a young man she did not recognize.

"There she is." Mark smiled, and Sally began to relax at the sight of her friends in the strange place.

The young man stood and bowed several times, his excitement plain. "My lady, it is an honor! Your brother was just regaling me with tales of your excellent charity."

"Was he now?" Sally raised an eyebrow at Mark. "I fear my *brother* talks to much."

"Not at all." The young man looked flustered. "May I ask, why did you take it upon yourself to feed the wretched at Newgate?"

Mark smiled and nodded from the table behind the man.

"Just as you say; charity, of course. Everyone needs to eat."

"Quite so, quite so!" His grin split his face. "I will not keep you from your luncheon. It was the greatest pleasure to meet you, my lady. Mister Virtue." He excused himself with another series of bows.

Sally took his vacated seat. "What was that about?"

Mark sipped his beer. "He was a journalist, already heard of you. This is where they drink."

She felt the blood drain from her face. "A journalist? Like the pamphlet?" she whispered.

Mark shrugged. "Like the pamphlet, but less sensational. More reputable. Never fear, Sally, I got rid of him."

Sally took a deep breath, unable to shake the creeping feeling of dread. Nick smiled at her reassuringly and reached for her hand under the table.

The feel of his warm hand grasping hers eclipsed every other thought she had. Sally laced her fingers through his and met his eyes, calmed by his proximity.

A barmaid brought a round of beer and Sally heard the ceiling creak above them.

She sipped the beer with her free hand, not wanting to let go of Nick for even for a moment. The creaks continued, followed by a muffled moan.

Sally felt a chill run down her spine.

"What manner of place is this?" she asked Nick.

He patted her hand under the table. "I think it's just a bar, I've never been here before. Mark?"

"Just a bar," he agreed with a shrug. "But I think they do a little extra business upstairs, if you catch my meaning."

The floor creaked again in response.

Sally felt sick to her stomach. She closed her eyes and reminded herself to breathe.

"Sally?" Nick asked.

She opened her eyes and saw Charlie barrel up the stairs behind Nick's head.

Sally gasped.

"Sally, you've gone quite pale. What is it?"

"They're here." She nodded toward the stairwell, her voice shaking. "We need to go."

Nick nodded his understanding and shot Mark a look. The

four of them stood, quickly finished their beer, and surrounded Sally on all sides as they left the bar.

Sally gasped for air once they reached the street outside. Nick threw his arm around her but did not slow his pace. Even Mark was quiet as they hurried down the alley toward the river. He smiled down at her and over his shoulder, Sally saw Wrath walk into a familiar-looking dressmaker's with Camille on his arm.

Chapter 36

Nick trudged through the rain to the shops, his collar turned up against the morning chill. The vendors in Southwark were just opening their shutters as he passed, headed for the Royal Exchange.

The short walk to London Bridge passed quickly. The remaining tall shops and houses that lined it provided some temporary shelter from the rain with their overhanging roofs near meeting in the middle. Relief though it was, these houses would not be part of the re-building of the City, as their proximity had helped the fire to spread quickly across the short distances between the streets.

That any of these had not been damaged was remarkable. Most of the City had burned to the ground, and as Nick crossed the bridge into it, he felt as though he were walking into another world.

Five years had passed since the fire, and London would not be kept down. Every way he looked, men were engaged in the rebuilding of houses, churches, stables, and shops. Some rebuilt for themselves, many took whatever work was going on the day, and still others had begun to work for Wren, the King's Surveyor of Works, on his new plan for the City. Masons and draughtsmen had begun to travel from the surrounding villages to lay foundations for new churches.

"Nick!"

He turned to see Mark approaching from a narrow lane and smiled in greeting. "Where are you off to?"

"On my way to see about a contract to furnish this new cathedral they're planning. Will and Jack are out here somewhere."

Nick nodded and they fell into step with each other as they walked deeper into the chaos of the City. "I'll be back at Hereford's soon enough. I'm off to the Exchange to pick up some things for Sally."

It had been days since their Newgate adventure. Sally didn't speak of it, but busied herself with cooking. Every day she made some new delight--bread, pies, and tarts. The hearth was put to constant use boiling or spit roasting something delicious. Even the coffee seemed to taste better.

As much as he had enjoyed abundance of lovely food, he did worry about her. She had withdrawn since they had narrowly avoided her captor on Fleet Street. Every day she seemed a little further away.

"Nick?"

"Did you say something?"

Mark smiled knowingly. "Not even listening to me, is he? Why don't you marry her already?"

Nick flushed to his ears. "Thought you might beat me to it, to be honest."

Mark waved his hand. "Don't be soft. Me and your bird, we have an understanding. She's a treat, she is, but she's only got eyes for your sorry arse, don't she?"

"I wish I knew. She always seems so frightened whenever I get close to her."

Mark gave a dirty laugh. "That's not fear, mate. If you think that, you and me need to sit down and have a little talk."

As they reached the newly finished Royal Exchange, Nick paused a moment to take in the sight of it. Vendors were packed tightly within the gleaming courtyard, using every available inch of space to display their wares. Gloves, silver, and imported luxuries covered every surface. The pillared courtyard was surrounded on all sides by four spacious galleries packed full of new shops with fixed glass windows that sparkled in the light. Sally had probably never seen anything so grand. He wanted to take her there and buy her more treasures than she could carry. He wished he could.

"Think about it." Mark began to walk away.

"Think about what?"

"Kiss her! See what happens!"

Nick rolled his eyes as Mark disappeared into the early morning fog, trailing a path of echoing laughter.

Shaking his head, he ducked into the crowd.

The spice merchant's stall was set into the back corner of the ground floor of the exchange. The crowd before it was teeming with servants purchasing chocolate, pepper, and cakes of sugar to take back to their kitchens. Nick read the jars on the back wall as he waited, seeing nutmeg, cinnamon, cubeb, ginger, and galingale.

Most of these he had not seen since Lord Somerton's kitchen. His mother could cook, but rarely did, as she was engaged with the greater task of putting the house in order. She had doted on him and Mark, though, and she would often sit them down at the small table and make them dishes of hot chocolate when the servants had cleared the kitchen after the midday meal.

She and Somerton had survived the plague only to succumb to a fever the following year. Nick had still been away at Cambridge. They had waited to tell him of the illness, afraid to pass it on to him. By the time he had received word and tried to return home, both of them were gone.

"Sir?"

Nick heard the merchant addressing him and remembered himself. "Brown sugar, cinnamon, and cloves please."

The merchant ducked behind the counter and withdrew three pre-measured parcels. "Ten pence."

Nick withdrew some coins from his pocket and gave them to the merchant, slipping the parcels into his deep pockets. He tipped his hat in thanks, and headed toward the exit.

The flower vendor stood in the doorway just out of the rain, his small cart covered in flowers of every color; roses, lavender, daffodils, dog roses, and cuckooflower. Nick paid a penny for a bunch of small pink roses, carefully tucked them inside his long coat, and headed back toward Southwark.

Sally was in the kitchen when he returned. She smiled as he came through the kitchen door. "I wondered where you had gotten to," she said. "I've made a little coffee."

Nick pulled the parcels of spices and sugar from his pocket and stacked them on the table. "I got you something." He took the roses from his coat, relieved to find them not too badly crushed.

Her face lit up as she took them. "These are for me?"

"Of course, and some spices besides." He unwrapped the parcels as she smelled the roses. "I got cinnamon, cloves, and sugar. Can you do something with these?"

"Cinnamon!" Sally's eyes widened. "I can do much with these. Thank you, Nick." She smiled up at him so warmly that he forgot he was soaked through with rain.

"Come, sit. You must be freezing." She took the small cauldron off of the pot hook and poured two cups of boiled coffee.

Nick took off his coat and hung it on the peg beside the door. He sat down at the table as she set the coffee in front of him with a plate of almond tarts and a small block of cheese.

"I'm afraid the others ate almost everything in the kitchen before they left this morning. I will need to bake more bread while they are out." Sally sat across from him and took an almond tart from the plate with a smile. "I saved these, though."

"These are exquisite." Nick took one from the plate.

Sally took a bite of hers with a sip of black coffee. "I'm glad you like them. What shall I make today?"

"Whatever you like," he said. "Everything you make is wonderful."

"I'm not as good as I should be." She shrugged. "My marchpane has never been as good as Madame's. She had a way with almonds."

Nick took a bite of the tart and closed his eyes in bliss as he chewed. "It tastes perfect to me," he assured her. "Who is Madame?"

"Madame Toulouse ran the kitchens of the Chateau where I grew up. My father left me there when I was a child, and she took me in. She taught me everything she knew. I can bake, cook, sew, and garden. And I can balance ledgers and read French tolerably well."

Nick set down his coffee. "That's a great deal most than most girls are taught, I can tell you. What of your parents?"

Sally gave a little shrug. "My mother died after I was born, and her husband was a drunk. He sold me to the Chateau when I was three, and Madame raised me."

"She sounds like a remarkable woman."

"She was. I miss her."

Sally had a faraway expression and Nick wondered at the life she had had. "You say your father sold you?"

"He wasn't my real father, but he beat me just the same. I know little of my mother, and I have been told that my real father was an Englishman passing through. I thought I would come to England to find him." She gave a little laugh.

"Have you?"

"No, and I wouldn't know where to begin to look. I have given up for now. I guess I have had other things to worry about." She took a sip of her coffee. "What about your parents?"

Nick took a breath. *What could he say?* "My mother was the housekeeper to Lord Somerton and I grew up there. Somerton took a liking to me and saw to my education. Mark's father was my mother's husband, but he died fighting the Royalist cause before I was born."

"He was a Royalist? Was he a servant?"

"He managed the stables. He was a good man, and loyal. Somerton loved his horses, and he and Henry became good friends. They fought together for the cause, though Somerton lost much. He went into exile with Charles for a few years, and our mother looked after the estate while he was away. What was left of it, that is."

"And your father?" she asked.

Nick shook his head. "I never asked. She was alone for a long time. I was afraid of the answer."

Sally regarded him quietly for a moment. "You are a good son, I think."

Nick gave a weak smile. "I hope so."

Sally set down her cup suddenly. "I want you to know something."

Nick sat up straighter. "Yes?"

"I did not become a whore because I wanted to."

Nick reached for a second pastry. "You don't need to tell me."

"I want to," she insisted. "When I got to London I was hired as a cook to a hotel, or I thought it was a kind of hotel, because I was very foolish. This man, Wrath, he...he ravished me, beat me, imprisoned me. I thought I would die."

"Dear God!"

"That's not all. They ruined me. They did something..." She

184

brushed away a tear with the back of her hand. "They made me barren. I would be useless to an honest man, should any want me."

Nick felt a current of murderous rage running through his veins and struggled to control it. He had heard of such things in university, but they were very rare, as the women seldom survived the ordeal. But to do it to an unwilling woman? "How could someone do such a thing?"

"I don't know. They did." Sally took a deep breath. "I tried to escape, but they found me every time I ran. They nearly killed me many times."

Nick involuntarily clenched his fists. "Is that what happened when I found you?"

"Yes." Sally blinked back tears. "He killed my friend, Bettie. I didn't know where to go, so I ran to Beaumont, and he killed him, too. Now they are dead because of me."

Nick reached out and took her hand. "It's not your fault."

"It was my fault," she insisted, "because I knew he would do it. He killed every friend I had. If he sees me with you, he will kill us both."

"He thinks you're dead. He has no reason to look."

Sally wiped the tears from her eyes, flowing freely now. "He always finds me. I used to think I could see Death..."

Nick thought of her strange fever and his heart sank. "Did he drug you?"

"Drug me?"

Nick stroked her hand. "When you were recovering from your fever, you were showing signs of withdrawal from a poison. Wormwood, if I had to guess."

"Wormwood?"

"Wormwood. It's a common medicine. Somerton took it for digestive problems before he passed. A spoonful is fairly harmless, but in large quantities, it can cause hallucination, sleep, and..." he cleared his throat, "miscarriage."

"Miscarriage?"

"Are you certain that you're unable to bear children? If you had been receiving wormwood for long enough..."

Sally sat in silence, staring into her coffee cup.

"It may yet be possible," he said. "When the drug has run its

185

course."

"I cannot bear to hope." She held up a hand, her eyes clouding with tears. "Wrath was drugging me? For years? What does it do?"

Nick swallowed hard. "You sleep, you have strange dreams, then you hallucinate, and eventually, you can lose your mind, or go blind. But you have to take a great deal of it. You would probably know," he dismissed.

"What does it taste like?"

Nick shrugged. "Sickly sweet, like licorice, or poor gin."

All of the color drained from Sally's face.

"Sally?"

She slapped her fist against the table top. "The gin! How could I have been so foolish? Who knows what he could have been doing to me?"

He held her hands. "You're safe now," he assured.

"He'll do it again, to other people. He's doing it right now. He'll--" Her voice broke off in a sob.

Nick stood quickly and took her in his arms, holding her as she cried. He felt her shoulders shaking against his chest and buried his face in her hair.

"He killed my friends...Claude, Bettie, Beaumont..."

He held her until her crying slowed. "You're going to be fine, Sally," he whispered into her hair. "No one is going to look for you here. We will protect you."

Nick felt her arms hesitantly wrap around his waist, her face resting against his chest.

"Who will protect you?" she sniffed.

"I can look after myself."

Nick stroked her hair, listening to the sound of her breathing slowing, when she lifted her head and looked up at him, her wide, dark eyes sparkling with unshed tears.

He wanted, very badly, to kiss her.

Mark's advice echoed in his head. He thought about it too long.

"The bread," she said.

"Hmmm?"

"I need to start the bread..."

186

Nick held her closer. "They can fend for themselves."

Sally placed a hand on his chest and gently lifted herself away from him. "I want to be useful."

"If you must." Nick shrugged. "I've never baked anything before. Would you like to show me how?"

Sally's smile returned and she nodded.

Chapter 37

She had been poisoned.

For months, likely years.

The others were in their beds, early in anticipation of the next day's honest work. The street outside was dark as a tomb. Sally couldn't sleep, so she cleaned.

They had eaten every scrap of bread in the kitchen, every oyster, most of the cheese, and they had drunk all of beer she had not hidden from them in reserve for the next day. Mark and the lads had labored from dawn until dusk, and when they had returned home, they were hungry and bone-tired.

She could tell by the smell of the bread in the oven that the next morning's loaves were nearly done. The dishes cleaned and stacked on the shelf, she put out the small fire in the hearth as the kitchen was still warmed by the heat of the oven, and began to sweep.

The past week should have been perfect. The Ramseys not yet returned, Nick had stayed in with her, helping with the shop's daily tasks in Mark's absence. Every day they talked as they worked alongside each other, spending long hours getting to know one another, sharing bread and stories, happy and otherwise. He was a dream of a man, but as much as she wanted to enjoy his company, the days were bittersweet. Nick wouldn't want her around forever, and she had no idea where she would go when he tired of her, as all men eventually had. She had no direction, no real hope for a future, and she could not make peace with the knowledge that she had been poisoned.

Her sanity, her life, even her sight--had been willingly jeopardized, for what?

The years at Wrath's had been a haze of fear, violence, and debauchery. Sally had fought him every step of the way until the gin had started to appear on her nightstand. She had thought it an apology at the time, a way to cope with the ache of her bruised body after the first beating that had left her hopeless and broken, tied to a bed.

She had drained that bottle willingly enough, and every bottle that followed until he finally finished her off, leaving her leaking her life's blood into a gutter.

There were plenty of girls in London who had willingly chosen the life for themselves. Sally had never wanted it, and he didn't need more girls. *Why go to such lengths to keep her?*

He had lost her. Now he was doing it to someone else.

Sweeping the last of the crumbs and dirt out the back door, she brushed against Nick's coat and knocked a bit of crumpled parchment out of the pocket.

She closed the door and leaned the broom against the wall. As she picked up the heavy parchment, she felt the smooth wax of a seal against her fingers. Curiosity piqued, she turned it over to see a broken blue seal with a lion on it, and the edge of a word written in a flowing, feminine hand.

Against her better judgment, she opened the letter.

"My Dear Mister Virtue," it began.

She could not read every word of the letter, written as it was in English with an abundance of flourishes, but she read the closing, and understood.

"Until we meet again, Jane."

Nick was courting someone.

He had never mentioned anyone named Jane, but that did not surprise her. Judging by the paper, the seal, and the needlessly ornamental writing, she was a lady.

Sally's heart sank as she folded the letter and placed it back into the pocket of his coat.

How could she compete with that?

As much as she had chided herself for her attraction to him, she had wanted, very badly, to believe he could be hers. It was plain now that it could never be.

She hoped Jane deserved him.

Pulling the bread out of the oven and extinguishing the fire, Sally put everything back into its place in the kitchen and trudged slowly up the stairs.

Nick sat beside the bed in his long shirt and loose trousers, bathed in candlelight. Sally wanted to climb into his lap and cry.

"You're awake." She smiled sadly.

"I was waiting for you," he replied.

"You don't have to do that." She pulled her dress over her head and draped it across the chair, self-consciously climbing onto the pallet in her long shift with her arms crossed over her chest.

"I don't mind. I was thinking we should talk."

Every night he slept on the floor beside her. Sally felt guilty accepting the bed, but she slept better knowing he was so close. She wished he would join her. "What about?"

He hesitated. "What do you want out of life, Sally?"

Nick was always asking these ridiculous questions. He was a dreamer, and liked to believe she had a choice.

"What do you mean by that?"

He rested his arms on the edge of the little bed and looked up at her with a mad sparkle in his eye and a smile on his face. "You've been reborn. How many people get a chance like that? You can have a new name. You can be anyone you want. You can do as you please."

Sally smiled at him in spite of herself. "A new name, maybe, but how many options do you think I have?"

"You can bake," he offered.

She hugged her arms around her knees. "I want to bake," she said honestly. "I loved the kitchens."

"You could have your own kitchen." He watched her carefully. His unfashionably short, dark hair had bits of sawdust in it and her fingers tingled with the desire to touch it.

She sat on her hands instead.

"You think I should open a bakery?" She asked, thinking of her hidden treasure box back at the opera house with a heavy heart, positive someone would have found it without her standing constant guard over it. *All those years of saving for nothing.* Of course, the girls were very stupid. If she could somehow get back inside without being seen, could it still be there?

"Sally?"

She snapped back into the present and found herself warmed considerably by a pair of soft green eyes. "I'm sorry, what did you say?"

He smiled shyly and looked down at his hands. "I meant your

190

own kitchen, in your own house. Something small. If you married."

Sally stared at him for a moment, feeling the weight of unshed tears in her chest. She could have cried easily. She gave a short, ugly laugh. "I'm a barren ex-harlot and a nameless bastard. I don't have two pennies to rub together, and everyone I care about seems to die. Who in their right mind would marry me?"

He was quiet for a moment before he met her eyes. "Are you still seeing Death?"

She let out a long breath. "Not in weeks. That's something, right?" She tried to smile.

"Sally, you are beautiful, and kind, and very clever, and I think that anyone in their right mind would marry you."

A shame the only man she wanted appeared to be taken. Her eyes drifted back to the sawdust in his hair and she said nothing.

"You can do anything. What do you want?"

She tried to think back to her childhood at the Chateau. It seemed so much longer than three years since she had left. *What had she been like then, before everything happened?*

"I would love my own kitchen, of course," she admitted, after some time. "I want a kitchen, and a big family, and a good husband with a beautiful heart. Who wouldn't?"

He had rested his face on his hands and was looking up at her with a strange, soft smile. The lamplight warmed his complexion until he appeared to be glowing from inside. It made her think of the sun setting over the fields of flax that surrounded the Chateau. She could almost smell summer again.

She looked away. "It's a beautiful dream, but it could never happen."

His face fell. "Why not?"

"Because when I find Wrath, I am going to kill him."

Nick sat up, taking her hand in his. "He will never find you again. I will protect you."

She shook her head. "It's not up to you to protect me. You're a good man, Nick, and I will not have you wasting your time on someone like me. Think of your own future. Your work will start again soon, and you can marry if you like..." Her voice cracked.

"I would," he said honestly.

191

"You would," she repeated, her heart breaking. "Of course."

He held her eyes. "I would, but you cannot think to endanger yourself bringing this villain to justice. Stay here with me, and think no more of it."

Sally pulled the coverlet up to her chin, the few words she had read of the letter burned into her mind. Surely this Jane of his would love having a harlot under her roof.

She felt Nick's hand on her cheek, and turned toward him, opening her eyes.

"Promise me you won't endanger yourself?"

"I will...*try* not to endanger myself."

Hardly satisfied with her answer, Nick kissed her cheek in goodnight. She closed her eyes in pleasure at the touch of his lips, the warmth of his skin like the sun on those fields. In spite of her better judgment, her heart longed for something she could never have.

Chapter 38

The moment night settled over the Hereford estate, Nick swung his coat over his shoulder and headed for the maze. Once he was certain he had not been followed, he scanned the west-facing windows for unwanted observers and, finding none, rushed into the forest. In the safety of the trees, he thrust his arms into his coat and put on his hat as he trudged through the undergrowth.

The Ramseys had returned to the estate that morning, and Hereford was no closer to paying him than he had been before he had left London. He had refused to see him when he was announced, but sent Julian to meet him at the door with instructions to return the following week. The boys, he had explained, had taken ill during the journey, and would need time to recuperate.

Nick had seen them happily playing soldiers from the front door and knew it for the excuse it was.

He shrugged it off. He was in no hurry to leave Sally.

In his haste to return to the warehouse, he almost missed her. Fortunately, the new red dress offered little camouflage in the forest, even at night. He paused behind a tree and watched her. She was lying on her stomach behind a fallen log, her chin cradled in her hands, watching the road. In her concentration, she hadn't heard him approach. He carefully tied his mask around his face and walked toward her, fireflies like floating cinders flickering through the trees.

She jumped as he stepped on a twig but relaxed as she saw him. "Oh, it's you!"

Nick lowered himself onto his stomach beside her in the dirt and she handed him one of the little knot rolls she had baked the day before. He smiled to himself as he took it. He had eaten another like it only that morning. "I like these."

She glanced at him. "It's a recipe from Normandy. Have you had them before?"

He realized with a start that she still didn't know who he was.

It was dark, he supposed, and he was wearing a mask, but surely she recognized his voice? "I have," he said. "A girl gave me one once."

She smiled to herself. "I'm sure ladies are very fond of you."

"Not the ones that count," he mumbled to himself.

"What was that?"

"What are you doing out here?" he asked.

She wiggled herself further into the undergrowth. "I'm watching for the bastard that ruined me. He comes this way sometimes."

Nick put the roll in his pocket and looked at her. Her skin had a slight blue tinge in the fading light. She shivered lightly, the leaves beneath her arms rustling softly at the movement. She hadn't worn a coat, so she must have left home when the afternoon was still heavy with heat. How long had she been out here?

Nick slipped his black coat off his shoulders. "What will you do if you see him?"

"I want to get a good look at his coach. I've seen it before, but never paid much attention to the crest. Now I'm wondering if it's his."

The idea that Wrath might be a peer had never occurred to him, but if that was the case, he had some idea of the danger she was in. "Let me take you home. I'll come back and watch for him." He draped the coat over her shoulders.

As she felt the weight of the wool, she sat up, pulling the coat across her chest. "You would do that? For me?"

Nick shrugged, sitting up. "Of course."

Her eyes were bright in the moonlight, shining with something that might have been tears. She looked away, rubbing the heel of her hand across them absently. "Perhaps we could stay a little longer."

They sat together in silence for several moments, settling into the growing darkness among the grasses and brambles, the whirring of insects and the swish of the trees in the wind growing more deafening with each passing breath. Sally sat with her knees to her chest, huddled inside the long coat like it was a blanket, the cuffs reaching her fingertips. With any luck, the coat might hold a trace of her scent when she returned it.

Nick cursed himself silently. What was he doing? What would she think of him if she knew what he was, knew that he had been hiding it from her? *What kind of a man accosts women in the dark while wearing a mask?*

He ran a hand over his face. Not the kind of man he wanted to be, and yet, the "upstanding tutor" strategy was working so well. He'd been prepared to beg her to marry him the night before and she'd dismissed him before he had gotten around to making his point. Did he even have a chance?

Nick cleared his throat. "Why do you want to find this man so badly? Why not leave London?"

She went very still. After several moments, she spoke. "He ravished me, he ruined me, and he made me a whore. I can't bear children, I am no maiden," she gave a humorless laugh, "and he murdered every person I loved on this earth. Now he's doing it all over again to somebody new."

Nick swallowed.

"If I can bring him to justice, my life will have been worth something."

"But it's your life," he protested. "Why not live it for yourself?"

"I'm a whore. How long do you think I've got?"

In Nick's medical opinion, Sally was in excellent health, recent attacks aside. He thought it might be best to keep this to himself until he was...himself again. "You're not anymore, though, are you?"

"God, no! But I will never make a lady."

"Is that what you want? To be a lady?"

She laughed and leaned back on her hands. "Not in that sense, no. I only meant...no matter."

He watched her, waiting for her to continue.

"It's only that ladies aren't meant to enjoy the act, are they? I do, and I make no apologies, and so I will always be a whore in their eyes."

Nick realized he was holding his breath. "You *enjoy* it?"

"Not always." She shrugged. "But when it's good, you know, it's wonderful. Or so I've been told."

Sally was usually so shy around him that he couldn't believe he was having this conversation with her. He marveled at the difference a little anonymity made. "While we're being honest, are you seeing anyone?"

She blushed to the roots of her hair. "Not exactly."

"What about that man I've seen you around with?"

Even in the dark he could see her face pale. "What man?"

"Tall, dark hair. Brown coat."

"Oh, Nick? He's my friend."

"He's in love with you."

"You're mad," she said. "He knows what I am. He's trying to save me."

"What, just for the sake of saving someone?"

"He's a good man, but he would never want me."

Was that really the impression he had given her? He shook his head. *What about the flowers?* He wanted to shout. *Can't you see I'm courting you?* "If you believe that, you're the mad one."

"That would be nice," she said. "I don't see anyone coming yet. Do you?"

He ignored the question. "Do you like him?"

"Are you jealous?"

"Curious."

"It's a strange thing to be curious about."

"Just weighing up the competition."

She laughed. "Go on then, what about you?"

"What about me?"

"Tell me about your little girlfriends. I'm sure you have ladies waiting for you all over the country."

Nick grinned. "Not a single one."

She wrinkled her nose at him. "Boyfriends?"

He shook his head. "No."

"There's nothing to be ashamed of, you know. Bettie only liked boys, and he was my best friend in this world."

He'd only heard her mention a Bettie once. She was opening up to him, albeit in disguise. "What was he like?"

"You don't have a chance, I'm afraid. He's dead. But you're just his type."

Nick realized she was teasing and told her what he suspected she was really asking. "I like women. You, especially."

"Good." Her smile was unguarded and lovely. Nick returned her smile, realizing he still had his mask on like a fool and she couldn't see it. To his considerable surprise, she climbed into his lap, settling between his legs with her back to him.

"What are you doing?" he asked.

"You looked cold. Would you rather I didn't touch you?"

"No," he answered, perhaps too quickly.

She rested the length of her back against his chest and sighed.

Relaxing a little, he took off his mask and bent his head to smell her hair. She smelled like cinnamon and nutmeg and all of the new spices he had brought her. Smiling to himself, he reached out, fitting his hands over hers to hold her wrapped up in his coat.

Sally leaned her head back into his shoulder, her temple against the pulse point of his neck. He shifted slightly, liking the feel of her in his arms. He felt her soft hair against his jaw, and thought about how close her lips were.

This was not a situation Nick the tutor had ever found himself in. Nick the physician hadn't fared much better.

But Nick the highwayman...

Shrugging the mantle of respectability and all of the restrictions he had worn with it, Nick raised his fingers to her chin. He carefully tipped her face upward and found her lips in the dark.

Sally was waiting for him. Her lips parted and soft, she met his kiss with a quiet sigh, the heat of her mouth the only warmth in the night. He trembled involuntarily as he felt her smile against his lips, his blood singing *finally*.

Nick broke the kiss only long enough to turn her around in his lap. Sally closed the distance between them by sitting on his outstretched thighs, sliding her legs around his waist. Her cinnamon scent covered his senses in a fog and he lost himself to the hunger he had been hiding for weeks, claiming her mouth with his own. She responded with a ferocity that surprised him, wrapping her arms around his neck and drinking him in like a woman dying of thirst. She covered his mouth in light kisses before taking the swell of his lower lip playfully between her teeth.

She was the sweetest thing he had ever tasted. He wanted to know how the rest of her tasted, too.

The coat discarded and forgotten, Nick ran his hands up the laces of her dress, tugging at the bow that held them together. Sally sank her hands into his hair, knocking his hat into the brush. Her skirt fell in heavy waves around his hips and he could feel the heat of her pressed against his near painful arousal. He thought he might die if he couldn't have her.

Sally seemed to be thinking the same thing as she reached for the tie of his breeches and pulled.

This was what he had wanted. She brightened his days and haunted his dreams. Every day, watching her, laughing with her, he had wanted so badly to touch her. Now she was in his arms, halfway into his trousers, and very nearly his.

Nick stopped abruptly as he remembered that she didn't know who he was.

What would she think of him?

It took everything he had to break off that kiss. "Forgive me."

She smiled and kissed him again. "For what?"

He almost didn't survive that one. Nick took a deep breath, willing his blood to cool. "You deserve better than this. I apologize."

She sat back on his legs, resting her curvaceous arse above his knees. "Are you serious?"

"I am not some villain who mauls girls in the forest."

"I did not think you were." She shrugged. "You know what I am. You can use me as you like, there will be no repercussions."

Nick put his hat back on, looking away. "Only what little regard I have for myself."

"Do I displease you?"

"Displease me? No," he took her hand in his, "nothing about you displeases me. Only I should hope that you act to please yourself, and that you are treated with the honor you deserve. I'm making a mess of this, aren't I?"

She looked at him carefully, and he hoped she couldn't see his embarrassment. Finally, she rested her hands on the expanse of his chest and said, "It would please me very much to make love to you."

Nick swallowed hard.

Sally moved closer to him and before he came to his senses, began to untie his shirt.

He caught her hands in his to stop her. "You're not a whore."

Sally sat back, hurt. "You think that's why I'm doing this? That I want you to pay me?"

"That's not what I meant."

Sally stood and began to walk off into the forest.

Nick grabbed his coat and ran after her. "Sally, wait. Please." She didn't slow down.

He caught up to her in a few long strides. "You should be courted and married, not used cheaply and discarded. You're better than that, don't you understand?"

Sally gave a disbelieving huff. "Who would court someone like me?"

"I would!" He nearly shouted, forgetting for a moment that she didn't know who he was. Nick felt a twinge of panic as he realized he had called her by her name. She had never told the highwayman her name. Had she noticed?

"You don't even know me."

He caught her in his arms, holding her still. *Tell her*, he urged himself. *Tell her now.*

Nick couldn't see her eyes. What would he see in them if he told her the truth? Disappointment? Horror?

Love?

He bent toward her upturned face and felt her breath against his lips. "I know enough about you. You're generous and kind, you're thoughtful and beautiful, and I can't get you out of my mind. I would like nothing more on this earth than to take you right here, or anywhere else, for that matter, but I want you to be mine."

"You got all that from half a chicken?"

He kissed her, and felt wetness touch his cheeks.

She turned away from him, and he knew she was crying. "I can't bear children."

"I don't care," he said, meaning it. "I don't have any money."

She laughed and wiped her eyes. "We're a good pair. Why don't you tell me who you are?" She reached for his hat.

"You might not want to know," he replied, dodging her

grasp.

"You might not want me if you knew me better."

"I'd like to decide that for myself."

A few stray lanterns began to appear as they reached the edge of the forest.

He stopped. "I'll watch for that carriage awhile longer. Keep to the main roads and you'll be safe."

She turned to face him. "I want to see you again."

"Tomorrow?"

She nodded.

"Go home. We can watch for him together then."

He took her cold hand in his and kissed the palm. Maybe by tomorrow, he would find a way to tell her. After some hesitation, she turned and began the long walk to Southwark.

Nick watched her walk down the middle of the empty street. He waited until she was perhaps one hundred yards ahead, pulled up his collar, and followed her, keeping to the shadows.

Chapter 39

Lady Jane was in a mood.

On the trip back to London, she had brought up the subject of marrying Nicodemus with her father only to receive a vehement and immediate denial. He did not explain his reasons beyond the fact that Nicodemus was a penniless tutor with no family to speak of, and he seemed to believe this was an adequate answer for a young woman in love.

He had withstood three days of fits and tears by putting her into a separate carriage for the remainder of the journey home. Her father was foolish to believe this punishment would dissuade her. She was determined to renew her efforts when they returned home. Once he saw how in love they were, he could not possibly deny them, and would forget all talk of the mystery suitor he wanted her to meet.

This suitor was a younger friend of his, he had explained, a wealthy earl with a house in town and a substantial estate in the West Country. She had rolled her eyes until he had mentioned that the earl might be considered handsome, and would not be averse to supplying her with endless dresses and fripperies should she agree to become his countess.

She had looked at her father with suspicion then, and regarded the proposition with growing apprehension as she endured a long session of hairdressing in early preparation for her first meeting with this nameless earl.

The whole situation disgusted her. Since returning the day before, she had not once seen Nicodemus. He had gone to his family's house in town to care for an ailing relative, and would not be back until they had fully recovered.

How admirable he was, she had thought, buffing her nails, to look after a relative when he could be delighting in her presence. *How very selfless!* She had carelessly dropped the buffer as a scheme popped into her head.

Now, as her carriage rounded the corner of Nicodemus'

street, she held the parcel of stew a kitchen maid had quietly wrapped up for her for the price of a penny, and tipped her perfectly coiffed head out the window.

Before her was squalor the likes of which she had never seen. The muddy street was brimming with excrement, rubbish, and rotting produce. So many common, toothless people bustled about that the carriage was unable to move at any pace. A man shouted incomprehensibly from a stall that looked to be selling fish. They were putrid, from the smell of them. Everywhere she looked, people were glancing at her, eyeing up the carriage as if they thought to take some piece of it for themselves. To her horror, a woman passed below her, nursing a baby in broad daylight, and thrust her hand under Jane's nose.

"Spare some pennies for the poor, m'lady?"

Jane recoiled into the safety of her carriage, wrinkling her nose in disgust.

The woman uttered some colorful curse that Jane didn't quite understand, and spat on the wheel of the carriage. With a shudder, Jane slid to the far side of the bench, and carefully peeked out the other window.

Several doors down, Nicodemus emerged from a shop, and her heart leapt at the serendipity of seeing him. How he could bear to live in such squalor was beyond her.

She smiled to herself. Soon he would be living with her and would never have to endure this frightful place again.

Jane was about to call to him from the window when Nicodemus ducked back into the shop, only to reappear with a young woman on his arm. Struggling to get a good look at her, Jane leaned out the window on her elbow as the carriage crept forward.

She was striking and dark, with masses of black hair braided over her shoulder and tied with a red ribbon. Although clean and obviously new, her dress was the dress of a common woman, made of simple homespun or linen dyed the red of the roses in Jane's garden. The woman held Nicodemus' arm with one hand, and carried a parcel of sewing supplies in the other.

Was *this* Nicodemus' ailing relative? She looked to be quite healthy and young, but if she was not ill, what cause could she have

202

to hold his arm? The carriage drew closer and Jane wondered if the woman could be a sister, or perhaps a married cousin. They had similar coloring, it was true, so surely that was the most likely explanation?

The woman said something she could not hear, causing Nicodemus to laugh. Jane had never once heard Nicodemus laugh. *What could she have said?* Jane was witty, everyone said so. She could make him laugh, too, and certainly would, once they were married.

Nicodemus and the woman stopped at a stall on the side of the road, and before Jane realized what was happening, he had purchased a small posy of flowers and gave it to the woman, who smiled prettily.

Jane gasped and jerked the curtain shut, holding her breath for a moment and closing her eyes. Holding the stew dumbly, she rapped sharply on the front wall of the carriage, and sat back into her seat as the driver turned toward home.

Nicodemus was courting someone! Perhaps he was already married? "Nonsense!" Jane seethed to herself. "I would know if he was married."

Married or not, Jane had seen the look on his face, and knew it was over.

Staring out of the window feeling an uneasiness in her chest that she thought might be heartbreak, she did not see the oncoming carriage.

Jane was knocked out of her seat as the carriage collided into the side of hers, knocking the back wheel off of its axle. Sitting on the floor, bruised and badly stunned, Jane looked down to see she was still clutching the stew, which was miraculously unharmed.

Hearing shouting in common accents mere feet away from her person, Jane held perfectly still on the floor of the carriage until the commotion passed.

There was a sharp knock on the door. The curtain fluttered and Bennett, the new driver, popped his head in. "Are you unharmed, Miss?"

Jane nodded and threw an arm over the seat in an attempt to pull herself up. Her ankle gave way and she stumbled against the upholstered cushion.

"Here, Miss, allow me." Bennett leaned against the carriage

to stabilize the floor and offered her his arm. Jane took it gratefully and stepped out of the carriage into a mud puddle.

Looking at her slippers, thoroughly ruined, Jane was without words.

"It will take a moment to get this fixed, Miss. There's an inn here on the corner; best you wait inside and keep warm."

"Inside?" She looked up at the inn in question. The sign was a painting of three compasses. It had been built in the Tudor fashion, four stories high and no more than four yards across. Very dark inside, there was no telling how far it went back. Jane could hear the heavy sound of mugs hitting table tops and the smell of burning tobacco reached her even in the middle of the street. "Bennett, are you certain this is a place for ladies?"

Bennett looked at the inn and shrugged. "It's early in the day, Miss, and I know this inn. You won't come to any harm."

Jane looked around the street. It was indeed early in the day and the sun was shining, but the streets heaved with strange people looking at her in her rich clothing as if they were estimating its resale value. Taking a deep breath of foul, salty air, Jane handed the parcel of stew to a beggar and followed Bennett into the tavern without a backward glance.

Once her eyes adjusted to the relative darkness of the interior, the narrow room appeared to go on forever. Scores of small tables cluttered the walls and filled the small space, the low ceilings holding in the warmth of the smoke and so many cheerful bodies. Every table was occupied by men, laborers from the looks of them, drinking beer and having a laugh. Though unfamiliar, Jane had to admit that the atmosphere was inviting. She began to relax, and took a seat at the bar.

"Maurice," Bennett greeted the landlord, "we've had a bit of a wreck outside. Keep an eye on milady while I get it sorted?"

"Aye, mate," he replied, accepting a few coins from Bennett for her needs. Bennett gave her a reassuring smile, and disappeared back out into the street.

Jane looked at the old barman with uneasy curiosity. "Good afternoon."

"It's a pleasure to make your acquaintance," he replied with a mock bow. "You look like you been through the wars."

Jane sat up straight and touched her hair. The coif that had taken all morning had begun to unpin itself, and was now listing heavily to the side. Reaching up to unpin the rest of it, Jane noticed a tear in the sleeve of her pink gown. "Damnation," she cursed under her breath, then silently chided herself for the impropriety. Her father was going to be very cross with her.

Maurice chuckled and grabbed a glass from behind the bar, pouring a dark amber liquid into it. Glass full, he set it before her with a smile. "That will sort you out."

Removing the last of the pins from her hair, Jane shook the tangled red mass down her back and heard an appreciative whistle. Realizing with a start that she was the only lady in the bar, Jane blushed a deep crimson and carefully took the glass. "What is this?"

"It's sherry. Don't they drink that where you live?"

"Father doesn't permit ladies to drink anything more than small beer or watered wine," she said with a shrug. "Is it strong?"

"It's sweet."

Jane examined the sherry in the light, fascinated by glint of the lanterns against the poorly cut crystal. Maurice seemed to be a kindly older man, certainly her father's age or older, and was likely to have her best interests at heart. Cautiously, she took a drink.

Sweet fire touched her lips and lit her insides aflame as she tasted her first sip. It was more than decadent, it was positively sinful. No wonder her father didn't approve.

Jane closed her eyes and emptied the glass.

When she opened them again, she glanced right to see a man beside her at the bar, watching her, and she jumped.

"I didn't mean to startle you," he said. "I was just enjoying the view. Can I buy you another?"

Jane's eyes widened at the presumption. No one had ever spoken to her like that. "I beg your pardon?"

The man smiled a slow, cheeky smile. "You are stunning, you are. May I buy you a drink?"

Jane regarded him carefully. Younger than many of the laborers in the bar, he was surely no older than Nicodemus. He was a large, well-formed man with a broad accent in a footpad's long brown coat. Removing his hat, he revealed a wave of thick, dark blond hair. Where Nicodemus was dark and brooding, this man was fair with deep blue eyes and an easy smile. He had the peculiar beauty of an angel who had been very wicked indeed. Jane found herself smiling back at him.

"You're not so bad yourself," she said, shocked by her brazen reply.

"I like you." He smiled and gestured to the barman.

Maurice returned, cleaning a glass. "What will it be?"

"Beer for me, and for the lady...?"

"The sherry was nice, Maurice. Have you anything else?"

"Certainly, Miss." He turned away with a smile, returning moments later with a short, fat glass of the same shining crystal.

Jane accepted the glass, sniffing the rich, golden liquid. "What is this?"

"Brandy," he replied.

Both men watched her carefully as she took a cautious sip.

Rolling the liquid around her tongue, she savored what tasted like layers of fire, sunlight, and burnt sugar. "Exquisite."

Maurice smiled and spread his hands. "We aim to please."

Feeling the warmth of the sherry tingling to the ends of her toes, Jane raised her glass to him as he turned to serve another patron.

The handsome man was still watching her.

"Thank you," she said. "This brandy is delightful. I am indebted to you, sir."

"You're not from around here, are you?" He furrowed his brow even as he smiled at her.

Thinking of the people appraising her clothes in the street, she lied. "No, I'm from..." She struggled to remember places her father said he visited, and remembered one. "Drury Lane."

The man raised his eyebrows. "Drury Lane? Are you an actress?"

An actress. Jane liked that idea. "Yes," she said, ignoring the look of surprise on Maurice's face as he passed.

"Have I seen you in anything?"

Jane took a sip of her brandy and looked away. "*Tristan and Isolde*," she answered quickly, unsure if that was even a play.

The man nodded carefully. "I haven't seen it. What are you

doing all the way out here?"

"Visiting an ailing relative," she said, feeling charitable.

He smiled and nodded, watching her every movement as though she were something he would very much like to eat.

It may have been the brandy, but Jane felt as though she would like to let him.

"What do you do?" she asked, congratulating herself for remembering that common people were often obligated to work.

"I have a carpenter's down the road. I am the master carpenter."

"Aren't you a bit young to be a master?"

"I'm very good."

Taking her small hand in his large rough one, he raised it slowly to his lips and kissed her smooth white knuckles, the brush of his firm lips a shock to her senses.

"What's your name?"

She tried to remember.

Bennett appeared suddenly by the door, glaring his disapproval at the handsome man. It was time to go.

Thoroughly disappointed, Jane shot him a look of warning, and returned her attention to the man. Draining the rest of her brandy, she gave him her best smile, and was more than a little satisfied to see him looking dumbstruck. "Thank you for the drink, Mister..."

"Mark."

"Mark." She smiled, liking the short punctuation of the word on her tongue. "I'm afraid I must go."

Mark watched with hunger as she gracefully stood, straightening her torn dress. She liked the way he was looking at her, believing she was an actress. Perhaps she was a beauty, after all.

Jane saw Bennett turn away to the street. Emboldened by the brandy, she leaned in and kissed Mark sweetly on the lips.

It was not the first time Jane had kissed a man. Expecting a harmless flirtation, she was quite surprised when the floor disappeared beneath her.

His lips were warm and his skin smelled of tobacco, sawdust, and sweat. Forgetting she had intended to leave, her arms found themselves wrapping around his strong waist. He gently held her head in his hand as he kissed her, running his rough fingertips down the length of her neck. Jane felt a wave of pleasure roll down her spine. She sighed against his lips and he held her fast, deepening the kiss.

Suddenly, another pair of hands closed around Jane's shoulders and before she knew it, Bennett was dragging her back to the carriage, leaving Mark, stunned and alone, at the bar.

As Jane returned to the Hereford estate, she saw an unfamiliar black carriage waiting near the front entrance. Her father's earl must have arrived early in his haste to beg her hand. Jane groaned and patted her messy hair despondently. The best she could do would be to try to sneak up to her room before she was seen.

Bennett opened the door of the carriage and looked at her reproachfully.

Jane groaned and alighted from the carriage. "Say it."

"I should not have left you alone."

Jane scoffed, her steps still swaying a little from the brandy. "I was in no danger."

"Obviously you don't know what kind of danger you were in."

Jane rolled her eyes. "I suppose you are going to tell my father."

"I most certainly am not. You think he'd react well to my leaving his only daughter to get manhandled by some scoundrel in a tavern?"

Jane smiled lazily at the memory. *Scoundrel.* She liked that word.

"I ain't telling him, and if you value your freedom, such as it is, you won't tell him, either."

"Such as it is," she repeated with a smirk.

"Don't let it happen again," he warned, "or he'll have both our necks. Come on, let's get you sobered up."

With a heavy heart, Jane followed Bennett into the hall through the open door.

"You mean to have her all to yourself!" She heard her father hiss from the study.

The man replied in a low voice. She could not make out his words.

"Another then. Better. Disappoint me and the deal's off."

Jane sobered suddenly at her father's aggression. She had not given her consent, and already he was negotiating for better circumstances for his only daughter.

He did have her best interests at heart, after all. She was ashamed at her behavior.

Intending to see to her hair, Jane bolted for the stairs.

"Jane? Is that you?" her father called.

Cursing silently, she stopped, took a deep breath, and walked back down the stair to his study.

"Father," she greeted, appearing in the doorway.

Her father's face was red with fury. At her sudden appearance, he cleared his throat and attempted to compose himself. "Jane! My word, what happened to you?"

She coughed delicately. "I went to give some provisions to charity in town and there was a collision. I apologize for my appearance."

Hereford pounded his fist against that table. "It's that new driver, isn't it? I told him--"

"No, Father," Jane stopped him. "Bennett handled the situation perfectly, only I was shaken up when we were hit."

Satisfied, Hereford gave a sharp nod. "I am pleased to see you unharmed. Allow me to introduce you to my good friend, Lord Arthur Rothschild, the Earl of Somerton. Somerton, this is my lovely daughter, Jane."

The man turned toward her and took her proffered hand, giving her knuckles a chaste kiss. Jane took her hand back, the warmth of Mark's kiss driven out of her skin. She flexed her fingers in disappointment.

"It is a pleasure to meet you at last, Lady Jane. I hope will be seeing more of each other in the future."

Lord Somerton was handsome, in a cold, hawkish way. Although he was younger than most of her father's friends, he was by no means young, and not half as handsome as Mark. His dress and deportment were infallible, but his complexion had an odd, sallow tone to it that put her in mind of parchment.

"Not so fast, Somerton," her father interjected. "There are still a few matters we need to clear up between us before that can be discussed."

"Father," Jane chided.

"That's quite enough for today." Her father shot her a weary look. "You may return to your rooms and rest. I will send Greta with tea."

With a last glance at the earl, Jane curtsied dutifully and returned to her room.

Once inside, Jane shook off a sudden chill. Earl or no, Lord Somerton would not do. He was too old, for one thing, and something about him gave her goose bumps. For all his smiles and bows, his eyes were cold.

Impatiently tugging at the laces of her dress, Jane caught sight of the tear in her sleeve and noticed patches of dirt spotting her skirt. What a sight she must have been! With any luck, her appearance would have put him off entirely, and she would be free to explore town on her own, kissing handsome men in taverns all over the city.

She swooned onto her bed with a secret smile, touching her lips gently with her fingertips. "Mark." She sighed.

While it was true that she didn't know what the tavern was called or if she would ever be able to find it again, she had a vague idea of the direction it was in and assumed that if she traveled that way, she would eventually get there.

She was certainly going to try.

Chapter 40

As Sally walked to the Hereford estate the second night, she didn't know what to expect.

Mark had left some time before to check on Harry and his progress with his bars. Nick had followed close behind, presumably going to check on the state of Harry's foot. She waited a little while, grabbed her shawl and sped off into the night, feeling guilty even as she increased her pace.

There was no reason to feel guilt. She reminded herself that in spite of her feelings for him, Nick was only her friend, and he was courting someone else. He had never made any claims on her, as much as she wished he would have. She rationalized that being faithful to someone who didn't love her was madness. Her life was her own.

So why did she feel guilty?

Her feelings of worry disappeared as she saw the highwayman, waiting for her on the hill where they had met the night before. She sat beside him on the log, her nerves on edge at his proximity. The guilt was gone, and her mission to hunt down Wrath all but forgotten. She listened to him breathe, feeling his minute movements in the trembling of the log beneath them.

The night before had been the best night of her life and all they had done was *kiss*.

Although she barely knew him, she felt a comfort when she was with him that she could not explain. They fit together in a way she had never before experienced. Her head on his shoulder, his mouth on hers. Her legs had fit around his waist like they belonged there.

He had said he wanted to court her. He had said beautiful things to her, and she had acted like a lunatic and stormed off. Now he was here again, for *her*. *Why?*

He was insane, clearly, but she was willing to overlook that for someone who could kiss the way he did.

She was trying to think of something to say when she felt his hand close over hers.

She wanted him, badly. She might be damned for that, along with everything else, but she wanted him with an intensity that frightened her.

They sat like that for maybe an hour, holding hands in tense silence, when at last he said, "No one will be leaving this late. Why don't I walk you back home?"

She agreed quietly and they walked back toward town.

Darkness had fully settled over the forest and he was in no danger of being seen as they headed for the city. There were no new street lamps so far out of town, and as often as she glanced at his face, all she could see was the outline of his profile by the light of the moon. He moved soundlessly through the night as criminals must, the warmth of his hand in hers the only reassurance she had that he was still beside her.

They reached the edge of Hyde Park and Sally felt Tyburn looming near before she saw it, the residual tragedy of the gallows rippling along the field in a mournful, near perceptible howl. Because she could not look away, she turned toward the evil and saw the fearful silhouette of the triple tree dark against the violet sky.

This is your future, they seemed to whisper.

In her heart, she answered, *I know.*

She heard the brutal crack of Claude's strong, young neck reverberate through the darkest corners of her memory, felt his cold lips against hers once more in a terrible promise, and in her bones she felt the stillness of one who is certain they are about to die. She was immediately aware of the unique texture of every breath she drew, the sweet sigh of the breeze whispering through her hair, and the dirt, the calluses, the very fingerprints of the hand in hers.

So little of Sally's life had been left up to her.

She might have days, hours, mere moments left, but she would be damned if she wasted them.

Tugging the hand, Sally led the highwayman off course into a cluster of trees beside the stream.

He followed her hesitantly, knowing the way back as well as she did.

"Wait..." he started.

For all of his talk of marriage and restraint, Sally was under no illusions and she knew enough to take what she could get when it was offered. There would be no marriage for her, no children, no home, only illicit passion and, God willing, revenge.

She turned to face him and pulled off his mask. She held his face and looked to his eyes though all she could see was darkness, and whispered, "There's no time."

Sally kissed him with everything she had left. Every drop of passion, lust, rage, fear, and hope she had poured out of her in a relentless onslaught of desperate, searing kisses. In spite of his earlier protestations, he kissed her back, his hot, lush mouth bruising hers with the force of his want.

There was no teasing this time, only frantic desire as she tugged the laces of his trousers and grasped his thick, hard cock in her hand. She felt him gasp against her mouth and she bit his lip in response. He slid his hands down her waist to cup her arse and all but threw her against the nearest tree, driving into her aching body with blinding force.

She wrapped her legs around his waist and let herself go in his arms, his hungry mouth on her throat as the cold tree bark scratched her skin. He held her easily, his body so young and strong and alive, his every thrust an answer to a sinful prayer. *Yes,* her body sighed, *this is what I have been waiting for. Yes, this is what this is supposed to feel like. Yes, you are mine, mine, mine,* on and on, until she heard her own voice gasping, "Yes!"

With one final, blissful thrust, the highwayman gave a rapturous moan against her neck and spent deep inside her. Sally shuddered in pleasure and wrapped her limbs around him, holding his body against hers, keeping him there for as long as he would stay.

He kissed her deliriously, possessively, until they heard the sound of a horse galloping down the lane nearby.

The sound still made her hair stand on end.

Sensing her hesitation, he soothed. "Don't be afraid."

"I should get home," she whispered.

The highwayman gently lowered her from the tree and steadied her as she tried to stand on shaking legs. After quickly

213

retying his trousers, he offered her his arm, and the gesture was so like Nick that Sally felt a twinge of regret. He might feel nothing for her, but she still cared for him in spite of herself, and she didn't want him to worry at her absence.

They walked in silence to the edge of Southwark, keeping to the darkest lanes and deserted alleys, before they stopped a few short streets from the warehouse. He took her face gently in his hand, and asked, "Will you be all right from here?"

She nodded and kissed his palm. "Will I see you again?"

"Oh, yes." He nodded.

"What's your name?"

He kissed her once more in response.

She sighed. He had his secrets and she had hers.

Sally watched him disappear into the shadows of the nearest alley, headed back toward the bridge. She wanted to follow him, to run away from the all of the madness with him, but she didn't know what she would find if she did. So many highwaymen, she knew, had lovers all over the countryside. In spite of his protestations, he could be returning to even now.

Turning away at last, she walked to the warehouse on aching legs, so thoroughly loved that the shame she believed she should feel did not hit her until she opened the back door to see Nick reading in a chair in front of the fire.

He looked up at her with wide, shining eyes, and she stared dumbly at him in response.

Setting down the book, he took a blanket from the back of the chair. "You look cold. Come sit with me by the fire."

His fingers felt oddly chilled as he wrapped the blanket around her shoulders. He didn't ask where she had been.

Sally sat in front of him on the floor before the hearth and felt her cheeks begin to burn in the soft warmth of the fire. Nick's feet were propped up on a small stool and she noticed he still had his boots on. Without a second thought, she tugged them off his feet and dropped them to the floor.

Mark crossed the room from the workshop to grab a bun from the basket above the oven. He looked at them curiously as he walked by, but said nothing.

As Sally heard his steps retreat from the kitchen, she let her head rest against Nick's thigh, and closed her eyes as he began to read.

Chapter 41

Nick sat dumbly in the chair in front of the hearth, holding his book of poems open to the page he had been pretending to read as Sally had entered the back gate.

After running the long way home in order to beat Sally there by mere moments, he had flung off his long coat, grabbed the book from the mantle, and dropped himself into the chair without so much as removing his boots.

Mark looked up from his carving. "What the--"

He had shot him a look of warning. Mark snickered to himself as he returned to his work.

Nick's coat still swung gently on its hook as Sally had come through the door, cheeks flushed and looking not half as loved as he wanted to have left her.

She glowed in the firelight, breathless and beautiful, and Nick knew, as he had never known anything else, that he loved her.

He didn't know what he had expected her to do when she came home, but he didn't think for a moment that she would come to him as she had. Now, wrapped in the coarse wool blanket, she rested her head on his thigh and sighed.

He watched the flickering light play off the formidable black waves of her hair, listened to the sated whisper of her breath, and stretched his fingers to caress her cheek, stopping short of touching her.

Did she know?

Mark tiptoed past them into the kitchen, meeting Nick's eyes as he passed. He held up his hand, pointed to his ring and nodded in Sally's direction. Nick choked on a laugh that was more than a little bit terror. He had talked to her about marriage in both of his guises now, but she had been dismissive both times. He knew what he wanted, but what did she want?

Nick took a deep breath and willed his pounding heart to slow to a sensible pace. He took up the book and began to read Spenser's *The Faerie Queene*. It was a little over-wrought for his taste, but Sally had seemed to like it while she had recovered from her fever.

He had barely finished a Canto before Jack and Will burst through the back door, swinging an enormous trunk between them.

"What have you got there?" Mark set down his tools.

They dropped it heavily on the table, and even the oak of the discarded door groaned in protest.

"Didn't get a good look."

Will took up a chisel from the work bench and had the lock off with a single well-placed blow.

"Silk!" Jack laughed as he buried his arms in the sumptuous fabric. "Lace and all!"

"Any wigs in there?" Mark asked. "Fetch a fair few bob."

Roused by the commotion, Sally joined them at the table, blinking sleepily at the bright jewel-toned fabric. "They look like costumes," she said, stifling a yawn.

Mark withdrew an ornamental rapier from the trunk. "Tell me you didn't accost a troupe of actors."

Nick reluctantly left the warmth of the hearth to join them at the table. "These are real." He nodded toward the starched ruff Jack was attempting to fasten around his own neck. "Elizabethan, if I had to guess."

Mark gave a low whistle. "Where did you come by it?"

"Down Sussex way. Fell off the back of a carriage, didn't it?" Will dismissed.

"The theatre," Sally said to herself.

"What's that, darling?" Nick blushed as the endearment escaped his lips. The lads would think nothing of it, but it wasn't like Nick to be so familiar.

Sally didn't blink. "Wrath used to take me around the theatres in the Piazza and Bridges Street. He never misses an opening night. What's opening this week?"

"I can find out," offered Mark.

Nick didn't like the direction this was taking. "What are you thinking?"

"We can blend in with the crowd, and I can point him out to you if he's there."

"Then we follow him home and run him through?" Mark joked.

"No, he'll have Charlie with him, so that might be difficult. We will discover his identity and run him through later."

Nick felt a twinge of worry for her safety and struggled to think of a reason not to go. "How will we know who he is? You're the only one who has seen him."

"I suppose I will have to go with you. But what if he sees me?"

Mark shuffled through the trunk of clothing and withdrew a fan, fluttering it delicately below his eyes, drawing laughs. "We will make you unrecognizable."

"He keeps to the upper tiers," she remembered. "He will be difficult to see from the pit."

"Then we will get you a box," said Mark. "I know a bloke."

"What if he sees me?"

Sally was clearly beginning to panic. Nick took her hand in reassurance and she looked up at him curiously. If hunting down her madman was what it took to bring her peace, he would do what he could to help. "No one will be looking for you. I will go with you, and you'll be safe."

"I don't mind going," offered Mark. "Been awhile since I've been to the theatre."

"You went yesterday," said Jack.

"Yeah, that's what I said. Awhile."

Near the bottom of the trunk, Sally found a high-necked russet gown with an enormous skirt made for a Spanish farthingale. She looked at it appraisingly and asked, "May I keep this one?"

"Yeah, sure. You sure you don't want something a bit...newer?"

"No," she said, appearing to deconstruct it in her mind. "This will be easier to alter."

Mark shrugged his assent and continued to sort through the remaining silks and ornaments at the bottom of the trunk.

Nick watched uneasily as Sally held the gown up to herself with a look of great concentration. "This will do nicely," she said finally. "I will start in the morning. Sleep well, lads."

They bid her goodnight as she ascended the stairs, trailing the long dress behind her.

The upstairs door shut softly and Mark pounced. "What was all that about?"

Nick stared at the place on the stairs where she had just been.

"Nick."

"What?" Nick returned his attention to the table to find his friends grinning at him.

Mark groaned loudly. "You daft old git. Go get her, then."

Nick made an obscene gesture to let Mark know what he thought of him, to the delight of the others, and ascended to stairs to the sound of laughter.

Opening the door to his room, he found Sally already fast asleep. The dress had been hung over the stool below the window, and she had left a candle burning to light his way to bed.

Nick undressed quietly and crept into the makeshift pallet he had built for himself beside the bed. It was mad that after the intimacy they had shared perhaps an hour before, he did not presume he could share her bed.

Of course, she didn't know it had been him.

Did she?

Nick rolled to his back, his arms aching to hold her, and settled in for a long night without any sleep.

Chapter 42

"Sit down, Wrath."

Standing in Hereford's periwinkle study at an unfashionably early hour of the day, Wrath was nervous. His back stiffened at Hereford's tone, his newly tailored coat a touch too tight across the chest. He leisurely sat in the gilded chair opposite Hereford, affecting an expression of cool indifference.

Hereford leaned forward across the table, touching his fingertips together in a peak. "It's time we re-think our bargain."

His arms began to itch. There would be time to burn the coat later. "Were you not pleased with the girl? There are others."

Hereford sunk back into his chair. "I wanted *her*."

"Sally was quite remarkable, to be sure, but there are others. Younger, more pliant."

Hereford smacked his fist on the table. "I don't want pliant, don't you understand?"

Wrath took a deep breath. "Sally was a murderess. Shall I go pluck one off the gallows for you?"

Once the words were out, he immediately regretted them.

Hereford was not amused. "You pride yourself on your ability to procure anything for anyone, and yet the only thing I ask for, I am told I cannot have."

"Sally's dead. Allow me to find something better for you. We have a new girl, fair haired and nearly a virgin. Let me send her over for--"

Lifting a hand to silence him, Hereford interrupted, "I don't mean to discontinue your services, but I'm no longer certain they warrant the cost of my only daughter's hand. I do have her happiness to consider, you understand."

Wrath might have laughed out loud, if he wasn't so suddenly terrified. "As you know, I have reasonable holdings and I pledge that I will treat her gently. She will never want for anything."

"I do wonder. She does so admire young Mister Virtue. Are you certain he has no portion? As you say, the Somerton estate may be wounded, but it may yet recover and I would so like to strengthen our relationship by supporting your family."

"Nicholas! He has nothing and he will receive nothing. Think not of it, Hereford; do not waste your daughter on a *tutor.*" He spat the word.

"Would a whoremonger be preferable?"

Wrath's blood turned to ice. "Need I remind you of my station?"

"That's not necessary. I believe I have made up my mind." Hereford leaned over the table and lowered his voice. "Either you find me a girl who will give me exactly what I want, or the deal's off, and I may yet give Jane to Mr. Virtue simply because it amuses me. Do not irk me, Wrath."

A hundred obscenities leapt to mind and Wrath bit back every one. "I shall prepare a girl for you for tomorrow. What time shall I bring her here?"

"To Bridges Street, if you please. Bring her to my box, and I will decide if I've a mind to take things further. Do not disappoint me."

Chapter 43

Looking into the borrowed mirror in Nick's room at the warehouse, Sally barely recognized herself.

Gone was the green dress, the kohl, the gaunt, paper-thin skin. The person staring back at her in the copper silk dress was a vision of health and loveliness, all soft curves and glowing skin, with a cascade of glossy black curls arranged in a wave over her right shoulder, held up with pins of pearls and gold. This was no downtrodden harlot, no naïve Norman baker; this was someone so different, so glamorous, that at first she didn't recognize herself. In the few weeks since her death, as she had thought of it, she had become a different person.

Her appearance wasn't the only difference she could see in the mirror.

Behind her, illuminated by candlelight, Nicodemus Virtue--not his real name--was carefully lacing up the back of her dress. She felt every gentle tug, heard the whisper of silk sliding through eyelets, and closed her eyes at the pleasure of the barely perceptible touch of his fingertips through the linen against her back.

"Are you nervous?" He asked over her shoulder, his breath on her skin sending an illicit shiver up her spine.

Sally opened her eyes with a start to see his handsome face reflected in the mirror, close enough to kiss. "A little," she admitted. "But it's our best chance, isn't it?"

"It's the best I can think of under the circumstances. Hereford goes to the theatre most nights and tonight's the opening of a new comedy. I can't imagine he'd miss it."

Dress tied, Nick crossed the room to get the coat that Maggie had found and altered for him last minute.

It had only taken a couple of days for Sally to alter the dress to her taste, distractions aside. Madame Toulouse would be impressed. She had taken a high-collared curtain made for a wheel farthingale and had changed it into something she hoped would pass in modern circles, if only for a night. The bodice had been taken in to fit her corset exactly, the neckline lowered and filled with the gold lace from the removed collar, the fitted sleeves removed completely and replaced with more of the sheer gold filigree, and the dress drastically reduced in volume to a gently curving bell. The skirt had a panel embroidered all over with gold beads and pearls in a pattern of tiny fleurs-de-lis, which she left intact save for a sample she had extracted for her mask.

The little mask they called a vizard, being a fashionable accessory for fashionable women in less savory surroundings, suited her purpose perfectly. She pinned the half-mask over her eyes, straightened her long ivory gloves, which covered much of the skin her dress left bare, and steeled herself for a night at the theatre.

Sally caught a glimpse of Nick's downcast face in the mirror's hazy reflection. He opened his mouth to say something, then changed his mind and turned to take his coat from the stool.

She heard the swish of silk as he slid his arms into the sleeves just behind her. After a moment's hesitation, he took her hand and kissed her knuckles. "You are beautiful."

The low reverberation of his voice soothed her nerves and the touch of his lips made her skin tingle, even through the gloves.

Any more of that and she would need to forgo the play to seek out her highwayman for some much-needed relief.

Sally withdrew her hand with a heavy heart, silently cursing his Jane and whatever unhappy twist of fate had allowed her to win him and attempted a smile. "So are you," she allowed, trying to sound more carefree than she felt. She cleared her throat. "Shall we retrieve Mark?"

Nick gave a half-bow and extinguished the candles.

Downstairs, Mark was sifting through the coffin that had regained its place of honor on the long table. He looked up at their approach with a wide smile, resplendent in a burgundy coat of finely embroidered brocade. "You're looking gorgeous as ever, Miss Sally! But Nick," he tsked playfully, "blue ain't your color."

Nick's coat was somber and black, as befitted an educated man, set off by a waistcoat of brilliant blue the color of the sea in a storm. Blue was precisely his color, but Sally imagined he would look tempting even in dirt.

Nick rolled his eyes and joined Mark at the side of the coffin. "What are you after?"

"Just a few bits and bobs for this evening. Got to look the part, eh?"

True to his word, Mark's unnamed contact had procured a small box on the lowest tier for the opening of *Generous Enemies* at the Theatre Royal on Bridges Street in Covent Garden.

"With stolen goods? Are you mad?"

"Keep it down, eh? Nothing recognizable, give me some credit. Here." He handed Nick a plain-looking pocket watch.

"You can't be serious."

Mark pulled a second one out of his pocket. "In case we get separated, we can pick a time to meet up."

"Are we likely to get separated?"

"If you must know, I've got my eye on a certain actress and if I see her, I plan for us to be separated for quite a long time, yes."

Nick's face reddened but he took the watch, shoving it into his coat.

Sally smiled brightly. "Anyone I would know?"

Mark shrugged. "Jane something or another. Stunning. Red hair down to there. You know her?"

"You just described half the girls in Covent Garden. They're all called Mary or Jane."

He smiled. "If it don't work out, you can introduce me to every single one. Come on then."

Mark handed her a necklace of half a dozen strands of pearls and she slipped it around her neck as they headed out the door.

The boys had gone to the theatre often enough in their everyday clothes, but carpenters did not commonly purchase well-situated boxes for opening nights. Perversely, they would draw less attention the more ostentatiously they dressed.

Sally reminded herself of this as she became aware of the significant weight of the pearls around her neck, struggling with the knowledge that the sale of them alone would bring in enough money for a house on Mark's street.

She said a silent prayer that the dainty clasp would not fail.

The coffin of treasure they had left under Jack's protection held the spoils of dozens of robberies and as dangerous as it was to keep and transport, when it was sold off it would make the four of them wealthy men. Still, when the penalty for stealing anything worth more than a shilling was death, Sally wondered if the risk was worth it.

It was, of course. Over the short time she had stayed at the warehouse, she was well aware that it had fed them during the uncertain weeks when there was no work, and it was no secret Nick hadn't been paid in months. She did not judge them as they had not judged her. One did what one must to survive, but she did wish they would not endanger themselves so.

Sally's feelings of apprehension increased as they approached St. Giles. Nick sensed her hesitation as she pulled her cloak close around the pearls and shivered. "Are you all right?"

"Do you think it was clever to walk, dressed as we are?"

Mark shook his head. "Darling, nobody's gonna give you any trouble when you're with us."

Sally looked up at Nick and he smiled gently. As kind as she knew he was, she had to admit he cut an imposing figure.

Returning his smile, she let her hand slip down from where it rested in the crook of his arm to take his hand.

Jane be damned.

As they drew near the theatre, only one street over from the dreadful place Wrath had held her captive for nearly three years, Sally attempted to distract herself by imagining she was someone else.

Sally's dead, she reminded herself. *I can be anyone I want.*

She imagined herself a great lady, universally respected and wealthy beyond reason. She stood up straighter and lifted her head beneath the considerable weight of the pearls as if they were nothing. *Why, they are only my very smallest set of pearls! I am so accustomed to the trifling little things, that I often wear them to bed!*

Sally squeezed Nick's hand and looked up at his profile as they ascended the steps to the theatre. *While we're wishing foolish wishes, I'll wear him to bed, too.*

We'll be married, and have dozens of children, and live in a splendid house, and--

"Oranges! Get your oranges! Four pence a pop!"

The shrill call of the evening's first orange seller brought her

225

back to earth and she emitted an involuntary groan.

Nick turned to her and smiled encouragingly as he led her through the lobby, Mark leagues ahead.

The theatre was as vulgar as Sally remembered it. Scores of unwashed, rowdy men, already clumsy with drink, hollered at the girls onstage and roughly handled the orange sellers making their rounds, sticky with the juices of overripe fruit.

The girls were almost as bad, foul-mouthed and covered in rouge and taffeta, all but falling out of their ill-made gowns, exposing themselves for spare change. Sally wrinkled her nose and averted her eyes, following Nick down the corridor toward a box on the first tier.

It was an excellent spot; the best stolen money could buy on short notice, and the view was very different from above the crowd. The noise was nearly as bad, but the stale smell of barrels of spilled ale and sawdust only barely reached her behind the vizard.

Sally sat on the sticky bench between Nick and Mark and had a look around the theatre.

There were three tiers of boxes above the pit, she well knew, but she could see the people seated within them much better from there than from the stage, and they all seemed to be looking at her. Sally turned her attention back to the stage and whispered to Nick, "They're all staring."

"Of course they are, you're beautiful. They're probably trying to figure out who you are."

Terror seized her and she began to fan herself. "They're trying to figure out who I am? Why would they do that?"

He took her hand reassuringly. "For the sake of gossip, nothing more. Don't worry--no one knows who I am, and as far as they're concerned, you're dead. No one will recognize you. Try not to draw attention."

Sally took a deep breath and lowered the fan. A woman appeared onstage in an enormous wig, breasts spilling out of a bodice too low to be believed. The crowd roared. Sally rolled her eyes and glanced to the left, only to see a pair of women eyeing her and whispering. She clutched Nick's hand.

"Don't panic," he said. "Everyone is looking at everyone else.

Take a look around and tell me if you see him."

Still grasping his hand, she did. Dozens of people filled the upper tiers, mostly men, gentlemen of all ranks and every age, many of whom frequented Wrath's theatre, some she'd had the misfortune of entertaining. She recognized a couple of Claude's old friends, and felt the full force of the danger she was in.

It was remarkable that she had lived with such terror every day until Nick had found her. She turned to him, took his handsome face in her white-gloved hand, and whispered, "Thank you."

His face reddened slightly. It was charming. "For what?"

"For everything."

He raised his hand to hers where it rested on his cheek and they held each other's gaze for perhaps a moment too long, when she heard the first whisper.

"...looks like the Green Devil..."

Sally's skin went cold and her eyes darted to the boxes around them, looking for the person who had recognized her.

"What is it?"

"Someone saw me. Someone knows. Oh, Nick!"

He held her shoulders gently. "She's dead, remember? You are a foreign lady just here to see a play."

Taking another deep breath, Sally straightened her posture, directing her gaze once more to the atrocity of a play. Pretending she didn't care was something she had been very good at once. She would just have to do it again. Keeping her eyes on the stage, she set her shoulders back, lifted her chin, and sat perfectly still in the haughtiest position she could muster.

Nick chuckled under his breath. "That's perfect."

As intermission was announced, Mark leaned in and said, "If you will excuse me, I've got an actress to find."

He disappeared in a flash as much of the audience situated in the boxes stood to socialize amongst themselves. Sally looked around the crowd and quickly spotted Hereford in the middle second tier with a number of other gentlemen and a lady in a gaudy red dress. She squinted and recognized Camille.

Behind her loomed the shadow of a familiar hat, and Sally watched as Wrath emerged, briefly, wearing a great deal of uncharacteristic finery.

She straightened her mask and tugged gently on Nick's sleeve. He looked in the direction she indicated. Wrath was standing in plain sight, at the edge of the box in a violet waistcoat that looked very much like a garment of Beaumont's.

He looked at them and Sally froze, certain she had been spotted, but Wrath wasn't looking at her. He was looking past her at Nick.

"I think we should go," she whispered.

"Do you see him?"

"There." She nodded toward Hereford's box as Wrath ducked behind the curtain. "Damnation. He's gone."

"Why don't we go after Mark? If you see him out there, tug on my hand."

Sally pulled her vizard further over her eyes and nodded, rather more bravely than she felt.

You're a lady, she told herself as they stepped into the hallway. *You have every right to be here. You are safe, you are respected...*

A well-dressed man passed rather too close to her and managed to brush to side of her breast with the back of his hand.

Sally shuddered in disgust.

Nick held her hand, carefully leading her through the crowd. As they descended the staircase, they passed three gentlemen who openly ogled her exposed flesh, one after another, as they became eye-level with her décolletage.

I am a lady, Sally chanted in her head. *Ladies do not have to disguise their revulsion, ladies do not have to suffer the indignity of...*

As they reached the foyer, Sally felt a hand slither across her arse. A voice whispered in her ear with fetid breath. "How much?

Sally's back went rigid with fear. She crushed Nick's hand in hers and turned to see, not Wrath as she had imagined, but a courtier she vaguely recognized. He leered at her with hooded eyes, reaching for his purse as he licked the excess saliva from his lips.

Mercury. Pox.

"I beg your pardon, Sir," she said in a tiny voice. "I am a lady."

"Like hell you are." He laughed. "You let me know when

228

you're finished with this one and I'll give you a pound for your trouble."

Nick drew himself up to his full height and put himself between Sally and the horrible man. "Sir, you are inebriated. Apologize to the lady and go home to your wife."

The courtier postured and curled his too-wet lip with distaste. "Step aside, pup, and let a man show you how it's done."

Nick's voice lowered to a menacing growl. "Apologize to the lady."

Sally was painfully aware that people were beginning to watch the commotion. She looked around the crowd and saw many faces from her old life, but Wrath was not among them. Mark was nowhere to be seen.

The courtier gave a humorless laugh and gestured to her. "Perhaps she has you fooled, but there has never been a lady who walks like that."

The crowd openly cheered as Nick's sizeable fist connected with the man's jaw.

"Get him!" A man shouted from the stairs.

The courtier attempted a feeble swing, but he was outmatched by Nick, who was much larger, much stronger, and much angrier than he was.

Three punches in, Nick had him on the floor, bruised and streaming blood onto the rug. Nick had him by the neck and seemed to be telling him something about the importance of respecting ladies when Sally noticed that everyone was watching her.

The attention was the last thing she had wanted. She backed up slowly toward the wall, wishing she could blend in with the paint, when a warm hand grasped her arm from behind.

Mark leaned in and whispered, "Time to go."

They skirted the edge of the crowd to the front door where Mark left her momentarily to grab Nick. They fled the theatre and darted down the nearest alley to the sound of shouts and cheers.

"Come on." Sally huffed, leading them through the labyrinth of alleys she knew so well out of Covent Garden and some ways into St. Giles before they stopped to catch their breath.

"Did you see him?" Mark asked.

Sally nodded, feeling for the pearls and relieved to find they were still firmly clasped around her neck. The vizard had fallen off during their flight, lost to the night.

"Did you?"

"No." Nick grimaced, flexing his bloodied knuckles.

"Well, you got to hit a guy. Night's not a total bust." Mark smiled. "I'll meet you back home."

"Where are you going?" Nick asked.

"Drury Lane," he called. "Night ain't over yet!"

Mark rounded the corner and disappeared, leaving them alone in the alley.

"Are you unharmed?" His eyes searched hers.

"You're hurt." She took his hand, examining his knuckles. "Why did you do that?"

Nick looked back toward the theatre in disgust. "That prick, the way he insulted you--"

"Why do you care?"

He looked at her in disbelief. "Don't you know?"

Sally looked up into the kindest eyes in Covent Garden, or anywhere, for that matter, and she did.

Because he cared, because he was wonderful, and because he had defended her when no one else ever really had, Sally took his stubbled face in her hands and kissed his perfect lips.

He grasped her waist and held her against the shadow of the wall, kissing her like a man utterly lost.

She lost herself, too.

His firm lips, his strong, rough hands, the delicious smell of his warm skin; he was as quiet as a criminal must be as he kissed her in that alley in St. Giles.

Sally didn't need to see his profile in the dark to know who held her. He'd changed his coat, but those shoulders were the same. Who could have guessed the mask had hidden such a face? His kiss, at once new and familiar, told her what Nick never could.

He was hers.

Sally caught her breath as he pulled away. His face was flushed, his expression uncertain. For all the heat in his eyes, he looked nervous as a boy.

She ran her thumb along the swell of his bottom lip, dizzy

with relief. "Why didn't you tell me?"

He swallowed. "I didn't think you would want to be with a footpad...I wanted to be better, for you. I'm sorry."

"Nick?"

"Yes?"

"Unless you want me up against another tree, you had better take me home."

Chapter 44

Wrath shifted uneasily in his seat.

Halfway through the first act of the new comedy, Hereford had not given any indication that Camille had met his approval.

Leaning his face on his hand, Wrath could almost see the ashes of his dream of Jane Ramsey's dowry floating carelessly into the rafters. Charlie sat at his left, watching the comedy, oblivious to his master's despair.

Camille should have been a safe bet. She was young and delicately beautiful, obedient and willing to do anything for a price. Even her name was French, although what her real name was, he could not say. He had briefed her on Hereford's particular perversions and she was game, but accepting as she was of her lot in life, she could not seem to muster the raw contempt for it all that Sally had not been able to disguise. Camille sat in her seat at Hereford's side in the new scarlet dress he had purchased at no small loss, clean, coiffed, and mostly sober.

Hereford did not so much as glance in her direction.

Clenching his fists, Wrath cursed his father, his King, and his country for bringing him to this dreadful place. That his father's loyalty had cost him to lose half his holdings to the Parliamentarians seemed to him a cruel joke. Torn from his place at Court too early as the war began in earnest, Wrath's education had been left to his father's hopeless servants in the country as Edward fled with Charles to The Hague. Wrath had been an adult when the King had been restored, and by then, their estate was in ruins, his manners were in shambles, and he had been utterly forgotten by a fickle Court.

Now more than forty years of age and still too coarse for polite society, Jane was to have been his way back in.

He knew he should have taken Sally back after dispatching Beaumont, that tiresome pup, but he could not seem to stop himself from punishing her for lying to him, and for running again. With her effortless popularity and that face--that face that everyone recognized and loved, she had seemed to him to embody the life that he had been robbed of, the life that he should have had. He caught her, saw only Court escaping him once more, and he killed her.

He had immediately regretted it.

The few possessions he had lifted from Beaumont's house had boosted his wardrobe, for all the good it did him. He tugged at the violet waistcoat, a bit too short for his wiry frame, and decided the color suited him.

He heard a collective murmur and looked around to see what had taken the boxes' attention away from the play.

It was Nicholas.

Nicholas, his cursed half-brother, was sitting happily in a lower box, immaculately dressed and accompanied by the most glamorous woman Wrath had seen in years.

Wrath knew precisely what he was doing. Nicholas must have begun making appearances ahead of receiving Jane's dowry and before long, he would be formally introduced at Court, where he would, no doubt, endear himself, as he endeared himself every damned place he went. He wouldn't need his share of the Somerton estate with Hereford's money.

Nicholas, with his good looks, perfect accent, and careful manners, was sure to be a favorite, certainly among the ladies hungry for fresh blood. Oh yes, Wrath knew his plan because it had been his plan, before it was snatched from his grasp, like everything else.

He watched Nicholas flirt with the lady, likely the bored wife of some lord or another, and struggled to contain his rage.

He needed some air.

Wrath stormed down the back stairs to the nearest exit and let himself out of the heat of the theatre with a groan.

He looked out over the tall, fashionable inns and bars of Bridges Street. The street had been rebuilt some years before while his little playhouse had been allowed to decay, a forgotten, moldering corner of Bedford Street.

All of this should have been his by now.

He had the Somerton estate, for all the good it did him. A dusty Tudor country house presiding over a handful of tenant farms and orchards, it was dreadfully rustic.

Wrath snorted.

There had been a time when the Rothschilds had been favorites of the Court. He had been a part of it for a moment in time, had tasted its intrigues and its sinful delights. How could he ever bear to leave?

Now, rapidly aging and thoroughly excluded, he pimped and he pandered, but he was no worse than anyone at Court. He might be limited to a dung heap, but in that slum, by God, he was King!

He would have burned it down, the whores and all, to wrap himself in Jane Ramsey's lovely money.

Then Nicholas came back, taking what should have been his just as he had when he had come squealing into the world.

He would not let him take one more thing that should have been his.

Wrath straightened his jacket and returned through a side door, just in time to walk into a plan.

Nicholas, reeking with the self-righteous honor that he wore like an ermine cloak, appeared to be beating Lord Lewes to within an inch of his life.

The stunner he had been sitting with trembled becomingly at a safe distance. No doubt that bastard boy would be fucked senseless before the night was through.

Wrath simmered with hatred, watching from behind the curtain until a tinkling noise caught his attention and he looked down to see a silver pocket watch land at his feet.

He held it in place with the toe of his boot as he reached down to pick it up with his handkerchief. As he caressed the polished silver with his thumb, an engraving caught the light and he immediately recognized the Earl of Hereford's personal crest.

Wrath smiled.

Chapter 45

The smell of rain filled the small room, mingling with the dry, earthy smell of the rushes. Nick crossed the floor, his worn boots softly padding across the boards to the windowsill. Taking the flint in his hand, he lit the taper in the brass candleholder, its small light casting wild shadows against the walls.

Thunder clapped in the distance somewhere over Southwark, the sound of rain hitting the angled rooftops, old and new, a quiet roar. Sally stepped out of her soft leather slippers, feeling the grain of the straw against the arches of her feet.

Nick turned and smiled his quiet smile in the candlelight, shrugging off his coat and laying it across the chair. He closed the short distance between them with short, careful steps, his wide green eyes seeking hers. Sally stood, barefoot in her finery, all of her earlier assurance lost. The candlelight flickered across his high, smooth cheekbones, his skin glowing golden and warm.

Wanting to touch that skin with every nerve in her body, Sally waited for him to come to her, a desperate hunger aching in her chest. He carefully raised a hand to her cheek and her breath caught as he dragged his callused thumb over her cold skin.

Lightning shot silver across the sky, casting Nick's face in heavenly light for one fractured moment. Thunder answered in a resounding clap and Sally tasted wet wood and lavender in her sharp intake of breath.

She took Nick's injured hand in both of hers, avoiding his swollen knuckles. "We should wrap this. It must hurt."

"I can't feel it."

Holding his gaze steadily, Sally asked. "Did you mean it? What you said about...wanting to be with me?"

"Every word."

She felt his warmth draw closer, his breath against her face as he kissed her eyelids, her temple, her cheekbone, her jaw, tracking the angles of her face in a trail of almost imperceptible kisses. Sally shivered with pleasure at the touch of his lips on her still cold skin.

Nick sank his hand deep into her hair, pins popping as they hit the floor, pearls following with a crash. He wrapped his arm around the small of her back, holding her hips flush against his as he kissed the length of her neck.

Her hands ran up his firm waist of their own accord, the silk of his pilfered waistcoat cool against her palms. She traced her fingers across his broad chest to the top button and pushed it softly through the embroidered buttonhole.

The rest opened easily and she slid the waistcoat over the broad planes of his shoulders and let it drop, silently, to the floor.

His lips claimed hers in the darkness, taking her breath entirely in a warm, deep kiss. He took her lip between his teeth in a gentle bite and she moaned low in her throat, her arms winding around his neck.

She felt him smile against her lips and he spun her so her back was to him, his hands traveling the curve of her waist. She felt his fingertips trace a line from her ear to the base of her neck as he draped her hair over her shoulder, kissing every inch of flesh as it was exposed, his breath caressing her skin.

The silk strings of the dress loosened, grommet by grommet, from her shoulders to the base of her back, and before she thought to protest, he slid the dress off her shoulders and let it fall, the watered silk pooling heavily around her feet.

"Nick," she gasped, remembering herself from within a daze. "My scars..."

He leaned his jaw over her shoulder and her toes curled at the feel of his rough stubble against her throat. "You are perfect," he said, his breath warm against her ear.

She felt a tug at the knot that held her corset strings and took a deep breath as the whalebone cage loosened around her ribs. She raised her arms as Nick slipped the corset over her head and set it on the chair. Standing in her thin shift in the chill of the room, Sally was vulnerable. Few had seen her completely undressed. Would she please him?

Her shivering subsided as Nick returned to her and held her arms, kissing her thoroughly. Craving his heat, Sally yanked his long linen shirt from his trousers impatiently. It ruffled his hair as it came over his shoulders, and she was rewarded for her efforts with her first sight of his bare chest. Acres of warm, golden skin stretched across taut ridges and planes of hard muscle. Eating properly after a long period of hunger, he was beginning, slowly, to fill out.

So distracted was she by his beauty and by the curious smile that played across his lips that she didn't notice his hands gripping her shift until he had it bunched around her waist. This was where things usually stopped, so when he eased it over her ribs and pulled it off, she didn't know what to expect.

He dropped the shift. Sally felt her cheeks warm as he regarded her naked body with exquisite hunger. "Beautiful," he sighed, taking her in his arms and rendering her speechless with kisses.

He ducked his head to take one aching nipple into his mouth, tracing hot circles around it with his tongue. Sally moaned, curling her fingers into his thick hair at last. Her bare back sank against the rough grain of the wall, and Sally thought of their previous encounter in the park. She smiled, delirious with pleasure. *My highwayman.*

Nick swept her up into his arms and she squealed in surprise. He carried her the short distance to the bed and set her on top of the coverlet. She reclined on her elbows as she watched him hastily undress. His shirt gone, he tugged off his boots, revealing a fine pair of strong calves. He untied his trousers and dropped them without hesitation, allowing her to look her fill in the flickering light.

Long, muscular legs and a strong, taut belly completed the picture of masculine beauty she had glimpsed as she had taken his shirt. He had a man's body, well-formed and tall, his silhouette at once graceful and predatory. As he removed his smallclothes, Sally bit back a gasp at the sight of his arousal.

He reclined beside her on the bed, and she opened her arms to him, crushing her breasts against his hard chest. He kissed her deeply, savoring her mouth, and she reached down, grasping him in her hand.

Nick gasped against her lips before angling his hips away. "Patience, my love."

Laying her on her back, Nick began to explore her body with

237

his hands and his mouth. Running his hands up her thighs and over the swell of her hips, he kissed her breasts, her ribs, and the soft plane of her belly.

Sally relaxed against the coverlet, losing herself in the moment. Experienced as she was, no one had ever made love to her. More than that, Nick made it feel like worship. A kiss inside her elbow, a stroke behind her knee; he touched every inch of her flesh with his big hands, leaving waves of tingling nerves with every caress.

At last he lowered himself above her. Sally sighed with contentment as she felt his weight settle against her, reaching for him once more.

Nick paused. He watched her face as he ran his hand down her arm to her wrist. He grasped it, lifted it over her head, and gently pinned it to the pallet.

Sally's lips dropped open in surprise. Nick gave her a wicked smile and wordlessly parted her legs. She looked at him askance, and he answered by sliding a thick finger into her.

She gasped, holding his gaze as he tormented her with his fingers. He contracted them inside her, and a bolt of energy shot through her body, causing her to cry out. Delighted by her reaction, he did it again, caressing a part of her she was certain had never been touched. Her body responded to his every movement, her legs gripping his waist, her cries muffled as she buried her face in his shoulder. Just as she thought she could take no more, Nick shifted, taking himself in his hand and entering her, pausing maddeningly at the threshold.

Sally tilted her hips upward, needing to feel him inside her. He let go of her arm with a wicked smile, slipped his hands beneath the small of her back, and thrust home.

She cried out in sheer relief. His strong arms held her fast, his breath hot against her throat. Her back arched against the pallet, her breasts crushed against his chest. She tightened around him as he thrust into her slowly, inch by delicious inch.

His pace quickened with his breath, filling her deeper, wider, harder, further into oblivion until they came together with a crash.

Nick collapsed against her, catching his breath. Sally held him, dumbstruck. Her hands caressed the wide expanse of his back, and she listened to him breathe. She could feel his heart beating against her breasts and she was nearly overcome. It was nothing short of a miracle to have him in her arms.

She stroked his hair, breathing his heady, masculine smell, and sighed. "I love you, Nick."

"Marry me," he said. "Right now."

Sally giggled and moved to sit up. "It must be after midnight."

"Then marry me in the morning. Forget about tracking down this villain and run away with me."

She frowned, weary. "I won't let him take you from me."

"I'm not going anywhere."

Sally kissed him, relaxing into his arms. His hand stroked her back, moving gently over the ridges of old scars, until he reached the largest and she heard his sharp intake of breath. He was up and examining her back in a matter of seconds.

"What? What is it?" Sally asked.

She could feel the rough edge of his thumb running carefully over the lion on her hip. "This is a brand."

"I warned you about my scars."

"No, I've seen this one before." Nick's voice sounded bitter. "I know who he is."

Sally turned around and grasped his arms. "Who is he?"

A hint of movement caught her eye above Nick's shoulder and she looked up to see a face watching them through the window.

Sally screamed.

Chapter 46

Mark threw open the kitchen door with a crash, Will following closely behind. "He got away," Mark panted between heaving breaths, his face red from exertion. "Didn't get a good look at him. Big bloke."

"They found me. It's over." Sally despaired from the edge of the table, resting her head on the edge of the pine coffin.

Nick gently rested his hand on her back. He would have expected more tears. After the initial shock had worn off, Sally had been overcome with hopelessness, but she had not cried. "You don't know that for certain. He could have been some madman happening by..."

"It was Charlie. He knows where I am. Wrath will come for me." She sat up suddenly, looking around the room. "Would one of you happen to have a pistol you could lend me?"

Mark reached into his coat pocket with a shrug before he noticed Nick shaking his head at him in warning. "Why would you need that?"

Sally looked at him like he was slow-witted. "I'm going to kill him first." She stood, steeling herself. "You said you know who he is? Do you know where he lives?"

"Sally--"

"The Opera House will never do. There would be too many witnesses, you see, and there is the small problem of Charlie."

"Sally--"

"Are you lads coming or am I going to have to commit murder by myself?"

"Sally!" Nick exclaimed, even as Mark was taking his hat off the wall to leave with her.

"What?"

Nick looked at her worshipfully, drinking in her enraged beauty, knowing he may never see her again once he told her what he knew. "Sally, perhaps you should sit down."

She shrugged and turned toward the door. "There's no time.

I'll get my cloak and--"

"Wrath is Nick's brother," Mark interjected from the doorway.

Sally turned back toward them carefully, looking as though she might shatter.

"Half-brother, maybe..." said Nick.

Sally walked silently across the room and sank into her chair. "How long have you known?"

"The brand," he said. "He was at the theatre earlier, but I knew for certain when I saw the brand."

Sally covered her face with her hands.

Nick was well aware that Wrath's man hadn't come for Sally. Even watching them for as long as he may have been, he wouldn't have recognized her. Without the kohl and looking as healthy as she did, Sally was a new person. He was spying, certainly, but he all he would have seen was Nick making love to a beautiful woman, and it wasn't the woman he had followed.

It was Nick.

Whether or not she wanted anything to do with him ever again, he would give her the truth, and he would make sure Wrath never found her.

"Wrath, as you know him, is Arthur Rothschild. He is the only legitimate son of my benefactor, Lord Edward Rothschild, and is the Earl of Somerton. He may be a murderer, but he is quite untouchable."

"I'll bloody touch him," Mark cursed.

Tears began to cloud Sally's eyes, "How is he your brother?"

"As you know, my mother was the elder Lord Somerton's housekeeper. Mark believes he may have been my father."

"He bloody was," Mark said under his breath.

"Not now," Nick warned.

Sally looked at him strangely. He wondered what she was feeling. Fear? Disgust?

"He will be surrounded by people at all times. He will be very difficult to get to, and he is far more dangerous than either of us suspected. We need to get you away from London."

Sally wiped her eyes with the back of her hand. "What about you?"

"I would follow you to the ends of the earth." He took her hand. "I need to get some things together here to make that possible, but we need to get you out of here now to make sure that you are safe. Do you understand?"

She nodded. "They could be anywhere. How could I leave without them seeing me?"

"We'll think of something," said Nick. "Why don't you get your things together and I'll round up the boys."

♠

"Stark, raving mad," said Mark. "You are out of your bleeding mind if you think for one moment that I am going to leave you here to get yourself killed."

Nick and Mark stood opposite each other over the open coffin, loot glittering angrily in the lamplight. The last few hauls had nearly filled the compartment, and it would fetch a great deal when it was sold. "We don't know why he was following me. Maybe he's taken up spying on me again like in University. Maybe he wants something. I'm going to have a quiet word with him, is all. Why does your mind leap to murder?"

"Because I know what he did to her, and I'm not having it! You know precisely where he lives, and you're going to kill him!"

"I didn't think you would mind."

"Of course I bloody mind! You're going to get yourself hanged!"

"Please, Mark." Nick leaned forward over the coffin. "You're the only one I trust to look after her."

They heard the sound of footsteps on the stairs and Sally appeared in the doorway, clutching her cloak. "I heard shouting. Is something wrong?"

Both men straightened. Nick attempted a reassuring smile. "There's nothing wrong. We're just making plans. Mark is going to take you to Dover."

Chapter 47

Everything happened very quickly.

One moment she was being proposed to by a kind, beautiful, fascinating man, and in the next, his friends were winding her loosely in a woolen shroud, dashing handfuls of her good cooking herbs between the layers.

Well-played, Death.

When Nick and Mark told her of their plan to get her away from London unseen, Sally was struck by such terror that she found herself unable to react appropriately. She wanted to scream, she wanted to cry, she wanted to run, but what did she do? She nodded almost imperceptibly, unsure of whether she was more afraid of the plan or Wrath, and watched as they fitted the false bottom over their stolen treasure and lifted her immobilized body over the table and into the waiting coffin.

"Here you go, Sally." Mark leaned over the coffin and placed something soft behind her head. "I brought you a little pillow. Is that better?"

Sally nodded. She was able to move her arms only slightly beneath the shroud before the wool tugged and her elbows hit the sides of the coffin. Were all coffins so small?

Nick leaned over the side, clearly worried. He must have seen the fear on her face. Smiling at her sadly, he stroked her cheek. "Don't be afraid, Mark will look after you."

"When will you come?" she asked, her voice shaking.

"I won't be long," he assured her. "I will try to meet you in Dover." He leaned into the coffin and kissed her softly. "If you need anything at all, you must tell Mark. You can trust him."

Sally nodded and watched his face until they lowered the lid.

She gasped at the sudden darkness, her eyes widening almost painfully, trying to detect some light in the all the black. They had made a hole beside her head so she could breathe. She craned her neck toward it to try to look out, but saw nothing. The coffin heaved and swayed as they lifted it off the table, the treasure in the compartment beneath her hissing as it rushed toward her head. She closed her eyes and felt herself shaking. It had been so long since she had seen Death that she had begun to feel he had loosed his hold on her, but there she was, trapped in his embrace.

Sally could hear her heart pounding in her ears as they set her down. They were walking around the outside conversing, but she could not hear what was said. She closed her eyes and focused on her breathing to assure herself she still lived, and was tormented with visions of her life before she had escaped; Wrath's beatings, the men, the hunger, the endless, endless gin. A dark figure hovering over her bed in the night, always there.

The carriage began to roll and the creaking of the wheels became the sound of Claude's cart winding through the crowd. The gallows were approaching and before her all she could see was the life draining from Bettie's surprised face.

Overcome with terror, Sally lost consciousness.

♠

Every mile was agony.

Encased in the narrow coffin, she was painfully aware of every dip in the road, every hole, and every pebble the cart rolled over. She felt the precise moment they left cobblestones for the dirt roads of the country, and she cursed them both for different reasons. While the maddening popping over cobblestones had ceased, the dirt roads were uneven and sloping, and the cart dragged when they hit patches of mud.

No matter the state of the roads, Sally would have gladly walked them for miles rather than travel in the guise of a corpse.

The coffin was certainly large enough for her, but being so enclosed, it felt unbearably constrictive. Her heart beat wildly and her breathing came in shallow, silent puffs.

Her hands gripped her shoulders in the woolen shroud and she turned her head toward the hole the lads had drilled. The comforting smell of the herbs they had covered her in mingled with the sweet night air. She closed her eyes against the darkness and willed herself to breathe.

She was face to face with her greatest fear.

She could have been in the coffin for ten minutes or ten hours. She had no way of telling the passage of time, and no way of seeing any landmarks as they passed. She could barely move, and she was afraid she would run out of air if she did not die of terror first.

Trying to distract herself, she thought about how much it was like sleeping in a bed. If she did not think about the confines, it was almost as if they weren't there. She imagined herself in the room at the warehouse, lying in Nick's arms under the thick, warm bedclothes, and tried to sleep.

The thought of Nick brought tears to her eyes. She felt them roll down her temples and into her hairline.

He wanted to marry her. Knowing every defect of her person, he wanted to marry her. She didn't care that he was penniless, and it didn't matter where they were going. Her dark dream of exacting revenge upon Wrath was fading in the face of death. It was no longer enough for her to see him pay for his sins; confronted as she was with a vision of her own fate, she wanted more than anything to have a future, however uncertain, with Nick.

Sally didn't care who his brother was. If they had a chance, any chance at all, she would take it.

He told her he would meet her in Dover, where they planned to cross to Calais. There would be no return to Chateau Lenormand, in case she found herself wanted for the murder of Bertrand Remi, but France was a large country, and bakers always useful.

Nick had tucked her into the coffin as if tucking her into a bed, and looked down at her with great sadness as he kissed her goodbye. He needn't be worried for her; while she was travelling with Mark in such careful concealment, she was as safe as could be. He would only need to collect his things and he would follow later, so as to not look suspicious.

He was more than happy to leave Hereford's employ, Sally was certain, so she did not understand his sadness. Was it regret, then, that he was leaving his friends? Was he unsure he wanted to leave with her?

She seemed to be missing some important detail. A vision of

his face as he kissed her kept running through her mind. Sad, distant, resigned.

He had looked a bit like Claude on his way to the gallows.

Choking on a sob, Sally struggled for breath, fighting to pull her arms out of the shroud. She didn't know what Nick was planning, but she had to stop him.

Chapter 48

The sun had begun its slow creep above the horizon when Nick arrived at Somerton House.

He had walked there in the dark of early morning and was careful not to make any sound that might warn of his arrival. Nick did not plan on being there very long, and did not want to cause a scene.

As much as Arthur had always disliked him, the same couldn't be said of the rest of the household. Nick was counting on their affection to help him if things went badly. They wouldn't be involved at all if he could help it. He would sneak in, corner Arthur in his chambers, and attempt to ascertain what he wanted and how much he knew.

He needed to know Sally was safe.

Nick walked past the house to cut through a narrow lane that ran down the side and connected to the back garden through a light wooden door. Sliding his hand through the narrow gap between two loose planks, he popped the latch free. He had done the same thing many times when he was a child, although it was considerably more difficult with larger hands.

The door swung open with a soft whine. From the back of the garden, Nick could see that every light in the great house was out. Unusual, given that someone was always up and about. He moved quickly through the garden to the servants' kitchen entrance and tried the door. It was unlocked.

The kitchen was cold, and Nick felt a twinge of unease. By this time of the morning, there should have been at least one servant awake preparing the day's bread for the house, but no one had started a fire in the hearth. Judging by the thick coat of ash around the base, it hadn't been cleaned in some time.

Walking softly into the hall, Nick listened for signs of life and found none. The house appeared to be empty. He knew Arthur had not taken the household to the country because he had seen him only the night before, and even so, some would have stayed on. *Could it be possible no one lived here?*

The great foyer was empty. A thin white sheet hung limply over the chandelier, the shadows in the hollows like so many teeth, creating the impression of a huge, pendulous skull. Sheets were scattered everywhere, over banisters and pooling around the furniture on the floor, discarded. Nick moved toward the front door to find months, maybe years' worth of mud caked onto the rug. The floor itself was reasonably clean, but there were fresh footprints leading to the stairs.

A voice in his head told him it wasn't too late to turn back, but he thought of the brand on Sally's skin and he marched up the stairs.

The door to the master suite was open and a faint light burned from inside. Nick closed his hand over the pistol in his pocket, and walked quietly toward the door.

Inside, the bed was perfectly made, and empty.

Nick looked around in confusion. Suddenly, he felt an intense, blunt pain as something struck his temple, and he lost consciousness.

♠

When Nick came to, he was tied to a chair. His coat and his pistol were gone. The room was black, and smelled of damp and lime. The sound of dripping in the distance was familiar, and he realized with a start that he must be in the wine cellar.

He started the fumble with the ropes around his wrists, when a match was struck and a single candle lit.

A flintlock cocked and a voice said, "Don't bother trying."

Nick looked up toward the light to see Arthur sitting on the stairs, an enormous man in livery behind him.

"Is this really necessary?" Nick asked.

The candle cast menacing shadows over the angles of his face. "You broke into my house. I would say so." Arthur stood and crept toward him, a leisurely wraith. "It's not every day one catches a highwayman so easily. Imagine the authorities' surprise when I tell them you were in my cellar."

Nick's head was still aching from being struck. He didn't know how long he had been unconscious. He could have been in the cellar for hours, or days. "You have no proof."

"I have your pistol, I have your coat." He counted off on his fingers. "And there is the small matter of Hereford's missing pocket watch that you dropped at the theatre."

Nick cursed himself. "Hereford is bringing charges?"

"I am bringing charges on Hereford's behalf. It's high time you pay for your crimes."

"All this for a pocket watch? I've never taken anything of yours."

"Yes, you have," Arthur growled, his eyes wild, and Nick realized that Arthur may not be completely sane. "Father doted on you. He kept you and your mother in comfort for years when he should have tossed you both out on the street. Filthy, papist bitch. You went up to bloody Cambridge with money that should have been mine, and mine alone, and now you think you can steal my woman?"

Nick's breath caught in his throat. He prayed Sally had escaped the city undetected.

"You do not deny it?" Arthur laughed. "Everything was settled. I was going to marry her, and then you started courting her."

He was going to *marry* her?

"I know what you did," Nick said. "I know everything, and I would sooner hang for your murder than allow you to marry her."

Arthur struck him across the face. "Insufferable child. You couldn't touch me. Hang you shall, nevertheless. With you gone, I will have her, willingly or no."

Nick struggled against the ropes in vain. "You cannot!"

"I can and I will," he promised. "Then Hereford will have no choice but to give her to me, and her fat dowry as well. I will have to raise the price, of course, being damaged goods, but I'm certain he will oblige."

Hereford?

It was then that Nick understood Arthur was not referring to Sally at all. "Jane is nothing to me," he said slowly, wondering how quickly he could get to Hereford's estate to warn him. "Let me out of here and you can have her."

Arthur shook his head at him. "I'm wounded you think I'm that stupid. Get some rest. Tomorrow's a big day for you."

Chapter 49

The coffin stopped its travels with a jolt.

Sally could smell damp earth, horse manure, and the sour-sweet smell of a brewery through the air hole. Assuming they had reached their first stop, she listened for Mark's approach and waited to be let out.

Instead, she heard the furious pounding of hooves growing closer. The sound was so rapid that she could not tell how many horses there were. The pounding grew louder and began to slow, until the horse outside came to a halt beside the coffin, radiating heat and the smell of lather. Had they been caught?

Sally heard the cadence of frantic conversation, and the lid of the coffin was hastily pried off, letting in a gust of cold night air. "It's all right, Sally," Mark said.

Sitting up cautiously, she saw Jack standing there, his cheeks scarlet from the wind.

Her heart sank. "Jack, what is it?"

Jack rested his hands on his knees and tried to catch his breath in deep, choking gasps. "It's Nick," he huffed. "He's been taken."

Mark swore. "Damned fool! How long do we have?"

"Not long." Jack shook his head. "It's a rush job, Somerton's behind it. Tomorrow afternoon."

"Hellfire and damnation!" Mark cursed. "I'll go back now, you take Sally to Dover."

Jack nodded.

"The hell he will!" Sally climbed out of the coffin on shaking legs.

Both men looked at her in surprise.

"I will not let that cretin take one more thing away from me! I'm going with you."

"Sally--"

"You can't!"

"I'm going with you and there's not a damned thing you can

do to stop me. I assume we're going to save him. What's the plan?"

They left Jack with the coffin at the coach house, having used what few coins they had between them for food and lodgings for the night for him and his tired horse. Mark took a portion of the hidden loot inside with him to barter for a new horse. The horse that had dragged the coffin from the city was strong, but slow, and with two people on its back, could never hope to make it back in time. They would need at least one more, and if they could obtain a swift pair, so much the better.

With Mark inside and Jack distracted by a bowl of stew, Sally wandered the stables.

The inn was not busy that evening. Few horses slept in the stables, slight and thin, with a solitary brown pack horse at the far end leisurely eating his oats. Sally frowned. None of the horses would be up to racing long distances, and she would hate to make them try.

Hearing a resounding snort behind her, she turned slowly to face the final stall and gasped. The horse inside was so black that he was almost invisible in the night. She looked up at his huge head, so much higher than her own, in fear. She had never seen a beast so big. He was easily twice the size of some of the other horses, with a glossy black coat, and enormous, shining eyes.

His name was carved on a plaque on the stall door. *Goliath.*

Sally shuddered in fear as Goliath leaned his gigantic head out of the stall and sniffed her hair, his hot breath blowing across her face.

Slowly, she reached up to stroke his muzzle, and was pleasantly surprised when he did not immediately eat her.

"He's just a horse," she told herself.

Unlocking the stall, Sally slipped inside to find the space much larger than the others. There was a mounting stool, to her great relief, along with a grand saddle, large and black with gold trim. She had seen one like it before, but had difficulty immediately placing it.

Pushing the stool up beside Goliath, she quickly saddled him the way she remembered seeing it done as a child. Seeing it and actually doing it were two very different things, however, and Sally found she could barely lift the thing, let alone lift it above her head

251

over the back of an enormous horse. Nevertheless, she persevered, and felt a jolt of uneasy satisfaction as she secured it comfortably across Goliath's huge belly.

He stood quite still, making the task a great deal easier. Heartened by this, she climbed up into the saddle, swinging her leg over the other side like a man, and took the reins in her hands. Goliath perked up, and if she did not miss her guess, he was excited for a bit of exercise. Sally reached forward to stroke his thick mane, her skirt sliding down his back in red ripples to reveal the pattern of gold etching along the leather saddle before her, and she remembered where she had seen such a horse.

He looked very much like the horse that driven Claude to his execution.

Not long before, just the sight of a horse had scared her out of her wits. Now the threat of losing Nick was such that the horse seemed almost incidental. Steeling herself for the journey to come, she gently pressed her heels against Goliath's ribs and her heart leapt into her throat as he began to trot out of the stable.

Seeing a thin, black cloak hanging off a peg at the front of his stall, Sally grabbed it as they passed as an afterthought, swinging it around her shoulders. It would be cold, after all.

As they neared the front of the inn, Jack and Mark came into view. Mark held his horse by the reins, freed of the coffin cart.

"Where's Sally?"

"I don't know. I didn't see her leave."

Mark was frantic. "We don't have time, we have to go back--"

Goliath began to pick up speed on the open road, and both men looked up as she passed, bewildered.

"I found a horse," she called. "Come on, Mark."

The wind caught the cloak as Goliath began to run. Sally clutched the reins and gripped the saddle with her legs as firmly as she could, afraid of falling off. Within moments, she heard another set of hoof beats as Mark caught up to her on his horse. Trees and farms passed with blinding speed as they shot through the countryside by the light of the full moon. Goliath knew where they were going even if Sally was less confident. Once they got closer to the city, she was sure she would be able to find her way.

252

Chapter 50

Jane barely touched her breakfast.

She pushed the eggs around her plate and nibbled a piece of buttered toast fresh from the hearth, its smoky flavor lost on her.

Her brothers were arguing again, tugging each other's shirts and pulling tufts of red hair. "He hit me!" one of them cried. When they were in motion, even Jane could barely tell them apart.

"Boys," Hereford warned. "Behave yourselves, or I shall give all your chocolate to Jane."

Gaping at her with matching flushed, freckled faces, they reluctantly separated, pouting over their upturned plates, the tablecloth asunder.

Jane lifted the little dish haughtily to her lips and raised her eyebrows at them over the rim.

This morning's chocolate tasted of chalk. Her mind filled with plots, she little care for her food. She persevered with the chocolate, knowing she would need it to warm her for her walk.

A maid came in and began to clear the table. Jane raised the back of her hand to her head in a little swoon. "My word, my head aches all of the sudden. May I be excused to my room?"

Paying her little attention as he rose to escape himself, Hereford replied, "Of course. Shall I send Greta with a tonic?"

"No, Father, that won't be necessary. I will only lie down for a little while."

"Very well," he replied over his shoulder as he walked into the hallway.

As soon as he had left, the boys started fighting again. Jane rolled her eyes and went up the stairs to her room.

After waiting several moments to be sure no one was coming, she went into her closet and retrieved her mother's trunk, removing the blue dress from the bottom with a smile.

Jane carelessly tugged the laces at her back, shimmying out of her slim-fitting ivory morning dress. Standing in her corset and shift, she reverently took the blue dress from the bed and slipped it over her head, delighting in the feel of the smooth velvet against her skin. She pulled it down over her hips and shook the dust off the skirt.

It fit perfectly.

Rather than laces, the back of the dress fastened with a neat row of tiny buttons that started below her waist and traced a straight line up her spine, ending in a low V at her shoulder blades. It was very daring. Jane reached her hands behind her back and began to fasten the buttons, one by one, as far as she could reach. Irritatingly enough, she could not quite grasp the highest two.

Jane threw her hair over her shoulder with a swish. Two buttons didn't matter to her. She was feeling a little daring herself, and her hair was likely to cover it anyway.

Picking up a pair of silk walking shoes with short heels in one hand, Jane glanced at herself in the mirror. The deep blue of the gown emphasized the blue tones in her pale skin and the stormy depths of her eyes. In contrast, her hair was fiery bright.

Satisfied that she was quite irresistible, Jane tucked her hair behind her ear and headed for the door.

The hallway was silent. Through the window at the end of the hallway, Jane noticed a black carriage stopped outside the house.

Had Lord Somerton come to call? If he was here, she may be summoned, and then they would find her missing.

Wrinkling her nose in distaste, she tiptoed to the top of the stairs, and listened.

Silence. Raised voices. A rumble of furniture. The door to Hereford's office burst open and Somerton stormed out, his long strides eating up the length of the foyer. "Jane!"

Where was her father?

Somerton stepped to the base of the stairs, his heels clicking across the black and white tiles.

Jane saw him coming and rushed to the far end of the hallway, praying he did not see her. She didn't know what he was playing at, but it made her blood run cold.

Somerton said nothing more, but waited, listening.

Hereford stumbled out of his office and shouted, "Jane! Do not come down!"

Jane heard a smack and a crash. Her father was being assaulted!

Running the length of the hall, Jane slipped down the servants' staircase into the kitchen to where the footmen and servants were eating an early lunch. They looked up at her panicked face in shock. "Father is being attacked! Somebody help him!"

Pausing only a moment, Bennett, Julian, and a stable hand rushed out of kitchen, the rest of the servants following closely behind to watch or offer assistance. The kitchen cleared of people, Jane looked out into the garden in terror, searching for a place to hide until the commotion was over. Spying the storage pantry open, she considered ducking inside, but disliked the thought of being trapped.

The garden was empty and perfectly quiet. If she could make it to the maze, she could wait in the forest until he was gone.

With a last look behind her, Jane quietly opened the door and darted for the maze.

She knew the way through it by heart, easily turning right, then left, then right again, passing the fountain at the center to escape the other side.

Once she passed the tree line, the forest was altogether different. Trees loomed above her, casting menacing shadows over the forest floor even in the bright light of the morning. No time to feel frightened, Jane ran as fast as she could through the undergrowth, her breath coming in hard, painful puffs. She pushed low branches away from her hair, her skirt tangling in brambles. Unable to keep the pace, she ran for an enormous oak at the edge of a pond and hid behind it, pressing her face against the trunk.

Trying to slow her breath, Jane listened, heard nothing, and glanced back toward the house. She could barely see it now. She would wait for as long as she could before returning, and would try to sneak back up to her room without her father seeing the dress.

Praying silently for her father's safety, Jane sighed.

Hearing a twig break behind her, Jane whipped around and was grabbed by an enormous man. She screamed as he threw her over his shoulder, and carried her further into the woods.

Jane kicked wildly and hit his back as hard as she could, screaming as they went. In a matter of minutes, they came upon a narrow road, and Jane was shocked to see Somerton's carriage stopped there, horses at the ready.

As they approached, Somerton threw open the door from inside and greeted her with a smile. "Good morning, darling."

The large man set her down on the ground and tied her hands together. He tossed her into the carriage and shut the door behind her.

Jane screamed as loud as she was able, the sound echoing through the trees and setting a tree of birds into flight.

"Scream all you like, I want them to hear you."

Jane glared at him with contempt.

Somerton smiled at her across the carriage, and his smile did not reach his eyes. "Come now, Jane, it won't be so very bad. You will be a countess. Isn't that what you wanted?"

"I will never marry you!"

Somerton slapped her hard. He loomed over her, and Jane recoiled from the rage in his eyes. "You will. You will obey me in this and all things. I have taken and broken better women than you. By the time I am done with you, you won't remember your own name. Your lover will be dead, and I will be your lord."

Jane knit her eyebrows together. "Lover?"

Somerton slapped her again. "Don't play coy with me! My brother, Nicholas, or Mr. Virtue, as he is calling himself—virtue, ha!—is being hanged this very day for highway robbery. Didn't they tell you?" He gave an ugly laugh.

Jane fought against her ropes. "Your brother? What are you talking about? He's only a tutor, for pity's sake!"

"He is a usurper and I will not let him take what is mine."

Jane sat back in her seat, her bound hands in her lap, really seeing Somerton for the first time. Clearly mad, he was nearly foaming at the mouth. "What do you mean to do with me?"

"Why, I mean to marry you, my dear." He laughed his ugly laugh as the carriage pulled up in front of a grand house and stopped.

The door opened and the large man pulled her out, throwing

her over his shoulder once more. Jane looked up and around to see a long, paved street of grand houses, but did not see anything she recognized. She screamed as she was taken into the house, pounding the man's huge back as they ascended the stairs.

The house was empty of servants, and every surface was covered in white cloth. "Where are you taking me?"

He did not answer, but led the way into a bedroom suite. The large man dropped her onto a high bed draped in green curtains and left the room.

Sitting beside her on the bed, Somerton stroked her cheek with his cold fingers. "You are most lovely, Jane. I'm afraid I have a prior engagement I must attend, but I will enjoy you later, you can be sure of that."

Clenching her hands together into a large fist, Jane bent her elbows and punched him as hard as she could.

Somerton raised a hand to his face. He smiled at her, revealing a row of teeth, red with blood. He shoved her casually to her back and stood.

"There's no use in getting impatient, darling, I'm afraid I really must be off. After all, it is not every day one gets to attend a good hanging."

Jane screamed as he locked the door. She listened helplessly against the wood as he retreated down the stairs, whistling.

Chapter 51

Looking down at the crowd from the cart, Nick wondered how it had come to this.

Scores of people filled the stalls around Tyburn, none of them knowing who he was and few of them caring. Some people had packed picnic baskets and were sitting on the ground at the front of the stalls within throwing distance of the gallows. He had no coin to pay them, but if he was lucky, one of them might tug his legs if he lingered.

The horse stopped at the gates and he was led off the cart and slowly along the path through the crowd toward the looming gallows. It didn't matter that he had not committed the crime he was accused of. He was guilty of highway robbery and highwaymen were seldom given trials. He had always feared this day would come.

He struggled to remain dignified as he approached his fate. He did not look at the crowd. If he saw the faces of any of the lads, he did not trust himself not to weep openly.

Sally would be halfway to Paris by now, and Mark would never make it back in time. Maybe he would stay with her. At least she would not be alone.

She was finally safe. Arthur did not know she lived. She would sail over the Channel and in the vastness of the continent, she would have her freedom. He only wished he could be with her.

Hearing the hammering of his coffin in the distance, Nick thought of Mark and wished he could have said goodbye.

As he reached the gallows, he climbed into the cart and they turned him to face the crowd and the hangman lowered a thick rope around his neck. In the heat of the summer, it was almost warm. He would not think of what was to come.

"Last words?" the Ordinary asked.

Nick leaned toward him, only to be jerked back to his position beneath the rope. "There is a girl being held against her will at Somerton House in St. James Square. Her name is Lady Jane Ramsey. You have to save her."

The Ordinary wrinkled his nose in disbelief. As he announced his sentence, the hangman cleared his throat insistently.

Nick looked at him weakly.

"Tilt your head forward."

"What?"

"I'm not speaking. Look away. Tilt your head forward, and play dead."

Chapter 52

Slipping inside the East Gate, Sally saw the crowd gathered around the empty gallows, and it was as if a wraith had driven the breath from her body. She shivered and drew her hood closer around her throat, feeling the icy winds of Claude's January execution in spite of the summer's dying heat.

The crowd was smaller this time, though no less bloodthirsty. *Who didn't enjoy a good hanging, after all?* Sally had known she would be seen, weaving through the fetid throng as they bayed for the blood of Nicodemus Virtue, disgraced tutor and terror of Hyde Park.

She had known she would be seen, and she depended upon it, preparing herself for the stage with a cold rage burning through her veins, every heavy-handed brush of ceruse administered with grim determination that this, her final appearance, would be the most important—indeed, the most memorable—of her short life. Short it would be, as well. As she closed in on the spotless black frock coat at the center of the crowd, not so near the aisle that he would be in any danger of being spat upon, Sally breathed a silent sigh of relief.

She had him.

Arthur Rothschild was his name, it so happened. Roth had been corrupted into Wrath, a fitting moniker so maddeningly close to the reality that she might have laughed. He must have cherished the mistake. An earl in the end, with a residence in St. James Square and blood as blue as you please, who enslaved, tortured, and murdered harlots because it was dreadfully diverting.

Not only harlots, but Wrath had cast out his own half-brother, capturing and arranging today's hasty execution after Nick had been driven to highway robbery to feed himself.

The cart arrived and Sally stifled a sob as Nick was led up the aisle in shackles. His head was held high, defiantly handsome in the face of barbaric cruelty. He did not look at the crowd. Believing she was safely hidden on the coast, he had no reason to look into the faces of those who would see him dead.

Sally took a deep breath and focused on the task at hand. It may cost her life and what was left of her soul, but if she had anything to say about it, Nick would not die today.

Glancing at the hangman, she felt a twinge of panic. He was not a man she recognized, and yet Mark had assured her he was on their side. She prayed that he was right.

As Nick reached the gallows, she heard the sharp whack of a hammer on pine and turned her head to see the undertaker pound an errant nail into the open coffin. He wore a wide-brimmed hat that obscured his face from the crowd. Hefting the hammer, he braced the joint with his left hand and struck the nail twice, three times, and Sally saw the glint of gold as the sun caught the ring on his left forefinger.

She smiled.

Her heart beat wildly as the hangman lifted the rope over Nick's head and adjusted it around his strong neck. Nick turned to the judge to say his last words. She could not hear the words he said over the pounding of the blood in her veins, except for one.

"...Jane..."

Sally caught the short name before it was lost on the wind and her heart shattered.

Jane had mattered after all.

The hangman put a hand on Nick's shoulder and although he didn't say a word that Sally could hear, she saw Nick's face change and she knew it was time.

She hoped her sacrifice would save him, and she hoped he would by happy long after she was dead. He was the truest friend she had, and she loved him with every piece of her broken heart. The sacrifice was for him.

The vengeance, that was for Sally.

She pulled the little stiletto blade from the secret pocket of her famous green dress and gripped it silently in her palm. She allowed the cape to fall open, revealing her ghastly white décolletage and the shimmering, blood-stained velvet beneath. Stepping behind Wrath, she snaked one white painted arm around his chest and pressed the tip of the blade between his ribs.

He stiffened instinctively, believing he was being robbed. At the moment the rope was pulled, dragging Nick into the air, Sally plunged the knife deftly into Wrath's black heart. As his weight fell against her, she leaned into his neck and whispered into his ear. "Silly bitch. You can't escape me."

Sally let the hood fall from her face, revealing ghostly pale skin and her painted black eyes, her hair released in wild waves over her shoulders. She heard a high-pitched scream, followed by several more as the crowd turned away from the spectacle of the execution to watch Somerton leaking his life's blood into the Tyburn mud. As spectators rushed to his side, Sally ducked, pulled up her hood, and walked briskly through the ensuing riot.

A young blond man separated her from the crowd and she recognized Harry. He had made it out of the gaol.

Harry winked at her before striding headlong into the crowd in the opposite direction, shouting at the top of his voice, "The Green Devil! 'Twas the murderous ghost of the Green Devil! Disappeared before my very eyes! Dragged him back to hell!"

Nick quite forgotten, men, women, and children nearly trampled Sally in their haste to escape the park. Charlie was back there somewhere, no doubt looking for her, and this unsavory thought spurred her heels toward Whitehall. She heard Mark hammering the lid onto Nick's coffin and she steeled herself.

There was one more thing she had to do.

Chapter 53

Running down the paved alleyway to the back entrance of the Opera House as fast as his short legs would carry him, Hereford cried, "Jane! Jane!"

Struggling to catch his breath, he shoved the side door open with the strength of a much younger man.

"Allow me, my lord." Julian slid past him into the kitchens, holding his pistol at arm's length. Hereford followed close behind, hastily adjusting his wig.

Julian stopped short and raised a finger to his lips. Hereford held his breath as Julian pushed open the door to the larder. Finding nothing inside apart from a murky looking jar and half a dozen rats, Julian curled his lip in disgust and moved on.

Hereford withdrew a scented handkerchief from his coat and held it over his mouth, choking on a cough. The whole vicinity had a rancid, sour odor that he could not immediately place. It was clear that the kitchen had been disused for some time.

Cautiously following Julian through the narrow hallway beneath layer upon layer of tattered curtains hanging unevenly to disguise the path to the filthy kitchen, he emerged into the bright light of the great room. While the house had glittered with candlelight in the evenings, a veritable den of smoke and temptation, by day, the squalor was revolting.

Every surface was covered in a thin, sticky film. The floor had not been cleaned in recent memory and boot tracks crisscrossed it this way and that, leaving crazy patterns over the stage and up the staircase. Thick dark mold crept up the walls from the floor boards, disappearing into wet pockets of damp partially obscured by ancient curtains draping the walls in a garish red.

Among the filth and debris of discarded wine bottles and empty casks were half a dozen sleeping women.

Thin, dirty wretches with filthy, matted hair slept in various positions at the foot of the stage, and beneath the stairs. A far cry from the goddess he had met at the play earlier in the week,

Camille was there in her new red dress, shivering as she slept beneath the loose edge of a curtain hanging from the wall.

They did not stir as he and Julian walked softly past; it was well into the afternoon and they slept the heavy sleep of the dead.

Creeping up the stairs, Julian led the way with his pistol, checking the rooms for Jane and finding nothing more than poverty and filth. There was no sign of his daughter.

Reaching the last door on the right, Hereford felt a chill run up his spine as he realized it was Sally's room. Julian had not been there with him and knew nothing of its previous occupant, so he unceremoniously trudged into the empty room.

The stillness of it set Hereford at unease. It was clear that no one had used the room recently; the window stood open, the chipped wash basin filled with cold water and shriveled flower petals floating limply on the surface. A drying bouquet lay discarded on the floor, the flowers brown and soft, smelling of musk and decay. Julian approached the dressing table and raised a clear green bottle to his nose, recoiling at the sweet scent. "This is not wine, my lord."

"She liked gin," Hereford said, unsure where to look.

"It is not gin, my lord. Unless I miss my guess, this is wormwood."

"Wormwood? That sounds foul."

"'Tis." He set down the bottle. "It causes madness. It's a kind of poison."

Hereford turned to spy the peephole in the wall and immediately felt sick to his stomach. Wrath had told him she had been willing.

A dark spot on the bed caught his eye. Emboldened, Hereford threw aside the heavy curtain. He bellowed at the sight. Most of the thin mattress was covered in a deep stain of darkest brown that could only be blood. Sally's green slippers lay discarded at the foot of the bed. Whatever had happened, she had left without her shoes.

"St. James," he said.

"I beg your pardon, my lord?"

"The pamphlet said she was found in St. James Square. How did she get there without shoes?"

"Pamphlet, my lord? You are not referring to that Sally Green?"

"Yes," he said, seeing the room in daylight for the first time. "This was her room."

Julian sucked in a breath through his teeth. "Nasty business. It doesn't look like she got very far, does it?"

"No, indeed."

Julian turned from the bed in disgust. "They're saying she was murdered, you know. Beaumont's dead, to be sure, but they never found her body, and there's no proof it was suicide. No one saw it. Susie from the kitchen went to Virtue's hanging today, and says there are a hundred people who swear blind that they saw her ghost strike Somerton dead. Nasty business," he repeated.

Murdered.

Hereford's blood ran cold. Sally had been his favorite, certainly, but it had never crossed his mind that she was not a willing participant, let alone that she was in any danger. That Somerton could keep women in such conditions, that he could poison them and drive them to madness or suicide; it sickened him to his very bones.

His heart sank. The signs had been there, but he had not wished to see them. He had been prepared, for the sake of vice, to relinquish his only daughter, his dearest, darling Jane, to a madman.

Wordlessly, Hereford sunk to his knees on the floor, and wept.

Hesitantly placing a hand on his shoulder, Julian said, "Take heart, my lord. We will find her. Somerton is dead and he cannot harm her."

"What if he already has?"

"Come, my lord. We will keep looking."

Julian patiently led him from the horrors of Sally's empty room down the stairs to the great room. Hereford did not attempt to step quietly, and the women began to sit up, silently awaiting instruction.

Hereford cleared his throat and dried his eyes. "Wrath is dead," he said simply. "You are free to go or stay as you please."

One by one, the women stood, looking to each other for

265

reassurance. Neither Wrath nor Charlie was there, and finding them gone, they began to run. One ran up the stairs and began whispering the news into the occupied rooms, while others took what they could carry and left.

The whole house was empty in a matter of minutes, and Hereford and Julian were left alone, standing on the bottom stair.

Chapter 54

Wood splintered and creaked as the lid was pried off Nick's pine coffin. A sliver of late afternoon sunlight broke through, followed by the shock of full daylight as the lid was torn off completely and discarded. Nick sat up, gripping his throat and sucking in as much fresh air as his lungs could hold.

His eyes adjusted to the light as he focused on Mark's grinning face.

"You made it," he said. "Will was worried here, on accounta' you looking dead and all, but I told him, our Nick is gonna pull through."

Nick looked around himself to see Will sitting beside the coffin, looking at him sadly.

"I'm alive," he rasped, feeling the pain of his bruised throat. "How did you manage that?"

Mark shrugged and gave a crooked smile. "Ketch owed me a favor. Got his shackles taken off for him."

As Nick began to climb out of the coffin, he was hit with a wave of dizziness and sat back down. "The hangman was in Newgate?"

"Where else do you think they'd find them?"

Nick didn't have an answer for him. He gingerly touched his aching neck, not quite believing his luck. "They should be dissecting me about now."

"Lucky for us a student stepped in to collect your body. Had to fend off some boys from the College of Physicians, but he got you in the end."

On cue, Harry emerged from behind the coffin lid wearing Nick's old clothes from university, grinning.

"Harry, you got out!"

Harry laughed and threw an arm around Nick, helping him out of the coffin. "Thanks to you and Lady Virtue."

"Lady Virtue? Mark, you didn't get married, did you? How long was I in that cellar?"

Mark laughed and handed Nick a crisp pamphlet. "See for yourself. Came out yesterday."

Nick looked down at the pamphlet in his hands. It featured a likeness of Sally apparently dressed as the Virgin Mary beside the headline, "*Ladye Vertue, the angel of Newgate.*"

"She's all anyone talked about in gaol. She's a hero."

Nick looked around the room, missing the one person he most wanted see. "If you're here, where is she?"

Mark's smile faded. "We needed a diversion."

Nick nodded. "So?"

"Sally was the diversion." Mark took a deep breath and began to explain, "Jack came and found us and told us what had happened, and before we know it, she'd taken a horse and gone back for you. She saved your life. The diversion was all her idea. We didn't know what she had in mind, exactly..."

Nick's vision began to blur around the edges and he gripped the sides of the coffin. "Mark. What happened?"

"She killed Arthur."

"She what?"

"Ran him through, right in front of everyone, and snuck out in the melee."

"Where is she?"

Will cleared his throat. "We don't know. We looked all over for her, and she hasn't come back yet."

Nick knew what kind of danger Sally was in. For the second time that day, he was terrified. "How could you let her do that? They thought she was dead."

"There wasn't a lot of letting involved." Mark shook his head. "She was determined she was gonna save you, and she did. In any case, they still think she's dead."

"What?"

"It was brilliant, really," said Will. "She put on that awful green dress and made herself up like a dead harlot. Then Harry starts shouting that he saw her dragging Arthur's ghost to hell, and they believed it. Everyone in London's saying it was a ghost what done it."

"You mean to tell me," Nick started, "that Sally murdered a peer and is roaming the streets dressed up like a dead harlot?"

Will shrugged. "It sounds bad when you put it that way, but yeah."

Nick resolutely climbed out of the coffin. Grabbing his black cloak and tricorn from his peg on the wall, he dressed quickly and prepared to leave.

Mark stopped him. "Stay here. You're supposed to dead, remember?"

"We have to find her." Nick sidestepped him.

"She'll come back." Scurrying into his path, Mark pleaded, "Nick, you were just hanged for highway robbery. You can't go out looking like a highway robber."

Barely pausing to answer, Nick replied, "If she's out there, I have to find her."

Sighing, Mark conceded. "Let's split up. Will, check the park. Harry, you stay here. I'll keep an eye on this one."

Nick grabbed Mark's arm. "Wait! When they took me from the cellar, I heard a scream. He's taken another girl. She may still be at the house."

Grabbing his pistol, Mark said, "We'll start there."

An hour later, Nick found himself looking up into the imposing face of his childhood home once again.

He knocked on the door with the enormous brass knocker and waited. Mark fidgeted beside him. "It's a bit strange being back, innit?"

Nick nodded. "When I left here this morning, Arthur was dragging me to my execution."

"Not gonna do that this time, is he?"

Minutes passed before the door was slowly opened by Edward Rothschild's favorite, ancient servant, Mr. Crowley.

"Good afternoon, Crowley. May I beg a word?"

Crowley stood in the doorway, blinking his watery eyes.

Mark rocked back on his heels, his hands in his pockets. "Crowley." He smiled. "It's Nick, and Mark Virtue. Remember us? Nick went to university, and I was always building things in the garden? Mum worked in the kitchen?"

Crowley's eyes didn't leave Nick's face, and he found this disconcerting. Nick smiled nervously. "Crowley, we've come to ask if you've seen some girls."

"Master Nicholas," he said, finally. "You were dead. That's why you didn't come."

"I beg your pardon?"

"Lord Arthur told us you had died just after Lord Edward, God rest his soul. That was why you didn't come."

Nick took off his hat. "I wanted to come to the funeral, very badly, but Arthur made it clear I was not welcome."

Crowley shook his grey head. "Not that. You never came to claim your share. Why wouldn't you do that if you weren't dead?"

Nick looked at Mark, confused. Mark offered a smug smile and raised his eyebrows.

Crowley frowned in puzzlement. "Some big chap came around here earlier and told me that Lord Arthur had been murdered and then he took the candlesticks. Is he really dead?"

Mark nodded vigorously as Nick replied, "I'm afraid so, Crowley. I'm sorry for your loss."

"Sorry, hell," Crowley spat. "It's all yours now. You had better come in out of the cold, Lord Nicholas."

Nick heard Mark snickering to himself as he followed Crowley inside the mansion. The foyer was dusty from misuse, and the enormous hallways were woefully silent. When he had been a child here, the house had been full of light, music, and laughter. He half expected his mother to walk in from the kitchens, carrying a tray of coffee and Lord Edward's favorite cakes.

Crowley led them into the kitchen and offered them wine. Nick gently took the bottle from his fragile hands, led him to a chair, and poured glasses for all three of them. "You said that everyone has left?"

"Everyone," Crowley repeated. "Of course most had gone already, when they could."

Crowley had seemed old when Nick had been a child. Now he looked older still, and Nick wondered how he was able to work. "Who looks after you?" Nick asked.

"Oh, I get by. I cook, when Lord Arthur leaves money behind, but it's been ages since I could get to the means to tend to this place properly."

Nick looked around the kitchen from the dusty workspaces to the empty cupboards. "He didn't feed you? Pay you?"

270

Crowley leaned back in his chair and sipped his wine. "He was never here, you see, and he was a right villain. I beg your pardon for saying so, my lord, but you were always the good one."

Nick sighed. Crowley was obviously confused. He would have to take him back to the warehouse, and find a way to look after him somehow. Maybe he could come to the coast with him and Sally, when he found her. He hated the thought of this poor old man left to rot in an empty house with no food. "Crowley, you don't have to call me that. You can call me Nick, remember?"

"Not anymore, my lord. It wouldn't be proper."

Taking a sip of his wine, Nick tried to be patient. He obviously hadn't seen any young ladies running about the house, but he couldn't leave him in this state. "Crowley, I need to go looking for my lady, but I promise you, I won't leave you alone here. I'll come back as soon as I can, and I'll find a way to look after you."

"I know you will, Lord Nicholas." Crowley closed his eyes slowly and nodded. "You're the good one."

"Crowley, why –"

"God's blood, Nick," Mark interjected. "He's trying to tell you that you're next in line but you're not hearing it."

"That's impossible." Nick dismissed the ridiculous statement with a shake of his head. "I really must be going."

Crowley opened his pale blue eyes and frowned, "It is quite possible, my lord. As Lord Edward's second son, the title, the lands, and holdings now belong to you. Didn't he tell you?"

Nick looked in shock at Mark, who had crossed his arms over his chest. "I told him," Mark said. "But did he listen?"

Shaking his head, Nick asked, "I can accept that Lord Edward might have been my father, but wouldn't the estate pass to a legitimate heir? A cousin, perhaps?"

Leaning forward conspiratorially, Crowley explained, "They were papists, you see, aside from the fact that your mother was of a much lower station, of course. They were married in secret, and I should know. I was there. I can assure you that you are quite legitimate, my lord, and it was Lord Edward's fondest wish that you would run the estate. He left you half of it when he passed."

Half of it? No wonder Arthur had been so determined to see him dead. Nick looked at Mark. "You knew."

Mark shrugged. "I suspected. I didn't know for certain. But Christ, Nick, you don't half look like him."

"Why wouldn't they tell me?"

Crowley raised a gnarled finger and explained, "By the time you were born, Arthur was nearly grown and already a rotten little shit. Your mother, God rest her soul, wanted you two to grow up together as common boys, so you wouldn't turn out like him. They left you a good portion, too, Mister Virtue. Lord Edward always liked you."

Mark's eyebrows shot into his hairline and he laughed.

Nick sighed and took a long drink of his wine. All this time, when he had been starving, working long hours for an imbecile, certain he would never be able to provide for Sally in the way that he wanted to, he'd been part of the nobility. Neither his mother nor his father, as he now knew him to be, thought to tell him while they were able.

Now that Arthur was dead and the threat on his life had been removed, he would be free to live out his life as Nicholas Rothschild.

None of it mattered if he couldn't find her.

He cleared his throat. "Thank you for telling me, Crowley. I promise you, I will look after you and I will be sure you have everything you deserve. I must leave now to look for my lady, but I will return. You haven't seen her, have you? A pretty girl, about this tall, possibly wearing a green dress? Or another girl, red hair, about the same height?"

"No, my lord, I haven't seen any girls around here." Crowley set down his empty cup. "Shall I bring around the carriage?"

"No, that won't be necessary." He smiled gently. Turning to Mark, he said, "I need to get to the forest before it gets dark. I'll take one of the horses. Would you stay here in case she comes back?"

Mark, grinning ear to ear, replied, "Of course, Lord Nick." He winked. "I'll just pick out my room, shall I?"

Nick stood and shrugged. "Just make sure Crowley gets a good dinner in him." He lowered his voice, "Jane might yet be here. I'm not certain Crowley would have heard her. I expect she is out of harm's way now, but we must find her and return her home. Will you check the rooms?"

"Of course."

Chapter 55

When Jane had wished to be kidnapped, this was not what she had in mind.

Lying in the dusty bed, Jane looked up at the green brocade canopy, listened, and waited.

It had been hours since Lord Somerton had disappeared and outside the diamond-paned glass, the sun was beginning to set. He would return before long, but she would be ready. Clutching the iron poker in her tied hands, she steeled herself. He might try to break her as he had threatened, but she would put up one hell of a fight.

At the sound of footsteps running up the stairs, Jane sat up, her skin prickling with goose bumps and her heart rising into her throat. This was it. She stood, swung the poker over her shoulder, and braced herself as the door burst open.

Jane swung the poker with all of her strength and missed as the man threw himself backward, the poker lodging into the hard oak door in a shower of splinters.

"Whoa! Wait!"

Jane tugged on the poker, trying in vain to remove it from the door. "Stay back!"

"I'm not here to hurt you." He threw up his hands. "Nick sent me."

"Nick's dead. Who are you?"

"I'm Mark," he said from a safe distance. "I'm his brother."

"How many brothers does he have?" She snarled.

"One less now." He shrugged. "Really, Nick's fine. He sent me to save you."

Jane raised an eyebrow. "You're here to save me?"

Mark doffed his hat. "Such as I am. You look like you're doing a fair job of it yourself."

He cautiously ducked under the iron shaft of the poker into the soft light of the bedroom, and Jane gasped. "You!"

Mark's eyes widened in recognition. "Hello!"

Her voice faltering, Jane demanded, "Where's Somerton? Is this part of his plan?"

"I daresay it's not. He's dead."

Jane sat heavily on the bed. "Dead."

"Dead." He smiled cheerfully.

"You seem awfully happy about it. If you are Nick's brother, isn't he your brother as well?"

"Not mine. Didn't like him."

Jane peered around him, checking for any villains that might by lurking in the hallway. Finding none, she regarded Mark with suspicion.

"He said Nick was–is–a footpad."

Mark shrugged as he took her hands in his, easily untying the ropes. "I reckon he is."

Jane's hands began to warm beneath his touch. She was close enough to his downturned face that she could feel his breath. "Are you a footpad?"

He looked up at her with arch of one golden eyebrow, seemingly unfazed by their close proximity. "I prefer rogue. Scoundrel, even. I--"

Hands free, Jane slid her arms around his neck and silenced him with a kiss.

"My hero." Jane smiled against his lips.

Mark deepened the kiss, drinking the sweetness of her mouth, half of her dress' little buttons undone before he stopped short, and pulled away.

"I should take you home. You're alone in a house with a strange man pawing at you. You don't need that."

Feeling very daring indeed, Jane loosed the remaining buttons and let the dress pool to the floor.

Chapter 56

Darting between alleyways, Sally clutched her thin black cape to her throat and kept to the shadows. Keeping an even, swift, pace, she knew no one would notice a lone harlot making her way toward town in a torn dress. As she passed the kitchen entrance of the King's Arms on Maiden Lane, a boy hung an iron lantern above the door, illuminating the blood stains on her dress for one horrible moment.

Sally swirled the cape around her skirts in a halfhearted attempt to conceal the stain, knowing her best chance of making it to Whitehall without capture was to not draw undue attention to herself, and to move quickly. She had avoided the riot by hiding in an empty coal bin until it had passed, and from there took her time slipping down alleys in every direction in an effort to throw any would-be pursuers off of her trail. Charlie was still alive, and although she didn't know if his devotion to Wrath was strong enough to drive him to kill her, she would not take any risks that might prevent her from seeing the King.

A rat scurried across her path. Every meaningless sound became terrible to her, every hoof's clatter a sure sign that the black horse of her nightmares was closing in on her at last. How could it not smell the death she had left in her wake?

Well and good. I am ready.

But first…

After what felt like hours of manic sneaking, hiding in plain sight, Sally finally spotted the spires of Whitehall. It would hardly do to knock on the front door; tonight it would have to be the garden.

She kept to the shadows of the high cobbled walls until she spied an accommodating yew branch creeping over the edge. Glancing over her shoulder, her view was obscured by her breath fogging the slowly setting darkness. The branch curled into a crevice in the stones, forming a kind of loop that might be used as a handle, a stirrup, or a noose.

Her heart thundered in her chest. She took a deep breath, and jumped for it.

Her fingertips scraped it on her first attempt, her soft leather shoes slapping the cold ground as she landed, rather too loudly. She held her breath for a moment, and listened.

Satisfied no one had heard her, she tried the branch once more. This time she caught it, the soft wood snaking further over the wall at the sudden pull of her weight. She swung her left arm to grip the branch, her right immediately relieved of the full burden of holding her suspended above the ground. Struggling to find a foothold, she kicked against the wall and found none. Frustrated, she braced her feet against the wall and pulled the branch with all of her strength until suddenly, she was climbing.

At last nearing the top, Sally crept up the branch until she was able to swing her legs over the side to sit above the tangle of a yew path, their branches grown together in a living canopy for lovers, or intruders, in her case. Looking down into the thicket, the ground beneath the yew path had a sinister darkness from the total absence of moonlight. There was no telling how far she would have to fall to reach the ground.

Sitting at the top of the wall, she closed her eyes, slowed her breath, and again, she listened.

The garden was quiet, and far enough from the noise of town that the loudest sound she heard was the beating of her own heart in her ears, a frantic drumming over the wind's eerie howling through the branches below.

Spotting a gap in the branches she hoped was large enough to fit through, Sally inched her feet into it, and flung the hem of her skirt through it. Gripping the branch across her lap, she lowered herself into the darkness and found herself kicking against air.

She held her breath and let go.

Mercifully, the ground was not as far away as she had feared. She dusted her gown as she stood, feeling soft, sore patches of flesh on her arm and hip where bruises might form if she lived long enough to see them.

Her eyes adjusted to the darkness of the yew path and she was heartened to see the night's first stars glittering through the branches above. Sally walked down the meandering trail, past secluded benches and small clearings where musicians might play. Listening for any unwanted company, she found the gardens quiet save for the soft buzz of the season's last insects and the occasional squirrel rustling through fallen leaves.

The path joined a larger, central path sparsely lit with hanging lanterns. Leaving the path to move among the trees, Sally followed the side of the path until it met the courtyard. There was a guard posted at a small door partially disguised by a trellis of ivy and night blooming flowers. The King had taste, to be sure, but in this respect he was not a subtle man. She hid herself beneath an apple tree with a clear view of the trellis, and waited.

Minutes, hours passed. The cold of the night sunk into her bones and she felt hunger for the first time since she had heard Nick had been captured. Heavy with fruit, the tree's branches beckoned to her, daring her to take. The flesh of the fruit shone smooth and blood red, even in the darkness, and she wanted, so badly, to eat.

After being so careful not to disturb a single branch or fallen leaf, Sally would not risk drawing attention to herself by crunching her way through an apple, no matter how delicious they looked.

And yet, it might be her last.

Carefully picking a fallen apple from the ground, she rubbed it on the fabric of her cloak until it was clean, and slipped it into her pocket.

At last, the trellis swung open and the King's procurer emerged. Sally had never heard his name, but she recognized him from the theatres. There wasn't a harlot worth her salt who didn't know precisely who he was. He would be gone for a while, but was not known to take all night at his task.

Her timing had to be perfect.

She waited until he had been gone perhaps twenty, thirty minutes, counting seconds in her head, before she prepared herself to make her move. Re-pinning her hair, she removed a twig from the tangles. She straightened her dress and tried to conceal the stains with her cloak by holding it low under her breasts, fuller since her escape, trusting the guard to look no further. Pulling the neckline of the battered dress down over her right shoulder, she transformed herself into Sally Green once more.

As she sauntered up the path toward the trellis, Sally swung her hips lazily and held her head high. The guard saw her approach, and immediately stood at attention. Sally flashed him a slow, cheeky smile.

He looked behind her and around the garden, searching for the King's man. Finding her alone, he demanded, "Who are you?"

Sally sighed, leaning against the trellis, the ivy tangling gently in her hair. "I'm Rosey. Who are you?" She borrowed the name without a second thought. When Sally had seen her in Newgate, she had been half-crazed with syphilis. She doubted Rosey would mind.

"Where's Chiffinch?" His voice cracked as he spoke.

So he was new to his post. *Good.*

"He's just picking up one of my friends." Sally smirked. Arching her back against the trellis, she looked up at the guard through lowered lashes and asked, "Are you going to let me in?"

Without another word, the guard cleared his throat and opened the hidden door.

Sally smiled at him as she brushed past toward the narrow back staircase, hearing the door shut firmly behind her. Shaking, she paused to straighten her dress and cover herself properly with the cloak. It was good to know that even covered in blood and filth and wearing the makeup of a ghoul, she still had the ability to make men forget themselves.

The staircase was covered in a long rug the color of claret, and was invitingly lit by a series of small sconces leading the way to the King's chambers. As a favorite of the working classes and the lesser nobility, Sally had never been chosen to keep the King company, but unlike those who had entered into the profession willingly, she had never the slightest desire to see to anyone who had been chosen for her, regardless of who they were.

As she reached the top of the stairs, the sconces led around a sharp corner to a plain wooden door. She knew she was very likely going to her death, but she reminded herself why she was doing it. Chiffinch had been gone awhile now, and she wouldn't have much time. She took a deep breath and opened the door.

Chapter 57

Charles looked at the wraith curtseying before him, and his lips quirked in amusement.

When Chiffinch had left to discreetly procure him a woman, Sally Green was the last person Charles had expected to find in his chambers. She was young and beautiful, to be sure, and though many of his paramours had come from the stages of Covent Garden, he was reasonably certain none of them were wanted for murder. There was also the fact that she was meant to be dead.

If Charles were to imagine a resurrected murderess running amok, as he seldom had occasion to do, Sally would not have been what immediately came to mind. Having washed her face into an altogether more lively hue at his request, he could see she was little more than a scared young woman. In spite of the ruined green dress, he could hardly imagine her as the voracious harlot so famous among the perverts and playhouses, let alone a bloodthirsty spirit risen from the grave. She looked up at him imploringly with her enormous, black-rimmed eyes, and brought to mind a perfectly harmless child.

"Have you come to kill me?" he asked, deadpan.

Sally started at the question. She was little more than a slip of a girl, and did not appear to be armed. She wrung her skirt in her hands, clearly nervous. "No, Sire."

Charles stood and nonchalantly draped a plush scarlet dressing gown around his lanky frame. "Hundreds of people claim to have seen you murder the Earl of Somerton this very afternoon. Do you deny it?"

Sally cleared her throat. "No, Sire. But I would tell you why I did it."

Charles raised his eyebrows in interest. He could guess why she'd done it. He'd had the misfortune of meeting the blackguard on a number of occasions and had been tempted to do him in himself. He poured two glasses of wine and offered one to Sally. "Perhaps some fortification is in order."

She accepted it hesitantly, her hand shaking.

Charles sank back into his favorite chair, sipping his wine.

Sally didn't move. He could see her trembling from across the room. She would drop that glass before long.

"Sit," he motioned to the empty chair across from his. "Drink."

She obeyed, sitting on the edge of the chair gingerly, as if expecting a trap.

Sally sipped her wine, involuntarily closing her eyes as she savored the taste. It was his favorite vintage, and it was unlikely that she had tasted any so fine. Her dress was in tatters and stained with what he could only assume was blood, but she appeared to be glowing with health and her shoes were new. Charles frowned, unsure what to make of the contrast.

"Please begin." He waved a hand. "I haven't heard a good story in ages."

"My name is Celeste Remi," she confided, her voice shaking, "and my story begins in France."

♠

Hours later, Sally paused for breath, taking a second sip of wine.

Charles held the empty decanter in his lap, little of the intense fascination he felt showing on his face. Dawn was fast approaching, and the room was filled with a cold, blue light, allowing him to see her gradually, shade by shade as the sun drew closer to the horizon. She was a pretty thing, tall for a girl with long limbs and raven hair. It was the look about her eyes that he noticed first.

He didn't need to see Sally's nose to know who she was.

The way she moved her hands was pure Minette, and as he watched them flutter, he missed his sister. Seeing Sally was a little bit like having her back.

Her skin was paler than the others, and she would be the eldest. He wondered who her mother was. "What happened next?" he asked her, resting his cheek against his knuckles.

"Your Majesty?"

281

He raised an eyebrow and prompted, not unkindly, "Our heroine frees her lover by murdering her tormenter, and then?"

Sally bowed her head in deference, kneeling on the checkered floor. "I have come to beg you to pardon Nicodemus Virtue, because he is an honorable man, and his crimes were not his own. He only took money that was owed to him, and he never hurt anybody. He—"

"Yes, I daresay," he interrupted. "But what of Sally Green?"

Although her voice cracked, she did not cry. "I have come to surrender myself to your justice. I murdered Arthur Rothschild for the crimes he committed against my person, and against many others like me, and I would do it again."

Charles did smile at her admission. She would attempt no pretty tears or pleas for mercy. She showed bravery he had seen in few, and he admired her for it. "Get up, get up."

Sally sat back into the chair, her heart showing in her eyes.

"Tell me, my dear, are there any other foes you believe Sally Green might take it upon herself to punish?"

"No, Sire." She shook her head. "She would have done away with them before coming to you."

Stifling a laugh, Charles composed his face into his best impression of a stern ruler. "Your honesty is quite refreshing. Allow me to beg your indulgence further; you say you only just discovered that Arthur Rothschild was half-brother to young Mr. Virtue. Were you aware that Mr. Virtue was legitimate?"

Sally sipped her wine. "No, Sire, Nicodemus is the illegitimate son of the elder Lord Somerton and his housekeeper."

Charles nodded sharply. "You believe this to be true?"

"Yes, Sire, Nicodemus told me himself, but I don't think he should be judged for the crimes of his brother; really, they couldn't be more different--"

"Celeste." Her eyes widened as he referred to her by her Christian name. He smiled at her gently. "The man you know as Nicodemus Virtue is Nicholas Rothschild, the legitimate son of Lord Edward Rothschild and his legal wife, his former housekeeper Lillian Page. He has been informed of his brother's death, and as he is the sole heir, I believe you will find him installed at Somerton House."

Tears sparkled in Sally's eyes as she raised her hand to her face in a sob. "I beg your pardon, Sire, but I cannot believe he would lie to me!"

Charles withdrew a monogrammed handkerchief from a drawer and gallantly offered it to her. "He was unaware. When he did not claim his share of the estate after his father passed, he was given up for dead, and was believed to be so until Arthur drew attention to the matter by forcing the execution without a trial. You see, he knew Nicholas could not have been tried for highway robbery as he is a peer, and as I'm sure you're aware, it is very difficult to convict a peer, no matter how dreadful his crimes may be."

Sally blinked, her mouth falling open in shock. "Nick's a peer?"

Charles nodded. "Quite so."

Sally swallowed the rest of her glass in one gulp.

Charles smiled. She was *definitely* his.

Sally delicately cleared her throat. "He is not in danger?"

"Quite the contrary, my dear," Charles assured her brightly. "As the new Earl of Somerton, he is very well situated, indeed."

Her shoulders sank and she let out a long sigh. "My thanks, Your Majesty. I am most relieved to hear he will come to no harm."

Whatever Charles had expected her to say, it was not that. He frowned. "And what of yourself, Celeste?"

Sally met his gaze with a startled expression, unsure of how to answer. She clearly still thought he was about to throw her into a dungeon somewhere. Surely she had some inkling…

Feeling mischievous, Charles tested her. "Did you ever discover the identity of your father?"

Sally regarded him carefully in the poor light of the chamber for a moment, and then she dropped her gaze to her hands. "No, Sire. I am told he was an Englishman who visited Chateau Lenormand the spring before I was born."

Chateau Lenormand. Twenty years had passed and he still remembered that bread. "Who was your mother?" he asked.

"Her name was Marie St-Jean, and she was a dairy maid."

Marie.

Charles took a deep breath. He remembered her, too. "You say that she has passed?"

"Yes, Sire. She was killed by her husband, Bertrand, when she bore a black-haired daughter."

After a long moment, Charles asked, "He is the other man you believe you have murdered?"

Sally did not look up. "Yes, Sire."

Charles longed for more wine, but was beginning to suspect it was time for coffee. "He beat you because you favor your father."

Sally sighed. "I wish I knew, Sire."

Charles almost laughed in disbelief. "You don't?"

Sally blinked in confusion, shaking her head slightly. "I never found him."

Charles took a breath. "You came here without any idea, fully expecting me to have you executed."

Sally paled at the mention of execution. She did not beg.

"You still do," he said, more to himself than to her. After a moment's consideration, he said, carefully, "Perhaps I can solve your great mystery. I passed through the Chateau that year. I knew your mother briefly. We were not sweethearts, precisely, but she was kind to me while I was there."

Sally sat stock-still, understanding dawning on her face.

"She was a good woman," Charles continued. "I am most grieved to hear of her fate, and of the many tragedies that have befallen you because of it. I would make amends in any way possible."

Of all the women he'd known, Charles had never seen such an expression. The girl looked as though she was torn between weeping and vomiting.

"You?" Her voice was little more than a squeak.

"Are you disappointed?"

Sally's eyelashes fluttered, sending a river of tears pouring down her cheeks. She wiped them away, embarrassed. "Are you certain?"

Charles bit back a laugh. "Quite. Someday soon I will introduce you to your siblings, and you'll see it."

"Siblings?"

"Many." He nodded toward her. "More every day. Bastards, the lot of them, but they do have their charm."

Sally gripped the arms of the chair. "That's why he never sent me here… he knew…"

"That I'd know you at once and have his head on a spike? I should think so."

Sally dropped her face into her hands, disbelieving.

Charles watched her with uncertainty, wondering if he'd said too much.

At last, she looked up. "A spike?"

"Oh, yes. I have a collection for just such a purpose." He almost smiled.

"You are too kind, Your Majesty." She almost laughed.

"Not at all," he dismissed. "Do you suppose young Somerton will still marry you, now that he has an estate to consider?"

Sally was caught off guard by the quick change of subject. "Sire?"

"Given your unhappy situation and your inability to bear children, do you think that he would?"

"I don't know," she said honestly. "The letter I found…he might love another."

"Impossible." Charles waved a hand. "And you? Would you still love him if he wasn't a criminal?"

With an indelicate shrug, Sally said, "I can live with it if he can. Sire."

Sharp as she was, the girl was young. For all the trials she had endured, she was innocent to the ways of Court. He had seen the way it could ruin people, and had lost his sister to its intrigues barely a month before. She had not been much older than Sally was now.

"I was a beggar once. In many ways, I still am." He shrugged. "There are merits to both lives, and you may find you have a choice. There is a freedom in poverty. You will struggle, but you can do as you like. If you enter the world of the Court, you are taking on more than you know. You will be unlikely to go hungry again, but you may find the responsibilities cumbersome, and Court--well, I wouldn't wish Court on anyone. Consider very carefully what you value, and ask yourself if this life is really what you want."

Sally spoke candidly and without hesitation. "I have never been free, Sire. In my experience, poverty brings more suffering than anything else. I want to be safe, and I want Nick. Nothing else matters."

Charles rose to his full height with a sad smile, towering over her as he crossed the room to ring a bell beside the door. "Well and good. I will arrange for a conveyance to take you home. I daresay Lord Somerton will be quite anxious to see you unharmed."

Sally leapt to her feet. "Home? What of my crimes?"

Charles wrapped a soft wool cloak around her shoulders and gently took her hand. "You and I both know that Sally Green is dead, and as such, cannot be punished in any meaningful way for the crimes she committed in life, let alone from beyond the grave. You would do well not to trouble yourself with her any longer, Celeste."

Sally blinked in astonishment.

"Come now," he chided. "Do you think I would let any more harm come to you?"

Sally held the cloak around her shoulders, a hint of color returning to her cheeks.

His footman arrived and Charles instructed him to convey Mademoiselle Remi to Somerton House, or anywhere else she would like to go. Smiling kindly to her, his footman bowed and motioned toward the hidden staircase she had ascended to reach his chambers.

Charles touched her shoulder in a gesture that he hoped was reassuring. "It has been a pleasure, Mademoiselle. I trust you will pass on my regards to Lord Somerton."

Sally curtsied awkwardly. "Your Majesty."

"Oh, and Celeste?"

She looked at him askance.

"Burn that dress."

Chapter 58

The moon had already set as she climbed into the inconspicuous carriage. The sky was a bewitching shade of deepest blue, and she could hear a cacophony of birds chirping as they descended upon St. James Park. Realizing she must have been in the King's rooms for hours, she pulled the soft woolen cloak tighter against the morning chill, and wondered what Nick was doing.

Sally touched the upholstery, trying to satisfy herself that she was truly in the king's carriage.

Had she dreamed the whole conversation?

In the space of a single day, she had murdered a man, stolen a horse, and surrendered herself with a confession so long it had taken all night to tell it.

After years of wondering, she had finally found her father.

If all of it was true and Nick was Lord of some great estate, would he still want her?

King's daughter or not, she was still illegitimate, barren, scarred, and burdened with a past that would make the most hardened sinner blush.

She was not the sort of the girl an earl ought to marry. Sally pulled the ribbon out of her hair and combed through the curls with her fingers. Although she had dressed the part for the day, she had come a long way from being Sally Green. Her hair was clean and soft to the touch, she was stronger and healthier, and she was no longer afraid.

Wrath was dead and so was Sally. At last she was at liberty to rule her own life, as Celeste or whomever she wanted to be, the way it should have been when she first came to London.

She was *free*.

Sally was confident she had friends in Mark and the lads. As for Nick, she could not believe he would turn her out, but as a landowner with an estate to consider, would he really take a barren wife? A woman with no name, no money, and a horrific past?

A harlot?

A murderess?

Now that he was an earl, he would be in a much better position to marry his Lady Jane. The best she could hope for was to be kept on as a mistress, regardless of who her father was.

Sally wondered if she could do it, even for Nick. She would love him with all of her being and then she would have to return him to another.

She couldn't do it.

This would have to be goodbye.

Sally shivered as the carriage stopped. They had reached Somerton House.

Looking up at an imposing face of pale grey stones, Sally wrapped the cloak tighter still and felt a rush of nervous anticipation settle into her bones. She needed to see for herself that he lived.

Could he ever forgive her?

"Miss?" The driver whispered. "The house looks empty. Is there somewhere else I can take you?"

Sally turned toward the driver beneath the street lamp and saw her breath turned to vapor in the cold. "No, but thank you, Sir. I will wait here for Lord Somerton."

"As you wish, Miss." He doffed his cap, climbed into the carriage seat, and drove away into the dawn.

The house did look empty. Sally could see no lights or movement from the street, but as she approached the door, she found it unlocked.

Pushing it open slowly, Sally ducked her head inside, looking for a servant. She saw no one. She stepped inside and closed the door.

Some kind soul had left a candle and matches on a shelf behind the door. Sally lit it, and between its small light and the gradually brightening sky outside, she was able to see her way around the mansion.

Somerton House was enormous. Every opulent inch from the high ceilings to the polished tile floors glittered with wealth and taste. Bustling through the foyer to a disused but grand hallway, she found the kitchens in a state of neglect, filthy and empty of food and servants.

Confused and more than a little frightened, Sally exited through another hallway, past a paneled dining room and through a second, larger hall at the center of the house. Covered paintings hung from the picture rail in double rows through a long gallery that led to a curving staircase wide enough for a dozen people to walk abreast. She paused beneath the staircase, steeled herself, and began her slow ascent.

Climbing the staircase, the only sound she could hear was the soft soles of her leather shoes padding against the marble. Every nerve in her body tingled with fear, half expecting Wrath's ghost to leap out of the shadows.

On the next floor, Sally came to a row of open, beautifully furnished bedrooms with no one inside. She was acutely aware of the racing of her own heart as she reached what she presumed to be the Master's suite at the end of the hallway facing the courtyard. Again, the door was slightly open, and there was a light burning inside.

From the hallway she could see a man's foot hanging off of the edge of a canopied bed. Sally wished she had taken a weapon from the kitchen in case she needed to defend herself.

As she pushed the door open, Sally spotted an iron poker embedded deep in the wood, and frowned in confusion. The wood emitted a quiet creak, and the man shot straight up in bed.

Sally screamed.

He screamed.

"Mark?" She shrieked in recognition. "Oh, thank God! You scared me half to death!"

"I scared you?" He asked, rubbing his eyes. "Where have you been? Are you well?"

"I'm fine. Where's Nick?"

A long, feminine arm snaked across Mark's bare chest and Sally realized, with a shock, that he was not alone.

She turned quickly and covered her eyes. "I beg your pardon," she apologized.

Sally heard a sharp gasp as the woman became aware of her presence and bolted for the closet.

Mark gave a heavy sigh. "You scared her off."

"Sorry," Sally said, turning to see Mark pulling his long shirt over his head. "What are you doing here? Where's Nick?"

"He's out looking for you. Just about killed me when I told him you were involved. Took to the streets looking like a madman with a rope burn around his neck. They've been looking for you since you disappeared. Will's been searching the streets, Harry's at the warehouse in case you'd thought to go back there, and Nick left me here. I figured this was the only chance I'd get to sleep in the Lord's room, seeing as how Nick's the big man now."

Mark lit a lamp beside the bed. Illuminated, the room was lovely. A large canopied bed draped in leaf green brocade dominated the wood paneled room. To the left of the door was a wide dresser and ornately carved wardrobe, and to the far side of the room, a matching writing desk and bench beside a high-backed chair upholstered in the same green brocade. Opposite the bed, glass doors trimmed in red and green diamond panes opened up onto a balcony overlooking the central courtyard.

Sally looked around the room in wonder. "It's beautiful."

"It's something, innit?" He gave the room an appraising look. "Ain't half dusty, though. Arthur didn't seem to sleep here none. When we got here, there was only Crowley, and the rest was the house full of this dust. What do you make of that?"

I know where he slept, Sally thought to herself with a shudder. "The house was disused?"

"Not entirely," he said. "Crowley lives here, he's the old butler. He's half-deaf, bless him. And that top drawer," he nodded toward the dresser, "it's full of treasure." He wiggled his eyebrows.

Sally stepped quickly to the dresser and yanked open the top drawer. Inside was her jewelry box. She opened it to find it just as she had left it, dozens of gemstones in all different colors winking up at her in the early morning light. Tears sprung to her eyes and she covered her mouth in a sob.

"I've never seen a girl cry at good jewelry. What is it, pet?"

Sinking down onto the edge of the bed, Sally wiped her eyes, and she sobbed into the cape. The jewelry was a connection to her old life, a reminder of the horror she had endured and how far she had come. The realization that Nick had nearly died hit her again, mercilessly, and she dearly needed to see him to assure herself he was alive.

Whether he would have her or not, Sally had to tell him how she felt.

"The jewelry was mine." She dried her tears. "I need to find Nick."

Just then, the woman sheepishly emerged from the closet wearing a stunning blue dress.

"There she is." Mark beamed. "Come here, darling."

The woman sat carefully beside Mark on the bed looking decidedly pale, from embarrassment or seeing her looking like a specter, Sally did not know. The woman was young, certainly, clean, and lovely, with a flawless complexion.

Mark looked at her in appreciation. "I thought you said you didn't have any friends." He smiled at Sally.

"I don't," Sally said. "Good morning."

She looked up at Sally uneasily.

"I'm Sally." She smiled. "You'll have to forgive me; I don't always look like this."

"This is Jane." Mark grinned.

Sally raised her eyebrows. "Not Nick's Jane?"

"Mark's Jane!" he protested. "She's an actress."

Jane blushed and remained silent.

Noting her shining, curled hair and her clean, buffed nails, Sally seriously doubted Jane had ever seen a stage. She was far too clean, too young, and too polished to be an actress. The dress alone was worth more than all of the dresses Sally had ever owned put together. Following her hunch, she asked her in French, "Does he know that you are a lady?"

Recognizing the language, Jane answered instantly, "No, please do not tell him."

Sally's hunch was confirmed. French was fashionable among the upper classes, and hers was perfect.

Jane had never been Nick's sweetheart. She had been Mark's Jane all along.

Sally laughed out loud. Jane looked at her in confusion and Mark watched with a smile on his face, not understanding a word.

"This man is my friend," Sally said. "What do you want with him?"

Jane blushed a deep shade of crimson, and Sally felt herself warming to her. "He is very handsome."

Sally nodded. "Yes, he is. You don't have a husband, do you? Or a father who will call him out?"

Jane shook her head, "I am not married, and I will not tell my father."

Sally looked pointedly at Jane's belly. "He will find out if you are with child."

Jane suddenly looked like she was going to be ill. She hadn't thought of that.

Sally sat beside Jane on the bed and gave her a reassuring hug. "Enjoy what's left of the evening, and he will return you to your father in the morning. What is your real name?"

"Jane Ramsey."

Mark gave a short laugh. "You're who now?"

They turned and looked at him in surprise.

"Come now, you don't think my French is that bad, do you?" He looked wounded. "Did you just say that you are Jane Ramsey?"

She smiled nervously and tucked a wave of red hair behind her ear, suddenly looking very young.

Switching back to English, she explained, "Somerton kidnapped me and thought to keep me here to force my father to allow me to marry him."

"So you ravished her instead," Sally said to Mark.

"She ravished me!" He reached for his trousers.

"I really did," Jane admitted.

"Your father is going to kill me," he declared, lacing his trousers. "Nick is going to kill me. I'm going to be dead. Come on, I'll take you home."

Chapter 59

Even in the dark, Jane could tell Mark was angry.

The cold blue dawn crept through the grate over the windows of the hired hack, allowing just enough light to see the muscle leap as he clenched his jaw.

Not angry. Mark Virtue was *livid*.

There was no reason to be so angry. He had rescued her from abduction most valiantly, and she had thanked him as enthusiastically as her imagination had allowed. It may have been ill advised to do so without first introducing herself properly, but to be fair, he hadn't seemed to be particularly interested in her father's name once she had discarded her gown.

Willing herself to look away from his rigid shoulders, she turned her attention to her hands resting in her lap, ghostly and gloveless against the worn velvet. In spite of the bite of the wind winding through the grate, her fingertips felt warm with the memory of his skin.

She glanced up to find him regarding her strangely, his blue eyes expressionless, caught between two thoughts. What could she say? *I must see you again.*

Surely a well-bred lady would never say something so desperate. Jane despaired quietly in her seat as the coach rattled furiously out of town. Her dancing master had never covered this situation in his lessons on conversing.

"I'm sorry," she offered.

He raised an eyebrow. "You're sorry?"

She swallowed. "I allow that perhaps I should have told you who I was, but to be honest, I don't see how it matters. I told you my name was Jane…"

"You're Jane-bloody-Ramsey," he said slowly, "and I am a dead man."

She made a face. "That's a bit dramatic."

He crossed his arms over his chest. "Dramatic? Oh right, because you're an actress!"

"Did I say that?"

"Yes, you did. You said you came from Drury Lane. Do you know who lives there? Actresses and whores, that's who, not harebrained Stewart heiresses out for a bit of rough!"

Jane's mouth dropped open. "You thought I was a whore?"

"Of course I did!"

Jane raised her hand to slap him and he caught her wrist.

Holding it, he lowered his face toward hers. Once again she caught the scent of tobacco and sawdust on his warm skin and in spite of her best intentions, her insides began to burn. Her gaze dropped to his lips and she wished fervently that he would kiss her.

Mark drew closer still and her breath caught in her throat.

"Some of the best women I know are whores. You can say what you like about them, but at least they're honest."

"Honest?" Jane scoffed. "So I told a lie about where I lived. I was alone in a strange inn and I lied because I was scared. I never lied about my name, and I never lied about what I wanted. I just wanted *you*."

"Why?"

She shrugged. "You saved my life."

"Not really."

"Close enough," she said, closing the distance between them with a kiss.

He held her fast, crushing her against his chest as he returned her kiss. His warm, firm lips almost painfully sweet against hers, swollen from a thousand kisses in the night.

The world fell away outside of his embrace. Too soon, he pulled away.

To Jane's immense satisfaction, his face was flushed and his dark gold hair was slightly mussed. He swallowed. "I'm not just something you can amuse yourself with."

"You amused yourself with me," she countered. "Are you courting anyone?"

"There isn't a lot of courting in Southwark."

"You could court me."

Mark blinked.

Jane shifted under his scrutiny, afraid she had been too bold.

"How old are you, Jane?"

She blushed. "Nineteen… in a fortnight…"

He stopped breathing. "Were you a maiden?"

Jane gave a little laugh. "Of course."

"Dead," he repeated. "Hung, drawn, and quartered. You've killed me, girl."

She rolled her eyes. "Now who's being dramatic? It's not as bad as all that…"

He laughed mirthlessly and looked out the window at Hereford's rapidly approaching estate, the warm hues of the vibrant dawn cast against the white stone, making it appear as if the great house was on fire.

"…we could marry," she suggested, "and no one need know."

Mark eyed her warily. "Marry?"

She nodded hopefully.

He snorted. "That's not going to happen."

Her shoulders fell. "Why not?"

Mark took her hands in his, and explained slowly, "Because you, darling, are Jane Ramsey. You're probably a lady, right?"

"Naturally."

"Naturally," he repeated. "You are *Lady* Jane Ramsey, and I am a carpenter."

She gave an irritated sigh. "It sounds silly when you say it like that."

"That's because it is silly."

"It is not!" Jane insisted, reddening. She could no more help her name than he could change his station, and she didn't want him to. "I am a grown woman and I will do as I please."

"Tell that to your father."

"I shall!"

"You might get your chance. Unless I miss my guess, that's him coming now."

Jane glanced out of the grate to see her father scrambling toward the carriage with something in his hand.

Mark squinted at the corpulent figure in the billowing nightclothes. "Is that a pistol?"

"Almost certainly." Jane cringed. "He's an excellent shot. Keeps it under his pillow when he sleeps in case the servants try to rob him in the night."

"I hope you're joking."

As the carriage slowed in front of the house, Jane set her hand on the top of the door and took a deep breath, preparing to confront her father.

Mark saw the look on her face and put his hand over hers. "I don't like what you're thinking."

"I didn't ask you."

"Jane." He took her face gently in his hands. "Think about this. Look at everything you've got here. You really want to throw all of that away?"

"Yes."

He sighed. "Look here, you don't know what the world is like. You think your life is hard because your servants burn your toast."

Jane made a squeak of protest.

"I'm not judging you," he continued. "But your life here is better than you think it is. Go back home, have a hot bath, and thank God that you don't have to go home to Southwark at night."

Jane felt tears gathering in her eyes. "What about you?"

"You'll have forgotten me by tomorrow."

"I will not!"

"You ought to." He looked away. "We were never meant to inhabit the same world."

"What if you're wrong?"

"I'm not," he said gently. "Go home to your father. He's worried about you."

"Jane!" She heard her father shout as he neared the carriage. "Jane!"

The carriage came to a halt. Her father was near enough that she could hear his heavy footsteps pounding the path outside. She wiped her eyes on her sleeve, and took one last look at Mark. "I'll find you," she promised, pushing open the door before she lost her courage.

Chapter 60

After Mark and Jane had left, Sally took her old jewelry box and sat on the bed.

Opening it, she took out every piece, laying them before her to see what was there.

Having left the smaller pieces to distract thieves in the brothel, all that remained were the largest and best pieces. There was an elaborate emerald collar, jade bangles, tourmaline beads, diamond earrings, a sapphire brooch, a bright yellow ring, a string of fat pink pearls, and Beaumont's ruby. Not a piece of it would sell for less than fifty guineas. Wrath was dead, Sally had been pardoned, and her jewels had been restored to her, making her a very rich woman, with or without the King's help. She could return to France or open a bakery as she pleased.

Underneath it all was the mark Nick had given her the night they met.

Enough for weeks in a clean boarding house.

Looking around the grand room with a sigh, Sally wondered if it could be true that Nick had inherited it. It would be her luck that by murdering Wrath to save Nick, she removed him from her arms forever. She had learned that Fate could be cruel, and she wondered why she was surprised.

Well and so, if she had truly saved him, that was good enough for her.

Removing the last enormous emerald pendant from the box, the sight of the wooden beads of her mother's rosary brought tears to her eyes. Perhaps it was a sign that God had not forgotten her after all.

Wrath had kept it. She wondered why.

Packing the jewels back into the box, she set the rosary on top and closed the lid. Overwhelmed by her sudden freedom, she reminded herself that no matter what happened with Nick, she would survive, and she would never have to sell herself again.

Hearing heavy footsteps on the stairs, Sally set the box on the writing desk and ran to the door. "Nick?"

At the sound of her voice, he began to run. "Sally?"

She met him at the top of the stairs, his face red from exertion. Without pausing to catch his breath, he took her in his arms and held her tightly, cradling her head and kissing her face.

"Sally," he whispered, breathless. "You're alive." Sally noticed the angry red mark of the rope looped around his neck and cried out, "My God! Your neck! We must find a physician!"

Nick's laugh spurred a hoarse cough and he pulled her to his chest in a hug. "I'm fine," he said, smelling her hair. "I'm fine, thanks to you. Where have you been?"

"There was something I needed to do..."

Without another word, Nick took her hand and led her down the stairs and out into the courtyard. They walked through overgrown grasses, damp with dew, to the trellis at the far side just as the rising sun burst over its vibrant riot of late summer roses.

Nick sat before them on a marble bench and pulled her down beside him, holding her hands in his. "I wanted to show you the garden before we go. It was one of my favorite places as a child."

"It is incredible." She smiled, inhaling the heady smell of the magnificent flowers. "Are we going somewhere?"

"I wasn't certain where." His brow furrowed. "I thought maybe the continent. We can travel by night until we are safely out of England, and then I was thinking perhaps the south of France, or perhaps Denmark. What do you think?"

Sally looked curiously into his lovely green eyes, and wondered why he had chosen that moment to go completely mad. "What are you talking about?"

"We need to go somewhere people don't know us. You already speak French, and mine is a bit out of practice, but I can learn..."

Sally's heart sank and she looked down at their joined hands. "You're a peer now; you will not be tried."

Nick took her cheek gently in his hand. "I will not have you hunted for murder."

Sally felt tears begin to prick her eyes and she tried to blink them away. "Can you ever forgive me?"

"Forgive you?" He took her in his arms. "I will never forgive you for putting yourself into such danger, but I am relieved to see you unharmed."

"I murdered your brother!"

Nick stroked her hair as she wept into his shoulder. "I would have killed him myself for what he did to you. It is just as well he is already dead. Please, do not cry over him."

"I'm not." Sally wiped her eyes with the heel of her hand. "Nick, I went to see the King."

The color drained from his face. "The King? Why on earth would you do that?"

"I begged him to pardon you. He said he didn't need to. He told me you were safe. I told him everything, Nick, and he pardoned me instead."

His eyes lit up and he embraced her once more. "That's marvelous! Why are you crying?"

"Now that you are Earl of--whatever--you will not want me." She sniffed.

He took her face in his hands and gently brushed a tear away with his thumb. "Sally," he searched her eyes, looking for words, "you must know that I love you. I will love you no matter who I am or what happens to me. I've been trying to ask you for weeks, but I'll ask you again. Marry me?"

Sally looked up into his face, so earnest as he held his breath, waiting for her answer.

Yes wasn't enough. It would never be enough. There were so many things she could have said to him at the moment, wanted to say, that she couldn't say a word. She threw her arms around his bruised neck and kissed him with all of the joy in her heart.

He laughed against her lips and asked, "Is that a yes?"

"Yes."

There would be time for all things she wanted to say. For the first time in many years, she could believe she had a future, and that future was better than anything she had ever imagined.

"Come on, Sally, let me show you our new home."

Epilogue

Marcheline Toulouse was tired.

Arthritis had set into her bones and her sight was not what it once was. The girls made up for her increasing slowness in the kitchens, treating her with care, but the respect she had once commanded had faded. Little Simone had grown and had Madame Toulouse's post set in her sights. Knowing she was waiting for her to grow infirm was unsettling.

After fifty years of baking in the kitchens of Chateau Lenormand, Madame had nothing to show for it but a bad back and a purse nowhere near large enough to keep her in her old age. Her sister had passed away and she had no children of her own to look after her.

She knew she would be cast out when her vision failed and she was too stiff to even knead bread, but her plan had been to hide her poor health and to continue to work as long as she could, knowing she would likely die in the poorhouse, if illness did not claim her first.

That is, until she had received the letter.

Arriving on thick paper etched in gold and closed with a red wax seal bearing the sigil of a lion rampant, the short missive had been written with care in French in a fluid, curving hand.

Madame Toulouse,

I have heard wondrous tales of your skill with pastry and I am in desperate need of an experienced cook to manage my kitchens.

My husband and I have recently come into the possession of an estate in Somerset as well as a sizeable townhouse in London.

If you would consider taking up the position, I will set you up in your own private quarters at both locations and triple your salary.

Please send word if you will accept our offer, and we will make travel arrangements immediately.

I do so hope you will consider it.

Faithfully Yours,

C.R.
P.S. Lord Somerton is very fond of your almond tarts.

Madame read the letter a dozen times before carefully folding it and dropping it into the pocket of her apron.

She had not the slightest idea how this Lord Somerton had ever managed to taste her almond tarts. The last English visitors had come to the estate some twenty years before.

Thinking of Celeste, Madame wiped her eyes and slowly ascended the staircase to her room.

She had not seen Celeste since she had disappeared years before, but had never given up hope that she might one day return, however unlikely that was.

After Celeste had knocked out Bertrand, he had been unconscious for several days before waking in a foul mood. She had certainly run away, and Madame would bet her life that Claude had helped her. What became of her after that, no one knew, but she knew the world was not a safe place for young girls traveling on their own.

Throwing her few possessions in a linen laundry bag, Madame composed her acceptance letter to Lady Somerton in her head. When she had finished packing, she sat down and put pen to paper.

My dear Lady Somerton,
I accept most graciously. Please do not trouble yourself in making arrangements; I will depart for England presently.
Your servant,
Mme Marcheline Toulouse

Wishing Simone good luck, she had left a short note of resignation and left the kitchens in a flurry of confusion.

Two days slow ride later, Madame met her boat in Calais, and she was off to England.

In all of her sixty-seven years, Madame had never travelled more than a few miles beyond the Chateau. She had grown up in the nearest village and began working in the kitchens after her father had died, leaving her an orphan at fifteen. Now facing a journey of two long weeks by boat and cart, Madame found she did not much care for travel.

She purchased fare to ride on top of the coach to save money, but had been offered a seat inside in respect of her advanced age, which she had accepted gratefully. Over the long, jerky ride up the hill from Dover, she had surreptitiously glanced out the window at the white cliffs as they rolled by and she shook her head. She hoped Lady Somerton was a kind mistress, for she had no desire to make the journey back down.

Madame spent many days looking wearily at her swollen knuckles and planning for her retirement. At three times her salary, she would reasonably be able to retire in relative comfort in five years, depending upon the accommodations available.

Her heart did a little flip in her chest as she considered the possibility that this Lady Somerton may not be so cruel as to cast out a poor old woman. Maybe she would be kind and allow her a room with the servants, or perhaps a little pension. No one she knew had ever received such consideration, but it had been known to happen. Grasping the letter in her hands, she had allowed herself to hope.

A fellow passenger announced their arrival to London with a joyous shout, and Madame looked out the window. Outside was a bustling city much larger than she had imagined. As they wound through the streets to the coach stop, they passed a hundred times as many people as Madame had seen in her whole lifetime. Madame watched them walking past, carrying children, buying produce, selling bread. Seeing a young, dark-haired girl, Madame again thought of her Celeste, the little wayward child she had thought of as her own, and wondered if she had come here when she disappeared all those years ago.

The houses were enormous and went on for miles. Madame furrowed her brow as they reached the coach stop. She had not expected London to be so very big; how could she hope to find Somerton House from here?

Alighting from the coach, Madame felt relief at once again touching solid ground. She swung the laundry bag over her shoulder, looked around at the shops and stalls surrounding the inn, and prepared herself for a long walk. Stopping at the nearest stall, she asked the fruit seller, "Please, Somerton House?"

"You what?" His mouth hung open like a fish.

Madame's English was limited and she found herself frustrated as she grasped for the words. She pulled the letter out of her pocket and pointed to the return address.

"St. James? Good Lord, love, you've got a ways to go."

His strange accent was nothing like that of the guests of the Chateau, and it was very difficult for Madame to understand. She turned to look in the direction he was pointing, said, "Thank you," and began to walk.

She had not gone more than a dozen yards before a young man ran up to her and stopped her. "Mrs. Toulouse, is it?"

Gripping her bag more tightly, she looked him over. He was a handsome young man, blonde with a mischievous face. "Toulouse?" He repeated, unsure.

She nodded, "*Oui, je m'appelle* Madame Toulouse."

"Madame Toulouse," he repeated, relieved. "I have come to take you to Lady Somerton."

Recognizing the name, she showed the letter to the young man. He glanced at it and nodded. "Yes, Lady Somerton. My name is Mark, and I'm the Lady's brother-in-law. Er...*frère?*"

Cocking her head at him, she had understood that this young man was the Lady's brother. He didn't look like an especially wealthy man, although his plain clothes were new and he looked to have a particularly fine ring. The Lady must have received her acceptance and had sent this young man to find her. Nodding her consent, she said, "Thank you," with a smile, and followed him with relief to a beautiful mahogany coach.

Once she had settled into the plush interior, Mark surprised her by climbing into the front of the carriage and driving the team of bays himself.

What a strange family, she thought to herself, watching the buildings go by.

After a long ride, the dirt roads turned into cobblestone streets and the houses grew bigger and grander. Some of them dwarfed the Chateau in both height and width, and Madame began to worry just how many people she would be baking for.

At last the carriage slowed and Madame saw an enormous

town house roll into view. It was not the biggest they had passed, but was certainly grand, with four or five stories and two wings that she could see. It had a wide, paved entrance decorated with a uniform line of short trees. She was very grateful for the ride as she thought she may have perished had she walked so far on her own.

As the house came closer into view, Madame saw that several people were gathered outside the house in a line. *What commotion was this?* Were they receiving visitors? In a flush of panic, Madame hoped that she would not begin her time here on an unpleasant note by interrupting the reception of some great person.

Her panic increased as Mark stopped the carriage before the front door. Madame sat perfectly still, trying not to make a sound, until the carriage began to move again.

To her surprise, Mark opened the door right there and offered her his arm. After a moment's pause, Madame cautiously took it, and alighted from the carriage.

Every member of the household watched her round the corner, smiling at her.

Dear God, she thought, *they're here for me.*

Mark led her toward the household, and the lord and lady slowly came into focus as they approached her.

The lady was walking very quickly, and Madame could see that she was wearing a simple but beautifully cut blue dress. She looked to be young and fair, and had very long, curling black hair.

"Madame?"

"Celestine?" Madame burst into tears as Celeste threw her arms around her in a warm embrace.

"I was so worried!" Madame sobbed in French. "What became of you? What are you doing here? Oh, my dear!"

Celeste replied, "It is so good to see you! I was afraid that you would not come."

Madame wiped her eyes. "*Mon dieu*! I must present myself to the lady, I thought you were she."

Celeste held her shoulders gently and looked into her eyes, "Madame, I am she. I am Lady Somerton, and this is my home."

Madame looked from Celeste to the magnificent edifice beside them and back again.

A tall, handsome man appeared and Celeste took his arm with a smile. "Madame, this is my husband. Nick, this is my childhood savior, Madame Marcheline Toulouse."

Lord Somerton took her hand in his and gallantly kissed it. "Madame, I am indebted to you."

Both Celeste and her young man looked comfortable, well-looked after, and very happy to see her. "I get to work for you, Celestine?"

"*Mais non*, Madame!" Celeste hugged her once more. "It was never my intention to make you work, I had only hoped to lure you to London so you might consider retiring here with us at Somerton House. We will take very good care of you, I promise."

Holding Celeste's gloved hand, Lord Somerton smiled at Madame and nodded reassuringly.

It was the last thing she saw before she fainted.

Jessica Cale is a historical romance author and journalist based in North Carolina. Originally from Minnesota, she lived in Wales for several years where she earned a BA in History and an MFA in Creative Writing while climbing castles and photographing mines for history magazines. She kidnapped ("married") her very own British prince (close enough) and is enjoying her happily ever after with him in a place where no one understands his accent. She is the editor of Dirty, Sexy History at www.dirtysexyhistory.com. You can visit her at www.authorjessicacale.com.

Made in the USA
Las Vegas, NV
21 November 2022

59992279R00184